The Three Muses of Milton

A Gaskell, Austen and Brontë Crossover

By Caroline Malcolm-Boulton

A Gaskell, Austen and Brontë Crossover

Copyright

Author: Caroline Malcolm-Boulton.
Published and printed by Amazon.
First Printed: 2024.
Current number of editions: 1.
This edition: 1.
ISBN: 9798879408393.

This book contains text from the works of Jane Austen, Elizabeth Gaskell and Charlotte Brontë. Their novels are no longer copyrighted, so restrictions are no longer applicable. However, this book does contain quotes and an original character from various screen adaptations of these texts. In these instances, the production companies and screenwriters have been contacted and written permission has been given to approve their use in this book.

Cover Illustration by Get Covers.
Internal illustrations by Victoria O. Fitzpatrick.
Internal illustration by Lana Dang (Page 274).

Dedication

I am delighted to dedicate this book to the three inspirational women who made it possible: Elizabeth Gaskell, Jane Austen and Charlotte Brontë.

Many of us know the works of these three iconic and inimitable female writers so well, their wit and wisdom having brought us joy from generation to generation, a special bond between author and reader that I am sure will last forever. Without their novels *North and South*, *Pride and Prejudice,* and *Jane Eyre*, this book would never have been written, and I can only hope that they would have approved of my humble efforts to take their exceptional literary gems and play with them to create something innovative of my own all these years later.

Ladies, you are an inspiration! Thank you for the many happy hours I have spent reading and re-reading your words, enjoying your scribbles, falling in love with your characters, and feeling at home within the pages of your stories. This one's for you!

I am also proud and privileged to say that 100% of the lifetime royalties for this book will be dedicated, with their blessing, to Elizabeth Gaskell's House, Jane Austen's House and the Brontë Parsonage.

Introduction

The Three Witches of Milton, which derives its title from Shakespeare's *Macbeth,* is a crossover of the world and words of Elizabeth Gaskell, Jane Austen and Charlotte Brontë, who each wrote in the early-mid 19th century. It is, I hope, a celebration of these three women and the concept of womanhood throughout time. To me, these three iconic authors wrote works that tried to make sense of the times they lived in and woven within their narratives, they were also writing a love letter to generations of women to come, reassuring them that being a woman at any time can be hard, but with a bravery that fosters an independent and self-appreciating spirit, women can prevail.

However, this book also has a further modest aim, which, I hope shines through. To me, while the words of these writers will forever remain iconic and inspirational, through experimentation, I want to see whether removing them from their original context and resettling them into new scenes and dialogue can give them a reinvigorated, reincarnated impact on readers.

Moreover, this book stands as a testament to the power of sisterhood. Regrettably, our world often witnesses women compelled to undermine and impede one another, driven either by self-interest or by their insecurities. It is truly disheartening that such a culture persists, considering the myriad challenges inherent in being a woman without adding unnecessary burdens onto each other. Thus, this book serves as a tribute to the virtues of kindness, empathy, respect, and acceptance among women, fostering a sphere where we can collectively strive to realise our fullest potential and lead lives of happiness and health.

In terms of the synopsis, this book intricately weaves elements from the literary legacies of Gaskell, Austen, and Brontë, offering a fresh perspective through a crossover and retelling of *North and South, Pride and Prejudice*, and *Jane Eyre*. While the narrative primarily delves into *North and South*, centring on the evolving love story between John Thornton and Margaret Hale, it commences midway through Gaskell's novel, navigating the aftermath of Thornton's rejected proposal and the pivotal events at Outwood station.

Locked within Thornton and Margaret's quest to unravel their emotions, the tale confronts the challenges posed by characters reminiscent of Caroline Bingley from *Pride and Prejudice*, Blanche Ingram from *Jane Eyre*, and the newly introduced Ann Latimer from *North and South's* 2004 adaptation. As these antagonists vie for Thornton's affections, his unwavering devotion to Margaret only intensifies. Their attempts to besmirch Margaret's character with petty jibes serve as poignant reminders to Thornton that women should strive not to undermine but uplift each other. Through these encounters, the narrative underscores the importance of solidarity and mutual support among women.

Criss - Cross - Crossovers

Caroline Malcolm-Boulton, also known as The Scribbler CMB, has written *North and South* retellings and continuations under the following patented titles:
Before We Were Us.
The Thornton Tales.
A Marriage of Inconvenience.
Parodies and Other Such Poppycock.
Criss-Cross-Crossovers.

This book belongs to the series *Criss-Cross-Crossovers.*

Criss-Cross-Crossovers is a series which explores the mixing and melding of the English classics, such as in this case, the works of Elizabeth Gaskell, Jane Austen, and Charlotte Brontë, most notably, their novels: *North and South*, *Pride and Prejudice,* and *Jane Eyre.*

In a World Full of Witches, Be a Margaret

Contents

Yet, unbeknownst to them, a love story like that of the one from the north and the one from the south could not be scripted, it could not be dictated to, but would organically unfold much like the poignant tales found within the pages of classic novels. Contrary to the belief that authors craft these words and determine their direction, I can attest otherwise. These characters not only exist on the page but extend their vitality beyond it. Their liberty in the name of love cannot be so easily edited or erased. They are free spirits, untouched by the constraints of writers with their wishes and whims. They live and breathe, surpassing the limits of mere prose. Love of the truest nature transcends the boundaries set by a world that often fails to recognise the profound and unbreakable bond fusing kindred spirits, their essence entwined in a dance that defies

reason. *Little-known to many is that in the divine act of creation, God sculpts each of us in our unique moulds. And yet, in exceedingly rare instances, a scarce anomaly occurs. Much like the conception of identical twins, the mould overflows, giving rise not to one but to two entities. Thus, twinned souls emerge, their matter combined, forming two hearts pulsating in unison within distinct bodies yet sharing allied spirits. If luck smiles upon these chosen few, these beings may serendipitously find each other, fulfilling God's plan for them that destiny awaits with bated breath, a future that fate prays for daily in faithful longing.*

The Three Witches of Milton

Chapter One

It is a Truth Universally Acknowledged

'It is a truth universally acknowledged, that a single man in possession of a good fortune, must be in want of a wife.'

What utter codswallop!

There, I said it!

I am quite sure that many of you, most of you, even, are currently sitting (or lying, or kneeling or slouching, however you choose to read), in abject shock, perhaps even disgust, to hear me sacrilegiously depreciate words which have become almost like fictional scripture, the phrase imprinted within the print of well-thumbed pages. But now that I have your attention, I bid that you hear me out and let me indulge in a moment of rational discourse on this matter, which I strongly feel warrants revision.

To begin with, it must be said with unashamed honesty, that here we have what may very possibly be the most recognisable sentence, the most famous opening line, in the history of English literature. And yet, despite its notoriety, it is arguably the most unfair, untruthful and downright unnatural drivel that was ever written, a fact which I believe the dear lady who composed it knew all too well. *Ha*! How she must have suppressed a smirk as her pen scratched the parchment, her humour itched, her insight tickled, as she began on a note of irony, her novel cultivated from the fertile seeds of female wisdom.

Still, despite her evident wit that shrewdly mocked the conventional poppycock of her own society, her sarcasm has often instead been mistaken for a hallowed veracity, and it is this that I must, before we go any further, correct. Therefore, if you will allow, I shall repair the grievously erroneous statement above.

'It is a truth universally acknowledged, that a single man in possession of a good fortune, <u>*might*</u> be in want of a wife.'

There, that is much better.
It is no longer overly romantic, nor overly ridiculous, but simply reasonable.

The truth is, whether it is known universally or not, a single man in possession of a good fortune, may or may not be in want of a wife. His inclination in either polar direction will doubtless be swayed by a few determining factors, most notably whether his heart is so inclined to lean in the direction of the inclination to enter into the role, nay the identity, of husband. For if one need not marry for any man-made purpose, such as that of capital, comfort or convenience, then surely to goodness, love must be the exclusive cause of his desire and decision to wed, his heart being the sole benefactor in this outcome that binds one to another until death sees fit to intervene and part them.

And, it is at this point, that I ought to justify why I am prattling on in this heretical way. It is very simply that in the case of the hero of this story, he had gone many years without having the slightest interest in taking a wife. He had, as rumour would have it, been too busy, too preoccupied with other matters to so much as glance at a woman with anything more meaningful than customary civility, and as far as the thought of matrimony was concerned, it was a binding contract that he had never thought of signing himself. He refused, as his grandmother would have put it, to become a reaper of the ring.

Why, one might solicit?

That is a most fair question.

In short, he was afraid.

It was an institution he was divided from by the void of fear, his conscience besieged by a tormenting foreboding that history would repeat itself and he would let his loved ones and dependants down through the bitter disgrace of failure, imperilling them to a life of want and worry, all because he was powerless to provide for them as a protector ought. Indeed, for thirty years, he had been content as he was to remain as a solitary soul in an unflinching state of bachelorhood. Although, one must concede to count the years that he was a babe and knew nothing of, and thought nothing about, the subject.

Moreover, now that he was in his prime, this man already held the titles of master and magistrate, and that was enough for him, or so he thought, the name of husband, one he deemed an unnecessary addition to his already demanding life. It was not helped that he was a man grounded in duty, so if he were to wed, he would naturally wish to devote everything he had, and everything he was, to the health and happiness of his family. But alas, he could never bring himself to be false, since dishonesty was not a word that appeared in his personal dictionary. Consequently, he knew, he had always known, that it would take a truly remarkable person to persuade him into proposing, given that she would be required to accomplish what no other had before her, and that would be to, by honest endeavour, and through nothing more than the sheer goodness of her authentic self, capture his heart, stimulate his intellect and challenge his character. She would, in essence, inspire him to be his best self, and in order to prove himself deserving of the loving faith she held for him, he would spend the rest of his days striving to be worthy of her. In the end, he would have no choice but to yield, since it would become impossible for him to endure this wretched world without her, his heart's mate, rendering it indispensable for both his sake and his sanity that she should agree, wholeheartedly, to be his partner in life.

However, while I may be portraying him as unfeeling, one who was unreceptive to human nature, he was no such thing, and so you must not think it for a minute, or else you and he can never hope to get along, and if so, that would be most unfortunate, not to mention detrimental to the story. For you see, if the reader cannot root for the hero, and if they fail to weep for him in times of trouble, or laugh with him in moments of mirth, then he is forsaken to perish in the abyss of literary insignificance. His world becomes locked away, shut up tight in the bind of a closed book, his existence dispelled as eyes still and cease to bear witness to the words that give him life, all memory of him lost, his history untold, unable to be resurrected through the imagination of the reader. And when this fatal fate befalls a man who bleeds the black blood of ink, his hopes die on the page along with your interest, and we cannot have that.

On the contrary, what you must understand is that far from being emotionless, he was a most decent man; honest, honourable, and of course, handsome, one cannot forget that crucial quality. He was steadfast in his sense of responsibility; his mind noble, his heart gallant, and there was nobody more qualified than him to make a fine husband. Still, for all his amiability, it would be fair to liken him to a soft-boiled egg; all tough on the outside, but once that impregnable shell had been cracked, he would prove to be delectably soft on the inside.

Only, as I said before, he was of the sort who was not inclined towards that particular inclination. Or, that is, not until he had met *her*, then everything had changed, and suddenly, and not to forget, most unexpectedly, he had never wanted anything more than to be a married man.

But who is she, I hear you ask? Well, if you know, *you know*, and if you do not know, then you shall have to wait and see.

Chapter Two

Nine Minutes Earlier

John Thornton settled himself beside the fire and stretched out his long legs as far as they would go, his tired limbs groaning in relief to be permitted the rare chance of relaxing, a luxury they seldom benefitted from, what with their master being a martyr to industriousness, as was his tenacious ilk.

Whistling a merry tune, Mr Thornton wiggled his toes as the flames lashed out their scorching tongues of blue, red and orange, the sparks of warmth attempting to lick at his feet that were encased in a pair of meticulously-polished shoes.

'Ah! There is nothing like staying at home, for real comfort,' he whispered, a contented, self-satisfied smile gracing his usually terse mouth.

It was a particularly harsh day out of doors, winter having not yet relinquished its grip upon the earth and giving way to its younger, sprightlier and more charismatic nursling: spring. The ground was still coated in snow, the windows frosted with snowflakes, and a chilly breeze whipped up about the place and nipped at people's hands and cheeks with teeth that nibbled as tiny mice made of ice.

'So foul and fair a day I have not seen,' said Mr Thornton to himself with an ominous glower, all the while rubbing his hands together like sticks of wood to stimulate heat to thrill his veins, or at the very least, to distract himself from the fact that he was frozen to the bone.

Still, in its weary moments, as this old winter day stopped to catch its breath, its hoarse cough sweeping across the mill yard with a gust, timid shafts of sunshine peaked out from behind the dreich clouds, promising that better days were soon to come.

Lounging in a manner that was bordering on idle, Mr Thornton slid down in his chair, ever so slightly, mind, as he read one of the four Sunday newspapers he traditionally enjoyed perusing after church, this being one of his few personal treats, an infrequent period of respite in his harassed week, a recreational repose which he savoured in that private and distinctive way that befitted the peculiarities of his personality. It was, in any case, true, that the overthrow of labour ushers in the reign of leisure, and it is a ritual that any man, whether he earns his bread through the employment of his hands or his head, may relish best after he has strived to deserve it following a week of honest work.

Nevertheless, it ought to be observed at this juncture, that Mr Thornton was not a fellow known for indulging in pleasure, for he was too conscientious to give himself over to frivolity or laziness. Not that he was dull, of course, only, he was a serious sort of man, was our Mr Thornton. He was not sombre, merely sober. Folks thereabouts said that he had such lofty thoughts because his head skimmed the heavens, what with him being so tall and all that.

He had almost been summoned elsewhere this afternoon, to court as a magistrate, only, thankfully, the ruffian had thought twice about coming up against the formidable Mr Thornton, so the reprobate had promptly confessed and complied most obligingly, affording the magistrate the rare chance to be alone.

At any rate, as a man who was always so busy, he appreciated his Sundays, the one time in the week when others did not hassle him to please them, instruct them, or provide for them. Yet, with a grieved scowl, he thought on how there had been, for a cruelly short period, another occasion when he had been permitted such ease, a time when he had been able to shrug off the cares of the world and just be himself, just be John. It was in the evening, at the other side of town, in a cramped house with a cosy parlour, talking of ethics and philosophy with a friend, all the while being so deliriously close to…

But that was all over now.

The point was, people said that Sunday was the Lord's day, but when it came to Mr Thornton, he liked to think that it was his day too.

That was… until today…

Now, the following fact may seem irrelevant at first glance, but given that Mr Thornton was a Justice of the Peace, he felt it imperative to accurately register the time of the ensuing offence for the record. Therefore, one should take note that at precisely eight minutes past two, Mr Thornton was moistening his thumb as he turned the page of his broadsheet, and this, he calculated, was exactly six minutes and five seconds after the whole sordid business that constitutes the subject of this story commenced, leaving him with a remainder of eleven minutes and three seconds before the sorry state of affairs which he found himself in moved from being bad, to infinitely worse.

Returning his thumb to his lips to ready it for its next flick, he then spat and spluttered when he tasted the tang of ink as it tingled his taste buds, the resin of varnish having run after the stack of cockcrow edition rags had been left loitering in the heavy rain by that heedless grocer boy. Nonetheless, his aggravated gripe was soon mollified when he began scrutinising a rather riveting-looking article regarding the Navigation Act, causing him to ponder on its potential effect on his trade. Chewing his lip, Mr Thornton scrunched up his eyes as they skimmed left to right, taking in the words printed in unreasonably small font. His eyesight was excellent, but it seemed to him as if people were trying to fit too much unnecessary tripe onto one page these days, and would do well to consult an editor. Much like this story, I hear you grumble. However, he had not got three sentences in before his attention was arrested by an unpleasant disruption. Peering up, the master found himself frowning as his finely-tuned ears were assaulted by a shrill squeak, a squawk, even, whichever is worse, we shall go with that. It was a disconcerting sound, to say the least, one which was blaring from across the room like a foghorn, and most rudely interrupting his prized hour of hard-earned leisure. Mr Thornton growled through the thin parting of his gritted teeth to be disgruntled thus.

Lord save him!

But he would not look. *No.* He would not give them the satisfaction.

Perhaps I had better explain.

When Mr Thornton had returned from the morning service, he briefly called into his mill office, as was his standard practice. After collecting a bundle of papers to occupy him throughout the rest of the day, he then headed back to the house to treat himself to an interlude of study by the drawing-room fire, something he had done every Sunday for the past five years without fail. This fixed appointment with himself had become so entrenched in Mr Thornton's routine, a man of habitual methodology, that the master found that he became like an irritable child out of sorts if he were deprived of it in any way, shape or form. It was essential, you see, because not only did these precious sixty minutes of seclusion serve to cheer his wearied bones, which were unfortunately not as young as they had once been, coaxing him into a passably affable mood, but it also helped to thaw his soul, because reading, as we know, is as close as any humble human may get to experiencing untainted bliss.

Then again, speaking of souls, a theme that had been on his mind a great deal of late, because, Mr Thornton, infuriatingly practical man that he was, opposed to being a sentimental fool, had never before cared tuppence for this hidden part of his person, his secret self, given that he hardly believed he harboured the capacity to possess such a tender thing. Bleak thought indeed. Yet, conceivably, this assessment was not merciless, but entirely rational, since perhaps it had wilted away in barren waste for too long, stifled by the weeds of loneliness that suffocated his hopes of true happiness. Through the ravages of time, the bracken of this austere discontent, with its thorns that sought to spear this bulldog's resilient spirit, had, over the years, cast a spell of reticence upon him that was now so desolate, that no rays of affection had penetrated the childlike crux of his being for God knows how long. That is, of course, not until—

Never mind.

Yes, it had been a suppressed and forgotten portion of him, a basic element and vital ingredient which we all need in order to distinguish us from beasts. Conversely, in Mr Thornton's case, it had long since been laid to rest, possibly forever subdued in deadened decay, rendered dormant through neglect. Still, something *had* changed, there was no denying it, and now as if for the first time, his soul was alive, it was awake, and *oh*— how it ached! How it pined in writhing pain when it thought of the one whom he lov—

Forgive me.

I have done it again. Ignore my ramblings, because it is not my place to speak of such things, it is not my role to interfere, he has sternly told me so before, many times. I must be quiet. But oh, dear! — I fear that without my prodding and pestering, there will be no hope left for him, stubborn darling that he is. Even so, it is what

I do, I *study* him, I *learn* him, and I *know* him through and through, better than I know myself. It is my calling in this life, I must do it, for you see, *the soul, fortunately, has an interpreter—often an unconscious but still a faithful interpreter.* But that is enough talk of me for now because a storyteller should be heard and not seen, no matter how personally involved he or she might be, or so I am told. Nonetheless, we shall return to me later, you can be sure of that, and then, I hope, all will become clear.

In any case, I should get back to the story, since I hear you impatiently press me to go on, and I shall oblige forthwith, seeing as *the eagerness of a listener quickens the tongue of a narrator,* and I must have compassion on your poor nerves. But where was I? Ah, yes, I remember. Perhaps it is best if I turn back the clock and start from the beginning, just nine minutes earlier.

Chapter Three

These Three Witches

It had all started with the prospect of being a perfectly innocent Sunday, and Mr Thornton, what with his sensitive mind being acutely troubled at present, both with the mill and with Marg—*and other matters*, he was looking forward to his rest more than usual this day. However, as soon as he ventured a single stride over the threshold of his drawing-room, he paused in abhorrent dissatisfaction, for rather than finding it the peaceful haven of tranquillity that he was accustomed to, Mr Thornton had discovered it under siege.

Stilling like a pillar of biblical salt, and with his brow sketched with brooding furrows, it did not take the shrewd man long to notice that he was very far from alone. Blinking in the hopes that he had been mistaken, Mr Thornton was appalled to discern that his sharp eyes did not deceive him. There was no refuting that there, before the mill master, in a somewhat satanic-looking circle of frills and bows, fans and baubles, garish trimmings that were attached to silken skirts with circumferences that would rival the equator, was a horde of unwelcome visitors seated around a nest of tables in the centre of the room, accompanied by his mother and sister.

As he felt his ears being assaulted by their strident giggles that resembled cattish titters, Mr Thornton was disappointed, *nay*—disturbed, to see that his parlour was currently occupied by the three most loathsome young ladies that he, or any other unlucky sod (excuse the profanity, but curses do occasionally slip out when one is vexed), had been burdened with the grave misfortune of being acquainted with.

Mr Thornton was not a man to be easily shaken. He was known for his grit in times of strife. He was renowned for his level-headedness in the face of disorder. He was acclaimed for the gravity of his bearing, making him a formidable adversary nobody dared cross in any sphere.

Nevertheless, a single man was no match for three guileful women, so with his instincts on high alert in a bid to protect himself and gird his loins, as they say, Mr Thornton attempted to swiftly and silently retreat unheard, unseen, undiscovered. But damn, dash and darn it, his gambit did not work, for no sooner did the master turn his back in an attempt to scarper, than his mother, with a tone that brooked no argument, halted him in his escaping tracks, formally announced his presence, and beckoned her son to come hither and join this dangerous lair of feminine frivolity.

Mr Thornton suppressed an involuntary gulp and slowly veered around, the broad frame of his sculpted shoulders huddled in a pointless effort to hide. Before him, he witnessed three pairs of eyes staring up at their prey with sparingly veiled covetousness, as if they planned to pin him down upon a plate and devour him for their luncheon, their vicious claws ripping him to shreds as they divided him up between them with selfish inequity. He grumbled at his hard luck. It was the sort of seething gripe that croaks in the throat, flares in the nostrils, flickers in the eyes, and constricts in the jaw, leaving nobody in any doubt that the dissenter is one pitifully unhappy fellow.

'Good afternoon, ladies,' he said blandly, hardly able to conceal his displeasure at having happened upon them most ominously. Then again, Mr Thornton was no dim-witted twit, so it would not surprise him in the least to learn that their attendance upon Marlborough House this hour was very far from an untimely coincidence, but rather, it was a pre-arranged and pre-meditated scheme contrived by none other than his nearest and dearest, all in the fickle hopes of enticing a smile out of him, maybe even a flirtation, and who knows, if the stars were aligned just right, possibly even a proposal.

Eyeing up his foes, the master recoiled as they each leered at him. They fluttered their eyelashes, rustled their gowns, fanned their chests, and twittered as if he had just said something tremendously amusing, and Mr Thornton being Mr Thornton, well, he knew that he might have one or two assets up his starched sleeve, but humour was definitely *not* one of them.

'Come join us, John,' his sister, Fanny, invited, a slight whine of spitefulness to her inflection, because even though she knew that her friends were only here to see her brother, she could not help but feel embarrassed by his demeanour, since to her, the celebrated man about town was nothing more than a dreary old stick-in-the-mud.

Miss Thornton cocked her head as she surveyed her elder sibling with a dissecting eye, wondering what on earth it was about him that made women turn into such giddy gooseberries at the mere idea of his court. She, for one, could not see the attraction and believed she never would, since relations are blind to the qualities of their relatives, especially if they overshadow their own inferior attributes.

'Yes, please do, Mr Thornton,' Caroline Bingley, the first of the three ladies welcomed as she extended an arm to summon him into their wily midst, her hands swathed in expensive silken gloves, the sickly sweetness in her tone enough to make him queasy, leaving him regretting his fourth kipper at breakfast, its remains gurgling somewhere between his stomach and throat, threatening to resurface at any moment. Seated closest to the door where he not only still stood but also stood still, Miss Bingley was adorned in a dress of the palest pink, a stark contrast to her raven hair that was kept in place with an extravagant pearl pin in the shape of a swan that rivalled her own long neck.

Miss Bingley could concede that Mr Thornton had not been her first choice of husband, the absence of ten thousand a year and an estate in Derbyshire a tactless oversight on his part. Nonetheless, beggars could not be choosers, and while he may never be considered a true gentleman in the exclusive salons of London society, here, in the north, he was undeniably a catch worth catching, his impressive business triumphs and dashing looks enough to inspire affection in any woman. Besides, Miss Bingley could begrudgingly acknowledge that despite her abhorrence for all things related to that distasteful word *trade*, it was responsible for her own family's prosperity, so who was she to turn up her nose at the suit of a successful mill master?

What was more, with the prestige of being the bride of the most respected man in Darkshire, Miss Bingley could forever hold her head high and consider herself, no, *crown* herself, the self-appointed Queen of Milton. He may have been a gruff sort of creature, both in appearance and attitude, and she herself was used to meeker natures that were easier to direct, her brother, Charles, before his disastrous marriage, to name just one. Still, Miss Bingley felt confident that with a little fortitude, and a great deal of cunning, Mr Thornton could be brought to heel, and if he complied, they could create a seamlessly cordial union that benefitted them both. After all, *happiness in marriage is entirely a matter of chance. If the dispositions of the parties are ever so well known to each other, or ever so similar beforehand, it does not advance their felicity in the least.* No, it was much better to venture into things without caring a fig for the tendencies and temperament of either person, for it is when rings are upon fingers that a wife begins to manage her husband and mould him into her image.

But alas, she was not alone in her designs, for wherever an eligible bachelor might be, he will assuredly be followed by a drove of admirers, the fans of his flesh, or perhaps his fortune, buzzing about him like a swarm of pesky flies.

'How pleased we are to see you, sir, come to join us, at last,' crooned Blanche Ingram, the second of the ladies turning to face Mr Thornton fully from her seat that was positioned beside a bookcase that housed his late father's collection, leaving him feeling they were somehow being violated by her close and careless proximity. In doing so, her back arched so vigorously that her chest thrust outwards, somewhat aggressively, her burgundy gown rather revealing for this time of day, but desperate times call for desperate measures, so never was there more call to lather up the bacon than now.

Miss Ingram had been attracted to Mr Thornton from the first moment she met him. It was true that she had been affronted by her irregular association with Miss Thornton to begin with, the thoroughbred Yorkshire lady far too genteel to be allied with a family who buttered their bread from the grubby manufacturing of cotton, a common commodity that nobody wanted to wear. Be that as it may, the undesirable friendship could not be helped, so when the flighty girl's brother had been introduced to Miss Ingram at a dinner party, she had been instantly enthralled, and so her cap had been firmly thus set. After all, *a lady's imagination is very rapid; it jumps from admiration to love, from love to matrimony in a moment.*

Then again, as far as first impressions went, it would be fair to say that Miss Ingram was not the sort of woman whom one would naturally describe as demonstrative, since aversion and apathy were more on par with her lukewarm nature. However, there was no disputing that if she were to marry at all, which she fully intended to, as all self-respecting women must, lest she be branded an old maid and an outcast of society, then she was well aware that she could do far worse than Mr Thornton.

Quite, for regardless of the dissimilarities in both their sensibilities and upbringing, he was precisely what she was looking for in a husband, just as if she had sent away her exact requirements to a tailor and he then furnished her with a made-to-measure representation of her wants to manipulate as if he were a mannequin, rather than a man. This was not surprising, given her history, because with Mr Thornton's excessively tall, dark and handsome features, the striking similarity reminded her of another gentleman, one who was just as remarkable as he was untamed in his rugged manners, the sort of rough spark of dynamism that is not shared by all Englishmen but is reserved to run through the red-blooded veins of northern males. To be sure, she had already lost one prince of the penny to a governess, of all creatures, and so, the spurned Miss Ingram would not be letting it happen again, her years of schooling in the art of ardour her weapon, and Mr Thornton, he was her quarry. He was her stag, her accolade, and she would mount him upon her wall like a trophy for all to admire, because, you see, while men hunt animals for sport and sustenance, women pursue the most prized game of all for the infinitely higher stakes of status and security: *husbands*.

But she was not the only hunter in this forest.

'There you are, *master*,' a coy voice purred, careful to give the man his due deference, his overbearing position as an unrivalled leader amongst men the very thing which set him apart from the crowd, not to mention above them, in every way.

'At last, we had almost given up on you,' Ann Latimer chuckled, the third lady shuffling along the settee and vacating a space for the unmarried gentleman to settle down beside her, all close and cosy.

Being sure to make a show of rearranging her billowing skirts, Miss Latimer's hand glided flirtatiously along the folds of her pleats, highlighting the outline of her leg, and so she lifted it ever so slightly, encouraging the silver material to cluster around its lean shape. Miss Latimer simpered to spy the way she caught his eye, his gaze narrowed as his breath grew ragged, his chest pounding with every vigorous boom of his heart.

However, it did not beat for her, but faithfully in honour of another. In reality, what was utterly unknown to Miss Latimer, was that Mr Thornton was not looking at her at all, instead, he was staring at the seat itself, his mind cast back to a fateful day when a certain lady had lain there, eerily still, almost as if she were asleep, his angel all in white, a few drops of harrowing crimson staining her dress the only mark of her mortality.

As for Mr Thornton, her distraught disciple had knelt by her side, muttering in feverish dedication while he prayed that she would wake, that she would come back to him safe and sound, because what was the point of living in this hideous world if she were not in it? In those few terrifying seconds when the stone struck her, his perspective had changed and his priorities rearranged. What did he care if the mill walls had been breached by the rioters and his property vandalised? What did it signify if he had wasted weeks of production and, as a result, lost many of his most prominent customers? And what did he care if he had to send his Irish families back home and face the wrath of his embittered workers? None of it mattered. All that mattered was that she lived, and lived she had, only, while he had dreaded the loss of her, the cataclysmic crisis that flung them so close to each other in an intimate embrace had only sought to remind her of how little she cared for him in return.

He had been afraid to lose her. She had reminded him that she was not his to lose.

Glowering, Mr Thornton tore his eyes away from the settee, the idea that these senseless ladies were seated upon it in place of his darling was more than he could stand. How he wished with all his might that she would be lying there now, only, this time, she would be wide awake, smiling up at him serenely, his hand coming to rest gently over her belly and cradling the precious babe she carried there, the testament of their consecrated love.

Fortunately for Miss Latimer, she had not noticed any of this, because if she had, she would have turned as red as a radish with envy, a hue that did not suit her colouring. In turn, she was not the least bit concerned by the presence of her rivals, no-no, not when she had the endorsement of her friend, Miss Thornton, hardly a chuckaboo, but she would have to do, and her suitor's sister, no less. It went without saying that she was the lady with the greatest prior claim to this prize they all fought over and sought after.

Miss Latimer was, after all, a Milton woman born and bred. She identified with the conventions of this city, including its people, its customs, its tenets, and most of all, its masters, the men who ruled hereabouts like feudal kings, and Mr Thornton was the greatest of them all. What was more, she understood Mr Thornton's bristly northern temperament, volatile traits that not all women would appreciate and know how to put up with, so it went without saying that she alone was qualified to govern and then train the animal that was the repressed and irresistibly wolfish Master of Marlborough Mills. It also helped that her father, a shrewd banker, was a gambler who had a nose for sniffing out successful studs. Therefore, he had advised his daughter to bet her hand on Thornton, the robust stallion, the surest ticket in town to secure her fortune. Moreover, she had given herself away once before, as a girl, to a thoroughly unsuitable knave in Switzerland, so now that she had returned, fully finished, Miss Latimer categorically refused to lose her head, and, more importantly, her heart. After all, marriage was purely business, nothing less, and certainly nothing more.

There, I have presented all three of them. The three witches of *Macbeth*, as Mr Thornton liked to call them as a private joke, or better yet, the three figurative witches of Milton, all here to ruin his day with their eye of newt and toe of frog, wool of bat and tongue of dog. But no potion of theirs could disarm him, piercing his armoured heart that had only once been penetrated by the blunt trauma of Cupid's arrow, the wound still raw, unlikely ever to heal. At any rate, as I say, here they all were, but no matter what charms or curses they wreaked upon him, he would not succumb to their witchcraft, no—not he! for how could he when Mr Thornton's heart had already been cast under a spell and stolen away, to the other side of town, its sweet keeper far more gentle and genuine than any of these conniving sycophants could ever hope to be?

Nevertheless, none of them were strangers to the callous sting of shattered dreams, but each woman, in her own way, understood that *there will be little rubs and disappointments everywhere, and we are all apt to expect too much; but then, if one scheme of happiness fails, human nature turns to another; if the first calculation is wrong, we make a second better: we* (as women), *find comfort somewhere.*

It was just unfortunate that in this instance, somewhere, or perhaps better defined as someone, equalled Mr Thornton.

'Should you like some tea?' Miss Bingley asked, hoping that he would come to sit with them, her hand hovering over the spotlessly polished pot as she awaited his response.

'No,' he answered brusquely with a sound that resembled a husky bark.

'Thank you,' he added tardily in a transparently spiritless attempt to recapture any remaining traces of his dwindling manners.

In truth, Mr Thornton did not particularly like tea, he never had, he only drank it infrequently and in small amounts by way of being polite. However, it occurred to him that if a certain someone were to offer him a cup, he would readily accept, requesting more and more as he drank his weight in the brown liquid, all the while enjoying watching her fiddling with the fine china, that insolent bracelet of hers amusing him for hours. *It seemed as if it fascinated him to see her push it up impatiently, until it tightened her soft flesh; and then to mark the loosening—the fall. He could almost have exclaimed—'There it goes, again!'*

The thought of this made him smile, but that curling of his lips soon curdled into a sour scowl. But alas, she was not here to serve it to him, so he had no interest in taking tea that afternoon.

Mr Thornton grumbled for the second time, and he felt sure as sure can be that it would not be the last. He could not understand how or why his sister knew these women, these fiends in human form. None of them were from these parts, aside from one, and as for the others, their social circles varied so drastically from the Thornton's own that it was a wonder their paths had ever crossed at all. He had asked her once, but in reply, his sister was vague, distractedly describing that she knew them because a friend of a friend, knew a friend, who had a friend, who was a friend, of goodness knows who, and they had introduced them, and so that is how she had apparently met them at some point in the near or distant past. Needless to say, Mr Thornton had walked away from the exchange with his sister more confused than when he had embarked upon it, and since that day, he avoided asking any more questions, lest his mind be left as scrambled as his morning eggs.

Now, it was not that Mr Thornton liked to criticise or condemn people, it was only that, as a magistrate, he judged that here before him sat *three of the silliest women in all of England*! However, their shortcomings were more unsettling than that, for while silliness may be irksome, he considered it no crime of character—a flaw, maybe, but an illegality, no. Nevertheless, what really worried him was the malice he saw lurking behind their eyes, orbs that were simultaneously unnervingly intense yet impersonal, crumbling their humanity to dust, their morals infected by the putrefaction of shallowness. These ladies, they lived for self-gain. He knew conceit was commonplace, but their self-interest was altogether uglier, and for someone who had lost a father to insatiable pursuits, and as a son who had built his livelihood on the back of his own uncomplaining and uncompromising selflessness, he was not ready to let anyone destroy it.

No, Mr Thornton did not respect them, and worse, he did not trust them, so on his guard, he must be.

If truth be told, half the problem was that Mr Thornton knew nothing about women. It would be entirely correct to say that he was a clever man, an uncommonly intelligent one, in fact, who knew a great deal about a great number of subjects. Even so, when it came to the fairer sex, he found that he knew them not, and when, only once, he had presumed to know one woman, just the one, he had been sorely mistaken, dragging him to the brink of indignity and compelling him over the cliffs of misery. Nonetheless, despite his lack of knowledge, that did not mean the man was stupid, and so he realised, with more than a mite of fright, that these women were not here for tea, but for him.

For you see, young ladies have a remarkable way of letting you know that they think you a "quiz" without actually saying the words. A certain superciliousness of look, coolness of manner, nonchalance of tone, express fully their sentiments on the point, without committing them by any positive rudeness in word or deed. But they would not succeed where he was concerned. To women who only sought to please him *by their faces,* he *was the very devil when* he *found out that they* had *neither souls nor hearts—when they open to* him *a perspective of flatness, triviality, and perhaps imbecility, coarseness, and ill-temper: but* in contrast, *to the clear eye and eloquent tongue, to the soul made of fire, and the character that bends but does not break—at once supple and stable, tractable and consistent*—Mr Thornton would be *ever tender and true.*

Sulking, Mr Thornton's temper was being sorely tested, and all he could think, all he cared about in the midst of this predicament in which he now found himself centre stage, was that his heart's true dearest, she was anything but nearest, and how that grieved him more than words can adequately express.

If only she were here, not them.

Despite their estrangement, irrespective of the frosty barrier of hot-headed hostility that their misunderstandings and petty squabbles had erected between them, an impediment which separated them with ruthless resentment, Mr Thornton knew that her presence would bring him solace. She need not say anything, she need not do anything, because her company alone would be efficacious enough to calm the storm that raged in his soul, her very existence a balm to his injured spirit. With just one look, and if he were lucky, one touch, her softness, her sweetness, her sunlight, they would melt the coldness of his loneliness and bring him peace. But no, it was not to be, she was not here, in his home, where he longed for her to live, bringing life and laughter to these walls of prison-like hopelessness. When night fell, and he had gone another day without seeing her, the woman shying away from his companionship whenever she could, in order to be spared from the hot and cold eruptions of his unpredictable considerations, a disguise which concealed his overwhelming despair, Mr Thornton feared more and more that she would never come here again, for why would she, when he meant nothing to her?

He scoffed.

He was her nothing; all the while, she was his everything.

The irony was laughable.

Mr Thornton sighed once more, the throbbing of that caged lump of muscle behind his ribs too sore for his strong body to withstand, that gnawing ache growing fiercer day-by-day, with every passing day that he missed her in a malady of desperate yearning.

I would attempt to describe his torment for you, I truly would, simple wordsmith that I am, but as I say, he has forbidden me to mention it, to reveal the very name…

No, I have said too much, I sense his censure boring into me, channelling from his core and burning my fingertips as I commit his inner-most thoughts to paper, rebuking me for reading his mind once again, even if I mean no harm, only kindness, so I best remain silent. Then again, perhaps if he is distracted later, preoccupied with thoughts of her, since think of her, he undoubtedly will, maybe then I can dare tell you more, but *shhh*, we shall have to wait and see.

'I think I shall go and sit beside the fire,' he decreed resolutely, nodding in the direction of the secluded shelter of the high-backed chair that rested beside the hearth, its isolation his only hope of acquiring some much-needed protection from their unwanted interest.

With his hands thrust in his pockets, and his head hung low in accepted despondency, Mr Thornton traipsed away, leaving all three ladies complaining in unison, pouting like children who had been denied the chance to play with their favourite toy.

Never mind, thought they, they would have their chance to ensnare him soon enough.

When Mr Thornton reached his sanctuary, he grabbed hold of the chair, and with the use of some forceful pushing and shoving, the master rotated it even further around so that it faced the fire completely, grunting as he did so, a most uncouth noise, I will admit, but the ladies did not mind, not when it was the most swoon-worthy display of masculine strength they had ever seen. Goodness, what a feral brute he was, and how delicious they found him.

It was at this point that the mistress of the house felt obliged to take charge, seeing as this gathering was not going at all as she had planned. Pouring a fresh cup of piping hot tea, and adding in a dash of sugar to sweeten his mood, Hannah Thornton rose from her chair with all the stately dignity that befitted her character and took the refreshment to her son. She knew he was not fond of this particular nourishment, even if he had developed a sudden taste for it in recent months, but she wanted an excuse to speak to him more privately, and so this was as good a pretext as any. Stepping close as she set it down, the mother patted his arm fondly.

'Come now, John, do make an effort, please,' she requested quietly. *She never called her son by any name but John; 'love' and 'dear', and such like terms, were reserved for Fanny.*

'You never know, you may grow to approve of one of them, maybe even admire them,' she suggested, although, even her son could sense the scepticism in her voice, since she recognised, deep down, that these hollow bit' o raspberries were not for him, their intelligence and integrity no match for his own punishing standards to which he held himself accountable. And besides, as much as she could not bear to think on it, Mrs Thornton understood that no matter how socially suitable these women might be, his love was no longer his gift to give, since he had already surrendered it willingly, his affections now in the hands of another who had cast it aside and asunder in disdain—*oh, that woman!*

Nonetheless, all Mr Thornton did in return was moan wearily.

'*Mother!*' he murmured with a strange sort of sadness that made him appear as vulnerable as both a child and an old man.

'You know me better than that,' said he, smiling at her affably, albeit weakly. 'I cannot flirt, I never could, and I will not degrade myself or them by pretending to like them. I am not that breed of man. I admire them not, you know that, how could I, when…,' Mr Thornton's deep tenor faded away as his eyes turned towards the window, looking south, the arrow of his inner compass magnetically pulled against all logic to point towards its heart's one desire. With his head sinking lower and lower in grief, Mr Thornton's expression echoed the torrent of torture that roared within.

She could hardly bear to hear the wretchedness that cracked his chords, the spores of resentment sprouting in her maternal breast.

'I am the mother that bore you, and your sorrow is my agony; and if you don't hate her, I do,' she near enough hissed in a whisper, but she soon regretted it when she saw the sorrow writ across his face.

'Then, Mother, you make me love her more,' he said softly in protest. *'She is unjustly treated by you, and I must make the balance even* by loving her twice as much to make up for it.'

Mrs Thornton could not help but smile. Her dear boy. He was always ready to compensate for a discrepancy, a debt that was not his to pay. He had been doing it since he was barely a man, but still a gangly boy of fifteen, and it seemed like he would never change, unable, or perhaps unwilling, to lay down that personal cross that he had been carrying for far too long.

Gently taking his head in her hands, Mrs Thornton raised her son's eye to meet hers, for she would not allow him to feel any shame, since shame was not his burden to suffer, not when he had done nothing wrong. Mrs Thornton, an intensely private sort of woman, did not wish for others to eavesdrop on their discussion, but on hearing the hubbub behind her as the ladies discussed the latest Parisian fashions, she took her chance to speak candidly to her eldest child. *She put her hands on his shoulders; she was a tall woman. She looked into his face; she made him look at her.*

'A mother's love is given by God, John. It holds fast forever and ever. A girl's love is like a puff of smoke,' she said, blowing her words like hot air, *'it changes with*

*every wind. And she would not have you, my own lad,
would not she?'*

'No, Mother,' he admitted once more, 'she would not,'
he said with a crooked smile, almost as if he admired
her for her refusal of him. He knew she could do better
than him, so, in a bewildering way, he only felt it right
that he should be denied her, for her sake, at least.

'But it is over now. Let me be, Mother, let me be,' he
concluded, taking his cup of tea with a grateful upward
twist of his lips. 'It seems that I am destined to remain
unloved, save by you, and so I must learn to accept that
I will be alone forever, because if she does not want me,
and I want no other, then there is nothing to be done. It
is all over now…all over.'

Mrs Thornton nodded with the compunction of one
who wishes to offer support but finds instead that they
can do nothing, so reluctantly she withdrew, mindful
that she was mithering as well as mothering him, her
conscience afflicted to think her son had been brought
so low in spirit, wondering how she could help him, all
the while silently loathing the one who had hurt her boy
by rejecting him with such careless cruelty.

At long last, once he considered himself safe, Mr
Thornton breathed a heavy sigh of relief. But, oh! How
rash he was, for while he may have removed himself
from them, the ladies, who had not even begun to
unleash their ruses, refused to be moved. A game was
afoot, that was for sure, but it was a contest of spite
these malicious spinsters would soon regret, because, in
the case of John Thornton, he was not a man to suffer
fools lightly, especially when they threatened the health

or happiness of those he loved best, and we all know of whom he loved best of all.

And so fools they be, albeit crafty ones, these witches of Milton: one, two and three.

Chapter Four

This War of Women

Clearing her throat, it was Miss Bingley who began a conversation—*the conversation*—which John Thornton would come to place in the top three most detestable discussions of his entire life, all eighty-four years of it. He could not have foreseen what was to come, but looking back, it all made sense, it all added up, and if he had known what he now knew, Mr Thornton would have got up and left the room there and then, both on principle and in the pitiful hopes of sparing his already fraught heart.

If only he had known!

Then again, if he had, the outcome of the day might have been very different, and what a crying shame that would have been, so perhaps it was for the best that he stayed the course, all so that our honourable hero might claim his reward by the time I declare: *the end*.

'Will you not join us in our conversation, Mr Thornton?' Miss Bingley begged. 'I am sure you will have many clever things to say.'

John grunted. 'Nay,' he replied plainly. 'It is better that I do not speak, for I am of *an unsocial, taciturn disposition, unwilling to speak, unless I am expected to say something that will amaze the whole room, and be handed down to posterity with all the eclat of a proverb*,' he remarked. 'And besides,' he added as an afterthought, 'I know nothing about fashion.'

Miss Bingley grumbled under her breath. It would appear that she would need to find another method of stealing his attention from his newspaper.

'Come now, Miss Thornton,' Miss Bingley solicited, all but hitting Mr Thornton's sister on the arm with her fan as she directed her to do her bidding.

'*Let me persuade you to follow my example, and take a turn about the room. I assure you it is very refreshing after sitting so long in one attitude.*' Miss Bingley then ascended imperiously from her chair and began to glide around the drawing-room as if on a cloud, the only sound that emitted from her was a faint rustling as her silken shoes stole along the floor as she went. It was fortunate for her that the length of her sumptuous gown hid the evidence that her stockings were encrusted in mud from all the muck that currently soiled the mill yard after a week of incessant rain, reminding her that she would insist upon her husband acquiring her a much more suitable property far away from his horrid factory once they were wed.

At first, Miss Thornton puckered her lips and her corkscrew ringlets bobbled up and down as her head wobbled in confusion, all the while looking around her to ascertain what she was supposed to do and why. Nevertheless, rise she did, and after having her arm first snatched and then squeezed tightly in an over-familiar grasp by her so-called friend, they began to promenade here and there in an arbitrary circle that may have been devoid of destination, but purpose, it most assuredly did boast. Miss Bingley liked Miss Thornton immensely. However, contrary to what one might think, her partiality towards the jelly-doll who was more than seven years her junior had nothing to do with a mutual bond of any kind that is forged between two people as a result of a shared intellect or interest, but rather, she admired how delightfully stupid the girl was. Miss Thornton was, in Miss Bingley's estimation, a thoroughly puerile creature, a wooden spoon, if you will, a foozler of the most irksome degree, and so she was easy to persuade, making it no effort at all to bend her to her will, rendering her Miss Bingley's witless mimic. Perhaps it did not help that Miss Thornton, the youngest of the set, was engaged to be married, agitating her friends to be infected by a venomous jealousy.

As they moved to and fro with the ease of leaves swaying in a summer's breeze, Miss Bingley grinned to herself. She was, to her mind, a thoroughly accomplished indoor walker, although whether that is a real talent, and how one comes to be proficient in it, I really cannot say. She knew what she was about, because she had exercised this ruse many a time, sailing, or perhaps we may say slithering, here and there in the hopes of catching a certain someone's eye, the swish of her skirt and the shadow of her figure forcing him to take notice of her as she swanned about the rooms of Netherfield Park of an evening. It was subtle, but it was a tried and tested means, and as far as Miss Bingley was concerned, *flirting* was a *woman's trade*, *one* she must *keep in* good *practice*. And it worked. Mr Thornton looked up, even if it were for the briefest of moments, so fast, that his neck must surely have hurt from the swift jerk as his tendons whipped his head first up, then down, and down it stayed, the man decidedly unimpressed by the diversion.

Envious of this ploy, Miss Ingram was quick to join the party. When Miss Bingley walked past, she extended her foot, just a smidge, and tripping her up, her adversary stumbled. Regaining her composure, and wincing to feel her ankle twinge, Miss Bingley turned to gape at her opponent, the glassy film of suppressed fury shimmering in her eyes. However, Miss Ingram merely sneered and rose to her feet with a measured and deliberate show of dignity. With a fleeting stride or two, the women stood close, the tips of their toes touching, the shorter of the two staring up mockingly, the taller looking down with suspicion. Circling each other like a pair of hissing cats, the women jostled one another with their elbows, and without realising what they were doing, Miss Thornton was knocked out of the way, leaving her ousted, alone and like a sore thumb dressed in purple silk, so after looking about her helplessly, she sat down again and left them to it.

Mr Thornton scoffed as he spied them from above the rim of his newspaper. Well, if they were trying to recommend themselves to him, they were doing a crass job of it by first using and then neglecting his sister, a further mark against their names in his black book. However, it was not long before Miss Bingley's scheme moved onto its next phase, making him grateful that his younger sibling was not being subjected to their guileful façade and exploited as nothing more than an expendable pawn.

'Will you not join us, Mr Thornton?' Miss Bingley invited with a tone so honeyed, it was sure to attract a swarm of bees.

'*No*,' he replied with a curt retort. 'I shall not. And besides,' he added with an impish click of his tongue, 'there can be but two motives for your inclination to walk about my parlour, and my participation would only serve to intrude on both, so I had much better remain where I am, thank you,' he went on, goading them glibly.

Miss Bingley then let out a shrill laugh, one, which if it had been a skimp of a pitch higher, may very well have burst an eardrum or two. *What could he mean? She was dying to know what could be his meaning,—and* so she *asked* Miss Ingram *whether she could at all understand him.*

'*Not at all,*' was the lady's answer; '*but depend upon it, he means to be severe on us, and our surest way of disappointing him will be to ask nothing about it,*' she jibed, trying her hand at a little light flirtation.

'But there you are wrong,' Mr Thornton countered, reeling them in so he might cast them back, '*I have not the smallest objection to explaining them,*' said he, as soon as she allowed him to speak. '*You either choose this method of passing the* afternoon *because you are in each other's confidence* (which he highly doubted), *and have secret affairs to discuss, or because you are conscious that your figures appear to the greatest advantage in walking; if the first, I would be completely in your way, and if the second, I can admire you much better* as I sit by the fire,' he enlightened.

'Oh! Shocking!' cried Miss Bingley. 'I never heard anything so abominable!' she charged, her voice theatrically stern, her face porky-pinched with the glow of the perceived compliment.

'How shall we punish him for such a speech?' she considered, thoroughly amused by this game, her walk having taken a most unexpected turn.

The two ladies were about to exclaim that this was most scandalous, giggling like a pair of schoolgirls in cahoots, readying themselves to debate on how they should scold him for his teasing speech. Nevertheless, their jubilation soon fell flat on its face when they caught a glimpse of their target as they rounded a vase of wax flowers and came to face him, his broad frame still tenaciously cemented upon his seat as if he were stuck to it. Much to their exasperation, far from taking the opportunity to admire their figures as he had implied, he chose instead to lift his broadsheet high, flap it out wider, and conceal his head behind it as if it were a barricade, he being in the crux of battle.

In short, he was mocking them.

In Mr Thornton's case, *he knew that it does good to no woman to be flattered by a man who does not intend to marry her; and it is madness in all women to let a secret love kindle within them, which, if unreturned and unknown, must devour the life that feeds it; and, if discovered and responded to, must lead, ignis-fatuus-like, into miry wilds whence there is no extrication.*

Angered by his derision, Miss Bingley was left seething, and throwing away Miss Ingram's arm like a redundant prop, she drooped back down into her chair with a huff-puff of breath, questioning how she should proceed, all the while attempting to ignore the way Miss Latimer sniggered behind her hand to have witnessed their humiliation, and all from the comfort of her ring-side seat, delighting in how she was the only one of the three of them whose poise was still intact. And it was then, in reprisal for the mill master's unapologetic contempt, that it all truly began, leaving him to wonder whether, if he had been just a fraction more civil, he could have avoided the whole sorry business that was to follow.

While she did not show it as visibly as her peeved companion, Miss Ingram too was seething, but if one looked closely, the signs of her inflamed indignation were plain to see. She eyed Mr Thornton with the sort of aggravation that prickles the skin and burns a blush upon it with the furious stain of mortified anger, the colour clashing with the ruby flowers on her bodice. It was infuriating to see him sitting there, his back turned to her as he read, his mind on other matters as he snubbed her, treating her as if she were nobody of significance. A rather unladylike snort escaped her nostrils as she sulked, which only served to intensify her ire. It was unthinkable that he should ignore her in this way, but then again, he was always impartial when it came to women. It was ironic, really, that the most eligible bachelor in Milton should be so indifferent to his admirers, this man who varied so greatly from the other lecherous bores in the master's circle, each of them loutish, piggish and lacking in everything but excess weight, the lot of them nothing but a bunch of pigeon-livered hornswoggles and gal-sneakers.

It vexed her greatly to realise that Mr Thornton, despite his unmatched credentials, was not a lady's man. He was so very different to anyone she had ever known before, and as for the man she had once thought to marry, he had most definitely not been a stranger to affairs of the heart, nor indeed, affairs of any kind. Or at least, that was the case until he reformed after his second marriage, a most degrading union if there ever was one. Then again, perhaps that is what he deserved for having lied to his friends about his situation by secretly keeping a madwoman in his attic for years.

As far as Miss Ingram could assess, Mr Thornton was always a gentleman, the kind who is more of an ideal than a reality. Miss Ingram had only been newly introduced into society when she had learnt, with a rude awakening that devastated her heart, that girls are taught to believe that men are noble creations that resembled gallant knights from fairytales—*what lies!* To be sure, she had discovered, as all women do, albeit too late, that fairytales are not real, and men are not princes, but slimy, slippery frogs. So, you see, that is why she had to be certain, that when she married, and in doing so, signed her rights away to her husband, legally giving herself to him body and soul, that she was not sentencing her own happiness to death by chaining herself to a brute, a wolf in man's clothing.

Still, Mr Thornton was not like that. He was not known for making licentious comments, nor did he ever let his hands wander when she detained him in shady corners of ballrooms (he did not dance), and never made her uncomfortable in his presence, save for his occasional menacing moods, such as today. No, Mr Thornton never took liberties and he never failed to treat the women around him with dignity, and in truth, Miss Ingram respected him for that, or rather, she would have, but his disinterest was making it intolerably difficult to win his favour, or any other woman's, for that matter. In fact, come to think of it, Miss Ingram could hardly think of a time when she had seen him look at a woman—her thoughts were rudely halted.

Suddenly, a sickly bile began to churn away inside her, and it affected a putrid sort of resentment to fizz there, and as it bubbled away, she felt an overwhelming need to launch a prompt and brutal retaliation, striking Mr Thornton where she knew it would hurt him the most.

Leaning to the side, and concealing her face behind her fan, she mouthed something to her two rivals. Neither Mrs nor Miss Thornton knew what she said, her words were but few, but if the smirks on the ladies' faces were anything to go by, then it had been something truly wicked indeed, and the conspiring bow of their combined heads was a sign that they had agreed to a temporary ceasefire and formed a coalition of callousness for, what they considered to be, the greater good.

'*How very ill* Miss Hale looked today at church. *I have never, in my life, seen a woman so altered as she is since the winter!'* Miss Bingley declared, conspicuously stridently, just to be sure she was heard loud and clear as the woman fired her opening shot in this contest, this war of women, of which she was determined to win and lay claim to the spoils.

Yet here we must pause and take stock, because before we continue any further with this script of their taunts, it is only right to ask ourselves why these three ladies would take the time and make the effort to besmirch Miss Hale's character at all. The reason is really very simple. As you clever set may have guessed, all three women had set their cap at Mr Thornton for many months, each one of them already disappointed in love, and vowing never to let it happen again, their new victim would be denied the right to slip through their fingers and escape their marital clutches. Nonetheless, no matter what wily methods they employed, none of them could get the master to pay them the slightest attention. It was almost as if, as far as he was concerned, none of them existed. As much as this had miffed them, offending their vanity, they had at least been appeased to learn that the secluded bachelor seemed disinterested in every young lady who fawned over him, showering him with their flattery and flirtation, his love and lust alike a prize that nobody could buy, bribe, or beg from this gentleman of staunch honour.

Then *she* had arrived.

It had not taken the ladies long to notice how Mr Thornton's awareness had been aroused by the somewhat disorientating presence of Miss Hale, this pious girl who had ridden in on her moral high horse and stolen his curiosity without any intention or endeavour. Even though nothing official had been declared on either side, it was obvious that the man was smitten with her, a hex she had cast upon him from the very first day they met. His fascination was plain for all to see, and while some men would make subtle public remarks about their passions, he was far too private for such publicity, but they could all see it. They could see it in the way he gazed at her with those lingering, longing stares. They glimpsed it in the way his chest thudded as his heart beat faster at the sight of her, the way his ears pricked at the mention of her, and the way his lips curled at the thought of her.

At first, they had mistaken his intrigue in Miss Hale as nothing more than esteem, an affiliation with her tedious integrity that was in harmony with his own immovable principles. But then, after the months passed, they realised it was an infatuation, a passion that was extreme, a fire, nay, a blaze, that was too intense to outshine. However, it was not until lately, after witnessing a shift in his demeanour and the cloaking of a depressive veil around him following Miss Hale being coupled with a young man, a station and the cloak of darkness, that it, at last, dawned on them all.

Mr Thornton was finally, and faithfully, in love.

And it was a true love, one that holds firm and steady.

There was that luminosity behind his eyes, you see. That unmistakable glint of love that gleams brighter than the purest gold. It was an awakening of a sleeping dream, a vision for the future, an imagining in his mind of what he could have with this woman if they were to wed.

It was difficult to explain, but they could all see it, and besides, whatever it was, regardless of whether Shakespeare had ever written about it, there was one thing for sure.

He had never looked at any of them that way.

But they could not, would not, let it be the end of their own hopes of marriage.

Yes, Mr Thornton was in love with the young lady, madly so, and as a result, it was their duty, not to mention their pleasure, to permanently destroy, or rather, dispel, his enchantment with Miss Hale, and that was what this gathering on the seemingly inoffensive Sunday afternoon was all about.

At any rate, I talk too much, as always, and I digress, so let us listen in once again to what they had to say about our dear Helstone rose. But first, perhaps we should hear her side of the story....

Chapter Five

Who Else?

Before we meet our leading lady, there is one thing you *must* understand: *No one who had ever seen Margaret Hale in her infancy, would have supposed her born to be a heroine...* but they would be wrong.

To begin with the old rigmarole of storytelling. In a country there was a shire, and in that shire there was a town, and in that town there was a house, and in that

house there was a room, and in that room there was a
bed, and in that bed there lay a young woman.

Thus, in this vein, Margaret Hale sat alone in her
bedroom on one perfectly unassuming Sunday
afternoon, on the very same Sunday afternoon that was
currently plaguing John Thornton, as it so happens, she
had no notion of the events that were soon to unfold.

After all, how could I—*I mean, she...* how could *she*
have possibly known?

On her return from church, Margaret loitered in the
hallway for an interval, at a loss of what to do as she
rolled up and down on the balls of her feet with jittery
unease, her fingers twitching for occupation, her mind
searching for diversion, her dear heart pleading for
calm. In the end, there was only one thing for it, and so
she made her way to the kitchen without delay, and after
just about pestering Dixon to the edge of madness, she
had insisted the maid put her to work at once.

At first, Dixon had been hesitant, wary of Miss
Margaret's unreserved willingness. That is to say,
Margaret was attentive by nature, and God alone knows
that Dixon was grateful for the assistance of a young
back and a strong set of arms and legs all these months
since she had become obliged to fetch and carry like a
skivvy rather than a lady's maid. Be that as it may, there
was something unnatural about the lass' eagerness this
day.

Still, help was help, and given that she was not in a
position to turn up her supercilious nose at anyone,
Dixon promptly pointed her charge in the direction of a

hefty mound of laundry that needed washing, starching and ironing, a playful simper curling her lips to see the grimace which briefly contorted Margaret's face at the sight of such a colossal heap.

Therefore, for the past three hours, Margaret had attacked it with zeal, working away with an energy that seemed boundless as she ignored the niggling spasms in her shoulders and the sweat that trickled from her brow with a mocking drip-drip-drip to see her adorn an apron and scrub high and low at every surface until her palms bled. All she could think was that she was glad her mother was no longer alive to see her reduced to this, God rest her soul, not that Margaret minded a little hard work, of course not, but she knew her dear mamma would have shuddered to see her toiling away as a plume-swish, rather than owning her place as mistress of the house.

In light of her gruelling service, when Margaret trailed back to her room quite sometime later, she was sorry to say that her limbs were groaning with a throbbing ache by way of thanks for her arguably ill-contrived dedication to the punishing task of being her servant's servant. It inspired within her an even greater sympathy towards those who laboured in the factories of Milton, their resilience enough to make her begrudge her own and pity its inferiority. Then again, Margaret ought not to complain, she had asked for employment, for an opportunity to be useful, and most crucially, for a chance to distract herself from languishing in the personal penitentiary that played host to her unhappy thoughts.

Stepping into her bedroom, Margaret glanced at the clock on her mantel.

It was one o'clock.

So... what would he be doing now?

Once she closed the door behind her, Margaret was overcome with the frightening realisation that the day was still young, so she would be compelled to continue in her exhausting endeavours if she wished to occupy herself until dusk. And what was more, to reach that finish line without sparing a thought for anything or anyone who existed outside the four walls of her refuge, lest she be saddened by thoughts of him—I mean, *them*.

With shaking fingers, Margaret rubbed at her temple which pulsated with a dull ache, and in that box of bone that contained her colliding thoughts, she sensed these distressing divinations forming in the interlude of her inaction. There they ripened into something inclement as they were at first sewn as tiny buds of no significance, but then she writhed as they rapidly grew into weeds that sprouted at an alarming pace, climbing up and twisting themselves round and round her subconscious, seizing at her already burdened heart with their vicious talons and suffocating them until she could scarcely breathe.

Fumbling behind her until she felt the brush of taciturn metal, Margaret hastily turned the lock, and with a wilting of her spirit, she slumped against the door frame with a defeatist thud. Her body was petite, so the thump was light, and this made her smirk in self-derision to recognise that she was so immeasurably small, powerless really, to overcome her demons.

Margaret hated feeling so helpless, it was not at all like her. Blinking rapidly, her vision was distorted, and with the wetting of her eyelashes, she saw that it was obscured by a deluge of salty tears that streamed down her cheeks in minuscule rivers of crystal-clear water. With a despondent snuffle, Margaret raised a hand to wipe them away, and as she breathed heavily, the scent of soap which had become lodged beneath her nails from washing the floors now seeped into her nostrils and stung the hairs with a pungent aroma that singed.

As a dainty sneeze escaped her, Margaret reached for her handkerchief, a small, equal patch of cotton that was nondescript, given that it was no more exceptional than any other of its mass-produced variety. All the same, on seeing it, as she clutched it in her hand marred by blackened blisters from the handle of the iron, Margaret began to weep more forcefully. Lifting it to her face, she sniffed it, and there she smelt the familiar fragrance of sweat, soot and smoke, a spicy scent that never failed to disturb something savage inside her.

It was *his*.

And who might *he* be?

Why, Mr Thornton, of course, *who else?*!

Chapter Six

The Vanquished Hercules

Mr Thornton stilled in an instant, his hands clutching his newspaper possessively, protectively, the whites of his knuckles showing as they shook, and with the froth of antipathy fermenting in his belly, he snarled. All thoughts of the Navigation Act flew from his mind. Mr Thornton did not care tuppence for anything else when his senses were alerted to the supremacy of that name, the one and only name that provoked him so, disturbing his sanity. *He shrank from hearing Margaret's very name mentioned; he, while he blamed her—while he was jealous of her—while he renounced her—he loved her sorely, in spite of himself.*

He silently thanked the Lord that his back was turned to them, or else they would have seen the ashen tint that faded his cheeks, the outline of his veins overridden by lines of angst that were carved into him like scores in stone.

Oh! So this was their game, was it? Of course! That would explain why they were here. They had not merely come to parade themselves before him, but they had an even uglier intention in mind, and that was to disparage Miss Hale.

Margaret.

His darling girl.

He knew that he should not think of her with such intimate fondness, but even if she was never to be his, Mr Thornton's heart was already married to her, and it always would be, so he felt that in the cloistered sanctuary of his most private thoughts, he, at least, had the right to call her by her given name.

Nevertheless, it was clear to him that the witches were once again up to their usual tricks, *for a charm of powerful trouble, like a hell-broth boil and bubble.*

While Mr Thornton felt it safe to assume that all that had passed between Margaret and himself was not common knowledge, it was possible that these three had worked him out. Was he really that obvious? Well, let them! Let them try and belittle Margaret—because he would be ready for them! In any case, if he had saved her from an inquest, risking his character and conscience on her behalf, then it was nothing to him to save her from their meanness.

Pausing, Mr Thornton mulled over how to respond, weighing up each and every possibility and assessing their merits, the short-term hope being that he could reclaim his parlour as his own as soon as possible by way of evicting these crones, and in the long-term, he would never need to hear Margaret spoken of with vicious spite again. He took a minute to calm himself, the colour slowly returning to his knuckles as the first intense stab of anger ebbed away. How sorely tempted he was to raise his voice to them, to demand they leave his house and leave (his!) Margaret alone, but he soon thought better of it. Instead, he broached the topic with a composed and calculated manner that, for now, gave him the upper hand.

'*Oh?*' said he, in response to Miss Bingley's earlier comment, which, despite being several pages ago, had only taken place a few short seconds previous. His single-syllable response was enough to cajole the ladies into continuing, all so that he could lay waste to their abominable duplicity.

'I noticed it too. *She is always so grave and disapproving,*' Miss Thornton agreed, nodding her head vigorously. It was not that she truly disliked Miss Hale, since while the young lady may have been maddeningly uninteresting, she had never been unkind to Miss Thornton, nor had she caused her any undue offence, other than insisting upon wearing her drab clothes, an affront which the spendthrift woman could not readily forgive. It was more that she was so severe, and a tiresome bluestocking to boot. Miss Hale possessed that way of looking down her nose at people, as if she were their better, and when she herself was no more than a clergyman's daughter who lived in a house that was so cramped that it could easily be squashed into one nook or cranny of Miss Thornton's own much larger home. She recollected with a pout the day that she had met her in town while purchasing a thing or two (or three or four), from Green's for her trousseau. Miss Thornton recalled telling Miss Hale about Watson's business proposition that was sure to make everyone as rich as Croesus, only to have her knit her brow and frown, going so far as to assert that she thought John would have nothing to do with anything so risky as speculation, as if she knew him better than his own sister. That had really nettled her. Miss Hale was undoubtedly the most dreary person Miss Thornton had ever met, other than John, that is. In fact, she often wondered whether her brother and Miss Hale might do very well for each other, they were both as dull as ditch water, perhaps even a shade or two duller still, with all their tedious pride and principles. But no, John was married to the mill, everyone said so. Moreover, he did not have a romantic bone in his body, he was far too gruff and grumpy for such a sentimental thing as feelings, so whatever her friends had in mind when it came to catching him, she knew they were wasting their time, for John would never marry, and nor would Miss Hale.

Indeed, the two of them were perfect for each other, and yet, Miss Thornton was quite sure that neither of them had even considered the other as a love match.

Smirking to herself, Miss Thornton loudly declared of Miss Hale, *'It is not as if she will ever get a husband!'* to which she saw her mother narrowing her eyes and shaking her head in chastisement, the daughter ducking her own and blushing at her pathetic attempt at mischief, her tongue not nearly as poisonous nor as practised in the art of malevolence as her friends'.

It was true that Miss Thornton may have had a snide side to her, but in reality, she was harmless, her heart much more sensitive than people often gave her credit for. On the other hand, as for Mrs Thornton, the censure of her daughter was not so much a rebuke of her childish disparagement but was a bid to spare her son any further distress, because as she knew, Miss Hale could very well have had a husband by now. Her son would have been the most loyal husband who had ever lived, but the silly girl had turned down her chance to be Mrs John Thornton, and as he said, there was nowt to be done about it now. Still, there was little time to ponder on this hopeless fact, given that the other ladies in question were far from finished with their assault on the character of the one whom they all spoke and thought of, the one who was not here to defend herself. 'Quite! On our return from church, your sister and I *were agreeing that we would hardly know her again,* what say you, Mr Thornton?' Miss Latimer pronounced, leaning back as she called towards him over her lace-trimmed shoulder, her enunciation cloying in its venomous quip. 'I thought she looked absolutely dreadful today, quite worn out.'

Mr Thornton dug his heels into the floor to assuage the anger that was mounting within him, his dander flaring up at hearing *that woman,* that saintly creature who was too good, too pure for all their hideous souls combined to ever rival, being demeaned in such a manner. And in her own hom—*no.* It was *not* her own home, he really should stop imagining that it was, but it ought to be, he wanted it to be, and even if she were never to step foot within these four walls again, he would still ensure it remained a refuge for her.

But alas, it was too much! He could hardly bear it. It was enough to make him want to shout and swear at

Miss Latimer, even if such vehemence of vulgarity was not in his nature. Why was hearing her mistreated so damned excruciating to him? This goddess who cared not whether he lived or died, he was her willing slave, she being his undisputed master who commanded him like a puppet on a string. Oh! How the mighty fall, good sir, how the powerful tumble down from their pedestals of crumbling dust, and there the vanquished Hercules collapses at the feet of a woman. There was no dispute amongst disappointed men that Cupid had a wicked sense of humour, and how his winged assailant must snigger with mirth to strike him thus and spear the armour that had for so long shielded Mr Thornton's heart.

How he wished he could tell her what she meant to him, and how he despised himself for being too stubborn as to shield his heart from her, choosing not to go to her and confess all the treasures reserved there in her name, jewels of ardour that he both concealed and cherished in that tomb of lonely longing. *Ha!*—how poetic, thought he. But even the poets could not save him now, since Mr Thornton was just a man, an ordinary man with nothing remarkable to say for himself, and how could one so inadequate in both word and deed ever be worthy of wooing a woman as incomparable as she?

Nevertheless, Mr Thornton refrained from any such brashness on his part, because not only would it be abominably rude to lash out at Miss Latimer, no matter how much she deserved his wrath, but his defensive outburst would also be revealing, far too enlightening, uncovering the truth of the sentiments he harboured in honour of that sweet lady of whom they scorned without shame. Taking a deep breath, Mr Thornton tried his best to moderate his tone, his rage simmering beneath the surface like a pot of stewing ire that was about to boil over and scald him, leaving him with the foetid blisters of rage to perpetually sting him as they seeped into the open wounds of his splintered soul. As if this young man did not wear enough scars, inside and out, to bitterly grieve him.

'I noticed no great difference,' he said coolly, congratulating himself on his bravado of indifference, even if within, his heart was screaming out in rebellion.

However, unable to help himself, he boldly ventured to add, 'Miss Hale is, as she always has been, entirely herself.'

Even Mr Thornton knew that this was a commendation too far, and so he bowed his head behind his newspaper and immersed himself once again in his reading, hoping that this would be enough to deter them and that they would soon lose interest, and so this despicable conversation would end as abruptly as it had started.

God help him if they continued!

But needless to say, they did.

Chapter Seven

A Very Different Cloth

Margaret held the handkerchief tightly in a steadfast grip.

He had left it behind on his last visit three months ago, not that Margaret was counting, that would suggest she cared, which she most definitely did not. He had given it to her after she accidentally poured tea on her wrist during one of his evening lessons with her father. She remembered feeling like such a clumsy fool, but the sound of his timbre had affected her to tremble so, as if she sat across from him as a harp, rather than a person, his baritone melody plucking at her quivering strings. She had not heard him speak all night. She had not heard him speak for weeks. In truth, she had not heard him utter a sound since they had stood at the foot of the stairs in a state of stalemate, he demanding answers, she unable to submit to his harassed request, and so he had informed her, in no uncertain terms, and without the aspiring expectation of eventual forgiveness, that he loved her no more.

The contents had cooled by the time it was spilt, soaking the cuff of her dress along with everything else it saturated as it flooded the table, the brown of liquid merging with the brown of wood, so it had thankfully not scalded her. Still, she instinctively flinched in fright and dabbing at her bracelet with a cloth that had also fallen victim to her carelessness, Margaret had sensed a shadow engulf her, and peering up, there he had been. With a face void of expression, Mr Thornton proceeded to wordlessly hand over his own handkerchief, his chin thrust into the air as he avoided looking into her eyes. It was so high, in fact, that she was able to examine every individual hair that made up the whiskers that stubbled his jaw like a black forest across a weather-beaten landscape, her height offering her the perfect vantage point to study him as the tip of her head sat level with his firm breast. On seeing him eye her wrist to discern whether she was injured, Margaret had tried to mutter her thanks as she lowered her head to evade his gaze and veil her blush, but only a muffled mumble stumbled ineloquently from her lips, and so, Mr Thornton walked away again with a fractious glower, but not before his eyes fluttered briefly to look at her bracelet one last time, a strange expression of vexation disturbing his stern features to see it come to harm.

Margaret meant to use it at the time, but she found herself unable to tarnish it with her tactlessness, something she had done too readily to his favours in the past with her impetuous misconceptions, so instead, she had pilfered it. The confession of her thievery shocked her still, leaving her wondering what on earth her father would say. Even so, she had fully intended to return it to Mr Thornton on the occasion of his next visit, as crisp and clean as she received it when it had been presented as a token of his chivalrous yet arbitrary kindness.

Nonetheless, she had done no such thing. Instead, Margaret had concealed it in her pocket, and there she had carried it every day from then until now, swapping it from one dress to the next, the symmetrical square of material caressing the folds of her skirts as it hid itself away in solitary confinement, and only now did it once again resurface to greet the light of day as she held it and thought of him. She had hoped it would force him to look at her again when she handed it over, his notice having been denied her for so very long, presumably as punishment for her unjust harshness towards him. But alas, she had not seen Mr Thornton in a terribly long time, he had stayed away, and all because she had disappointed his hopes and demeaned his character with her pride and her prejudice.

Nevertheless, her melancholic reverie of chapters past did not linger for long. Instead, she thrust the offending artefact back into her secret nook, and with purposeful strides, Margaret made her way to her bed, and there she threw herself down and longed for the ground to swallow her whole, all so she might escape the riot that raged in her heart.

What could it be? Why did she care for what he thought, in spite of all her pride in spite of herself? She believed that she could have borne the sense of almighty displeasure, because He knew all, and could read her penitence, and hear her cries for help in time to come. But Mr Thornton—why did she tremble, and hide her face in the pillow? What strong feeling had overtaken her at last?

Of course, deep down, she knew, of course she knew, but she was not yet ready to own it.

For a while, at least, *she lay down and never stirred. To move hand or foot, or even so much as one finger, would have been an exertion beyond the powers of either volition or motion. She was so tired, so stunned, her feverish thoughts passed and repassed the boundary between* lucidity and irrationality, *and kept their own miserable identity.*

There was so much to consider. So much to contemplate. Such a mess for her to muddle through. She knew she could not shy away from it indefinitely. She must screw her courage to the sticking place of her inborn heroism and confront her fears. There was no other way out of this. Then, and only then, with her head held high in the reassurance of her faith, Margaret would have no choice but to walk through the crucible of her discontent if she ever hoped to escape it and break free so that she might live in the light of peace that lay on the other side of this tunnel, though the path be a dark and disorientating trail to tread.

But, oh! Where to start? Margaret felt utterly lost in this confusing, chaotic disarray, and she had no hope of making sense of any of it, let alone all of it. It was like a ball of wool that had become tangled, impossible to unravel with its knotted strings, her feelings a jumbled mass of overlapping lines that ran in contradictory directions without knowing where one began and another ended. So much had come about that Margaret hardly knew what to think anymore, each emotion annulled by a fiercer and infinitely more impenetrable successor.

Looking back upon the year's accumulated heap of troubles, Margaret wondered how they had been borne. If she could have anticipated them, how she would have shrunk away and hid herself from the coming time!

'I am so tired,' she whispered to herself, her loneliness overpowering her, *'so tired of being whirled on through all these phases of my life, in which nothing abides by me, no creature, no place; it is like the circle in which the victims of earthly passion eddy continually.'*

In less than a twelve-month, Margaret had been uprooted in more ways than one, as if ripped from the sheltered soil of her familiar surroundings, and if she were honest, she hardly recognised herself any more, she scarcely knew who she was, and that both thrilled and terrified her with equal intensity. Her feelings were so feral that she was sure they could not be right, or at the very least, they could not be respectable. Wild as they were, they had sown a seed in her heart with their stubborn stems that embedded themselves in the very core of her being, winding themselves intrinsically into the integrity of her whole existence until she could no longer distinguish what was old and what was novel. What was fact and what was fiction. What parts of herself she wanted to preserve and nurture, and which parts she was ready to bid farewell to forever.

It was almost as if she could not fully remember who she had been before she had come here and met him, as if that girl no longer was, disappeared for good, usurped by womanhood, her spirit evolved while her body remained, a reincarnated, reinvented person dwelling within. She was to herself an unknown stranger that she somehow recognised, a new acquaintance who she must make the effort to befriend, or else she would be lost to herself.

The past year had been one of considerable trials and tribulations, and Margaret often wondered, in her quiet moments of self-doubt, whether she had braved them with all the resilience that she might have, and with the humility she knew she could muster if her will required it. Then again, it had not been as bad as all that, for you see, *day by day had, of itself, and by itself, been very endurable—small, keen, bright little spots of positive enjoyment having come sparkling into the very middle of sorrows.* Woven within the blackness of her despair, was laced a thin yet indissoluble length of thread, intertwining itself as a strand of irrepressible hope.

Him.

For what seemed like numerous harassed hours, although it must have been no time at all, Margaret shifted between sitting and lying as she wrung her hands, nibbled her lip, tapped her foot and dredged her powers of resourceful creativity, all in a vain effort to uncover a remedy. Curling up into a confined ball, as if she were a cat, Margaret tried to rest, willing away the lonely hours and clearing her mind so that it might sweep aside the cobwebs that cast their tangled threads about the place and clouded her thoughts, praying that sleep would whisk her away into a peaceful abyss of unconsciousness.

For anyone who might be inclined to chide Margaret and call her a watering pot, pestering her for her moroseness, she might well reply:

'Do you think if I could help it, I would sit still with folded hands, content to mourn? Do you not believe that as long as hope remained I would be up and doing? I mourn because what has occurred cannot be helped. The reason you give me for not grieving, is the very sole reason of my grief. Give me nobler and higher reasons for enduring meekly what my Father sees fit to send.'

Nonetheless, this plan proved futile. Far from falling asleep, all Margaret had been able to do was stare at the ceiling, her thoughts whirling in a chaotic windstorm of anguish, leaving her feeling all at sea and rather sick with it. After all, *a ruffled mind makes a restless pillow.* In the end, she gave up, and sitting upwards with vigorous intent, she opened the first book that came to hand, which was, as it happened, a rather weighty tome on the history of cotton. She had found it in the public library of Milton, the first of its kind in the city, an innovative setting that was accessible to all, and a place that Margaret had made a point of visiting at her earliest convenience.

However, despite her acute awareness of the significance of the occasion, she had been distracted from her enjoyment of it, disconcertingly certain that she had seen a tall man with black hair in the distance, his impressive bearing and brisk, indomitable stride hard to ignore, his head towering high above all others and appearing to float along the bookshelves. Margaret could have sworn that she knew him, but she must have been mistaken, for the man she supposed it to be would surely have been too busy with affairs of commerce to visit the library on a market day. Then again, he did hold reading in such high esteem. She had heard him tell her father that while he was not disposed to idleness, and while he would rather be a man of use than one of leisure, he often wished he could spend a greater portion of his day with his nose buried in a book of pleasure, rather than those of business.

Being sure to remain cautiously out of sight, Margaret had deftly edged nearer, and with the gentleman's back turned to her, she had spied that he was carrying works that bore the words, *"New F,"* in rather fine gold lettering, and for a moment, she half wondered whether it had been referring to the New Forest. Margaret tried to lean in to get a better look, but then the man had moved away most unhelpfully, so she discounted her foolish imaginings and returned to her carefree exploring.

Left alone once more, Margaret hummed serenely to find herself in such easy company as that of authors and their characters, poets and their sonnets, thinkers and their ideas, her fingers tracing the spines of the volumes as she wound in and out of neatly packed aisles of books stacked high, some tall, some short, some fat, some thin, drinking in the fresh smell of the virgin pages that longed to be opened and read.

This particular book had been sitting faithfully on her bedside table for the past few weeks and Margaret had dedicated herself to reading at least one chapter every night before she retired. At first, she expected that it would be terribly dull, but on the contrary, it was proving to be a most riveting and informative read.

Perhaps, if she were attentive in her studies, then she might have more to offer in her conversations with the townsfolk of Milton, her opinions grounded in fact, as opposed to conjecture. Besides, it would surely do no harm if when Mr Thornton came again—*if* he came again—Margaret could impress him with her knowledge, proving to him that she understood the ways of the north, thus demonstrating that its masters and men were no longer an enigma to her.

She liked the exultation in the sense of power which these Milton men had. It might be rather rampant in its display, and savour of boasting; but still they seemed to defy the old limits of possibility that persisted in the hackneyed, humdrum cities of the south, prevailing *in a kind of fine intoxication, caused by the recollection of what had been achieved, and what yet should be.*

Therefore, notwithstanding her wavering attitude toward them, Margaret wanted to properly comprehend these men so that she might assess them more fairly and determine once and for all the measure of their moral stock. Her exercise was not one of theory but was entirely practical. She wanted to respect them. She wanted to know them better. She wanted to be on friendly terms with them. Or at least, she wanted that with him. Nobody else mattered, really, not any more.

Margaret could not claim to know much about Milton, nor its people, nor its ways, but in the brief time that she had lived in this town, she had come to realise that there were two kinds of masters: those who were cruel and those who had a conscience, and as far as she was concerned, Mr Thornton was the only one who fell into the latter category. She had listened, she had listened carefully, and she had watched, she had watched attentively, and Margaret had established that Mr Thornton was cut from a very different cloth to his peers, a thicker, stronger, bolder, and more durable cloth, a more fitting robe for the role he had been ordained to perform. Consequently, she felt it only right that she should learn all she could about his world if she ever hoped, as modest and fragile as that hope might be, to one day be part of it.

Still, in spite of her best efforts, it soon transpired that reading was as pointless as everything else she put her mind to. It did not help her cause that the words kept disobligingly merging into one as her mind swam like a bowl of soup, so instead, Margaret elected to turn her attention to the sedative pursuit that is embroidery, a time-honoured means of occupation known to engage a woman for many a tedious hour, simultaneously numbing both her fingers and her faculties. That is to say, she did not mean that sewing in itself is frivolous, for it is undoubtedly an undertaking that requires considerable skill if it is to be exquisite in its depictions or delights, so those who appreciate its labours and art must not be offended. It was only that she keenly wished that a woman could hope to do more than commit herself to a tiny slither of silver as her bosom companion. Consequently, Margaret took up her frame and needle with an air of equanimity and set herself down for a period of serene repose as she commenced work on a present for Edith's twenty-first birthday.

Chapter Eight

A Pair of Fine Eyes

It was at this point, after the conversation taking place in the parlour of Marlborough House had been allowed to fall into a rut of stuffy silence for several minutes, that Miss Latimer decided that it was her turn to say her bit. She had remained fairly quiet thus far, having been brought up to believe that it was better for a woman to be seen and not heard, her role to listen, as opposed to prattling on so (as you can tell, I lacked such instruction), particularly in the presence of a man. Miss Latimer was not known for being talkative, but that was not on account of her having nothing to say, because the opposite was the way of it, and she dearly wished she was at liberty to express herself without inhibition, especially when men tended to be drivelling bores who rarely spoke two words of sense put together. Nonetheless, she had been taught the inflexible tenet at finishing school that a woman's mouth was a redundant vessel that should only override a gentleman so that it might whisper honeyed sentiments into his ear, and therefore, while she may bend this uncompromising rule from time to time, she was not inclined to break it. However, on this occasion, she felt she had the right to dissent and manipulate this rule for her advantage, given that the other two ladies who had accompanied her to take tea with the Thorntons this afternoon appeared to be thoroughly ill-bred, speaking both in and out of turn, so she deemed it only natural that she too should offer up an opinion.

As she sipped her tea, Miss Latimer's tongue flexed in her mouth as she readied this whip of spite, and she simpered to herself when she landed upon a most dastardly scheme, her pearly teeth gleaming in the reflection of a silver tray, affecting her to resemble a dog bearing its fangs in preparation for a vicious attack. With measured grace, she set the teacup upon its saucer, porcelain meeting porcelain in a soft clink that resonated through the room. The amber liquid within swirled gently, a resonance of the tempest brewing beneath her calm façade.

What one must understand about Miss Latimer, was that as far as the banker's daughter was concerned, a woman's chief attribute and crowning glory was her beauty. Without this crucial quality that separated the heroines from the hags, any female, whether she be a lady or a skiv, may as well be scathed with the pox and hide away in obscure isolation, for an unattractive woman can be of no use to herself and is an affront to everyone else. Ugliness was a sin that no amount of soap could expunge. Therefore, armed with a nefarious grin, Miss Latimer, a lady who considered herself a cut above average when it came to her looks, opted to launch her maiden speech.

'I do wonder whether Miss Thornton might be right,' she said all of a sudden and without ceremony, judging it best to just come out with it, what with Milton folk preferring frankness above the niceties of inane jawing. Everyone present, save Mr Thornton, glanced at her duly, not in the least Miss Thornton, who was not inured to having her comments validated, her eyelashes flickering their surprise.

On seeing that the attention of the room was appropriately fixed upon her, Miss Latimer allowed herself a small sally-shiggle by way of a compliment.

'It is unlikely that Miss Hale will ever get herself a husband,' she decreed decisively. 'If one could overlook her lack of fortune and formal education, as well as her insistence on coming out with the most radical humbug, then there is still the unavoidable fact that she is plain,' she said bluntly, not that any of the ladies minded, quite the contrary, since any derision of Miss Hale was more than welcome to their collective cause.

Straightening herself so that she sat in a more august position that showed off her posture, Miss Latimer nodded her own agreement, as if inviting herself to continue.

'As for her silhouette, it juts in and out in a way that is neither here nor there, as if she cannot make up her mind as to what shape she wishes to be. Now I come to think of it, she reminds me of an hourglass,' she assessed with a squiffy nose, since while she esteemed the slender female form, she could not abide it when a woman dared to have a more lithe waist than she, her hungry stomach rumbling beneath her corset as she resisted the enticing display of mouth-watering delicacies that sat mere inches from her, taunting her with their golden pastry, ripe jam and fluffy cream. Smacking her lips with deft decorum, she spluttered ever so slightly when she felt a trace of the watered-down red ink she had painted on sting her buds. This application was a subtle trick her mother had passed down to her daughter as a means of heightening her allure. Her mother, who now resided abroad with her lover under the guise of being away on grounds of poor health, had always been distinctly critical of her only child, taking great pains to complain that motherhood had robbed her of her youth.

In the quiet corners of Miss Latimer's memory, there lingered the echoes of a childhood tainted by the words of a parent whose love was veiled in the shadows of criticism. From the earliest recollections, her likeness in the mirror was to become a source of contention, a canvas on which her mother smeared the stain of inadequacy. A child's innocence, like fragile glass, shattered under the relentless glower that dissected every feature, every imperfection. The mirror, once a playground of self-discovery, transformed into a cruel accomplice, reflecting the disapproval carved into her mother's eyes. Her words had been as thorns laced with venom, each syllable a prickle that pierced the delicate petals of Miss Latimer's self-esteem. *"You could be pretty if only...,"* became the repetitive refrain, a conditional melody that hissed through the corridors of her mind.

Mrs Latimer had been described as the most handsome woman in the county in her day, with all the men hanging on every word that dripped from her rosy lips, and so Miss Latimer pouted to think of the plump freshness of Miss Hale's lips that seemed to perpetually shift most prettily, the moist twins of oval skin, those half-moons, separating, on the cusp of speech and smiles with dreamy awe. Having once courted the admiration of the gentlemen of Milton, Miss Latimer sniffed with jealousy to confess that she had witnessed many a man cast a satisfied glance as the lady in question walked past, none the wiser to the mesmeric pull she possessed. It peeved Miss Latimer to consider that the girl, that country bumpkin of no discernible pedigree, had the audacity to be willowy and yet so unfairly well-rounded, a dual achievement that was more infuriating than she could say. Even so, there was at least one detail which brought her succour, and so she was as pleased as punch to tell of it to all.

'And,' she continued, her words lingering in the air like an enticing puff of scent, inviting attention before gracefully descending and settling, 'I confess, though it pains me to do so,' her abject attempt at sympathy sticking in her throat, 'that I must fall in with the rest of you: Miss Hale is looking terribly tired these days. She appears to be utterly worn out...like an old shoe,' she concluded contemptuously, reminding her of the pair of frayed leather bruns that she had bid her raily-daily-abigail dispose of this morning, wishing that Miss Hale could likewise be thrown upon the dustheap and swept away from whence she came, never again to be missed, never again causing the ladies of the town to misstep with her righteous words and refinement.

'Indeed,' affixed Miss Ingram, and for a trice, one might fancy she was about to plead Miss Hale's case, but one would be sadly wrong.

'I understand that she was required to leave her aunt's charming house in a smart part of London to come here and take up residence in Crampton of all places, next to the market, with all the hideous pig's heads!' she cried, her features screwing up to emphasise her expression of revulsion.

'I was told the very same, or that is, my maid, was told by our cook, who was told by the grocer, who was told by the butcher,' the first lady concurred with an equal display of repulsion to think of living on a street sullied by the stench of blood and meat, not to forget the unsightly sight of those snouts hanging high and looking down at everyone with the same haughty countenance that Miss Hale wore. Miss Latimer scoffed at the thought of the confining abode Miss Hale called home.

Whispers of the newcomer had reached her before their paths crossed, and upon learning her humble address, she had envisioned a dreary sprite dwelling in the shadows. Yet, at the Thorntons' dinner party, Miss Latimer's expectations crumbled. Instead of a pitiable figure shrinking into the background like a spectre, Miss Hale emerged as a regal presence, commanding the room with a magnetic allure that held every gaze captive.

The revelation had dismayed Miss Latimer. Far from being a drab nymph, Miss Hale stood as a majestic creature, an ethereal force that left an indelible impression.

It did not escape Miss Latimer's discerning eye that their host, who had minutes before greeted her with polite indifference, abruptly abandoned a conversation with Mr Hamper to approach the young lady standing like a statue of ice-blue in an out-of-the-way corner of the room.

Indeed, Mr Thornton had extended his hand to encounter Miss Latimer's with well-mannered gallantry, his touch light as the breath of evening air, but it was a scripted greeting exchanged as pleasantries in a social performance, nothing more. Still, within the choreography of civility, his eyes betrayed a faint shift. A young lady, a comet in the celestial congregation of guests, captured his glance. He regarded her with a semblance of awe as if blinded yet illuminated by her beauty.

The host's hand, once a mere formality in its contact with hers, now cradled another's with a quiet reverence, an admiration expressed in the unspoken language of an enduring meeting. Miss Latimer had observed this tableau, his fingers, previously unresponsive to her touch, now hesitated on the young lady's palm, as if reluctant to release a treasure discovered in the fleeting twinkling of connection. From that transformative moment, Miss Latimer saw Miss Hale not as an obscure bystander, nor a subject of irrelevance, but as a formidable threat.

'They were surely never rich, but now they really are miserably reduced,' she expounded with a spurious whisper of confidentiality, her Milton upbringing having entrenched within her a preoccupation with money and a confidence that material wealth was the only merit worth mentioning.

'She is, by all accounts, driven to keep house like a servant because they cannot entice anyone to work for them,' she guffawed, amused by the notion of such a queenly figure being lowered to nothing more than a common cinder, or a Cinderella, just like in the fairy-tale her nanny had read her as a child. I say nanny, but there had been several, eight, to be precise, all but the last having quit their posts, their wits not merely at their end, but countless miles past it.

The ladies all tittered, and so Miss Latimer congratulated herself on her petty slight that had been delivered wrapped in a pretty bow of concern.

'Truly, is it any wonder that she appears so forlorn? No, I say that Miss Hale's bloom has been snatched by the hand of hard luck, and is likely to fade away entirely before the winter is out. And what man, pray tell, wants such a wife?' she asked in a tone that invited but required no response

However, a reply was to be proffered after all, for it was as Miss Latimer was about to surrender to the pining pangs of her cravings and reach out to capture a piece of oral heaven in the form of a biscuit drenched in honey that she stopped, jolted by the sound of Mr Thornton's brusque rebuttal.

'As you say: Is it any wonder that Miss Hale is a little downcast, given that she has been obliged to endure so much misery in recent months?!' he challenged. 'She has had to contend with a great deal,' he argued, rustling his paper as he tried to find something to read, anything at all, to improve his plummeting mood. He had not said a word as the various insults above had been batted about, but each baseless slur was a blow to him, and he could no longer stand it.

With his eyes settling on an article regarding the contentious Smog Act, he reflected on all that she had suffered over the past year, and this compelled Mr Thornton to consider how it had been necessary for Margaret to leave her home, a paradise that was by all accounts idyllic, and come here, to a town where the people were surely strange to her, the pollution from the factories blighting her sensibilities and turning her against this metropolis of materialism and those she judged to be culpable as abettors to the iniquity of inexcusable greed. For pity's sake! Mr Thornton would count himself a warrior of a man indeed if he could stomach half the upheaval and unhappiness she had borne in such a short space of time and still hold his head high in all the stately dignity that she did with such effortless grace and good-humour. Margaret was the epitome of a leaena et dea, and as such, she should be venerated, not condemned, especially by those not even worthy to shine her boots.

'Not to mention the passing of her mother, God rest her soul,' Mrs Thornton interposed pensively, gently patting the cross which rested around her neck, one of the few trinkets she wore along with her wedding ring, a simple brass and silver symbol of her faith passed down to her by her grandmother. Mrs Thornton may have had a poor opinion of the late Mrs Hale, what with all her indulgent low spirits, but that was irrelevant, because death was a solemn matter that warranted sober deference, and she herself remembered only too well what it was like to lose a mother, she having been the same age as Miss Hale when it happened. In the quiet chambers of memorial, where the echoes of time dance with all the delicacy of elephants on stilts, there resides a woman who once trod the labyrinth of grief at the tender age of eighteen. As the sun dips low, she finds herself retracing the steps of her sorrow, a pilgrimage to a sacred space where loss etched its permanent mark. In the discoloured glow of retrospection, she revisits the distressed sepia-toned pages of her youth, each chapter adorned with the fragility of innocence, and loss had remained her constant companion ever since.

For all she despised the young woman her son had formed an unreciprocated attachment to, Mrs Thornton could at least admire her forbearance, so it did not rest easy on her conscience to hear others batty-fang her so readily. To be sure, all the ladies sat before her had led lives of intact comfort, their sheltered worlds unshaken by the storms of misfortune, whereas bereavement of innumerable natures had been the kismet of Miss Hale. *Of all the trite, worn-out, hollow mockeries of comfort that were ever uttered by people who will not take the trouble of sympathising with others.*

This niggled Mrs Thornton's attitude of aversion towards Miss Hale, for while she could not forgive the girl her transgressions, she would not wish this breed of unhappiness upon anyone, more so when it fell upon the shoulders of one merely starting out in life, since she knew what the heavy burden of grief and assumed responsibility could inflict, as it had done to her son when he had lost his father.

For this reason, Mrs Thornton trusted that these hardships had served Miss Hale well, for while they were cruel in their timing and their consequences, they had at least allowed her to hold fast to her valour, and both find and foster her inner strength. Though she would not admit it, least of all to herself, Mrs Thornton was beginning to see that, in some respects, John and Miss Hale were not all that different after all.

On heeding his mother's words, Mr Thornton grunted noisily in treaty.

'Aye, that too,' he granted, pleased that she had stepped in and spoken some sense, her surprising defence of Margaret being nearly enough to make him forgive the fact that she had coerced him to stay here this afternoon, trapped in this den of malignant mockery.

Nearly, but not quite.

As for Margaret, while Mr Thornton applauded her courage when it came to the premature death of her mother, coupled with her unflagging ability to hold her head high and keep that same head in times of trouble, *he would rather have heard that she was suffering the natural sorrow. In the first place, there was selfishness enough in him to have taken pleasure in the idea that his great love might come in to comfort and console her; much the same kind of strange passionate pleasure which comes stinging through a mother's heart, when her drooping infant nestles close to her, and is dependent upon her for everything.*

The thought of her feeling wretched was enough to make his soul squirm in sympathetic pain, and yet, it thrilled him with a curious form of manly gratification to hope that she would come to him in her grief and choose him as her comforter. He hated the idea of her alone in that house with none other than her father for company. Mr Hale was an excellent man, that was not the issue, but Margaret ought to be around people who could give her notice and lift her spirits, and as far as he knew, her only real friend here, one of his own workers, had died pitifully young, so now she was more alone than ever. Furthermore, it did not rest easy with him that Margaret was in Crampton. To be exact, Mr Thornton could never be accused of being condescending, and while he found the proportions of the Hale's home ample and the atmosphere cosy, he could not help but feel Margaret ought to have somewhere more befitting the magnificence of her character. When Mr Bell had first asked him to seek out a suitable property for a former clergyman with a wife and daughter, Mr Thornton had engaged minimal effort and deemed the house a sufficient prospect. However, once he laid eyes on *Margaret, with her superb ways of moving and looking, he began to feel ashamed of having imagined that it would do very well for the Hales, in spite of a certain vulgarity in it which had struck him at the time of his looking it over,* and he was abashed to have neglected his duties, feeling like he had somehow let her down. It seemed to him that he may as well have asked the queen herself to live in such a house when she, by right, ought to be in a palace. Once more, the thought of her labouring on her hands and knees to scrub floors, enduring the heat from the iron and stove, and straining to lift hefty pots did not sit well with him. But she would do it, and he knew that his questioning her about it would only encourage his stubborn darling further, so he dared not say a word on the matter. He knew her better than that.

Mr Thornton would much rather Margaret was here, under his roof, where he could care for her and give her the life she deserved, working every God-given hour to ensure that his wife never wanted for anything her heart desired. Oh, but if only she were to come to him. Mr Thornton had imagined it often enough during the lonely hours he spent in self-imposed solitude in his mill office late at night. That was his way nowadays. He had always been conscientious, but lately, with the difficulties that the factory walkout had unleashed, he found his work had increased tenfold, so he was kept employed at all hours trying to catch up with orders and setting everything the strike had clouted askew straight again. However, that was not the only reason, nor was it the primary one. He could easily have worked at the table in the dining room or his own chambers, but he stayed away on purpose. In truth, he could not bear the cold reality of coming home to find his bed empty, the space beside him vacant, a human-shaped-hollow that only she could fill, a place where he knew she should be, her figure rising and falling steadily as she drifted between sleep and wake, waiting patiently for her husband to return, burning for his embrace as fiercely as he burned for her. He had never minded it before, but now, the loneliness of his bachelorhood affected his very bones to ache with longing, and it almost hurt to go to bed, so he rarely did in the days after the disappointment of his failed proposal.

During those subdued evenings, Mr Thornton would fancy that he would look up, startled by a sound as the floorboards creaked, announcing he was not alone after all, and there she would be. In his mind's eye, Margaret had never looked so beautiful, appearing before him mild without being meek, coming as she did in peace, dressed all in white, heralding the truce she wished to propose. She no longer sought to do battle with him, she had simply come to find solace in the shelter of his love, her countenance softened by the joyful certainty that had dawned upon her and set her free, that truth being that she wanted him just as much as he yearned for her. Smiling, he would picture her impertinent lips parting and quivering as she deliberated on what to say. Then, at last, as he stood before her in mute entreaty with his arms opened wide, his core quaked to think how *she might droop, and flush, and flutter to his arms, as to her natural home and resting-place.* They need not say a word. Their hearts, once bereft and now restored, would do all the talking on their behalf, and what sweet songs they would sing.

The notion had been so inspiring, that he had often got up and made to leave, electing to throw caution to the wind so that he might go to Margaret and try out his plan, the idea of confiding his unbroken fidelity to her and having it returned enough to make Mr Thornton grow ten inches taller with pride. But it was not to be.

He always stopped himself just as he was about to walk out the door, insecurity plaguing him and dragging him into a vicious circle of uncertainty. *One moment, he glowed with impatience at the thought that she might do this,* that she might confess that she cared for him too, then *the next, he feared a passionate rejection, the very idea of which withered up his future with so deadly a blight that he refused to think of it.* And now he had left it too long, and so it was too late. He had missed his chance with her, as fragile as it had been, as fanciful as it was, as fictional as it were, as foolish as he remained.

Nevertheless, while this piece of theatre was playing out in his mind, an actual scene was unfolding around him, and the ladies present were not prepared to put up with their host's infuriating logic blinded by love, each of them having copious criticisms regarding Miss Hale primed.

Propelling her nose into the air, Miss Bingley wrinkled it in disdain, a strand of her hair falling across her forehead and irritating her nostrils, her tresses as black as coal.

'You are, of course, quite right, sir, madam' said she, feigning accord with Mr Thornton and his mother. 'The poor lamb has been unfortunate, to say the least,' she granted with a sympathetic pursing of her lips. 'It is heartbreaking to think of her so ill-used by fate,' she commiserated, her tone serious, her eyes smirking. 'And to lose her mamma!' she gasped. 'Why, the young lady will be lost without her, which I expect is the cause of her wanton behaviour, and just to think how she must deplore having to look after that buffoon of a father of hers!'

All the ladies cackled in chorus at the mention of the dull, feckless, mole-like man whom they insulted.

'Had-yur-wheest!' Mr Thornton barked. 'Do *not* speak of her father like that!' he retaliated, his head twisting round the side of his chair as he glared at them, his features menacing as his eyes flashed with tempestuous confrontation. His blue irises were ignited by the fitful blinking of the fire, a bewitching spectacle to behold, the effect defining the ends of his raven hair to glint like polished spikes, the vivid embers in the hearth swaying chaotically as a blustery northern breeze blew down the chimney to chill the party of not-so-merrymakers

'He has been the greatest friend I have ever known and is worth ten of any man I have ever met. Richard Hale is intelligent, unassuming and unfailingly generous, even in the face of his great loss. I cannot imagine what it must be like to be forever torn from the woman I lov—to lose a close relative, but I think he has endured it with commendable grit. Mr Hale defines what it is to be a gentleman, and he has welcomed me into his home, so I will not have him knocked in my presence, do you hear?!' he reprimanded, and nodded to himself sharply to see the three ladies shuffle awkwardly in their seats to have had their insensitivity challenged.

Miss Bingley waited for a semblance of calm to settle the atmosphere.

'Yes,' she conceded, rather half-heartedly, her tone dry in its stale empathy. 'But really, that is no excuse! Regardless of her circumstances, the girl is quite beyond the pale. And speaking of pale, she is no such thing. She is *so brown and coarse,* most unladylike,' she disparaged, shaking her head punitively, as if the sight of a slight tan upon the skin was an indefensible infringement on femininity.

Miss Latimer chuckled. 'That is what one gets for pigheadedly traipsing about outdoors at all hours with no chaperone,' she derided, underlining Miss Hale's disgraceful conduct, trudging about the town visiting the dirty and dissolute labourers of Princeton, not a care in the world regards her safety or the diseases she might contract from their grubby houses, if houses were what one could call those squalid hovels. No, there was one thing for sure, Mr Thornton would not like that, and so this ruse was sure to devalue his enamoured infatuation with the southern flower, the thought of her being sullied by mingling with the great unwashed enough to turn him green with disgust.

'Absolutely,' Miss Ingram acquiesced as her grey eyes rolled, the colour matching her grey gloves that were as insipid as her grey personality, 'she is insupportably tanned. It cannot be good for her health. I even spotted a freckle or two, undoubtedly the result of too much time being subjected to the elements. She ought to be careful; excessive exposure to sunlight can leave a woman quite unbalanced,' she warned, thinking on how the man she had once hoped to marry had acquired his first wife from the West Indies, a land where the sun baked the earth, and almost certainly baked the brain along with it.

Mr Thornton let out a boisterous, "*ha*!," his paper crumpling as he threw it down on his lap, odd, since he always took meticulous care of his belongings, no matter how small or significant they may be, years of hardship training him to be careful with what he had.

'I think it hardly surprising she is so tanned,' he maintained. 'It is to be expected when she spends every waking hour going here and there to attend to the needs of the sick and impoverished, never a thought for her own wants,' he went on, a mite resentful that Margaret did not care to fuss over his needs, but that was beside the point.

'It is easy for a woman to be as pale as milk if she sits inside all day long and does no more than gossip,' he ridiculed pointedly, the ladies behind him puffing in indignation as they fanned their palpitating bosoms, their temperatures rising along with their tempers. Really! This was not how a gentleman ought to address a lady, particularly three ladies of their eminence.

'It is only natural that a person, be it a man or a woman, will acquire a little ruddiness to their complexion if they go about some hard work and apply themselves, and in Miss Hale's case, I hardly think it has done her a disservice,' he lectured, choosing, most wisely, not to mention the fact that he had spent most of his time in church today happily counting the freckles on the back of her neck and sketching an atlas of them with his eyes, somewhat like outlining the patterns of the stars. He had used to enjoy mapping the twinkling eyes of Heaven as a boy through the tiny rips in God's carpet that let his eternal light shine through in the days when the Milton skyline was clearer, as was his future. However, now he had found a much more inspiring constellation to chart on a creamy landscape that was known to ripple with the lull of that woman's glorious form. His mind wandered further still to think of Margaret's delectably alluring skin with her tapered arms, slender neck and peeking shoulders, all dusted in a hue of russet, giving her a healthy glow that heated his own red blood, turning it into a frenzied splutter that pounded in his chest with the sole purpose of serving her, thrumming a beat of constancy.

'And as for her being unbalanced, I happen to know from my studies at that house that she has an exceptional mind; one that is sound and sensible. So I say let the woman walk if she wants to, let her be, let her alone,' he muttered.

With an affronted glower, it was once again Miss Ingram's turn to address the room. 'I am entirely of your opinion, sir, she is a most excellent walker, and bravo to her. I am sure we are all quite envious of her energy. Nonetheless, we must consider that *she has nothing else, in short, to recommend her, but being an excellent walker. Why, I shall never forget her appearance this morning. She really looked almost wild,'* Miss Ingram appraised, recalling how, through the dismal champagne weather, she had spotted Miss Hale appearing from over the hilltop in the distance where the graveyard lay as she herself descended from her gilded carriage to attend church. It had sent a cold shiver down her back to think of the woman walking there, a most unnerving place to spend one's time. After remembering this, Miss Ingram's cheeks bore an alarming streak of scarlet as she was driven to think of another person, for *lady*, she refused to call her, who had often strolled about the moors surrounding Thornfield Hall in the early hours of the morning. In doing so, she had happened upon a man whom she had no business happening upon at all, and causing him to topple from his horse, he had most likely exacted a serious head injury, that being the only explanation as to why he had taken leave of his senses and married the elfin being.

'*Yes, and her petticoat; I hope you saw her petticoat, six inches deep in mud, I am absolutely certain!*' Miss Thornton chimed in, gawking at her friends, appalled to so much as contemplate treating one of her silken garments thus, all carelessness and no care, even if she had enough of them to dress all the womenfolk of Milton for a month. Miss Thornton was about to say more, but she bit her tongue, the low growl that emitted from her brother enough to make her think better of her folly.

'*Your picture may be very exact,* Fanny,' said her mother; '*but this was all lost upon me. I thought* Miss Hale *looked remarkably well when she came into* church *this morning. Her dirty petticoat quite escaped my notice.*'

It was indeed true that Mrs Thornton had privately observed that Miss Hale was looking astonishingly well of late, taking into consideration the trying circumstances she had faced. Having let her eyes train over her in church, Mrs Thornton had been provoked to begrudgingly admit that Miss Hale was a rare beauty. She was perhaps not as obviously handsome as some, still, she had a natural elegance that could easily arrest any man. The way she talked. The way she moved. The way she looked at you, it was all enchanted by a hypnotic loveliness, an enthralling refinement that one could not cultivate, it being innate to the gravity of a person's self-possession. Thinking back, Mrs Thornton had always said that a Milton girl would do for her John well enough. They were his sort, they would know the ways of the north, and they would comprehend what was expected of them as a mill master's wife. But by Heavens!—Miss Hale was a true lady unlike anything she had ever seen, so it was no wonder that John, a man used to the gruffness and grime that came from living in a town where the air was perpetually scotched with smog, had been utterly overwhelmed by her refreshing grace. It was only a pity she had not been equally impressed by his unmatched honour.

Looking about her, Mrs Thornton found herself unexpectedly saying, 'It is a wonder you did not invite her along today, Fanny,' to which all of the other women coloured and glanced covertly at Mr Thornton.

Miss Thornton hardly knew what to say, and with her mouth open in incredulity, all that stumbled from her was, 'But, Mamma…she is not…like us.'

Mrs Thornton paused, and with a sober sigh, replied, 'No, I suppose she is not.'

In the want of the fourth lady, the unwilling sentiment loitered like an unwelcome draught in the room—a subtle conviction that the missing presence might, in fact, withhold a sense of wisdom and commandability that surpassed the combined qualities of the three women currently gathered. There was a quiet acknowledgement that sometimes, the most profound virtues reside in the spaces left unfilled, prompting contemplation on the possibility that the absent lady, in her dearth, held a unique and admirable grace.

Miss Latimer, her gloved fingers gripping the edge of her chair, found herself ensnared in a silent struggle.

The object of the elder lady's admiration, a figure she held in ill favour, was not even present to bear witness to the covetous regard bestowed upon her.

'If you forgive me, Mrs Thornton, that is hardly the point!' Miss Bingley protested, daring to argue with her future mother-in-law, a dragon who would be promptly carted off to live with her feather-brained daughter the very instant she herself took up residence as the new Mrs Thornton. A house cannot have two mistresses, after all.

'*To walk three miles, or four miles, or five miles, or whatever it is, above her ankles in dirt, and alone, quite alone! What could she mean by it? It seems to me to show an abominable sort of conceited independence, a most country-town indifference to decorum!*' Miss Bingley persisted with animation, because, you see, the thought of a young lady scampering about and catching the eye of any passers-by was enough to make her scream, since it reminded her of another minx who had done just that. The insolent girl from Hertfordshire may have won out with all her walking, her ploys now giving her the right to roam the grounds of Pemberley as her own and pollute its shades, but mark her words, this time, Miss Bingley would not let a plain bit of frock ruin her chances.

'*I am afraid*, Mr Thornton,' observed Miss Ingram with a mean grin, '*that* her adventures may *rather have affected your admiration* for her eyes, which I once heard you refer to as "*fine*",' she *teased*. Reflecting upon a specific evening, as shadows lengthened in the embrace of twilight during a soirée, the reserved mill master, in a rare lapse of vulnerability, allowed his guarded demeanour to falter. With a wistful tone, he commented on the uncanny resemblance between Miss Hale's eyes and his cherished hue. The remark, initially irksome, acquired a deeper layer of discomfort as she surmised that it was not mere coincidence; instead, Miss Hale's distinct shade of cloudy blue appeared to have influenced and dictated the mill master's favoured colour palette, creating an intricate and disconcerting correlation between the tint of her gaze and the preferences of his heart.

'Not at all,' he retorted with deliberate nonchalance, keenly aware of how splendidly they had glittered in the dazzling sunlight this morning, much like sparkling sapphires, *'they were brightened by the exercise,'* he affixed with a smirk, not caring that he was getting dangerously close to disclosing exactly how he felt about Margaret to these unwelcome visitors. But he could not help himself, he could not help but admire her, both for her character and her beauty.

Still, Mr Thornton was brought back to the moment by yet another nit-picking comment, one which troubled him, because it made him wonder whether his guests (not that they were *his* guests), could read his mind.

'For my part, I must confess, I never saw any beauty in her face. Her features are not at all handsome. Her complexion has no brilliancy. Her nose wants character !—there is nothing marked in its lines,' Miss Latimer interjected.

Mr Thornton rumpled his own nose at this point. Here he had to disagree. He adored Margaret's nose. Unlike his own parish-pick-axe of a sharp beak, hers was not too pronounced in either direction, being neither too stubby, nor too angular. It was a sweet little thing that decorated the centre of her face most fittingly, and he had thought on many occasions of how he would like to lean down and kiss her there with a playful anointing of his lips, watching in rapture as she snuffled adorably in reply.

'*Oh, her teeth are tolerable, I suppose, but nothing out of the common way,*' Miss Bingley gibbered on, adding to the list of Miss Hale's apparent failings, grievous as they were.

Mr Thornton made a silent: *"what?!"* with his mouth, his face scrunched in exasperation. *Her teeth?!* Were they talking about a woman or a horse, here?

Before he had a chance to consider the candour of his refutation, Mr Thornton bit back with, 'Miss Hale has a simplicity about her that some men might find attractive. There are gentlemen who are not so easily thrilled by tawdry baubles that hang here, there and everywhere on a woman,' he continued, his eyes darting to take in the hideous ornaments that dribbled from the three ladies, and dribbled he meant, because it occurred to him that it looked rather as if a diamond mine had spat out its innards upon them, and it was not a comely look, as far as he was concerned.

'No, they are drawn to the aura of her character. While many a woman may need dresses and jewels to disarm her suitor, others require nought but her unadorned self, the grandeur of her mind, the magnificence of her force of nature, and the tenderness of her heart: these will be enough to charm any man and secure his good opinion, rendering him lost to her!'

On asserting this, Mr Thornton felt rather poked-up, causing him to redden beneath his bristles to think that, in essence, he was in effect depicting Margaret as being perfection itself in her exposed modesty, as in, naked.

Self-consciously, he finished, 'Yes, some women are arguably plain, but then again, some men find that... preferable.'

God save him!—Mr Thornton was helpless when it came to her. How could it be that she affected such a violent passion in him? What was completely unreasonable, was that Mr Thornton had managed to make it to thirty years of age without being remotely interested in a woman. He had never before felt the all-consuming, intoxicating lure of intense desire. Yet now, out of nowhere, he sensed that his sanity had been besieged, imprisoned, and now punished by an irresistible feeling of devotion for another. He had once prided himself on the belief that, unlike his contemporaries who easily succumbed to the whims of a beguiling smile in matters both personal and professional, he remained steadfast and impervious to such enticements. Ha! The irony of his present predicament did not elude him.

With a wistful sigh, Mr Thornton reached behind the cushion of his chair, retrieving a book on the villages of the New Forest—a recent acquisition from Milton's first public library. As he gently flipped through the pages, his fingers tracing the familiar texture of paper, he arrived at the section commencing with the letter "H." Yet, as his eyes scanned the lines in search of He...Hel...Helst..., his thoughts sailed far beyond the printed words, and he found himself utterly lost, adrift in the sea of a pair of fine eyes.

Chapter Nine

Masquerade

Quietly sewing away, minding her own business in her typically unobtrusive manner, Margaret could not have begun to imagine that, by the end of the day, within a few hours, in fact, her life would be very different indeed. There were no premonitions, not a single hint or warning, only a sense of unrelenting disquiet as Margaret lethargically threaded her needle and ambled it back and forth with minimal attentiveness as her diligent wrist did all the work on her behalf, her mind far away on other things, her thoughts wandering wistfully to think of her cousin and the life she had chosen.

Edith and the captain were so delightfully happy. It was truly that simple, and truly that serene. Their carefree world was one of sunshine, a paradise that was untroubled by gloomy clouds and devoid of rain, their sky painted with a palette of perfect blue, with not a blemish of black to worry it. It occurred to Margaret that the easy equilibrium Mr and Mrs Lennox enjoyed was almost certainly owing, in part, to the fact that they each held fast to the intractable philosophy that men and women belonged wholly to separate spheres and were in every sense distinct, a law that was as much set in stone as the Ten Commandments themselves, a concrete basis that made up the foundations of their marriage, as it did for all unions of their ilk. The pair coexisted in amiable reference to one another, ceaselessly circling their partner as Mars and Venus must in a cosmic dance composed by society, making sure to never collide with their partner's trajectory. This way, they were ensured to live in unobtrusive harmony, with the theoretical strengths of their sex complimenting the other, and their alleged weaknesses being carefully orchestrated so as to not inhibit their contentment or interfere with the proper order of things.

Nevertheless, as far as Margaret was concerned, while this arrangement may have worked very well for her kin, and had subsequently become the standard for her cousin to follow, even if Edith had ultimately been blessed by a love match and a man who worshipped the ground her dainty feet walked on, she had never been able to subscribe to that doctrine herself. To Margaret's mind, it was not her responsibility to warp herself to please the specifications her husband desired, or indeed, dictated, but rather, it was his to adapt his expectations so that he might wholly appreciate his wife. Marriage was surely about compromise, not conformity.

Margaret could not abide the thought of being dictated to, of being controlled or constricted in any way!—it would not do! No, she *valued* her *own independence so highly that* she could *fancy no degradation greater than that of having another man perpetually directing and advising and lecturing* her*, or even planning too closely in any way about* her *actions. He might be the wisest of men, or the most powerful*—but she *should equally rebel and resent his interference.*

In Margaret's case, she had made the conscious decision, from rather an early age, that only the most profound, and yes, passionate love would ever induce her to marry. While some dream as rosy-cheeked girls of beautiful weddings, Margaret merely dreamed of a good man to meet her at the altar. Her list of requirements for her groom was not long, exactly, but it was exact. She did not mind if he had money, so long as he had morals. She did not mind if he was handsome, so long as he was honest. She did not mind if he was celebrated, so long as he was compassionate. She did not mind if he was brilliant, so long as he was brave. She did not mind if he was impressive, so long as his integrity was intact. And, above all else, she did not mind if he agreed with everything she said or approved of everything she did, so long as she was free to be entirely herself when she took on his name. To be sure, while there were some areas where Margaret was willing to compromise when it came to her partner in life, for these principles she would refuse to sacrifice her convictions on the altar of convention and deny her wants!—nay, her needs. Marriage was far too serious a contract to be entered into lightly. After all, if a woman were to sign away her liberty, she ought not to freely become the slave of another, but strive to be free.

'*I can live alone, if self-respect, and circumstances require me so to do,*' she would whisper to herself. *I need not sell my soul to buy bliss. I have an inward treasure born with me, which can keep me alive if all extraneous delights should be withheld, or offered only at a price I cannot afford to give.*'

It was during Margaret's ten years living in London that she had slowly, surely and rather sadly, come to realise that finding such a species of man would be if not impossible, then at least incredible. For a start, Margaret was not unkind, but she was not inclined to like everybody she met. Her heart was open, but it was not incapable of closing if and when it felt the need to shut its doors to unwelcome visitors. Indeed, *there* were *few people whom* she *really* loved, *and still fewer of whom* she thought *well. The more* Margaret saw *of the world, the more* she was *dissatisfied with it; and every day confirmed* her *belief of the inconsistency of all human characters, and of the little dependence that can be placed on the appearance of merit or sense.* And besides, even if meeting with a man to whom she could envisage giving herself to in law, spirit and body, who was to say that he would return her esteem? Margaret had always been incontrovertibly sceptical when it came to love. It seemed unlikely to her that two such kindred souls should ever cross paths, and if they did, then the menaces of fate, which so often scheme to unsettle happiness, may well set them apart.

However, it was not until Henry Lennox proposed that Margaret had been thoroughly convinced that she would never find a man who could ignite the flames of devotion in her. Henry was a good sort and she did not doubt that he would make a perfectly adequate husband. She trusted that he would never harm her in any way, which was more than some men could promise. Nevertheless, she felt sure that, over time, he would come to regret his choice. He would be disappointed in her and dissatisfied with her, coming to think of her as a dog he wished to muzzle. He would grow increasingly frustrated with her, and the more he tried to quietly censor his wife, the more she would dissident, and, in the end, their marriage would wither from something regrettable where neither party truly felt respected and wilt as a weed marred by resentment, and that was a cruelty Margaret refused to inflict upon either of them.

Looking back, Margaret could scarcely recall Henry's proposal. It had been so markedly unexciting in every aspect. His address was been even-tempered, the vitality of his determination fickle, and his passion as dulled as a blunt sword, and so after a good night's sleep to get over the ordeal of her first offer of marriage, not to mention a degree of disappointment in its insipidness, Margaret managed to move on voluntarily and forget the whole uncomfortable incident. It was as if it had never even happened, so much so that she was quite sure a few more months would erase it from her memory, and it would be as a dream, one that was neither happy nor sad, simply...Margaret stifled a yawn.

Then again...*his* proposal had not been forgotten in such a hurry.

Oh! She would not think about that...she could not think about that...but she could not help herself...

It was only when a bird with orange and white feathers shot out into the room from behind a miniature oak door in the clock that Margaret jumped and was abruptly awakened from her trance. Startling, she peered up to see it bobble on the end of its spring perch, and with its beak opened wide in habitual salutation, it chirped its mechanical ditty which announced the passing of one hour and the heralding of the next. It had been a gift from her Uncle Shaw when she first went to live with them in London. He had been such a kindly man, one who was distinctly more receptive than her aunt. He appreciated that at the tender age of eight his niece would likely be missing her home and may well feel terribly out of place in the capital, her usual landscape of green fields and blue horizons having been replaced by grey streets and skies. Therefore, he wanted her to have something that reminded her of her natural habitat when she woke to greet the morn, persuading her into wakefulness with its tune and cheering her with its pleasant song that contained the uplifting notes of hope for the day ahead.

Stealing a stealthy glance in the direction of the slender hands that stated that it was now one o'clock, Margaret wondered if they were still there, in a place and in a presence she herself sorely wished to be. Trying not to think on it, all she could do was think on it, and she guessed that they were no doubt there now, at this precise moment, sipping tea and enjoying his company, or more to the point, he would be delighting in theirs, all thoughts of her banished from his mind.

Preoccupied with this miserable notion, Margaret's finger slipped, and so the needle pierced her skin, causing her to yelp, waggle it, and then suck it like a child. Overcome by a nauseating sensation in the pit of her stomach, Margaret abandoned her sewing and unceremoniously tossed it aside, knowing full well that she could not concentrate, and so there was no point spoiling Edith's present all for the sake of pretending to be indifferent to the changing tides of her emotions that lapped over her like waves upon an ever-shifting shore. In any case, she was not in company, so there was no need to feign nonchalance and deceive herself into believing her façade of apathy, feeble as it was in its transparent charade. No, Margaret was alone with her feelings, and so she was permitted to let them out to roam free so that they might roar and weep at their pleasure, and all for her displeasure.

It was better this way. Margaret could not stand pretences. Feelings should be honest. People who disguised the condition of their spirit were ratified by fakery and chastened by falsehood, and while she appreciated that there were always occasions when it may be wise to keep one's sentiments private in order to protect them, she judged that there was nothing more ailing to integrity than to lie to oneself. Fooling others was one thing, but to mislead your own sense of self was a grievous mistake, possibly even a transgression against the soul. It would mean excluding one's closest friend and confidante from examining one's motivations, guiding one's actions and ministering to one's heart.

Standing up, she began to pace about the room, her tapered hands fidgeting before her in restless frustration, desperately seeking something to do that would see her through this particularly agonising afternoon. As she did so, Margaret spotted the mask that stood beside her mirror, a gift from Edith, brought back from her honeymoon in Venice. It was exquisite, with its white visage that glittered with specks of gold dust. Holding it up, Margaret pressed it against her face, and through the hollow slits that sought to hide the complexion and character of the presence behind, she regarded herself, and she did not like what she saw, so she instantly stripped the veneer away, as if it repelled her.

No. Margaret did not like masks. She did not like masquerades. She wanted to be herself, her authentic self. Only through owning both the perils and pearls that came and went with the seasons of life could she hope to mature into the Margaret she was always meant to be.

On placing the prop aside, Margaret noticed the smudges that stained her skin, her fingernails a grubby bed of grit and grime, an acknowledgement of all her efforts below stairs. Sighing, she went to her washbasin and prepared an infusion of rosewater and lavender to cleanse her of this blight. It was not so much that she minded for herself, but even though her mother was no longer with them, she would have frowned and tutted to see her daughter turned out like a ragamuffin, reminding Margaret of her childhood days running about the countryside with her brother, the pair of them returning home covered from tip-to-toe in mud, grass and water from the stream.

Plunging her hands into the warm pool that swilled with the swirling dyes of purple and pink, Margaret let out a long and shuddering breath, the heat doing her the world of good as it sharpened her senses and revived her wits. With a tired tilt of her head, she found that her eyes lifted shyly towards the mirror that hung opposite, staring back at her unblinkingly with unapologetic scrutiny. Crinkling her nose in disparagement, Margaret quickly turned away in self-disdain. How plain she was. Her face was by no means what one would call ugly, but it was too commonplace to be considered remarkable.

Her complexion was uncomplicated, with a smooth dermis and a soft glow, her jawline usually to be found tinted with the natural hue of a rubicund blush that dimpled her cheeks and was known to become inflamed with the red blotch of mortification that spread like a wildfire when she was embarrassed.

Her features were comfortably proportioned, with nothing being too big, nor too small, nor too high, nor too low, and this was fortunate, she reasoned, since it was more than some could boast, but it also meant that there was nothing arresting about her.

Edith has used to try and bolster her by saying: *'The French girls would tell you, to believe that you were pretty would make you so.'* However, given that she was English, Margaret had found her cousin's advice rather unhelpful.

With her eyes dipping to skim the length of her body, Margaret once again cockled her brow. Her figure had consistently been too little in longitude and too curved in latitude around her hips and breasts to be deemed pleasing. With a self-conscious sniff, Margaret distinctly remembered several of Edith's friends from London whose physiques had been as flat as a plank of wood, the ladies sneering at the comely flower from Helstone at various coming-out balls, always teasing her and pointing out with a waspish sting that no man would ever approve of her crimped looks. She had felt like a specimen being pinned down and anatomised, the entirety of her form uncovered as they poked and prodded her with their fans in jest, all the while pricking her with their snide insults. Perhaps that is why she had grown immune over the years, she had developed a thick skin to protect her feelings, so it no longer upset her when she was talked of with ridicule, something which was now a relentless occurrence following her move to Milton, and she had been displaced, a flower entreated to bloom when subtracted from its natural soil, and so she willed herself to stand tall against the gales of antipathy that battered the bedrock of her resolve.

However, unknown to an unworldly Margaret, far from belittling her shapely figure, the spiteful mademoiselles from her girlhood had been seething with jealousy at the way their beaus all eyed the pretty parson's daughter with palpable rapaciousness, the girl blessedly ignorant to both the cattiness and covetousness which followed her about the room like a bad smell. If truth be told, it was one of the many reasons why Margaret wore such dreary clothes; it was because the insecure part of her that always felt ill at ease in her own skin disliked drawing attention to herself, and bland dresses with their simple designs and unexceptional fabrics were just the thing to stop people looking at her. And it had worked well enough, or that is, it had until *he* had first looked her way.

Mr Thornton. *Again*. It was always him. *Always*.

As she sensed a prickling on the back of her neck, a flush akin to a pair of watchful eyes resting on her nape, Margaret trembled, and after chastising herself, she determined that she would not give in to her low spirits. On balance, it surely did a woman good to be visited by mysterious feelings now and again, and so she would resist this self-doubt and retaliate with a disposition of unswerving courage. But what could she do? Well, for a start, she may as well write to Frederick. Margaret had not heard from him in several weeks, not since his most welcome letter that assured his family of his safe return to Spain. She recalled its arrival and the relief it brought. Taking it to her father, they had ripped it open hurriedly and scanned the pages with nerves of jelly, fearing the worst, that the navy had at last caught up with him, and he was to be tried for treason. However, that had mercifully not been the case, and no such tragedy had struck the Hales to this date. On the contrary, by the evidence of scratches made in ink, Fred testified in his untidy hand that he was out of immediate danger, and so he was getting on with his life in the wake of his mother's untimely death, an end Margaret knew she must likewise try to achieve.

Yes, that was it, that was what to do. Margaret would write to her brother, and then perhaps to her dear friends Elizabeth Darcy and Jane Rochester, both of whom she had profoundly missed in recent months, their sensible advice invaluable to her. But first, she ought to change, her current attire musty from the steam of the iron. Margaret was pleased with herself for having settled on a plan. She *was at an age when any apprehension, not absolutely based on a knowledge of facts, is easily banished for a time by a bright sunny day, or some happy outward circumstance.* Therefore, encouraged by the pleasant intent of corresponding with her kin, Margaret hummed cheerfully as she sifted through her day dresses. Now, the pale blue or the dark blue? With a faint hint of a smile, she vaguely speculated as to which cloth and colour Mr Thornton would like best—

Oh! Stop it, Margaret! What an extraordinary notion; what a silly fancy.

With a groan gargling deep in her throat, Margaret's head dropped forward and bumped the door of the wardrobe, and there she slowly knocked it again and again with gentle frustration by way of penance.

She *would not* let everything be about him. It had never been so before, and so it must be that way again. She would make sure of it. Breathing steadily, in through her nose and out through her mouth, just as her governess had taught her, Margaret fought to calm herself, permitting the abyss of nothingness to wash over her and whitewash her thoughts into a blank canvas, the strokes blotting out the image of him that had become so melded, so meshed into her psyche that she could almost trace every curve and contour of his form. She had endeavoured to pay it no heed, but with every day it only grew larger and more distinct.

Oh, but no!

There he was again.

How was it that he haunted her imagination so persistently?

She could not run. She could not retreat.

She could not escape him.

But then again, did she truly want to?

Chapter Ten

Gentlemen and Highwaymen

Feeling abandoned, the ladies all coughed in chorus as they rearranged themselves daintily upon their respective chairs, their orchestrated attempt to discredit Miss Hale and ingratiate themselves with the gentleman in their midst not at all going how they had planned.

However, the interim of their neglect was not entirely wasted, because it was in this interval that they each realised something both separately and simultaneously. Upon reflection, they privately concluded that to undermine their romantic competitor, adopting a significantly different strategy might be more effective. It would appear that Mr Thornton, ever a man of staunch honour, could not be influenced by something as ephemeral as a woman's good looks, so perhaps they had been imprudent to focus on this at all, especially given that Miss Hale, much to their frustration, was rather handsome. Instead, they ought to be interrogating Miss Hale's suitability to be the wife of a specific breed of man: a Milton master. In this, at least, they could all agree that she was unsuitable to an unpardonable fault.

For a start, the lady in question hailed not from the same city that had birthed their future husband, and this geographical as well as cultural divide was as palpable as the criss-cross of symbols comprising patchwork fields and stone boundaries that had separated not only counties but an entire country for centuries. What was more, her every action seemed to defy the expectations of those around her, as if she were determined to break the stiff cast society had cast for her.

Their united displeasure had only intensified over the past months with each unconventional choice she made, yet she remained steadfast in her commitment to charting her own course and would not be dissuaded by the disapproval of others. In effect, their censure only served to reinforce her, as if her individuality, rather than deterring her, became a source of empowerment. She wore it like armour, facing judgement with a steely resolve that left many baffled and others secretly envious. It was as though she had unlocked a hidden strength within herself, born from the courage to embrace her distinctiveness in a world that constantly sought to suffocate her with its conformity. Miss Hale moved through life with an air of independence that both intrigued and unsettled those who sought to categorise her. In the face of adversity, she did not waver; instead, she turned challenges into stepping stones, proving that originality could be a catalyst for growth and self-discovery. While opinions about her continued to diverge, there was an undeniable allure to her unapologetic authenticity, and this, more than anything, made the three women loathe her beyond all others.

No, Miss Hale would not do for Mr Thornton: of this, they could all agree.

Yet, unbeknownst to them, a love story like that of the one from the north and the one from the south could not be scripted, it could not be dictated to, but would organically unfold much like the poignant tales found within the pages of classic novels. Contrary to the belief that authors craft these words and determine their direction, I can attest otherwise. These characters not only exist on the page but extend their vitality beyond it. Their liberty in the name of love cannot be so easily edited or erased. They are free spirits, untouched by the constraints of writers with their wishes and whims. They live and breathe, surpassing the limits of mere prose. Love of the truest nature transcends the boundaries set by a world that often fails to recognise the profound and unbreakable bond fusing kindred spirits, their essence entwined in a dance that defies reason. Little-known to many is that in the divine act of creation, God sculpts each of us in our unique moulds. And yet, in exceedingly rare instances, a scarce anomaly occurs. Much like the conception of identical twins, the mould overflows, giving rise not to one but to two entities. Thus, twinned souls emerge, their matter combined, forming two hearts pulsating in unison within distinct bodies yet sharing allied spirits. If luck smiles upon these chosen few, these beings may serendipitously find each other, fulfilling God's plan for them that destiny awaits with bated breath, a future that fate prays for daily in faithful longing.

Such an affinity flows like the river that fed this very mill, oblivious to the social dams constructed to impede its course. Nevertheless, the ladies in their limited wisdom were not to know this, and as far as they were concerned, a rose plucked from foreign soil may bloom, but it shall never possess the fragrance of familiarity, and what else, other than a woman of his own kind, could Mr Thornton possibly want as a wife?

Eyeing each other in what could only be called a momentary truce, Miss Bingley was the one to take up the mantle.

'Alas, Mr Thornton, we are entirely with you. We have no choice,' said she, throwing up her hands in surrender, as if to throw in her hand at a game of cards, 'we must concede that Miss Hale does have a natural…adequacy of appearance to her that is quite refreshing,' she commenced, and for a ticking-trice, he almost believed she was sincere.

Then she spoke again.

'But that is why I feel for her so. She is probably so foolhardy because while she may have a degree of abstract beauty, she lacks any true brains or breeding to fall back on.'

Mr Thornton's eyes, having just unearthed the elusive passage sought in his library book for the past half hour, swiftly ascended and darted around the periphery of his chair.

'How so?' he bit back, terribly gruffly, since to his mind, there was no woman alive with more striking wit or refinement than Margaret.

'Well, for a start, *she gives herself airs, and they're not rich—never have been*!' Miss Latimer substantiated, grateful for the fortune her banker father had amassed, not to forget the impressive dowry he would bestow upon her when she married the man of her choice. That is, if only said man would relinquish his silly infatuation with another and realise that she, *not she*, was the obvious and only candidate to become his wife.

Nevertheless, the next comment was to come from her intended's sister, the youngest of the set feeling left out, and out of place, the woman used to being the biggest sauce-box in the room. 'And *she cannot even play the piano!*' Miss Thornton exclaimed stridently.

Her brother laughed sarcastically at this vain assertion. 'Ha! Is that all her faults amount to? *Go on, Fanny. What else does she lack to bring'er up to your standard?*' he demanded to know, his native drawl thick with provocation.

On heeding this, Mrs Thornton felt it only right to interrupt in defence of her daughter, because while Fanny (dear heart), could be, at times (or most of the time), a scatty girl who rarely spoke a word of sense, when she was right, she was right, and there was no denying she was right on this occasion.

As the animated chatter had been allowed to continue, each lady seemed determined to outdo the others in their critique of Miss Hale's alleged shortcomings. Mrs Thornton, however, sat with a stoic expression, her thoughts eddying beneath the surface. While she found most of the chatter nonsensical, she could not shake the notion that there might be some truth hidden amongst the poppycock, for Miss Hale had admitted in the matriarch's presence that she played both ill and hardly at all.

'*I heard Miss Hale say she cannot play herself, John,*' his mother corroborated, glancing up briefly from her sewing to say her bit.

Mr Thornton huffed in exasperation, crossing his arms with a displeased demeanour. Sulking, he wore a frown that sunk lower and lower, so low, in fact, one might think it would drop off the bottom of his face altogether. He apparently stood alone amongst those present in his readiness to defend Margaret's honour. Whether or not the lady herself appreciated it, defend her, he damn well would.

On seeing her son descend into one of his sullen moods, Mrs Thornton began to regret granting her daughter leave to invite her friends for tea. She had hoped that it would be a quiet affair and a chance for her son to forget Miss Hale for an hour or two, mollified by the company of others and distracted from matters at the mill, but on the contrary, it had morphed into an incessant litany of the young woman. It seemed as if

Miss Hale was the only topic of conversation to be had, her name ripe and ready on everyone's lips.

Amid the friction, Mrs Thornton only wished that she could divert the discussion away from Miss Hale for a time, and then perhaps her son's brooding mood might lift. Yet, every attempt to steer the discourse in a different direction was met with resistance, as the trio were resolved to dissect and disparage the young lady's every characteristic. Sighing inwardly at the unfolding scene, the mother felt torn between a desire for peace in her parlour and loyalty to her son.

Nonetheless, while she was thinking this, Miss Bingley was preoccupied with the revelation of Miss Hale's lack of musical talent. She could hardly believe her ears, and so revelled in a thinly veiled snigger.

'There we have it! She is scarcely a lady worth mentioning,' she decreed with confidence of conviction. *'No one can be really esteemed accomplished* and fit for society *who does not greatly surpass what is usually met with. A woman must have a thorough knowledge of music, singing, drawing, dancing, and the modern languages, to deserve the word; and besides all this, she must possess a certain something in her air and manner of walking, the tone of her voice, her address and expressions, or the word will be but half deserved,'* she expounded, her voice growing lofty.

'Sounds exhausting,' Mr Thornton rated, silently praying that his home would never be invaded by a woman, be it a wife or daughter, who took up even a quarter of these tiresome pastimes listed.

'Oh! It *can* be exhausting, particularly if a woman is not made for it,' Miss Bingley agreed, mistaking his comment for one of concern as opposed to cynicism.

'It takes considerable time, patience and aptitude to become thoroughly engrossed in these attainments. It does not happen by chance. A woman may be born into a role of distinction, and she may have an intuitive sense of superiority, but in the end, it is up to her to cultivate her gentility if she wishes to come into her own. For my part, I have only met say six women who can claim to have achieved such a degree of accomplishment, and four of them are sitting in this room,' she complimented, her hand gesturing towards her companions, all the ladies smiling in thanks, all the while detesting each other in that underhand way that is particular to the fairer (and feistier) sex. For, you see, *people who are only in each other's company for amusement never really like each other so well, or esteem each other so highly, as those who work together, and perhaps suffer together.*

Mr Thornton massaged his temple, the thought of so many tedious fortes making his head swim. Thank the Lord that Fanny had only taken up an interest in the piano. Heaven help him if she ever developed attentiveness for any other activity, but this was thankfully an unlikely difficulty, given that she usually gave up on any new pursuit mere days after starting, exasperated by the effort required. However, he would not remain tight-lipped on this one, not when he could have his fun, a reward he sorely deserved today.

'I am no longer surprised at your knowing only six accomplished women,' he mused, a mischievous grin

amusing his face. *'I rather wonder now at your knowing any,'* he batted back, ignoring his mother's tutting to hear him joke so.

'We do exist!' Miss Latimer reminded him querulously, not at all pleased at having her years cooped up in a dreary Swiss finishing school overlooked, something Miss Hale had never been forced to endure. She recoiled to remember it. The echoes of polished footsteps on marble floors, jeered tales of rigid etiquette and suppressed laughter. In the hallowed halls, she wore the stays of societal expectations, each laced restraint a reminder of the boundaries that had imprisoned her. The chandeliers, dripping with crystal tears, mirrored the gleaming veneer she was expected to maintain, even as her true self longed to break free, only now, she had forgotten how. It had been a chilly mausoleum that had turned her soul to ice, and so, she was not prepared to let her time there go to waste. After all, her education had been founded on the rudimentary art of acquiring a husband, so get her hands on him, she fully intended to.

'I am quite sure you do,' Mr Thornton conceded. 'However, I think you have left out some accomplishments that a woman should lay claim to,' he deliberated aloud, taking the matter seriously for a moment. 'I am no expert, naturally, but it seems to me that a woman ought to boast more than fine accomplishments. *People may talk as they will about the little respect that is paid to virtue, unaccompanied by the outward accidents of wealth or station; but I rather think it will be found that, in the long run, true and simple virtue always has its proportionate reward in the respect and reverence of everyone whose esteem is worth having. To be sure, it is not rewarded after the way of the world as mere worldly possessions are, with low obeisance and lip-service; but all the better and more noble qualities in the hearts of others make ready and go forth to meet it on its approach, provided only it be pure, simple, and unconscious of its own existence.'*

His sister grumbled at his stuffy moralising.

'And what are women meant to do, then, John?' she asked huffily, her new French-style fringe blowing as she puffed.

'Well, should she not add something *more substantial, in the improvement of her mind by extensive reading?'* Mr Thornton questioned, unable to conceive his life without his books, and equally unable to imagine having a wife who did not likewise share his love of the written word, even if she did have her personal tastes that differed from his own. With a nostalgic twitch of his lips, he recalled how his headmaster used to say, *"I declare after all there is no enjoyment like reading! For the person, be it gentleman or lady, who has not pleasure in a good novel, must be intolerably stupid."*

To which the eager and intelligent lad had replied, *"How much sooner one tires of anything than of a book! When I have a house of my own, I shall be miserable if I have not an excellent library."* This philosophy had stood as a cornerstone in his pursuit of re-establishing himself in business and society. Indifferent to his dwelling's size or location, he harboured no concern for the grandeur or modesty of the house. His sole preoccupation lay in securing a comfortable residence for his mother and sister, preferably one with an adequate library that he could add to. Grieving the departure of their family's prized books following his father's passing and the subsequent necessity to sell them, he found solace and satisfaction in this tradition. From the moment he assumed the role of Master of Marlborough Mills, endowed with the means to indulge his wants somewhat, he had taken it upon himself to enrich his private collection with a new volume each month. This periodic addition became both a pleasure and a privilege, a testament to his enduring love for literature and a poignant reminder that joy of a humble and honest sort could be found, even during the challenges of life.

Smiling to himself, Mr Thornton thought on all the evenings he had sat in that cosy Crampton drawing room, discussing prose and philosophy with his tutor, only to peer stealthily to the side a thousand times to see her sitting there, quietly reading away in her own little world, her clever head bent over a book, her curiosity as immovable as her will of iron. Mr Thornton remembered how, on one evening, he had watched his darling in rapt fascination as that insolent bracelet of hers slid up and down her wrist every time she turned the page. As he peeked at Miss Hale, he had seen a strand of chestnut hair escaping its pins and coiling over her face, her hand reaching up distractedly every now and again to push it aside. He had hardly been able to look, the desire too insufferably overwhelming as he fought the urgent impulse to go to her, tuck it behind her ear, and kiss her lobe with the lingering daubing of his trembling mouth, all the while whispering how much he adored her.

A relentless yearning gripped him, an incessant desire to be near her at all times. He envisioned himself by her side, eager to discover the enchantment that captivated her within the pages of that enigmatic book. The temptation to beseech her to divulge its secrets drove him to distraction. Her melodic voice held the power to soothe the wild disturbance stirred by the mere thought of her. He longed to sit in rapt attention, her Southern lilt resonating like a lute, plucking the strings of his heart. Unbeknownst to her, she possessed a captivating influence, a mastery that she, his lovely lass, had yet to fathom.

Mr Thornton had dreamt of this so often, the man having been forced to anchor himself in his chair during his lessons to prevent himself from taking leave of his senses and throwing himself at her feet, imploring her for just a morsel of her attention, a scrap of her glorious affection.

'Reading is all very well,' Miss Bingley answered, disturbing his musings, 'but a woman has better ways to occupy her time. Thinking and theorising are for men.'

'Hear, hear!' Miss Ingram concurred.

Mrs Thornton was appalled by the audacity of such a boldfaced statement, for she could not endorse the opinion that a woman's intellect should be shrouded in the shadows of ignorance.

'Preposterous!' Mr Thornton retorted. 'Is it not within a woman's realm to excel in a myriad of skills?' he championed, his thoughts drifting to Margaret's unparalleled competence as she coordinated the affairs of her household and bore the weight of her family's struggles single-handedly. Yet, this was merely a fraction of her character when contrasted with her benevolent spirit—a genuine goodness that surpassed the virtues of any mortal on earth.

On perceiving his vehemence, the ladies exchanged tentative glances, a collective tension settling over the room like a heavy mist. Whispers of uncertainty floated among them. The air hummed with stifled doubts as they reassessed Mr Thornton's manner.

Thinking on her feet, Miss Ingram carried on with the cause.

'That is all very well, and good deeds are, of course, a Christian duty which we must all adhere to,' she went on, trying to remember when she had last lifted a finger for anybody other than herself, 'but there is a time and a place for such things,' she explained. 'For example, did you know that Miss Hale makes garments for the poor?!' she laughed, her hands flying before her theatrically as she mimicked the art of knitting.

'No!' gasped Miss Thornton, visibly appalled.

'It is true,' affirmed Miss Latimer. 'I have heard she crafts hats and mittens for the factory workers and their children. She's been spotted distributing them during winter.'

'How dreadful!' snorted Miss Bingley, aghast at the notion. 'What if one of those wretched urchins were to lay a hand on her?' The three ladies recoiled in unison, as if the mere thought were as contagious as a plague itself.

Even so, and oddly enough, it was Mrs Thornton who held the strongest opinion when it came to this comment. In truth, she found herself caught in the intricate web of incompatible sentiments. On the one hand, there lingered a palpable disapproval to think of Miss Hale distributing alms to the proud people of Milton, implying they needed her charity, as if the mills did not pay them a reasonable wage. Nevertheless, amidst this scepticism, she could not deny a certain admiration for Miss Hale's enterprising spirit. She had keenly observed her competence with a needle during her visits to the Hale's home when the mother was ailing. Each time, the proof of Miss Hale's crafts(woman)ship lay meticulously arranged on various table-tops. Leaning in for a closer inspection, Mrs Thornton, an expert in such matters, appraised the girl's handiwork. To her judicious eye, Miss Hale's sewing exceeded the scope of mere acceptability; it was nothing short of exceptional. The fine stitches, the precise folds, all bespoke a level of skill that commanded respect. Mrs Thornton, though reserved in her expressions, was obliged to acknowledge the undeniable talent that Miss Hale possessed, a talent that spoke louder than any preconceived niggles she may have had about her aberrant ways.

As Mrs Thornton grappled with the nuances of her contrary opinions that were at odds with each other, she could not escape the realisation that, in the tapestry of complexities that defined Miss Hale, there existed filaments of aptitude and diligence that demanded recognition, even from the sternest of critics.

'I think it a fine pursuit,' she deemed at last, causing the women to turn in their seats and squint at her reproachfully, amazed by her endorsement. 'Miss Hale is certainly proficient, and while I do not approve of who she gives it to and why, I cannot fault her for her initiative and innovation, two traits that are valued hereabouts.'

A smile graced Mr Thornton's lips at the commendation of Margaret, instilling a sense of pride for his beloved. It also heartened him to discern his mother's subtle indication, hinting at the possibility of Margaret assimilating into Milton society and, more importantly, their family. Identifying the mutual qualities of intelligence, capability, resourcefulness, and loyalty between his mother and Margaret, he foresaw a potential camaraderie, foretelling two Mrs Thorntons coexisting harmoniously, each contributing to the family name in her unique way. Nevertheless, Mr Thornton had to regrettably acknowledge the present rift between his mother and Margaret. The realisation stung him, contemplating how a more welcoming and kind reception from his mother might have influenced Margaret's perception of his suit more favourably. He could not help but wonder if, with a little more warmth and acceptance, the woman he loved might have viewed their future together with greater enthusiasm and confidence.

At any rate, it was while he was busy imagining Margaret sitting in a chair beside the fire as she worked away, envisaging her knitting little socks for their babes and perhaps even a scarf for him to wear proudly about town, that the ladies initiated their next insult.

'And one cannot forget how she goes about visiting the new-found and ill-conceived schools for the children of the dissolute, helping them teach the reprobates,' Miss Bingley added with a noticeable sneer.

'I cannot abide this ridiculous fashion for educating the poor,' said Miss Latimer sternly, rolling her eyes. 'It is irrational, pointless and most irresponsible. Why on earth do these people insist on learning to read and write when they are only fit to work in our mills? I say it will do them no good and they will forget their place,' she assessed. 'Society as a whole will suffer for their greedy ambition to have more than they deserve, mark my words.'

Mr Thornton had to bite his tongue at this. Perhaps they were only fit to work in mills because they could not read or write. To him, equality of education was not a vague ideal, but a fundamental necessity. It was not just about providing desks and textbooks; it was about dismantling the barriers that denied entry to the hallowed halls of knowledge. In his mind's eye, he saw a world where the pursuit of wisdom was not a luxury based on gender and status but a birthright, where the seeds of curiosity were nurtured in the fertile terrain of unbiased erudition. Scholars should be advanced on the merit of their wisdom, not the prestige of the purse of their patronage. In the silence of his contemplation, he resolved that the edifice of humanity could only endure if built upon the solid foundation of learning, a foundation that could withstand the tremors of ignorance and intolerance. To him, true progress lay not in the accumulation of wealth but in the collective elevation of minds, for a culture enlightened was a civilisation emancipated.

'Then there are the hospitals!' Miss Ingram added. 'Miss Hale has been seen attending the workhouse infirmaries to nurse the sick and dying. I hear she sits with the elderly and comforts the grieving,' she said, wondering why anyone would wish to do anything so needlessly melancholy. 'I am loath to imagine what form of sickness she might contract in those flea-infested tombs of disease and decay,' she shuddered.

Mr Thornton huffed to hear this. On this point, at least, he was conflicted. In principle, he had no issue with Margaret attending these places, and in fact, he was rather jealous of the idea of her giving her time and care to everyone and anyone other than him, his latent jealousy once again rearing its ugly head. Still, in her acts of kindness, he discerned the beauty of her spirit—a beauty not diminished by his fleeting gloom of envy, but one that shines all the brighter in the selfless glow of her deeds. However, while he felt his soul puff out in pride for her tenderness of heart, he did not like to think of Margaret placing herself in any danger. Her mother had been prone to poor health, after all, so what if Margaret was similarly inclined to catching any passing sickness? And then there were those she mingled with. Poverty was no crime to his magistrate mind, and while most of the people in the workhouses were honest sorts who had fallen on hard times, many more were there because they had not led wholesome lives. Thus, it worried him to think of her going about here and there with God knows who—Mr Thornton ground his teeth, the thought of a handsome man with blonde hair and Grecian features stealing into his mind and ransacking it with his mockery.

'And let's not overlook the company she keeps,' Miss Bingley interposed. 'I have heard that she not only spends time with the factory workers but even counts some of them as friends.'

'What a lark!' cried Miss Latimer, clapping her hands together like a child. 'Most likely because nobody in polite society in Milton cares to befriend her,' Miss Latimer speculated.

'Well, perhaps that's because there are no friends worth having!' he snapped.

'There is no need to be such an ogre, John!' his sister pouted, peeved that she should have her friends over, only for her brother to behave like such a knave.

'Oh! Do not speak of your brother so,' Miss Latimer chastised. 'He is nothing if not the very definition of a gentleman,' she simpered. 'He is everything a man ought to be. He is clever, conscientious, and of course, charming, three attributes which cannot see a man wrong. To be sure, I have found myself thinking that all men should model themselves upon Mr Thornton: otherwise, I consider them quite disappointing.'

'My word,' Mr Thornton was heard to mumble from his lair, 'I do not think I have ever been so highly praised in my life, not even by you, Mother,' he quipped. '*It is happy for you*, Miss Latimer, *that you possess the talent of flattering with delicacy. May I ask whether these pleasing attentions proceed from the impulse of the moment, or are the result of previous study?*' he asked, sick and tired of hearing her father not-so-subtly recommend his daughter to him by referencing her extensive and expensive foreign education. He regaled no regard for the allure of costly schooling or the notion of sending his children away. If he were ever fortunate to be blessed with children, then he would keep his daughters and sons close at home, cherishing every moment with them. Recognising that their time under his roof was brief and that they would soon grow up and fly the nest, he would wish to make the most of his time with them and to prioritise meaningful connections over superficialities, ensuring their education delved into matters of substance that would equip them for the challenges of the real world.

'And besides, it is not true,' he refuted. '*I have faults enough, but they are not, I hope, of understanding.* I am predisposed to be sullen. I like to sulk. I like to scowl, and I am not sorry for it. *My temper I dare not vouch for. It is, I believe, too little yielding—certainly too little for the convenience of the world. I cannot forget the follies and vices of others so soon as I ought, nor their offences against myself. My feelings are not puffed about with every attempt to move them. My temper would perhaps be called resentful. My good opinion once lost, is lost forever,'* he finished, his voice lowering into a wounded groan as he thought about her. He had been resentful, had he not? He had made it clear that he thought little of her, and through forcing himself to behave with abysmal aloofness in her presence, he had no doubt convinced her of his indifference to her, an apathy that conceivably bordered on intolerance. After all, *there is nothing like wounded affection for giving poignancy to anger.* In the months that had rolled by, no matter how frosty their estranged relationship had become after her rejection of him, followed by her unbearable preference for another man, Mr Thornton was helpless but to pine for her, no matter what falsehoods he had shouted in her startled face about his passion for her being both foolish and done with, the woman being of no consequence when it came to his hopes for the future. But while his charade may have been a lie, Mr Thornton was privately terrified that while he loved her more than ever, he had forfeited her good opinion forever with his childish resentment borne of heartbreak.

In feeling frustrated by her lack of headway in convincing Mr Thornton that they were entirely in the right and that Miss Hale was entirely in the wrong, Miss Ingram decided to play another card, because, at the end of the day, there was nothing that pleased a man more than being soft-soaped and buttered-up by a woman.

'Oh, I am quite sure we can forgive you a fault or two, Mr Thornton, but that is because you are a man,' she explained. 'A woman must employ what attributes she has to make herself agreeable. A man, on the other hand, is a different animal entirely. *A man should pay no heed to his good looks, he should only possess strength and valour. Gentleman or highwayman, his beauty lies in his power,*' she theorised, projecting her well-polished voice, given that she knew the man sitting irksomely far away from her was keen on philosophy, his few precious hours of leisure spent with his nose buried in a book. However, when they were wed, she would ensure that his attention was firmly transferred and transfixed upon her at all times.

It was at this point that Mr Thornton began to wonder whether there was anything at all wholesome in Miss Ingram's nature, her character as rotten in his estimation as the bark of a dead tree. *Miss Ingram was a mark beneath jealousy: she was too inferior to excite feeling. Pardon the seeming paradox; I mean what I say. She was very showy, but she was not genuine; she had a fine person, many brilliant attainments, but her mind was poor, her heart barren by nature; nothing bloomed spontaneously on that soil; no unforced natural fruit delighted by its freshness. She was not good; she was not original; she used to repeat sounding phrases from books; she never offered, nor had, an opinion of her own. She advocated a high tone of sentiment, but she did not know the sensations of sympathy and pity; tenderness and truth were not in her.*

Mr Thornton did not *look on self-indulgent, sensual people as worthy of hatred; he simply looked upon them with contempt for their poorness of character.* Then again, he really ought not to cast stones, not when his character was protected by nothing more than a house of glass. He was not perfect, and nor could he ever hope to be. Human frailty, you see, whether it be in the mind, body or soul, is uncurable. It is our cross to bear, our God-given curse.

'What do you mean by that?' he found himself asking against his better judgement, his head, influenced by the weight of curiosity, turned ever so slightly towards her.

Miss Ingram falsely thought this meant he approved. 'A man need only be a man,' said she with perfect simplicity. 'And a gentleman may rest easy in his exaltation, for he need be nothing more than great. That is all that God requires of him to crown him king of his little portion of this world. Women are limited. Men are limitless. You are everything. We are nothing, not without *you.*'

Listening to this speech, Mr Thornton scoffed, and this time, he stood up, bounding out of his chair and disturbing it enough to make it scrape backwards across the wooden floor with alarming vigour, impressive if one took into account the heft of its solid build. Soaring to his feet, the master loomed above them all, tall and terrifying with his intimidating stance. His shoulders, muscular sculptures of bone and flesh, were hunched over forebodingly as he stooped, his arched bearing almost affecting him to appear deformed, like an aggrieved beast that might strike out spontaneously at any moment. With his eyes flashing with the blaze of outrage, he stared at the women beneath the hood of his thick brows.

They had well and truly gone and done it now!

'You think a man, *a true man*, so shallow?' he disputed in abhorrence at being branded as such a contemptible sod just because of his sex, a stigmatisation that was dictated by nothing more than a shaft between his legs that he had no say or sway over whether it was there.

'Yes, power gives us options, it gives us privilege, and I daresay, a degree of gratification, for we are human, after all, and as such, we are corrupted by a hunger to chase self-promotion. But a gentleman is so much more than that! Or, at least, he should be,' Mr Thornton appealed with gravity. 'What of decency? Humility? Compassion? Should a man not be grounded in veracity as well as brute strength? Does adversity not give us courage more than achievement does? Because while one is fickle and fleeting, the other endures if it is authentic, allowing us to be resilient in withstanding the trials of life,' he reasoned still.

Approaching with the stealth of a tiger, he advanced towards the ladies, who instinctively leaned back in fear whilst also somehow tilting forward in unison, drawn by the irresistible allure of his ferocity, eager to be consumed by the intense thrill he emanated.

Miss Ingram swallowed the bubbling ball of tension in her throat, her gaze surrendered to him as she watched commanding presence inching closer. The sight of his striking form left her breathless, and she gulped at the overwhelming spectacle. His proximity was so immediate that she could almost discern the peppery scent of his masculine sweat. Her eyes were captivated, fixated on the rhythmic bobbing of his Adam's apple.

'I only meant…,' she began, licking her lips, since they were as dry as parched mud in midsummer, fissuring into a labyrinth of dehydrated cracks. 'I was merely explaining that a woman should value these attributes of which I speak more in a man than in herself. She should seek them out in her partner and praise him for embodying them. In contrast, it would be wrong if she were to crave or advance these faculties in herself.'

Mr Thornton scrunched his temple sardonically. '*Why*?' he pressed, unimpressed by her baseless reasoning.

'I think I can answer that,' Miss Latimer voiced, a hint of envy colouring her words as she observed Mr Thornton's considerable investment of time and attention in Miss Ingram, even if it was tarnished by ridicule. 'It is in light of our *apparent* frailty compared to men.'

With a subtle flutter of her eyelashes, Miss Latimer pressed on, determined to assert herself in the ongoing debate. 'We merely have our good looks and charms to recommend us,' she explained, a hand lifting to fondle the ringlets of blonde which hung about the nape of her neck in daintily set spirals, her finger knocking a lengthy silver earring that hung there, and as it swung like a pendulum in its disruption, a small prism danced across her face, highlighting the shimmer of spite that lived in the crevices of her eyes like specks of engrained grit.

'We may indeed be validated through the utilisation of our accomplishments, but that is as far as our talents go. On the other hand, when it comes to a man, he can boast of greater things, since he is endowed with so much more than us inferior women. He can also be brave. He can be dominant. He can be energetic. He can be unique. And most of all, he can be autonomous, he can be the master of his own fate,' she described with slow and seductive repartee, deftly choosing her phrases as to define the attributes she recognised in him, ones which she misguidedly thought he championed also, the word: "*master*," being no blunder.

Here Mr Thornton stepped back, dumbfounded.

'And can a woman not claim any of these for herself?' he asked after a while, his voice now much weaker, reflecting the shock he felt to hear Miss Latimer casually condemn her own kind to a fate of subservience. It had never before occurred to him that a woman would be so ready, so willing, even, to bow down to a man and defer to him without question. What sort of life would that be for her? It was certainly not one he would ever wish to impose upon his wife.

Mrs Thornton was about to intervene and agree most adamantly with her son that a woman, while showing suitable deference to the men in her life, could, and indeed, should, foster these qualities, nurturing them in her own character, both for the sake of herself, and for the betterment of her family. *It is in vain to say human beings ought to be satisfied with tranquillity: they must have action; and they will make it if they cannot find it. Millions are condemned to a stiller doom than mine, and millions are in silent revolt against their lot. Nobody knows how many rebellions besides political rebellions ferment in the masses of life which people earth. Women are supposed to be very calm generally: but women feel just as men feel; they need exercise for their faculties, and a field for their efforts, as much as their brothers do; they suffer from too rigid a restraint, too absolute a stagnation, precisely as men would suffer; and it is narrow-minded in their more privileged fellow-creatures to say that they ought to confine themselves to making puddings and knitting stockings, to playing on the piano and embroidering bags. It is thoughtless to condemn them, or laugh at them, if they seek to do more or learn more than custom has pronounced necessary for their sex.*

Indeed, she was about to speak, but she never got the chance. Just as she was poised to speak, her words were rudely halted by the sharp interjection of another.

'*No*!' Miss Bingley hollered, rather brusquely, causing her companions to gawk at her in fright.

'Women who attempt to be the equal of a man are not praiseworthy characters. All this desire to be headstrong, obstinate and independent, it is not natural for a woman to aspire to such individuality, and so, she should not be rewarded for it,' she hissed severely, thinking of one such woman who had used her intrepid ways to capture the only man Miss Bingley had ever truly wanted. The forfeiture of ten thousand a year was disappointing enough, but what she had never admitted aloud, nor would she ever degrade herself to do so, was that the loss of a fine man was pointedly more grievous than the loss of his fortune. Initially, when they first arrived at Netherfield, Miss Bingley had not expected that woman, one of five obscure and penniless sisters, to be of any consequence to her circle of friends. However, she had been profoundly mistaken, and the painful lessons learned made her resolute in not allowing herself to be blind-sided again. The thought of enduring further hurt and humiliation from someone she once considered of no discernible significance was something she could not tolerate. 'No, there are not many women out there like that. They are rare, thank goodness!' she exclaimed, her voice laced with a palpable sense of relief.

'I see,' Mr Thornton said at last, rather flatly. 'Well, lucky me, and poor you,' he decreed, thinking that there was some truth in what they spoke, not that women were lesser, of course, but that men, through a right that they had not earned, had inherited the lion's share in life. His apology was not sarcastic, just as it was not necessary, but Mr Thornton, being a man who had been forced to assume the burdens of other people's debts for most of his life, always felt a sense of responsibility weighing on his shoulders, and so, he was compelled to make amends.

Returning to his chair, Mr Thornton slumped down with a thud and stared at the fire, his long fingers rubbing at the bristles which darkened his chiselled jaw in that way he did when he was deep in meditation, brooding over one who was wonderfully headstrong, obstinate and independent.

'And that is precisely why we bring up Miss Hale,' Miss Bingley muttered in irritation. 'You cannot deny her radical inclinations. She blatantly disregards our ways. Miss Hale is excessively outspoken and opinionated, qualities most unbecoming in a young lady—quite off-putting. Surely, she would not honour her husband.'

'And she would prove entirely unsuitable for a Milton man!' Miss Ingram chimed in, emphasising the obvious incompatibility of Miss Hale with the local sensibilities, customs which she knew the Thorntons took most seriously.

At this, Miss Latimer's eyes widened and sparkled with mischief. Ah-ha! This was just the ticket.

'As a matter of fact,' she began, her neck pivoting round to look at her host, the skin on her slender column creasing. 'I particularly recall one evening, Mr Thornton, when you remarked on the matter,' she goaded, delighted that she could evoke the recollection of that night, one which must still surely be offensive to him, even all these months later.

'Why, your comments were so severe, I could scarcely forget it.'

Mr Thornton rummaged through his memory, wondering when on earth he had said more than two words together to Miss Latimer.

'*Oh*?' he replied.

Miss Latimer grinned, an ugly, sardonic grin, and if one looked closely enough, then one could see her sharpening her claws beneath her gloves as she readied to rip apart the appeal of her opponent's faultless façade in the eyes of Miss Hale's admirer.

'Yes, it was at your dinner party,' she launched, sensing the air in the room shift instantaneously as both Mrs and Miss Thornton jolted, the man sitting across from them all stiffening, his reminiscence well and truly stirred up in revival.

'It was after Miss Hale had behaved so shockingly. Perhaps you remember it? I recollect that after she finished making her discourteous scene, you turned to talk to me,' she narrated wistfully, and Mr Thornton had to privately admit to having unequivocally directed his less than gallant courtesy towards Miss Latimer that evening and possibly bestowed upon her an excess of civility—an egregious lapse in judgement on his behalf. With a remorseful sigh, Mr Thornton conceded that, beneath his pride, a less-than-admirable inclination had driven him to intentionally provoke a sense of jealousy in Miss Hale, not that she would have taken the trouble to even notice, whereas if she had spoken to another man with equal enthusiasm for even a second, Mr Thornton would have been silently dismayed and secretly devastated.

'I told you how sorry I was for her behaviour, and I apologised on behalf of my mild and ignorant sex, mortified as I was. If I recall, you said, with the most earnest tone I have ever heard, that it was of no matter, for Miss Hale mattered not to you. You then said that a creature like her cannot be tamed, and as such, no man could ever hope to control or restrain her, *"she is no bird; and no net ensnares* her," you had whispered, as if to yourself, *"she is a free human being with an independent will,"'* she orated, delighted by the way everybody in the room gaped at her in enthralment. Still, much to Miss Latimer's annoyance, there was one who still refused to glance her way, his back still firmly set against the group, and little did she know, that far from throwing ice upon the fire of his fervour for Miss Hale, her words only sought to stoke it into a more vehement inferno of feverish passion.

'And then, if I remember correctly, you muttered under your breath, *"and nor should she be,"'* she finished, a little lamely, his silence not the reaction she had lobbied for.

'Really!' she added hastily, her voice splintering in its discomposure. 'You were hurt by the way she spoke to you, I know you were,' Miss Latimer avowed, her tone terse and curt, for she was stung by his refusal to acknowledge her jibe. At least this one was true, even if everything else had been a malicious fib, or at the very least, a gross exaggeration. Miss Hale *had* been rude to him, *she had!* Everybody had seen it, so why was he unwilling to condemn her for it?

As the clock on the mantel ticked away, passing the stifled time, still Mr Thornton said nothing, and as five pairs of eyes studied the back of his head hesitantly, he did not move, not a muscle, the cogs of his mind revolving as he thought, and thought…and thought.

'My-my, Miss Latimer,' Mrs Thornton rallied, attempting to muster all the cordial liveliness she could, disconcerted by her son's eerie hush. 'It seems as if you recall Mr Thornton's words better than he does himself.'

'You see!' upheld Miss Bingley with animation, convinced they had won at last. 'She is deplorable!'

'She is abhorrent!' Miss Ingram denounced, her eyes glaring slits of steel. 'I am sorry she ever came here!'

'She is barely tolerable!' Miss Bingley cried. 'And we want nothing to do with her!'

It was then that a timid voice spoke up. 'Is...is that really fair?' Miss Thornton interposed nervously, glancing about her, her eyes betraying her uncertainty. 'Miss Hale is perhaps different to what we are used to. But she is not a bad person. We should not be unkind,' she suggested, beginning to see, at long last, that her friends, though beautiful, were perhaps not quite so beautiful on the inside. It was all very well poking some harmless fun at Miss Hale, but to condemn her, and when she had done nothing truly wrong, seemed cruel. Her remark was met with grave silence, but this did not discourage her, for with a gulp of resilience, she added, 'After all, I feel sure she would never treat any of us as we have treated her today.'

True as this disparity was, it did not prick any consciences.

Yet, amidst the audience, one person remained unresponsive. Her scrutiny, uncompromising, stayed fixed on Mr Thornton. A simmering anger nestled in her breast as her brittle hopes collapsed and bowed down in defeat. Miss Latimer had intended for her speech to be the final nail in the coffin for Miss Hale, because even if Mr Thornton refused to accept all the other charges these ladies laid at her door, then surely he could not excuse being shamed in his own home. But no, thinking back, she realised her imprudence at once. Mr Thornton may have appeared to be enraged with the young lady that night for opposing him in front of his peers, the bachelor considered the monarch amongst the cotton merchants, a man nobody would ever dare contest, that is, not until *she* had stood up to him. Nonetheless, the woman seated to his left had seen the way his intense eyes had skimmed up every few minutes to glimpse the vision in icy blue who sat halfway down the table, checking to gauge her mood and see that she was well taken care of, his heart heavy as he sighed to think on how they had quarrelled so carelessly and caused a further fracture in their already fragile association.

Yes, Miss Latimer had seen it then, just as clearly as she saw it now. Mr Thornton, the man she coveted, was already taken. This was no mere foolish passion, this was love. And it did not matter a fig what that hoity-toity Miss Hale said, because regardless of her impression of indifference towards the mill master, Miss Latimer had seen the young lady glance hopefully at Mr Thornton almost as much as he had her, so it was obvious that she had feelings for him too, even if she were not yet ready to acknowledge them.

With her faith in her future ultimately crumbling to dust, Miss Latimer was determined to hear him speak, to witness the confession of his feelings. This final revelation would conclusively verify the hopelessness of her hopes.

'But afterwards,' she said slowly, 'as the night wore on, *she seemed to improve on you.*'

There was a pregnant pause that pierced the air, like the cry of a newborn babe.

'I even began to wonder whether you thought her rather wonderful,' she accused, withholding a sniff, 'Why, *I even believe you thought her rather pretty at one time,*' she continued, tears pricking in the corner of her eyes, once again thinking on how Mr Thornton had spent half the dinner slyly diverting his attention from his companion and offering it shyly instead to Miss Hale, even for a short-lived moment, his face awash with yearning as he took in her agreeable gown, twinkling eyes, glossy hair, and attractive form. Yet worst of all, Miss Latimer had perceived the palpable disappointment emanate from him to learn that Miss Hale, the only one he had eyes for, was not the one sitting by his side.

Still, nothing, a silence enveloping them all.

'*Yes, I did,*' said Mr Thornton finally, his answer absolute, not a trace of reservation diminishing it, strange for such a typically tight-lipped man.

'*But that was only when I first knew her,*' he added quickly. It did not escape his notice to hear the simultaneous breath of relief that issued from Miss Bingley and Miss Ingram, shortly followed by their smirks and cackles of glee, because cackles they were, to think that Miss Hale had without a doubt waned in his highly sought estimation. Nevertheless, Miss Latimer remained in stony stillness, her feelings numbed by her inevitable downfall, and her caution would be proved right.

'As I say,' he continued, his tone steady as he rose to stand before them once more, 'that was only when I first knew her.' Then, with the octaves of his voice lowering into a growl, he professed, 'But *it is many months since*

I have considered her as one of the most handsome women of my acquaintance.'

All at once, the ladies' silly grins distorted into frowns, and they all choked in chorus on their splutters of surprise, a most unladylike symphony erupting around the parlour.

'Wait, no! I take that back!' he revised, his height growing as his temper swelled. 'She *is* the most handsome woman of my acquaintance,' he corrected categorically. 'It cannot be otherwise, not when her beauty of face and integrity of heart is unrivalled, an enchanting combination of immense appeal which is enough to disarm any man of both his wits and soul.'

Mr Thornton's presence hung heavy, thunder gathering behind his eyes. The air fizzled with tension as three women wove a web of whispered cruelties about the absent enchantress, the one his heart held dear. These cutting words of derision against Margaret sliced through him like the thrusts of a razor-sharp knife. The rusty teeth of those remarks cut him, leaving it to bleed in the aftermath of first her rejection and now the scorn of others who only sought to smear salt upon his wounds. The pain, a poignant reminder of the challenges he faced defending the woman he held dear, only fuelled his determination to shield her from the judgement al scrutiny of those who failed to grasp the depth of her character. But in his inability to deter their vilification, he found that his love for her was not only unrequited but utterly useless.

Lost, and at a loss of what to do, he left the room abruptly, a hurricane deserting the eye of the storm. Taunts of disdain chased him down the corridor as he sought solace in the refuge of his study, the heavy oak door closing behind him with a muffled thud.

Alone amidst the hushed embrace of leather-bound volumes and the faint scent of aged mahogany, Mr Thornton locked himself away and sought escape from the venomous chatter. In the cocoon of taciturnity, Mr Thornton sought clarity, criss-crossing the filaments of affection and frustration into the material of introspection, the very matter of his soul, determined to emerge with a heart unburdened.

Chapter Eleven

Barely Bear

Enough!

This would not do. This would not do at all.

Launching herself into her commission, Margaret hunted in vain for some paper in her personal bureau so that she might write to her brother directly, but after hauling the drawers ajar with an air of desperation, she found that no spare parchment was to be had. She huffed at this irksome inconvenience. However, there was one drawer, the second from the bottom, to be precise, which she did not plunder, because she knew what loitered within, and so she could not bring herself to look, the contents too shocking to acknowledge, and if she should dare to peek, it would be too tempting not to take out and hold with reverence. If truth be told, there was paper in there, but it already occupied a purpose, a most private purpose that was not to be disturbed. As her fingers quivered over the handle of this secured compartment in vacillation, Margaret found herself muttering at her idiocy, so she promptly opted to slink down to the drawing room where she knew there were supplies to be retrieved.

Slipping away, she quietly stole through the house, and after peering around the doorframe of the parlour, Margaret was relieved to find it deserted and at the discretion of her disposal. On discovering the necessary materials easily enough, she nestled herself at the table that was reposed in an alcove and dipped the nib of her pen into the pond of blue ink, ready to etch her missive to her brother.

At first, her task commenced with optimism and with little room for distraction, leading Margaret to falsely congratulate herself into believing that she had at last parted ways with the distress of the day, the agitation that bubbled inside her taking rest to replenish its energies so that it might confront her again with invigorated gusto tomorrow.

Nonetheless, it would appear as if the naivety of youth had conspired to deceive her o'er, because as Margaret continued to scribble away as fast as her fingers would fly, she soon found that her disobedient mind was once again inclined to go a-wandering. She opened with the usual pleasantries. How did her brother fair? Was he in good health? Would he please thank Dolores for the beautiful Spanish shawl she had sent? Were their wedding plans progressing as they would hope?

Nevertheless, as Margaret penned these monotonous lines of civility, the mention of matrimony poked at a tender wound within her, insensitively mocking her and picking at it like a scab. As she squirmed in her seat to avoid this pestering, Margaret found that her eyes instinctively flickered first to the side, then upwards, falling with natural preference upon a tall armchair that rested in a corner of the room beside a small tea table. Blinking unhurriedly, she considered it in all its impassive triviality, and as she did, the inanimate object gave her a strange sense of comfort.

It was Mr Thornton's chair.

That is to say, it was not his chair expressly, but because they had so few visitors to the house, he seemed to be the only one who ever sat in it, rendering it his seat by default. Observing it with an aberrant sort of sadness, Margaret realised that the chair—*no*—the room—*no*—the house, somehow felt emptier without him situated there, a void that only Mr Thornton could fill, a space that had become moulded to his exact description, his shadow its silhouette. She knew that with this being Sunday, he would be reading his newspaper by the hearth, his favoured pastime in the few leisurely hours he could claim as his own after church. Margaret had heard him tell her father so, and ever since then, a queer part of her that she could not quite explain had taken to acquiring the same journals every week. If she were undisturbed, Margaret would sit in the parlour and read them, but if she were in company, then she would attempt to conceal them behind another paper, and then, if any degree of attention was fixed upon her, she would be obliged to wait until she was alone in her room to study the editorials. Ever since she had initiated this ritual, Margaret had amused herself by wondering which articles interested him the most and what he made of them. There had been one today on the Navigation Act which would surely pique his interest, what with it affecting his trade. Indeed, she was certain of it, so Margaret would wait and see what Mr Thornton said to her father on the matter during his next lesson, his thoughts on his Sabbath studies a periodic topic of conversation and one which filled Margaret with inexplicable diversion.

It softened her shell of provocation to imagine him reading away in this restful attitude. He worked so very hard, too hard, really, and so it was quite right that he should find an intermission in his harried week, however brief, to do as he pleased. It warmed Margaret's heart to think of how his countenance changed whenever he sat down to a discussion with her father, and she could not help but allow a tender flicker of a smile to caress her cheeks as the muscles there twitched in fondness.

Mr Thornton routinely arrived with a look of fatigue about him as he stepped into the shelter of their humble abode every Thursday; his shoulders heavy, his brows stern, and his lips fastened into a thin line of silence. His harshness was almost as reliable as his punctuality.

Nevertheless, as soon as their dialogue commenced, the mill master would shake off the shackles of the outside world, and together, the teacher and student would converse as freely and gaily as two old friends who knew of no barrier to their rapport, all thoughts of discrepancies in age, class, education or industry set aside for the evening, as if melted away by the fire and vanished into the ashes of irrelevance.

Mr Thornton was perhaps the oldest of Mr Hale's pupils. He was certainly the favourite. Mr Hale got into the habit of quoting his opinions so frequently, and with such regard, that it became a little domestic joke to wonder what time, during the hour appointed for instruction, could be given to absolute learning, so much of it appeared to have been spent in conversation. It had long been her impression that his visits to their home had become the highlight of Mr Thornton's week. To begin with, she could not comprehend why he should be so mollified by the minimalism of their four walls and the unworldliness of their company, but then she had grown to understand. Their home was one of the few places, if not the only place, where he could simply be himself, and nothing would be asked of him. And now that she considered it, Margaret judged that it too, in its own peculiarly intimate way, had likewise become the acme of her calendar.

Glumly, Margaret thought back on how despite her pretence of indifference, she had awaited his lessons every week, her eyebrows tensing as the clock ticked away with infuriating sluggishness until the designated hour of his arrival. Then, finally, once she was quite beside herself with impatience, Margaret had felt a thrill delight her from tip to toe as she heard his firm knock, a stirring in her that she had not fully recognised as she scurried to answer it. However, much to her regret, Margaret had taken great pains to shroud herself in a veil of aloofness before she opened the door to the mill master, all so that she might disguise the pandemonium of emotions that fluttered away inside her.

With lips that chaffed, initially hitching themselves upwards into a wistful smile, and then sagging downwards in desolation, she recalled the first time she had laid eyes on him. His face was simple and symmetrical, a no-nonsense sort of face that told you everything you needed to know about its wearer, and yet, at the same time, it gave nothing away, as secretive as an unopened tomb, with nobody quite knowing what lay underneath the surface. When it came to his features, she found them difficult to describe, given that they were simultaneously nondescript and somehow handsome beyond compare. His complexion was rough, hardened by being frequently compelled out of doors to do battle with the wind and cold. His visage was distinctly angular, with a straight nose and strong jaw, and with neither aspect being chiselled like that of a Greek statue, but which nonetheless gave one a sense of confidence in the man, the sturdiness to be found there a testament to his unshakable foundations. His black hair was thick, and while it was kept meticulously short and tidy, there was an unruliness to it, especially as it curled about his ears, which Margaret liked, and much preferred to when it was smoothed down as a black helmet. For you see, she could appraise his mood when it was ruffled, and the extent of his tousles revealed to her his temperament, and this helped her deduce what was going on in that head of his, the same head that did not wobble when confronted by the gales of life, but remained secure atop his shoulders with an immovable emphasis of purpose and constancy of principle.

The rest of his face consisted *of straight brows which fell over the clear deep-set earnest eyes, which, without being unpleasantly sharp, seemed intent enough to penetrate into the very heart and core of what he was looking at. The lines in the face were few but firm, as if they were carved in marble, and lay principally about the lips, which were slightly compressed over a set of teeth so faultless and beautiful as to give the effect of sudden sunlight when the rare bright smile, coming in an instant and shining out of the eyes, changed the whole look from the severe and resolved expression of a man ready to do and dare everything, to the keen honest enjoyment of the moment, which is seldom shown so fearlessly and instantaneously except by children.*

With a shiver that tickled her spine, she contemplated his smile. *Margaret liked this smile; it was the first thing she had admired in this new friend of her father's; and the opposition of character, shown in all these details of appearance she had just been noticing, seemed to explain the attraction they evidently felt towards each other—*

Had she really just used the word "*attraction?*" Margaret composed herself so that she might effectively ponder this slip of the mind's tongue. Yes, she supposed she had. Then again, attraction can encompass all manner of feelings, but in her case, or rather, their case, she could no longer disown that she and Mr Thornton had been drawn to each other from the very beginning. After all, opposites do attract. Then again, she was beginning to wonder whether they were exceptionally the opposite after all. They may be distinct in many ways, but when and where it mattered, she trusted that they were more similar than they had perhaps first supposed.

Mr Thornton did not smile often, and while she had at first chosen to believe that his stony exterior was a reflection of his disdain for those he considered beneath him and his dominance over them, and his expression of solemn severity was likewise a manifestation of his reserve, she had since decided that she respected his selective smiles. It made them all the more precious, you see, for a man who smiles often, his smiles may be cheerful, but they are also cheap, whereas a man who must have a smile coaxed out of him, a man who bestows his smile but seldomly, he must do so with great sincerity, and in this face of discernment worn by Mr Thornton, she found that she valued his smile all the more, leaving her touched and rather honoured that he had ever gifted one upon her humble self.

Margaret remembered the first time he had smiled at her. It had been when she attended him during that initial evening when he came to take tea with her parents. She had been tired after a day of ironing curtains with obstinate creases that refused to straighten and baking biscuits that were a hodgepodge of uneven shapes as they rose in crumbling heaps, poor Dixon muttering in the background to think of her rolling pin being so badly used. Margaret's senses had been inadequately attuned to her environment on that winter's eve as she nodded off in her chair while the scholars engaged in lively discourse. However, despite the drowsiness which had befuddled her, Margaret had keenly felt Mr Thornton's observation of her, even in her sleep, and she noticed the way he glanced towards her shyly, a mite mortified to think he had bored her as his tongue ran away with itself in its unbridled enthusiasm. Rising from her seat, Margaret had gone to prepare his tea, and peering up bashfully as she stopped by his side, she had been struck by the intensity of his gaze as he stared at her hands with an intimate fascination that seemed to have lulled him into a trance. It had caught her off guard, so unexpected as it was, so unseemly as it seemed, and with trembling fingers, she had nigh on dropped the strainer with an almighty clatter against her grandmother's china cups. Then he had done it again after her mother had remarked on the frightful wallpaper the landlord insisted they retain, and when the hostess commented, perhaps somewhat tactlessly, on the lack of suitable alternatives to be found, their guest looked embarrassed on behalf of his town's limitations, so he made a light-hearted joke about Milton having passed muster. As he spoke, Mr Thornton had turned to her and offered Margaret a familiar smile, and she had been forced to look away, unsure of how to respond to what she half suspected to be an effort at humour, and possibly, even an unpractised attempt at flirtation.

But, oh, to think of all that had occurred since that first night when she refused to shake his hand, a foreboding omen, if there ever was one, for it had ushered in all the hostility and hurt that had arisen amidst them in the devastating interlude between then and now.

With her awareness returning to his chair, Margaret comprehended that even though she was dreading his next visit, whenever that should be, she would not find rest until he was restored to his proper place in the chair, within their home, amongst their family, in...

She swallowed hard.

In her life.

But when would he come?

Mr Thornton had once been dedicated to his studies, the very model of dependability, the man making a point of attending this fixed appointment at the same time, on the same day, every week, for many months. He had come when it snowed, when it rained, and when the harsh northern wind blew, and no matter how beleaguered he was with matters at the mill or the court, he had never once failed to attend his engagement with both father and daughter, taking up his rightful place in his chair, by the fire, by Margaret's side. But ever since—

No! She would not think about that.

Not now.

Not yet.

It was at this point that Margaret's hand halted, and with her wrist wilting to the side in languid defeat, she gave up her writing. Realising that she had been gripping her pen so tightly that her knuckles were turning white. She laid it down and flexed her fingers. In doing so, Margaret tried to ignore the ache of guilt which gnawed away at her. She told herself that his absence was neither worthy of wonder nor worry. In any case, there were several perfectly equitable explanations for his frequent non-appearances. One such rationalisation would be that he was incontestably busy with all manner of matters relating to his business. She had heard from Mr Bell that things were not going at all well for the masters of Milton after the strike, that they were struggling to fulfil their orders and were losing trade as a result of the unexpected delays. In this instance, Margaret could well imagine that for a man of few scruples, he might resort to sloppiness or duplicity in order to meet expectations and preserve his purse, but as for Mr Thornton, he would never cut corners or waive standards, so she felt sure he was working diligently to do right by his customers and his workers. Yes, that would be the case, she was sure of it, and if she knew him, which she did, the whole effort was probably a great deal more taxing on his time and strenuous on his health than Mr Thornton was letting on, so was it any wonder that he no longer had the time to think of the Hales and their modest companionship that did not serve to aid or alleviate him in any way?

But then again, that had not prevented him from having the time to enjoy the company of others today.

The clock struck the hour.

Two o'clock. They would likely still be there.

Closing her eyes, Margaret suppressed a quivering breath as her heart fluttered with the frantic wings of one who is trapped in a dark and desolate place. There was no use in pretending anymore. Yes, Mr Thornton was an eminent man whose time was greatly in demand, but she knew that if he wanted to be here, he would, so it must have taken something important to prevent him from visiting with his friend, a man whom he loved almost like a father.

Her.

Pressing her palms down on the sheets of paper before her, Margaret shuffled them with a fitful swipe of her hands, sending them flying off in all directions across the polished wood until she could take it no more, and snatching the pages that had not yet succumbed to her outburst, she tore them to shreds, and she threw them up into the air. Her head fell back to watch as they floated down in a mass of flakes, reminding her of when she had first seen the factory, a snowy hell, as white as death itself.

She felt like a paper doll that had been whipped up into the atmosphere by a frenzied gust, before being tossed about at its whim, waiting, as she must, to be dropped and discarded as she fell back down to Earth, hurtling into the realm of insensible reality.

She was so very cross with herself for not being able to adequately convey, nor indeed, confess, how she truly felt. Margaret had always been a forthright person, but ever since Mr Thornton had proposed, it was as if she withheld a secret that she could not share, not because she was ashamed of it, but because she was afraid of how the truth of it might overwhelm her and drag her into the depths of the unknown.

It was agonising, carrying around this burden, and it distressed her to think that she would never be free of it, that it would follow her for the rest of her days, tracking her as a long shadow of repression and repentance, the ghost of what might have been.

However, whatever aggravation Margaret felt towards herself, this was nothing compared to the resentment she harboured towards Mr Thornton.

The nerve of the man!

What could he mean by infecting her mind so, *as if* she *were always thinking that he cared for* her, *when* she knew that he did not; *he* could not.

'But *I won't care for him!*' she whispered assertively to her audience of an empty room. *'I surely am mistress enough of myself to control this wild, strange, miserable feeling.'*

Blinking, his disappointed features stole into her fretful mind with startling clarity. Failing to pacify the pangs of unease that ceaselessly nipped at her, she strained to concentrate on something else, anything else, anybody else! But it was no use; his words rang in her ear like the clanging of an almighty bell that demanded to be heard, its boom resounding far and wide with a thunderous reverberation as it proclaimed its message.

'I love you.'

Margaret stopped and shuddered as her repressed reminiscence reluctantly drew her back to that disastrous day that seemed to belong to another lifetime, a faded prologue when she had believed herself to be a woman of mature sense and sensibility, but instead, she had found herself to be a girl, one who was untried in the risks of love.

Margaret knew that she could not go back, still, she visited that nightmare time and time again, only, she was helpless to change a single thing, forced to stand and watch as a silent witness while they each hurled denunciations and defamations at one another with infantile recklessness. If only she could explain to him. If only she could tell him the truth about her brother. Perhaps then there would be hope as the misunderstandings that divided them thawed, freeing them from their sentence of loneliness, both of them being too afraid at present to lay themselves bare, instead having no choice but to wallow in grief and lick their wounds inflicted by Cupid's arrow for which there is no cure other than love returned.

If only he would see the truth in her eyes.
But he refused to look.

Oh, but it was no use. Margaret flinched to hide from the imp of remorse that now sat upon her shoulder and taunted her relentlessly, and she omitted a self-pitying sigh that caught in her throat and let her head slowly droop so that it came to rest on the table, her face still buried within.

This had to end.

She had hidden from the uproar that writhed within her for too long. It was time she faced her feelings once and for all and determined who would come out as victor: them, or her. There was no compromise, no middle ground to be had, only one could emerge victorious. The thought of this battle frightened her, for she knew that she could not hope to be crowned conqueror over these sentiments and unlock the anarchy of Pandora's Box upon her small world, a vault which once revealed, unleashing its enigmas upon its trespasser, can never be closed again. Nodding, Margaret knew that it was too late, she could no longer snub them, their cries that demanded to be noticed too loud to be ignored, too pleading in their passion to be pushed aside in fallacious indifference. The thought of it made her sick with uncertainty, and yet, she welcomed it, this undercurrent that threatened to sweep her away and drown her in uncharted waters. *The vehemence of emotion, stirred by grief and love within* her, it *was claiming mastery, and struggling for full sway; and asserting a right to predominate: to overcome, to live, rise, and reign at last; yes,--and to speak.*

When she at last relented, Margaret could privately confess that despite her assumptions, the legacy of Mr Thornton's declarations still hung in the air like a haze that refused to dissipate, blurring her sagacity with its disorientating mist. She felt lost in it, a fog of feeling that was foreign, and yet, somehow familiar as it absorbed her into its fold.

The sheer conceit of it!

Margaret had been so sure that his words had been the offspring of impulsive irrationality; that both she and he would soon forget their impassioned speeches – but no! His insolence had not dissolved the moment he had so hastily departed from the house. It was quite the reverse. He had the nerve to linger, to persist, and to offensively claim her mind as his dwelling place, as if it were his right to remain there in stubborn disobedience, his avowals clinging to the skirts of her soul for dear life, refusing to let go until the bittersweet end.

Well, he could forget that scheme, for she would not allow it!

But then again, had she not been cruel in turn? Had she not refused to listen to Mr Thornton's confessions and rejected him with pitiless incivility? It had been no ordinary exchange, after all, but a man laying his heart at her feet, asking her to care for it, requesting that she be the sole benefactor of its treasure trove of riches. And what had she done? She had stomped on it and trampled his hopes into the dirt, all because he presumed to know her heart without even asking, assuming to understand its secrets long before she herself had listened to the thrum of its truths.

Massaging her temple wearily, Margaret tried to cast off the guilt that constantly clawed away at her conscience over the way she had censured and denied him with so little attempt at benevolence. It had almost been inhumane. She had seen his anguish, she had seen his sincerity, and she had seen the fevered appeal in his eyes, and still, she had abused his vulnerability most ashamedly, all because her pride had been nettled by the timing of his address, impulsive as it was, even if there was something wonderfully endearing and earnest about the wild rashness of his besotted revelation.

Nevertheless, it was over now, she must remember that, so there was no use scrikin over it. There was no resolution to be had, no possible way to revise her verdict, so she staunchly declined to permit him to dictate to her for a moment longer. Indeed, Margaret was convinced that by harnessing an abundance of indifference, she could seek to exile this invasive, unwanted trespasser from her head and her heart – *wait, no! Just* her head.

Possibly. Maybe. *Oh!* It was too confusing.

With an insubordinate snort, she scoffed, thinking of how he might be accustomed to playing the overbearing master of all he surveyed; but with God as her witness, John Thornton would not be the master of Margaret Hale!

'I don't want to possess you!'

Margaret closed her eyes and trembled as the hairs on her arm stood and bristled of their own volition, stirred as they were by the surge of desire that coursed through her veins. It was a heady sensation which Margaret had been wholly unaware of only a few short months before, having lain dormant in maidenly naivety, only, now, it gushed through her with such a ferocity that it was almost all-consuming. Margaret then proceeded to scold herself sharply, attempting to scatter this impenetrable daze. Nevertheless, strive as she might, the more she endeavoured to struggle free from…from…

His ardent words…
His searching scowl…
His provoking declarations…
His wounded expression…
His piercing eyes…

His effect on her…

His hold over her…

…then the more urgently…the more hungrily…the more fiercely she felt him, the more impatiently her whole body ached in want of the sensation of him – *John*!

Margaret stiffened.

How could she have foreseen what would transpire? How could she possibly have predicted his unexpected act? Oh, but Margaret, the signs were there, plain for her untrained eyes to see. She could remember it, even now, all too vividly. When she had first entered the room, there he had been, stalking by the window like an agitated beast that wanted taming. There was something in the hunched arch of his back, the steady, rhythmical sway of his body that revealed the tension that flowed through that mighty oak of a man from tip to toe. Then there was that look! It was so raw that she could hardly find the words to describe it, but she saw it, all too often, in her mind's eye, haunting her memories. That intense stare he had settled upon her when she arrived; that single, inspired gaze that lingered just a fraction longer than was proper, and in that interval of intimacy, it had foretold all, confirming what she had suspected all along, ever since she had returned home the day before, and that was that Mr Thornton would come and ask for her hand.

And here he was, there he had been, gallant to a fault as he did his duty by her, bound in honour to her as he was by her foolishness.

Still, his countenance had been perplexing, as if he were surprised to find her come to him at all. He must have been expecting her, he had requested a private audience with her, but he was surprisingly disorientated, as if awakening from a dream. He paused for what could only have been the briefest of moments, but as he did, Margaret could see him watching her in awe, as if he were greeting an angel, his eyes drinking in her every inch, taking in the form of the woman, who, by the time he laid his head on his pillow that night, may well be his fiancée, his hopes of happiness for the future resting upon her answering lips. It would only take one word, just one, a solitary syllable being enough to raise or dash a man's aspirations in one fell swoop. What immense power she possessed, and she had brandished it like an axe, fatal with its blow that felled that same mighty oak.

As Mr Thornton's interest had travelled across her, Margaret quivered, conscious of his regard gently alighting on her temple and concentrating upon the spot where she had been assaulted the day before, her carefully placed russet curls hiding the evidence of this violent, albeit accidental, crime against her person. With her pulse racing, she had felt the tender heat of his worry as he had studied her, asking himself whether she was well, torturing himself for ever having let a single hair on her head be harmed. She had been by his side, after all, and surely there she should have been safe, not struck down within the shelter of his strong arms. None of it had been his fault, she knew that was without question, but equally, she knew how he would be blaming himself for letting her take a clout that had always been intended for him.

Then he had begun, instigating their crisis of confessions, and there had been no turning back.

'I came... because... I think it... very likely... I know I've never found myself in this position before. It is... difficult to find the words...'

Without realising it, Margaret's mouth had been gliding along the length of her arm, and there she found that her teeth sunk into her hand, piercing it and leaving a mark on the same patch of skin that met with the edge of her finger where he had touched her for the first time, his own digit skimming it with leisurely inquisitiveness when she passed him his tea.

'My feelings for you... are very strong...'

Swallowing thickly, she pleaded with herself to pay no heed to the tingling thrill that slithered and tickled throughout her mortified flesh at the thought of his cavernous voice as it pulsated throughout her nerves. His words stayed with her so constantly; it was as if he had wilfully carved them into the bark of her very being in an act of rebellious defiance. *And so she shuddered away from the threat of his enduring love. What did he mean? Had she not the power to daunt him?*

'I wish to marry you because I love you!'

Loved? By him? *Outrageous*!

How could he have exploited such sacred sentiments? Surely he did not entertain any tenderness for her; it was not possible, let alone probable. They had known each other for so short a time; they had nothing in common and had done nothing but quarrel during every meeting kindled by their arrant magnetism. She never knew how they ended up in such a collie-shangles, but they always managed it between them. Their beliefs could not have been more divergent, their faith in the goodness and worth of their fellow man, and their emphasis on humanity were in constant conflict with one another. How could he take the liberty to be so bold as to use such a word as *love* after all their heated arguments? It was deceitful, it was dishonourable, it was…*darling.* Then again, the way he had beheld her…

'One word more. You look as if you thought it tainted you to be loved by me.'

The nerve of the man! Why did he believe he retained the authority to address her with such indecent language? All rough, unruly and downright magnificent? Had he no notion that a man beseeching a woman so fervently would forever discredit her unspoiled innocence? For irrefutably, such expressions of devotion—*nay*, of reverence, should only be uttered in the sweet and privileged intimacy that exists between steadfast lovers.

'I am a man. I claim the right of expressing my feelings.'

The scoundrel! What of her right not to hear of it? To think that he could toss about the idea of being in love so casually; when in truth, it should be treated with piety, with prudence, with sworn fidelity. But he was not committed to his offer, she was certain of this. Or that is, he was, in principle. Mr Thornton would have seen it through and seen her right without complaint, but in his heart of hearts, he must surely have been relieved that she had spurned him. In doing so, she may have temporarily injured his pride, but she had spared him the life sentence of surrendering his own happiness for her sake, a sacrifice he would never truly forgive, gradually infecting whatever regard they may have harboured for each other, curdling it into something insupportable that progressively poisoned their union. Margaret was well aware that Mr Thornton had only applied for her hand because he had been under pressure; he had deemed it his responsibility to salvage her character after the shameful scene she caused at the riot, an episode she was not sorry for in the least, other than that it had urged him unwillingly to the edge of reason, the brink of onus, until they were both left standing on the precipice of their precarious association, with no way of going back to how things were before.

'I spoke to you about my feelings because I love you. I had no thought for your reputation.'

Spoken to her of his feelings? Well, why had he not spoken to her of them before? It was not as if he had lacked the opportunity. He had seen her every week for eight months, and in that time they had spent many an uninterrupted minute together as she had first received and then retrieved his coat, scarf, gloves and hat as he came and went. Why had he not, during these secluded audiences, hinted that he admired her? That he preferred her to all others? That he, in his infinite generosity, cared for her?

However, it appeared that the more strictly Margaret tried to evict Mr Thornton from the inner sanctum of her most private thoughts, the more mulishly he dug in his heels and clasped her close.

'You cannot avoid it.'

What infuriated her the most, was the fact that she could be so feckless, so weak against his offensive. Truly, she had judged herself to be comprised of sterner stock than this. Did she not retain enough restraint to dismiss him? To command and abandon the feral, intolerable chaos that she bore in her breast? Evidently not, for she was helpless in hiding from him.

'You must have to disappoint so many men who offer you their heart.'

Offered her his heart, indeed! He had done no such thing, for he was heartless, so he had no such prize nor possession to bequeath. Then to imply that she was a flirt—the cheek of it! Yes, there had been others, one other, Henry, but that was not the same thing at all. How dare he allege that she courted the attention of other men?! That she allowed them to take hold of her in such a way as he had. Did he not know what he was to her? Did he not understand that his place in her life was distinctive and exclusive to him? That he was irreplaceable?

There was no other but him. There never had been, and there never would be. She was beginning to realise that; all too slowly, all too late

Possessed by a need for immediate distraction, Margaret undertook to arrange her curls more times than she had fingers to count. Removing a pin from within a mass of silken locks, she slid it back into position, pushing it down with greater force than was needed, hoping that the stab of discomfort would cause her to wince and then filch away her concentration, redirecting her to the here and now, not mislaid on matters that were already over and done with.

What Margaret could not fathom, was that when Henry Lennox had broached the subject of matrimony, she had managed to voluntarily move on and forget the whole unhappy incident with ease. She had made the very same private comment earlier today. Why, then, did Mr Thornton plague her so? She felt sure that he was somehow doing it on purpose; for such arrogance and tenacity would be just like him. Still, Margaret could not deny that on that morning, his commanding presence, his indulgent words, his imploring request for her hand, they had all roused something completely unfamiliar within the fibre of her very soul.

'Nay, *I, if I would, cannot cleanse you from it.*'

Margaret picked up a cloth and scrubbed at the splodges of ink on her fingers far more forcefully than was necessary, as if the clouded feelings she concealed could be wiped away through vigorous purification.

She disliked him more for having mastered her inner will. How dared he say that he would love her still, even though she shook him off with contempt? She wished she had spoken more—stronger. Sharp, decisive speeches came thronging to her mind, now that it was too late to utter them. The deep impression made by the interview was like that of a horror in a dream; that will not leave the room although we waken up, and rub our eyes, and force a stiff rigid smile upon our lips. It is there—there, cowering and gibbering, with fixed ghastly eyes, in some corner of the chamber, listening to hear whether we dare to breathe of its presence to anyone. And we dare not; poor cowards that we are!

But no, Margaret knew there was a reason why she had been powerless against him that day, she, who was anything but helpless. The thought of being a pitiful creature who could not govern her own conscience, direct her own body, or control her own mouth was ludicrous, but somehow, that fateful morn, she had been incapable of anything other than hurling weak accusations at him, falsehoods so feeble that surely even he could never have credited them, for how could they stand up against the strength of his noble character?

And yet, he had. He had believed her. He had believed her implicitly, trusting boy that he was. He had swallowed her lies and there they had stuck in his throat as he had spoken to her bitterly, but with not nearly as much spite as when she had rebuked and ridiculed him, unable to curb her tongue as it lashed its venom. Margaret had seen the tears welling in his eyes, the anguish which smouldered behind the glassy film of his unshed tears.

'...do not be afraid of too much expression on my part.'

Well, in this at least he had been all truth. He had barely looked at her from that day forth, barely spoken to her, her very presence an affliction he could barely bear.

The thought of him brought such pain and pleasure as she had never known, her heart drifting between these two poles in a dizzying miasma. How was it that, in the midst of her cataclysm, there he was?

She recalled the way he had swept from the room, his exit leaving behind a vacuum of screaming stillness that left her bereft of words, even now. Holding his gloves in her hands, Margaret tried to analyse what had just taken place, those three short minutes in which so much had been said, and worse, so much was left unsaid.

...even before he left the room,—and certainly, not five minutes after, the clear conviction dawned upon her, shined bright upon her, that he did love her; that he had loved her; that he would love her. And she shrank and shuddered as under the fascination of some great power, repugnant to her whole previous life. She crept away, and hid from his idea. But it was of no use.

Yet through it all, Margaret had come to realise one thing, one obstinate fact which she could no longer deny, try as she might with all her might.

Peering up from within the confines of her hands, Margaret caught sight of herself in the reflection of her inkwell, and with a whisper so soft, it scarcely existed at all, she breathed a sacred and most surprising truth:

'I miss him.'

Chapter Twelve

Perhaps, Perhaps... Perhaps

In the amber light of the study's glow, Mr Thornton withdrew into the sanctuary of privacy, a contrast from the world that lay outside the door, the clamour and demands vaping into a mere hassled silhouette beyond the veil of his solitude. Unwanted visitors, like unwelcome predators, lingered on the threshold of his seclusion, their voices a distant murmur, but he, the master of this hermitage, sought a respite from their intrusion. He closed the heavy oak door with a measured deliberateness, shutting out the prying gazes and pressing concerns that sought entry, attempting to barge unheeded into the recesses of his inner sanctum. Leather-bound volumes stood sentinel, their spines bearing witness to the stories of yesteryears, and yet, in this cocoon of contemplation, his own narrative unfolded. The room, filled with the hushed whispers of his thoughts, became a clandestine theatre where the drama of his emotions played out in scenes illuminated by the shuddering flame of introspection. Here, within the walls of his shelter, Mr Thornton conjured her presence—an apparition woven from the fabric of his desires. In the quietude, he envisioned conversations unspoken, moments not yet lived, echoing in the distorted chamber of shared silences. The ticking of the grandfather clock chimed in harmony with the rhythm of his heartbeat, a reminder that time, trapped in its unbroken shell, held a different cadence. In this retreat, Mr Thornton forged a communion with her, the woman who existed not in the realm of physical proximity but in the wraithlike expanse of his musings. His gaze, unfocused yet penetrating, delved into the nucleus of a world where they could be alone together, untethered from the obligations of the others. How had he allowed it to go this far? How had he allowed the void between them to grow so vast?

At the mere contemplation of her, an insidious agony gripped his entire being, a noxious pain intent on ruthlessly corroding and withering every vestige of his strength. He found himself incessantly tossed about, akin to a marionette manipulated by the capricious whims of an unseen puppeteer. Mr Thornton had gone thirty years without looking twice at a woman, and now, well now he had been knocked to his knees in worship, and he could not picture his life without one cherished maiden. It was like an addiction he could not, would not, relinquish. She alone engaged and satisfied an emptiness inside him, a loneliness that he had never known existed before she revealed it to him. Only now, she refused to abide there and had sought to rip herself from his reach, tearing away his tattered heart as she fled. Yet, entangled in the abyss of disorder that consumed him, comprehension remained elusive. Was love destined to be such a merciless mistress, wielding its influence to slash and strike away at every recess of his consciousness? No, he concluded, love was an irrational force, an ideal stripped of sanity. She served as a calming elixir for the tempest within him, yet paradoxically, she embodied the storm itself—the nature that had agitated his heart into a whirlwind of unfamiliarity.

God! How he loved her. His love for her knew no bounds. It was a love that was ferocious, fond and faithful, a flame that no misunderstanding or misfortune could ever extinguish. That would explain why he had abandoned his principles and protected Margaret from undergoing the ordeal of a public enquiry, keeping her out of danger from both the convicting punishment of the law and the reproachful verdict of society, even if it had been at the sacrificial cost of his own integrity. Even so, Mr Thornton did not regret it, nor did he begrudge her the service, nor the way it had risked his honour and held it at ransom, no, and he would do it all again, time and time again, if only it meant she could be spared, that she would be safe, no matter what became of him as a consequence.

Glancing up, his great height allowed him to stare out of the window from afar and regard his little world, one which had once been so preciously important to him, now seemed dyed with the grey hues of monotony. The mill yard, his empire of cobbled feet and inches, flecked with the white wisps of fallen cotton, appeared as a blur, its contours softened and indistinct. Shades of sunlight and shadows played hide-and-seek among the chimneys, clashing like long spindles as fencers must do, and as the light shifted in its sprightly sport, the mundane metamorphosed into the mysterious, as if changing both form and significance.

He cast his eyes to the ground and soberly thought on what the ladies had said about the rarity of such a woman as Margaret Hale. It occurred to Mr Thornton there and then that such people, not merely women, were as uncommon as stardust, and more precious still for all her astounding originality. Therefore, when a man found her amongst the masses of conventional people upon this earth, unexceptional souls that excited him not, if he were lucky enough to discover such a creature as she, he should do all he could to encourage her friendship, and, in time, strive to win her hand and thus secure the cherished gift that was her heart, something he would treasure always. So, why had he stopped trying? And what was more, had Margaret been right all along?

Had he never *really* tried in the first place?

Had his fears of rejection shackled him and prevented him from opening up to her?

Had he failed to be honest with her, sharing with her the sacred sentiments of his heart? Perhaps.

How could he ask her to be honest with him when he was unable, if not unwilling, to offer her honesty in return?

Perhaps he had been too reserved. Perhaps he had been too hasty. Perhaps he had been too officious. Perhaps he had been too impatient. Perhaps he had been far too unforgiving.

Perhaps he had deserved her refusal after all. Perhaps, perhaps... perhaps.

Chapter Thirteen

The Blue Devil

Mr Thornton had eternally been a logical man; a rational person. He liked solid and undeniable facts and figures; concepts that were not varied, but secure. He had always assumed that if he were ever to succumb to caring for a woman or make the decision to marry, it would be with the same self-assured intelligence that dictated every division of his life. But how naive he had been. It was now obvious that matters of the heart were anything but academic and held no relation to the quantifiable figures lodged in the ledgers of his mill and the mechanisms of his mind. The admission, though bitter, was a salve to the wounds concealed beneath the façade of composure.

The embers in the fireplace glowered, stoking the ashes of resentment that smouldered in the recesses of his soul. In the privacy of his vulnerability, he grappled with the knowledge that Margaret, the elusive figure of his affections, might harbour a love for another.

Miserably disturbed! that is not strong enough. He was haunted by the remembrance of the handsome young man, with whom she stood in an attitude of such familiar confidence; and the remembrance shot through him like an agony, till it made him clench his hands tight in order to subdue the pain.

The very falsehood that stained her, was a proof how blindly she loved another--this dark, slight, elegant, handsome man—while he himself was rough, and stern, and strongly made. He lashed himself into an agony of fierce jealousy. He thought of that look, that attitude! —how he would have laid his life at her feet for such tender glances, such fond detention! He mocked at himself, for having valued the mechanical way in which she had protected him from the fury of the mob; now he had seen how soft and bewitching she looked when with a man she really loved. He remembered, point by point, the sharpness of her words—'There was not a man in all that crowd for whom she would not have done as much, far more readily than for him.' He shared with the mob, in her desire of averting bloodshed from them; but this man, this hidden lover, shared with nobody; he had looks, words, hand-cleavings, lies, concealment, all to himself.

As he faced the truth of his lingering anger and the green-eyed monster named jealousy that clung to his heart, Mr Thornton, in the seclusion of his thoughts, embarked on a journey of acceptance—a journey towards healing and, perhaps, a revelation that would one day dispel the shadows that obscured the clarity of his emotions.

But he could not bring himself to believe that she was a bird of paradise, for the rumours must be nothing but fudge and be fudged in return.

Slumping against the wall in defeat, his legs gave way until he found himself sitting on the cold floor, a figure of desolation, in the grips of a fit of the blue-devils, and with his fingers restlessly combing through strands of ebony hair, he released a low, anguished moan. Margaret: she was an enigma. She remained an unsolvable puzzle in his turbulent world that longed for calm waters. His thoughts were overwhelmed by the haunting recollections of that ill-fated day, a mere four months ago, when he hurtled their association—if one could even dignify it as any form of relationship, more a pitiful acquaintance—over the cliffs, mercilessly shattering it into irreparable smithereens. How, for heaven's sake, had he fallen prey to such irrational folly?

Allowing himself to finally relive that encounter, after months of stubbornly refusing to revisit it, he replayed the scene as a pathetic spectacle. There he stood, bearing the most vulnerable longings of his heart to a woman who held him in disdain, recoiling from him. Good God! The haunting image of her aghast face persisted, a poignant reminder of his own descent into madness.

'Please! Stop. Pray, please don't go any further.'

Hell, ham and humbug! If only he had stopped. Lord! Could there have been a more star-crossed trio of minutes? Their brief audience, fleeting and far from sweet, left behind a wake of devastation. How was it conceivable that so little time elapsed, yet wrought so much havoc?

Her bewilderment must have been profound, a sudden gale that swept through the tranquil landscape of her understanding. What unseen force had eclipsed his customary restraint? Had he not, mere moments before, asserted himself as a man of meticulous and calculated reason? In his thirty years on this terrestrial stage, he had taken pride in never succumbing to the capricious winds of impulsivity or the perilous allure of recklessness. And yet, here he was, caught in the net of his primal yearnings, surrendering to a self-serving carelessness, an uproar that defied the very essence of his character.

With no sensible plan in hand, he approached her, flinging himself at the altar of her presence with no prior orchestration, no genuine reflection on the repercussions of his impromptu overture upon this precious soul. The graceful dance of consideration eluded him, leaving only the erratic cadence of his unbridled emotions to serenade the moment. Each step, a note of chaos, as he floundered where he should have waltzed into the delicate symphony of her world, oblivious to the dissonance he unwittingly composed.

Fool!

'Please don't continue in that way. It is not the way of a gentleman.'

Yes, she had accused him of not being a gentleman, and even though her allegation had grieved his sensitive self-esteem, he knew she was right. Had he not launched into the conversation by addressing her aggressively?

'Your way of speaking shocks me. It is blasphemous.'

He should have stopped there and then, escaping the scene with what little dignity he had left intact. But no, he had censored her enlightened opinions, resenting her endearing thoughtfulness for others. He scoffed at her friendships with those he deemed unsuitable. What kind of imbecile was he? What beastly breed? Damn it − what debased species of gentleman behaved in such a manner, particularly when he was supposed to be professing and proving his love? Then, to add insult to injury, he had failed to change course, to rectify his ways, to temper his harsh tongue. Instead, he careened into the most disastrous proposal known to fact or fiction. Had Shakespeare been privy to John Thornton's assaults on the exalted prose of love and his condemnations of the art of wooing, he would undoubtedly have crafted a tragedy exclusively shaped for his narrative. To exacerbate matters, Mr Thornton allowed his scorching temper to roam freely, subjecting her to an unrestrained barrage of uncouth harangues. Alas! He went so far as to accuse her of being a flirt, a temptress skilled in ensnaring the hearts of men.

Oh, John! John, John, John, what had you been thinking?

As he brooded on this, Mr Thornton returned to rummage through the miserable remains of the day. He had been as coarse as a tempest's howl, as unrelenting as the thunderous clash of waves against an unyielding shore, and as devastatingly blunt as a bull recklessly charging through a fragile china shop. Each word slipped over the next stumbling word, a desperate plea to be trusted, to be taken seriously. Yet, it had not worked. His insatiable craving for her had clouded his rationale, leaving him unable to think straight, let alone craft a sentence imbued with the poetic grace and credibility that such a moment deserved. Thus, the truth remained: he was never gifted in the urbane art of expression. His words, typically economical, steered clear of pointless tattle and superfluous eloquence. As you can imagine, he and your faithful narrator are not torn from the same page on this account. At any rate, in the crucible of his adolescent years and young adulthood, where he toiled tirelessly to mend the fabric of his frayed family life, leisure for excess was a luxury he had been unable to afford, so he had trained himself to be frugal in all things, including the sparing dialogue he employed.

Thus, when Margaret had cast her ethereal spell upon his sombre existence, Mr Thornton found himself woefully deficient in the refined finesse required to expertly flatter and earnestly pursue her. The intricate methods of complimenting a young lady, subtly revealing his ardent yearnings, and tenderly courting her care was a foreign language to him. He may as well have been translating Dutch, or double Dutch, at that. No, when it came to Mr Thornton, there were no artful embellishments—what you got was what was on the tin, and because of this, he had failed when his courage and good sense had been most sorely needed.

'It offends me that you should speak to me as if it were your duty to rescue my reputation!'

Oh, beloved one, how could she have imagined he owned such a barren plan? How could she have doubted that he was in love with her? He cared nothing for her reputation; for as far as he was concerned, she had behaved heroically at the riot. He owed his life to her and despite her refusal to accept his thanks, he would remain steadfast in his genuine gratitude. But now, with hindsight, he realised how negligent he had been. Of course! It must have looked as if he were proposing to her because of the incident on the front steps of the mill house. It was true, that all he had offered her before that day was subtle, secretive hints of his feelings, of his intentions towards her. Penitently, he accepted that his offer must have come as a jolt, and so it was no wonder she had been offended; thinking that he sought her hand merely in duty and not devotion.

'You think that because you are rich, and my father is in reduced circumstances, that you can have me for your possession! I suppose I should expect no less from someone in trade!'

Mother of mercy! How that cutting speech cleaved through him. Oh, Margaret, Margaret! It was all so painfully untrue! How could she not grasp the depth of his feelings? Her father's financial strains held no weight, for he desired her to abide by his side whether she was as opulent as an empress or as humble as a church mouse. He had known far worse poverty himself and survived it, so why should he shun or seek her in the name of money? The misconception that he aimed to possess her as if she were an abstract trinket was corruptly distorted. He had never thought of her as a derisory figurine, to be placed on his mantel, trained to remain silent, to carry out his bidding without dissent, a doll devoid of distinct personality, simply taking on the characteristics her owner assigns.

How wrong she was to believe he was so wanting in humanity, caring for nothing beyond the realms of commerce. Though a lowly tradesman, he bore a heart that beat with as much fervour as any man. He had no desire to possess her, for how could any man hope to own or tame her mysterious spirit? A tender smile played upon his lips at the thought of her indescribable individuality, but this soon vanished in the bleakness of his reality.

No, he harboured no aspirations to rule her—never that. His honest wish was to serve her, to provide, adore, respect, and treasure her, always, but never spoil her, never that. He wanted her to stay exactly as she was, only to watch her in ever-increasing esteem as she aged and matured into her magnificence. As he had almost wept at the time, he longed to marry her because he loved her. The depth of his affection transcended meagre possession, weaving a bond of selflessness that was committed to her welfare.

And yet, she cared nothing for him, being or wellbeing, he could be damned, as far as she was concerned. Therefore, Mr Thornton relented that all that remained following his vicious battle with love, was the hollowed-out, empty shell of his former self. The thought of this bewildering woman ravaged his mind morning, noon and night.

But no more, he had to stop.

'I do not like you, and never have.'
She had rejected him unequivocally, making it abundantly clear that her heart would forever elude his reach. Yet, how could he ever dismiss her from his thoughts? Contemplating her had become as innate as breathing. A quirk amused his frowning features as he envisioned those irresistibly impertinent lips that more often scolded him than graced him with a compliment. The desire to witness those rosette petals curve upward, even just slightly, consumed him. Oh, what he would sacrifice to see her smile directed at him. The wholesome thought of kissing them, of pressing his untrained mouth against hers, and feeling the soft, supple flesh of her virgin lips meld with his own was too exquisite to articulate. The longing drove Mr Thornton to the edge of madness, his nails digging into his palms to censor any cry that threatened to escape.

But saints preserve him, he understood that with the faintest whisper of a sign, the transitory bestowing of her gaze, or the gentlest touch, he would be at her mercy. Despite the torment that accompanied the mere mention of her name, as he had found in his parlour today, he had discovered himself inexplicably bound to her. She remained intrinsic to him, even if he existed in constant irrelevance to her.

But there was a problem.

Something, or rather, someone, had got in the way.

Him.

Chapter Fourteen

Love Her Well

Opening his eyes, Mr Thornton rose to his feet, a newfound resolution stirring. While his future lay still unmapped before him, he knew what he must do first.

Smiling to himself, he decided that this was the perfect time to set the record straight and explain to these women—*these three witches*—once and for all, that he was not the man destined to be theirs, and even more so, they were not the ladies for him, because there was only one he had ever wanted, only one who would suit his desire, his temperament, his passion, and alas, she was not here. Yes, with a smirk, for a man, even in despair, must find his pleasure somewhere, Mr Thornton resolved to leave them in no doubt as to where his immovable affections lay, because, after all, he was definitely not one to dabble. Poised to rise and carry out his task, a sudden knock at the door disrupted his intent. Looking up, he witnessed the door creak open, and, for a moment, hope fluttered in his heart like a feeble bird braving flight with broken wings. As he glimpsed the edge of a skirt swishing around the corner, he began to stand in anticipation, only for his expectations to quickly wane.

'Miss Latimer?!' he coughed in incredulity as her unexpected figure appeared.

The young lady entered his study, pausing provisionally before committing to her visit and stepping closer.

Mr Thornton lurched forward, voicing his discomfort. 'Madam, this is not appropriate. We should not be alone. I must ask that you—'

'I will be but a moment,' she cut in, her countenance serious, her tone insurmountable. 'I am leaving,' she announced, fixing him with an unflinching gaze, and he felt a twinge of relief mingled with ongoing wariness.

'I just have one thing to ask of you before I go,' she said, and there was something in her manner which made him believe he had no right to refuse her.

'Very well,' he replied nervously.

'Love her well.'

Mr Thornton cocked his eyebrow in confusion.

'Because, at the end of the day, that is all we want,' she said sadly, solemnly. 'To be loved…as you love her. So, on behalf of all women, I ask this of you: love her entirely, love her eternally, love her well.'

At first, Mr Thornton could not speak, but he recovered himself enough to nod his faithful assurances.

'Thank you,' she said with visible reprieve. 'And trust me when I say, that whatever happens between the two of you, she will love you for loving her with all the honesty and honourability that only you can.'

With that, satisfied in her quest, Miss Latimer turned to leave, whispering over her shoulder as she stole from the room, her voice free of regret, only cleansed by acceptance, 'Goodbye, Mr Thornton, I doubt we shall meet again.' And with that, she left.

He watched her departure and the way she closed the mill gates behind her with firm finality. The city beyond the rooftops seemed to pulsate with a myriad of promises, mirroring the possibilities that lingered in the wake of Miss Latimer's wisdom. Mr Thornton's gaze followed her silhouette until it melded into the glow of the sunshine, a solitary figure circumnavigating the labyrinthine paths of their divergent destinies. She never looked back at him as she exited by the wings of this play of people, this play of passions, and with all honesty, Mr Thornton could say he wished Miss Latimer well.

As he walked back to the parlour with slow, assessed steps, his mind occupied with deliberating on what to say and how to say it, Mr Thornton could hear the hushed hiss of words snaking down the corridor to ensnare him with their goading vindictiveness.

'What could he be thinking?'

'How can he defend her like that?'

'It beggars belief.'

'She does not deserve it.'

'Well…she does not deserve our unkindness,' came the familiar voice of his sister, to which there resounded a bluster of muffled scoffs.

Very well, thought he, as he listened to these absurd wheeze-sneezes, at least their persistent malevolence made his mission clearer and easier to execute. Therefore, Mr Thornton entered the room with an air of perfect calm about him. The ladies all looked up, startled at first, a little uneasy, unsure of themselves. Without taking a seat, he stood before them, his hands clasped behind his back.

'Ladies,' he began graciously, 'I have come to beg your pardon.'

At this, they all blew a sigh of relief and smiled forgivingly.

'My sister was right, I was an ogre, and what's more, I was not clear, so please, let me be clear now,' said he.

'You will leave this house and not return.'

All at once, the whole room took a sharp, shocked intake of breath.

His sister teetered on the verge of vocal protest, a gabster by nature, yet she was persuaded to hush—an inkling of comprehension, perhaps. She grasped that, for possibly the first time she could remember, she and her brother were of the same opinion, so, for once, she said nothing, and simply let him speak.

'And if I ever hear you speak of Miss Hale with such spite again, I will not hold back out of civility, but will tell you, and anyone present, how loathsome I find your sentiments, and I will defend Miss Hale until my last breath!'

'John!' his mother began cautiously, fully aware that when her son was in a foul mood, he tended to utter regrettable words—his ill-fated proposal to Miss Hale being a glaring example. Though John had never resorted to physical aggression with his robust physique, the acuity of his tongue and the sharpness of his intellect served as formidable weapons against any adversary. By nature, he was a reserved individual, but when the crimson haze of anger descended, he could drop his self-possession, speaking without the sieve of forethought. What made matters worse was Mrs Thornton's understanding that John could weather any personal insult directed at him, having endured such affronts since childhood amid his family's disgrace. However, she found it inconceivable that he would tolerate any slight aimed at his beloved Miss Hale.

But then again, *angry people are not always wise.*

Understandably, Miss Bingley and Miss Ingram were incensed, and one might swear they frothed at the mouth in fury.

'You are mad!' they accused.

At this, Miss Thornton rose to her feet and stood in solidarity with her brother, though, in her height, she only reached the lower rim of his shoulder.

'That is enough!' she insisted. 'My brother is not mad. He might be hopelessly dull, but he is a good man who has put up with you today even though you have been nothing but horrid. So, I also think you should leave!'

she ordered, pointing at the door, so cross, that she never noticed her mother smiling at her proudly.

However, her demands were ignored and Miss Bingley and Miss Ingram's indignant reactions were expressed in undignified splutters as they hurled a relentless volley of fresh insults at Miss Hale. The accusations collided and stumbled over each other, creating an anarchic commotion of condemnation.

'But she is insufferable!'

'She is reckless!'

'She is dreary!'

'She is unfashionable!'

'She is headstrong!'

'She is wilful!'

'She is unconventional!'

'She is *not* the woman for you!'

'She is everything a woman should be, and everything a man could wish for, because believe me, you can forget about all your superficial accomplishments, because at the end of the day, *men of sense, whatever you choose to say, do not want silly wives*! They do not want to be poisoned by a person who is sickly with spite,' he advocated, staring down at each of the ladies before him in turn, his gaze prolonged and unforgivably forbidding, telling them in no uncertain terms that he judged them to be rotten to the core.

'You talk of women as if they are lesser beings, but you are wrong! Yes, it is regrettable that women are made to feel they are insignificant, both by the law and society, but by God, that does not mean they should actively choose to demean themselves and thwart their cause. They should be crying out for recognition and demanding veneration, showing us men what women are truly worth. Truly, some women merit a higher regard than a hundred of their male counterparts combined. Why, my own mother is cleverer and more capable than any man I know!' he sponsored, nodding his head towards her, his mother's heart warmed by her son's words of encouragement, his sister confused as to why she too was not mentioned, but this was soon rectified.

'As is my sister,' he added with a touch of brotherly pride. 'I am relieved that she appears to have come to her senses, recognising you for who you truly are. Two persecutors of your fellow women—two witches! Though, at least that is better than three,' he admitted.

He was so unbelievably angry, not to mention confused.

Why did women insist on tormenting one another? Life's formidable challenges already weighed heavily upon them, prompting the question of why some actively seek deconstruction instead of construction. In a world that calls for unity, the collective effort of womanhood should be a harmonious symphony, resonating with the shared purpose of uplifting each other, fostering resilience, and fortifying the bonds that rise above the struggles inherent in every woman's journey. Perhaps It is a manifestation of societal pressures or the internalised competition ingrained in cultural narratives. In the pursuit of acceptance and recognition, some may mistakenly believe that tearing down others elevates their own standing. It is a paradoxical choice that hinders the potential for a sisterhood that could collectively overcome adversities.

'And as for Miss Hale, she is tremendous! I have never met a woman so exceptional in all my days. And that, ladies, is what a man wants in a wife. He wants somebody who not only cheers or champions him, but somebody who challenges him, inspiring him to be a better man, the best version of himself. Partnership, honesty and devotion are what make for a marriage of real substance, not wealth, position or influence. These do not bring happiness but are a retreating horizon that cannot be achieved, leaving us constantly empty and dissatisfied. They will not bring you comfort when you are miserable, when life proves hard, no, they will abandon you. They will not guide you when you are lost. They will not mend you when you are broken. They will not warm you when you are cold. And, they will not loyally remain with you as you shift through the changeable seasons of life. But true love, a genuine faith in one another, a sincere friendship, this is what I want.'

After a while, he exhaled, his rage dissipating as it peaked. Instead, he was overcome by a surge of remorse. 'There is only really one person who I want all of that with,' he said, so quietly, it was as if he were talking to himself. 'She is rational. She is intriguing. She is kind. She is competent. She is heroic. She is irreplaceable. She does not have a senseless or scheming bone in her body. And I will *not* let you treat her so wickedly,' he said with a judgemental glare.

Now, at this point in the story, one might be forgiven for asking why a man who is so notably reserved should suddenly find himself embroiled in such an uncharacteristic stream of confessions that exhibits his emotions, after all, he was known to be *the personification of sensible silence*, but the answer is quite simple. Firstly, I talk too much, which means these characters talk too much, so that fault lies with me. However, secondly, and more critically, we should remember that *reserved people often really need the frank discussion of their sentiments and griefs more than the expansive. The sternest-seeming stoic is human after all, and to burst with boldness into the silent sea of their souls is often to confer on them the first of obligations.*

So what was he to do about Margaret?

Deep down, he knew none of the hurt mattered. Not really. Because whatever she had done, and whomever she had done it with, none of that changed who and what she was. Indeed, regardless of how hard he tried to cruelly expel her from his mind, just like she had banished him from her cares, he could not remove her from his heart. There was no use in wishing he could change any of it. *What is done is done, and cannot be undone*, and yet, life appeared, to him, *too short to be spent in nursing animosity or registering wrongs. We are, and must be, one and all, burdened by faults in this world; but the time will soon come when, I trust,* dear reader, *that we shall put them off in putting off our corruptible bodies...I hold another creed, which no one ever taught me, and which I seldom mention, but in which I delight, and to which I cling; for it extends hope to all; it makes Eternity a rest—a mighty home, not a terror and an abyss. Besides, with this creed, I can so clearly distinguish between the criminal and his crime; I can so sincerely forgive the first while I abhor the last: with this creed revenge never worries my heart.*

Love was anarchy, love was brutal, love was unfair, love was intangible, love was undisciplined, love was glorious. Love...love was Margaret!

Walking towards the window, his eyes broadening as they darkened with the brooding hue of epiphany, he muttered in self-reproach, 'I really should not be telling you all these things.'

'No, John! You most certainly should not!' his mother agreed, shocked by her son's unexpected outburst of emotion, his words fated to become the tittle-tattle of Milton by the evening, and then what would become of him? John was without a doubt the most respected man in the town, a position of authority that he had spent many years cultivating: his blood, sweat and tears poured into forging his reputation as a person of sound acumen. Oh, but now his once sturdy status of repute would be brought into disrepute after tossing about a few careless words of ill-placed loyalty, his lauded standing in this town doomed to come crashing down in a matter of mere minutes, and all due to that girl who did not deserve his devotion.

Mr Thornton shook his head, his attention fixed on the window, indifferent to their opinions. His mind, besieged by thoughts of her, paid little heed to external judgement. Had he been more attuned to his surroundings, Mr Thornton might have discerned the subtle shift in the sturdy mill gates—once firmly closed, now stood subtly ajar.

'No…I should be telling *her*,' he meditated, a pithy laugh escaping his mouth. 'I need to tell Miss Hale that I think…that I feel…that she is—'

'That I am what?' came a quiet voice from across the way.

Chapter Fifteen

Sisterhood

In the subtle stillness, Margaret allowed the enormity of this realisation to settle over her. His absence resonated in the cavity of her loneliness, there was no denying it, this poignant pulse of longing that gripped her. Her heart insisted on seeing him again, a need that surpassed solely want and claiming necessity.

Amidst the imperceptible turbulence of feelings, Margaret's gaze fell upon a table adorned with an array of books—his books. A sudden rush of fascination compelled her to her feet, and with hands that trembled in anticipation, she reached for them, her fingers caressing the spines with an almost religious reverence, each tome telling a story of their shared love of literature. The sensible titles and sober covers imitated the taste and personality of the man she missed so dearly. Gathering the volumes in her arms, she held them close to her bosom, as if finding solace in the tangible remnants of his world.

As Margaret cradled the books like precious babes, a wealth of memories rushed back to her. Each book seemed to carry a piece of him, a fragment of the conversations they had shared, the debates they had relished, the laughter they had enjoyed, and the intimate moments they had experienced together. The scent of the well-thumbed pages enveloped her, a familiar and comforting aroma that transported her back to the countless hours spent in his company. Tears welled up in Margaret's eyes as she realised how much she had taken those meaningful encounters, those exchanges, for granted.

Alone, surrounded by the physical relics of their association, Margaret made a decision. She resolved to find him and mend the bridges between them so that they might have a chance, as small as it was, to reach each other again. The books became a symbol of their unfinished story, and she felt an obligation to return them to their rightful owner, hoping that in doing so, she could rewrite their narrative, thus repairing the torn pages in their relationship and restoring it to a semblance of...*of what?*

However, it was as this idea took seed in her heart that Margaret's resolution was delayed by an unexpected knock that reverberated from the front door, momentarily disrupting her intentions. Pausing for just a trice, she had no interest in answering it, wishing instead to be left to her plan, but then a thought occurred to her, and she wondered if, just possibly, it might be...

Her heart quickened as she hurried to answer it, and as Margaret flung open the door, a flood of first disappointment, shortly followed by relief, washed over her. Standing before her, on her Crampton doorstep, were two familiar faces, her dearest friends in all the world: Elizabeth Darcy, and Jane Rochester.

Their unexpected appearance was a radiant burst of warmth, like sunlight breaking through heavy clouds, instantly transforming the mood that had previously stifled the atmosphere. Elizabeth, exuding spirited vitality, and Jane, a paragon of gentle sincerity, rushed forward and held their friend close. Together, in a cluster of embraces, they migrated to the inviting parlour, creating an oasis of sisterhood amid Margaret's emotional tumult. What was initially an unwelcome interruption had now become a serendipitous intervention, bringing with it the empathy only true kindred spirits could provide. As cheerful chatter filled the room, Margaret felt a weight lifting from her shoulders. The companionship of Elizabeth and Jane became a consolation for her soul, and at that moment, the urgency of her earlier mission gave way to the comprehension that, perhaps, the journey ahead could be better navigated with the strength and support of wonderfully faithful and cherished friends. 'Why are you here?' Margaret inquired, her voice revealing a blend of surprise and intrigue.

'To buy and make cotton, naturally,' said Elizabeth with a droll laugh. 'Why do you think? We have come to see you, just as we promised,' she jollied.

'We missed you,' Jane affixed, depositing a tender kiss on Margaret's cheek.

However, Elizabeth's expression turned earnest.

'And, truth be told, we were worried about you,' she confessed, a look of compassionate unease etched on her face.

'Worried?' Margaret repeated, a faint blush betraying her conscience.

'Yes,' confirmed Jane with a trace of quiet sympathy. 'You have endured so much, Margaret. From your wrenching departure from Helstone, to your dear mother's passing, and not to forget that distressing affair with your brother and the magistrate.'

Margaret's cheeks coloured with the indignity of her past troubles.

Seating herself, Elizabeth gently guided Margaret to join her, while Jane settled down on the opposite side.

'Will you not confide in us?' Jane urged, her words an invitation for Margaret to unburden herself and disclose the veracity of her ordeals, her experience of coping with and overcoming the intricacies of life in Milton.

She hesitated, for beneath the surface of this reunion, a reluctant anxiety loitered. Margaret, with blue eyes that reflected the hues of a tempest-tossed sea, faced the inquiry of caring friends.

'Which of all my important nothings shall I tell you first?' she asked with subdued jest.

'Margaret?' Elizabeth encouraged, lightly rubbing her arm. 'Whatever is the matter? You look terribly sad.'

'Oh, *it is the town life,'* she insisted, trusting that they would understand, for they too were native creatures of the country and not the city.

'Life here is so vastly different. The people here are different, and I find myself quite lacking their resilience, it seems. *Their nerves are quickened by the haste and bustle and speed of everything around them, to say nothing of the confinement in these pent-up houses, which of itself is enough to induce depression and worry of spirits.'*

'And what depresses and worries *your* spirit?' Jane pressed with cautious, unassuming interest.

'I...,' Margaret faltered, this alone being enough to arouse concern, for she was usually the first to know her mind and to speak it, since this, their collective capacity to be self-governing, intrepid and forthright, had been the initial appeal, drawing these three women of immense strength of character to one another.

'I hardly know myself,' she said at last, unable to effectively express her unrest. 'I feel so helpless, so useless, so unlike myself.'

'Do not speak so,' Jane implored, distressed to hear her friend depreciate herself. 'Margaret, life is hard for us women. We have so much to give but are often unable to give it, our rights denied, our opportunities limited. We battle hardships in silence, expected to weather them without complaint, only compliance, and you have been through your own share of incalculable tribulations this year and endured them with commendable courage and integrity. You are the most heroic person we know. You are fiercely kind, brave, loyal, honest, and more. And it pains us to see you doubt it, so please, tell us what distresses you.'

'Does it have anything to do with those books you are holding as if your life depended on them?' Elizabeth asked keenly, her gaze lingering on the compilation in Margaret's protective hands, thinking how Darcy would approve of this fine collection.

'Oh, these?' she coughed awkwardly, like a schoolgirl being caught with something she ought not to have, causing her to nearly drop them onto her lap as if she were fumbling with pilfered treasures.

'They belong to... *him*.'

Her friends raised their eyebrows in quizzical bafflement. '*Him*?'

Margaret took a deep breath. 'Mr Thornton.'

The two women exchanged glances, their mouths mutely opening into an arched, "*ah*," for a mutual understanding now passed between them.

'The same Mr Thornton you have written to us about so often?' Jane asked knowingly.

'It has not been that often!' Margaret objected, a mite defensively.

'Often enough,' countered Elizabeth with a playful smirk.

'Indeed!' Jane agreed. 'He features in your every letter. You tell us, most ardently, how frustrating you find him. How thoughtful, pig-headed, conscientious, infuriating and fine-looking he is!'

'My-my! Could it be that our Margaret is finally in love?' Elizabeth teased, shoogling her by the shoulders.

Margaret let out an indignant huff. 'No, I—'

Mid-sentence, insight struck her. Her lips parted, quivering like leaves in the unsettling winds of change.

'Oh! That is it,' she exclaimed softly. *'I am in love!'*

She could not fix on the hour, or the spot, or the look or the words, which laid the foundation. It had been *too long ago.* She had been *in the middle before* she *knew that* she *had begun,* but somewhere, in the midst of it all, all her pride and her prejudice, he had captured her heart, and now, he held it captive, refusing to let it go, for it was his, he had won it, he had earned it, and so, he would rightly keep it for himself.

Margaret stood rooted to the spot for what felt like an age, an analogy that would prove to be most fitting, as it happens, for she felt as if she had somehow aged in those few minutes, her heart maturing from that of a girl into a woman, as it came to behold itself for the first time, the looking glass of awareness being held up, reflecting its truest desire for her to see in all its exposed honesty. In this image, she saw not merely herself, for she was no longer herself without another, and there he was, by her side, the other half of her complete self, and it made her tremble to see him with such clarity.

The truth was, that ever since Margaret had learned she was to come to Milton as a dutiful daughter who wanted nothing more than to chain herself to the railings of her Helstone home and refuse to forsake it, a shadow had appeared alongside hers in the mirror, an apparition, a prophecy. She had not known who he was or what he was to her, only that he was stubborn in his perseverance, telling her, whether she wished to hear it or not, that, in Milton, in that strange new world so far removed from her own experiences and expectations, she would meet her match, she would meet her man.

Struggling to suppress the lump of emotion rising in her throat, Margaret offered a solemn nod to her silent audience. It was undoubtedly him, a truth she had quietly acknowledged deep down all along. No man had ever affected her in the way he did, infecting her with his every word, his every deed, his every touch, and so it should not be surprising to discover that she was, despite her best efforts, irresistibly in love with John Thornton. Nevertheless, this would not do, it was not to be, so she deemed that it was more imperative than ever to distract herself from this most tremendously humbling realisation.

'*Margaret*?' echoed a distant call, jolting her back to the present. '*Margaret*?' floated Elizabeth's voice from the realm of reality.

'So, what is he like?' Jane asked eagerly.

'What is he like?' Margaret repeated, her lips dry.

How could she even begin to answer such a question? The thought of him brought such pain and pleasure as she had never known, her heart being wrenched between these two extremes with exhausting force. How was it that in her cataclysm, there he was, a pillar of stability? He was a lighthouse that shone a steady light upon her, constantly showing her time and time again who she was, steering her from the volatile seas of her misdoubt, guiding her home again. And yet, despite his unmatched decency, she had returned his goodness with nothing short of grievous ingratitude. She had been so unforgivably stupid. How could it be that she had not seen it? She had been so preoccupied with railing against him for all he stood for, that

Margaret had not fully understood what it was she was wrestling with. But she could see it now, as bright and beautiful as the sky on a clear spring morning. Margaret did not care that Mr Thornton was a tradesman, for what crime was that? She did not mind that he was rich while others were poor, that he was a master while others were oppressed, because he was not the enemy. No. He was all honour and justice. He was what was right in a world that was so very wrong. No, what she had been fighting, all this time, was her feelings for him.

She *had not intended to love him; the reader knows* she *had wrought hard to extirpate from* her *soul the germs of love there detected; and now, at the first renewed view of him, they spontaneously revived, great and strong!*

Margaret had said no for this precise reason, which was that she was afraid of caring for him too much. If only he knew that her denial was not borne of him, but of her, because by giving herself over to Mr Thornton, Margaret would be laying herself bare to her greatest fear, and that was being overtaken by a man.

But, oh! What a man he was. There was none like him. There never had been before, and there never would be again, she was sure of it.

It had been many months now since Margaret had understood that Mr Thornton had never, and would never, treat her with anything short of respect. It was true that they had argued over many topics, debate being the undertone of their exchanges, but never once had he made her feel that her opinions were any less valid than his own. At first, she had thought otherwise.

She had witnessed a passing flash of light in his eyes, and Margaret had mistaken this mirth for mockery of her observations that clashed so vehemently with his own. He no doubt thought her youthful, ignorant and inexperienced in the ways of the world, of his world, and so he was laughing at her for being nothing more than a silly girl who was barely a woman. Then, after a while, she realised that she had misinterpreted that glimmer that entertained his blue eyes. It was not scorn she saw there, but animation. It was amusement tickled by stimulation. Mr Thornton enjoyed their discussions, they roused him, they rallied him, and most of all, they dared to challenge him, something he had never before experienced, and something which he had found refreshing, and, in time, vital to his pleasure.

To Mr Thornton, Margaret's interrogation of his values did not seek to break down his integrity, but rather, to build it up, to secure it. She fortified him, inspiring him to be the very best version of himself, not merely to please her, but to satisfy himself and appease the standards he set for his own character. While some men would have discredited her for taking a stance and holding firm to what she knew to be right, he quietly encouraged her with his approving silence. While some men would have belittled her for being a woman who freely spoke her mind, he had never given her cause to think her sex was a hindrance to her capacity for intelligence, but rather, an advantage that gave her greater scope than his hardened experiences ever could. He was not intimidated by her, how could he be, when he was so impressive in comparison.

She began now to comprehend that he was exactly the man who, in disposition and talents, would most suit her. His understanding and temper, though unlike her own, would have answered all her wishes. It was a union that must have been to the advantage of both: by her ease and liveliness, his mind might have been softened, his manners improved; and from his judgement, information, and knowledge of the world, she must have received benefit of greater importance.

In short, he had been willing to love her for who and what she was, with no corrections to be made, and now, she saw, quite self-evidently, that there was nothing she wanted to change about him.

Looking up, Margaret could only breathe three uncomplicated words as an answer, three words that encompassed all she felt with perfect and profound simplicity:

'He is…*everything*.'

'So, what are you planning to do with those?' Jane asked, nodding toward the books.

Margaret held them tighter still, her expression disclosing a mixture of longing and hesitation.

'Why not take them to him?' Elizabeth suggested.

'I cannot go there,' Margaret confessed, her gaze briefly flickering with apprehension. What her friends did not understand was that, in her hands, she held chapters of her story left unfinished, passages unread, words unsaid, and echoes of a past that thrilled and terrified her alike, the final pages yet to be written. Still, while she longed for a happy ending, she feared she no longer held the power, she no longer held the pen.

Jane furrowed her brow in confusion. 'Why not?'

'Because *they* are there,' Margaret responded cryptically.

A perplexed look was traded between the two women, their shared incomprehension apparent in the meeting of their gazes.

'And who are *'they'*?'

It is now time that we (re)meet those referred to thus far in Margaret's story, in her account of this day, in her version of events, as *them*, *those* and *they*.

Miss Latimer. Miss Bingley. Miss Ingram.

On that particular afternoon, the assembly of these three women had left an indelible impression as they convened in the church, decorated in resplendent attire produced from exquisite fabrics and fashioned with eye-catching designs. Their features radiated with the brilliance of exquisite jewels, capturing the soft gleam of the winter sun. Nonetheless, amidst the opulence, each visage seemed conspicuously ostentatious in Margaret's modest estimation. The embellishments appeared gaudy and needlessly ornate, particularly when juxtaposed with the unassuming sanctity of the church. Nevertheless, it was hard to fault these women for their striking appearance, for when a woman demonstrates such undeniable elegance, critiquing her becomes a challenging task, and this difficulty only increases when there are three of them to contend with. There was no denying they were the definition of the Pink of the Ton, the Beau Monde, embodied.

It was in thinking this that a dim shadow of resentment cast itself upon Margaret's countenance, and an unkind notion took root. The unvarnished truth was that she harboured a strong dislike for them—Miss Latimer, Miss Bingley, and Miss Ingram. Despite frowning at her uncharacteristic deficiency of charity, Margaret could not escape the fact that her feelings towards these women were far from amiable. She found them too smoky by half. Margaret had attempted to be fair and appreciate the positive qualities in each of them, but no amount of tolerance had managed to convince her of their conviviality.

She struggled to put her finger on the exact cause of her dislike of them, or perhaps it would be more accurate to describe it as a vague distrust. To say that Margaret had spent any significant amount of time in their company would be inaccurate; their acquaintance amounted to no more than a trickle of fleeting happenstances. However, each time they had met,

Margaret had been left feeling distinctly uncomfortable. She had first encountered them at a dinner hosted by the Hampers, and in the middle of their grinning and giggling behind decorative fans, they unveiled themselves as frivolous, coquettish, and mean-spirited. Never did a kind word escape their lips about anyone; and beneath the veneer of pretty smiles, their inherent pettiness was unmistakable, their insincerity and insensitivity, incontestable. The soothing balm of genuine womanly affection was notably absent from their sentiments, and all around them there clung an aura of vindictiveness. They embodied an infantile mentality that derived satisfaction from demeaning other women for their puerile amusement. To be sure, each time they had crossed paths, Margaret had felt an icy chill encircle them, the enmity of their hearts leaching from them like a bitter winter frost that formed a nimbus of barrenness. Therefore, trusting her astute sense of intuition, Margaret had been sure to consciously distance herself from the trio, forsaking any potential friendship with them without a niggle of regret. That is perhaps why she had not been asked to spend the afternoon with them today.

Retreating to the safety of her bedroom, Margaret had spent the afternoon in a desperate attempt to engage herself and banish thoughts of anything, or anyone, beyond the four walls of her sanctuary.

If only she had not unintentionally overheard their conversation.

With a self-conscious snivel, Margaret vividly recalled the incident. When she had exited the church, she found herself ensnared in the narrow entryway along with the rest of the congregation. Amid the polite yet insistent jostling to escape the confines of the tightly packed flock—a throng of starched skirts with circumferences rivalling the equator and top hats towering to brush the moon—Margaret had been unable to help but overhear Miss Thornton asking the three young ladies to tea that afternoon, their enthusiastic acceptance heckling in her ears.

Margaret had observed the way Miss Thornton deliberately neglected to extend an invitation to her, the elevated pitch of her voice hinting at a calculated effort to leave Margaret keenly aware of her humiliating exclusion. It was a camouflet intentionnel. Standing right beside them, her left elbow nearly touching her would-be-sister-in-law had she accepted Mr Thornton's proposal all those months ago, Margaret felt the sting of rejection—ignored and dismissed not only by Miss Thornton, but also by her mother and brother.

A subtle sniff betrayed Margaret's comprehension of what had been bothering her, and she begrudgingly admitted to herself that the source of her discomfort was envy. *Margaret was not a ready lover, but where she loved she loved passionately, and with no small degree of jealousy.* She had tried to ignore it all day, but the truth was that she could not bear the thought of him being delighted by another woman's company, even if she had no right to be protective of his favour in the least. The problem was that while such a thing as a man and a woman conversing graciously may be innocent in itself, in this case, it could well lead to the unavoidable conclusion, which would be that woman becoming the recipient of his ardent love.

At this juncture, Margaret found herself contemplating whether these women possessed the capacity for genuine romantic sentiment and steady loyalty, wondering if they could truly bare their souls before him and request acceptance with the same unreserved love that she believed he was endowed with. Withholding a twinge of scepticism, Margaret concluded that their interest probably lay more in his social standing and the depth of his purse than in the unparalleled integrity of his character. He was certainly known for being plump in the pockets, as Mr Thornton had notably established Marlborough Mills as the most successful and lucrative mill in the county. His good looks, she surmised, were merely a fortunate asset that rendered their pursuit of him all the more enticing, as if he were a coveted trophy to be acquired and not a treasure to be cherished. People married for less, and was it not supposedly a woman's vocation in life to find and secure herself an appropriate husband? Much to her regret, Margaret knew it to be all too true, and after all, a man in possession of a good fortune must apparently be in want of a wife, so could it be that he would, *could*, fall in love with one of them?

Yes, Margaret supposed he could.

He had proposed to her, after all, and it was regardless of whether his proposition had originated from the seeds of affection or duty, because the fact remained that Mr Thornton had been considering taking a wife. Therefore, if Margaret were not to occupy that coveted vacancy, then there was no reason to think he would not offer it to another.

The image of them all seated there, engaging in playful banter, showering him with adoration, and inexorably succumbing to his charm—perhaps already enamoured—filled Margaret with a poignant sadness that threatened to overwhelm her. It was, of course, understandable that both unmarried and, conceivably, even some married ladies in the town were drawn to him. Even if Mr Thornton were not the sole eligible bachelor in Milton, he incontestably stood out as the most desirable one on the market. Here Margaret winced at her own inadvertently transactional phrasing, questioning if she had unwittingly adopted a mindset rooted in buying and selling. She was turning into a Milton woman, after all. At any rate, unlike the other unattached men hereabouts, who were coarse in appearance and uncouth in their appetites, Mr Thornton possessed a rare combination of handsomeness, intelligence, intrigue, and, above all, decency—a quality that set him apart as a truly exceptional human being.

So yes, Margaret could well believe what Mrs Thornton had told her time and time again, and that was that her son was a catch, meaning that every woman for miles without a ring on her finger sought to dangle herself before him like bait on a hook. However, while his good looks, manners and wealth may have attracted them, to begin with, Margaret knew all too well that a woman could fall genuinely, and entirely, in love with him. After all, if he could succeed in winning her heart, a prize which was once thought impregnable, then surely a less guarded woman could easily, and gladly, give herself over to him. Hence, was it as she feared, that the women who took tea with him today were all applicants for the coveted role of Mrs John Thornton?

It felt like an inevitability, leaving her wondering when, not if, she would hear of his engagement to another. It had only dawned on her this very day how the eventuality of this prospect taunted her. She had tried not to think about it, but now that she had, she sensed that it was perpetually on her mind. She wondered how it would be delivered, and by whom. It occurred to Margaret that Mr Bell would likely be the bearer of this grievous news. He would come to the house, and with his usual air of casual mischief, he would announce to the Hales that Mr Thornton, the man everyone had long thought married to his mill, was at last to take a wife. Margaret would stop, her heart responding to this bitter blow. At first, it would feel like it had jolted and halted, suspended in motion as it reeled from the shock. Then it would feel like a stab, as if a spear with a serrated end designed to amputate all one's happiness was plunged into her and pierced the clandestine hope she sheltered there. And then, finally, she would bleed to death, slowly, surely and secretly, never able to say a word as she grieved for what might have been.

To know that he would have that life with another.

But the question was: which one would it be?

Miss Latimer? Miss Bingley? Miss Ingram?

Lady one, lady two, or lady three?

However, she also knew that as far as his mother and sister were concerned, they believed that Mr Thornton would be far more likely to take a wife if another candidate were removed from the list.

It was after these fragile and fertile thoughts had traversed her harried heart, that Margaret professed the intricate events of the past year to her attentive friends, detailing the upheaval that began with her relocation to Milton and continued with the unexpected entrance of Mr Thornton into her life. Elizabeth and Jane listened with unwavering patience, their discreet expressions of shock and sadness their only response throughout. Margaret had clearly been obliged to keep a great deal to herself for far too long, so they would not interrupt now that she was at last able to divest herself of her distress. After commiserating with Margaret over the strains of the past twelve months, and feeling heartily sorry that they had not been able to offer more assistance until today, her friends quickly turned to advising her on the here and now.

'I would not believe a word Miss Ingram says. Do not let her intimidate you or diminish your self-confidence. That seems to be her particular talent and one she relishes,' Jane advised sympathetically, remembering, all too vividly, the cold, cutting way in which Miss

Ingram had belittled her when she was a governess at Thornfield Hall.

'But while she might make you feel like nothing and nobody, she herself is without substance. She is shallow and she is hollow. You are worth ten of her, a hundred, a thousand. She despises you because while she is a mere copy, you are an original. Her mundaneness is threatened by your uniqueness.'

'Quite! Well said,' Elizabeth concurred adamantly. 'Nor should you pay any heed to Miss Bingley,' she warned, sharpening her eyes shrewdly.

'Nothing brings her more pleasure than undermining others and fostering a sense of inferiority. It stems from her discontent. I genuinely feel sorry for her,' she said honestly. 'They are nothing but coffee-sisters and cheek-achers.'

'Oh, I am not so sure,' Margaret gently protested. 'Is that not unkind? *It is right to hope for the best about everybody, and not to expect the worst. This sounds like a truism, but it has comforted me before now, and some day you'll find it useful. One has always to try to think more of others than of oneself, and it is best not to prejudge people on the bad side.*'

Her friends laughed affectionately.

'You are too good, sweet one. They do not deserve your forgiveness. But what of this Miss Latimer?' the two women delved, unacquainted with this third entity. Margaret shook her head. 'I do not know,' she acknowledged.

If Margaret were to bet, not that she would, since she believed speculation to be the game of fools, then she would say Miss Latimer would be the most likely person to capture Mr Thornton's affections. She was beautiful, but then again, they all were. She was refined, but then again, they all were. She was wealthy, but then again, they all were. Nevertheless, there was one thing Miss Latimer could boast that none of the rest could, and that was that she was a Milton woman born and bred. In other words, she had been brought up to be the perfect mill master's wife.

I—I mean, Margaret,—saw he was going to marry her, for family, perhaps political reasons, because her rank and connections suited him; Margaret felt he had not given her his love, and that her qualifications were ill-adapted to win from him that treasure. This was the point—this was where the nerve was touched and teased—this was where the fever was sustained and fed: she could not charm him.

If she had managed the victory at once, and he had yielded and sincerely laid his heart at her feet, Margaret should have covered her face, turned to the wall, and (figuratively) have died to them. If Miss Latimer had been a good and noble woman, endowed with force, fervour, kindness, sense, Margaret should have had one vital struggle with two tigers—jealousy and despair: then, her heart torn out and devoured, Margaret should have admired her—acknowledged her excellence, and been quiet for the rest of her days: and the more absolute her superiority, the deeper would have been her admiration—the more truly tranquil her quiescence. But as matters really stood, to watch Miss Latimer's efforts at fascinating Mr Thornton, to witness their repeated failure—herself unconscious that they did fail; vainly fancying that each shaft launched hit the mark, and infatuatedly pluming herself on success, when her pride and self-complacency repelled further and further what she wished to allure—to witness this, was to be at once under ceaseless excitation and ruthless restraint.

Because, when she failed, Margaret saw how she might have succeeded. Arrows that continually glanced off from Mr Thornton's breast and fell harmless at his feet, might, she knew, if shot by a surer hand, have quivered keen in his proud heart—have called love into his stern eye, and softness into his sardonic face; or, better still, without weapons a silent conquest might have been won.

As she thought this, Margaret shuddered.

She knew that she could make him happy, if only he would let her.

Oh, how she longed to. She would love him unconditionally. She would aid him loyally. She would care for him tenderly. She would devote her whole self to him, but she knew that would never be enough. She could never bring herself to agree with him on everything, and if she felt it necessary, she would contest his opinions and actions. Still, there was an infinity between them that neither could renounce.

He is not to them what he is to me, she thought: he is not of their kind. I believe he is of mine; she thought further,—she was sure he was,—she felt akin to him,— I understand the language of his countenance and movements: though rank and wealth sever us widely, she had something in her brain and heart, in her blood and nerves, that assimilated her mentally to him. 'But,' said Margaret quietly, 'what can I possibly offer him? All I desire is for him to find joy, and all I have brought him is pain. Perhaps I do not deserve him. Perhaps the vision of our entwined happiness is no more than a dream.'

'Perfect happiness is elusive,' Jane told Margaret, reflecting on the trials she and Rochester had survived. 'Love and marriage are about finding someone whom you are willing to live and die for, and, in turn, who is willing to weather the storm that is life with you. Women are not blessed,' said Jane, 'and I long for a world where women are afforded the same rights and opportunities as men. But as it is, we are seen as lesser. We are viewed as companions, as property, but if you find someone who truly cares for you, who truly appreciates you, then he will see you as more than a woman; he will see you as an equal.'

'You see, Margaret,' Elizabeth explained, 'marriage need not be a surrender of one's freedom. It can be a partnership, a union of minds and hearts where both individuals uphold and uplift each other. It is about finding someone who values your independence as much as you do. It is a coalition that does not dissent against your differences but is a celebration of your distinct strengths that make you stronger as one. The right marriage is not a constraint on freedom but a harmonious blend of two souls, each contributing to the other's growth and fulfilment.'

Jane sensed Margaret's lingering self-doubt.

'Margaret, Miss Latimer, and these others may be an enigma for now, but time has a way of revealing the true nature of people. Trust your instincts and, in the meantime, focus on those who genuinely care about you. These are the ones who should influence you, to help you re-discover who you are, not those who seek to dampen your light.'

Elizabeth nodded in stalwart agreement.

'And do not let the opinions of those who seek to undermine you define your worth. You have faced challenges with strength and grace, and that is an unshakable testimony to the integrity and indestructibility of your spirit.'

Margaret, surrounded by the warmth of her friends' understanding, felt a renewed sense of fortitude. Indebted to their counsel, the shadows of imprecision seemed less daunting, and the path ahead, though unclear, appeared negotiable with the steadfast espousal of true sisterhood.

'I do not know what he wants. I do not know if he still cares for me as I now know I care for him,' Margaret confessed, her voice tinged with uncertainty.

'Then you must find out, once and for all,' Elizabeth declared with conviction. 'After all, he asked you to marry him, and if his feelings are fickle and fleeting, then he does not deserve you.'

'Indeed, Margaret, relationships of all natures should be built on a foundation of mutual understanding and unswerving commitment,' Jane surmised. 'If he asked you to be his wife, it is only fair for you to seek clarity on where his heart truly lies.'

'But I have done him so many wrongs,' she admitted.

'Margaret,' her friends soothed. 'You are not the first woman to underestimate a man and fail to see his value, and you will not be the last, trust us,' they said, knowing all too well their own experiences of initially misjudging the men who would ultimately become their beloved husbands.

Margaret absorbed their words, feeling a surge of determination forming. Brushing her brown curls away from her neck, Margaret appeared contemplative.

'I dare say there's many a woman makes as sad a mistake as I have done, and only finds it out too late.'

With her friends by her side, she realised the importance of confronting the doubts that had lingered in her heart. The path to love, she understood, required both vulnerability and courage, and she was ready to discover the truth that lay ahead. Besides, there was one stubborn fact that persisted.

'I suppose that I could not unlove him now, merely because I found that he had ceased to notice me,' she whispered sadly.

And yet, it was foolish to think that he could love her now after all they had put each other through. *She knew she must conceal her sentiments: she must smother hope; she must remember that he could not care much for her. For when she said that she was of his kind, she did not mean that she had his force to influence, and his spell to attract: she meant only that she had certain tastes and feelings in common with him. She must, then, repeat continually that they are forever sundered:—and yet, while she breathed and thought, she knew that she would love him, she must love him.*

Oh! How different men were from women! While a man can forget love in an instant and cast it aside as if it were a trifling nothing to be discarded for its inconvenience or its indecorous connotations, not to overlook the way it inflicts lamentations on the mind, a woman does not neglect these truths so easily, the mark of love forever engraved on her heart, a muscle which is significantly softer and more sensitive in a female than a male: its matter not brittle, but profoundly brave. While women could arguably be the more sympathetic sex, she could not allow that they were in any way less substantial. While men may be retiring when it came to the fidelity of affection, women were not so faint-hearted, but rather, they were fierce in their faithfulness, and so, Margaret would prove her constancy.

But he could not love anyone else! He had said he loved her. He had told her that he would love her with an unyielding devotion, even against her will if he must.

'One word more. You look as if you thought it tainted you to be loved by me. You cannot avoid it. Nay, I, if I would, cannot cleanse you from it. But I would not, if I could. I have never loved any woman before: my life has been too busy, my thoughts too much absorbed with other things. Now I love, and will love. But do not be afraid of too much expression on my part.'

She would not shake off her faith in him. She would give him a chance to return her love.

Therefore, Margaret resolved to go to Marlborough Mills at once and to confront him and to confront her feelings for him once and for all, provoking both man and matter to come to a head. But oh, she was afraid! What would he say? What would he do? Would he welcome her into his home, into his arms? Or, would he sneer and jeer and send her away like an unwanted memory of things that had passed and could never be?

There was only one way to find out.

With a mind that was fast devising a plan, Margaret scurried up to her bedroom and with stealthy resolve, she dragged open the drawer of her dressing table and liberating what was inside, she tucked it in her dress pocket and returned to the parlour to collect the stack of books and bid farewell to her friends.

'And, Margaret,' they called after her as she made to leave, 'you should not let these women tear you down.'

Raising her chin in all its innate dignity, Margaret's eyes twinkled, her usual self-assurance returned and restored.

'Oh, I do not intend to. For what they do not know, is that *there is a stubbornness about me that never can bear to be frightened at the will of others. My courage always rises at every attempt to intimidate me.*'

'After all,' she said, turning to smile at her friends as she closed the door behind her, her chin thrust up in defiance, 'if Mr Thornton is to marry anyone, it should be me.'

Chapter Sixteen

The Author Of This Story

Now, what one needs to understand is that when Margaret walked, her steps tended to be brisk and her stride purposeful as she marched ahead resolutely towards her destination. She did not lollygag. She was not one for dawdling, dilly-dallying or delaying, not to forget any other related verb that begins with the letter d. However, today, as she wound her way through the bustling streets of Milton, there was something decidedly lagging about her walk. Her legs felt as if they were made of a less substantial framework than bone and muscle as they wibbled and wobbled like the proverbial jelly on its plate. The harassed influx of nerves proved highly vexing for Margaret, as she was not accustomed to being of a nervy disposition. With an irked scoff, she chided herself for her aberrant silliness. Why, she had been brimming with the confidence of conviction mere minutes before when she had left the house, so it made no sense that she should find herself all at sea now that she had set sail.

Nevertheless, as Margaret made her way across the town towards Marlborough Mills, her mind pursued a trail of insurgence. It quarrelled with its own reasoning as it convinced her that, on the one hand, she had no reason to be nervous, that she had every right to go to him, and yet, on the other, it whispered that she was being foolish and that this was nothing but a mission of folly.

Coming to a curt standstill, Margaret halted in her tracks and took a moment to pause and think, unaware that her sudden movements were drawing attention and soliciting comment. As she pondered on how best to proceed, or indeed, retreat, Margaret was completely oblivious to the horde of confused pedestrians who passed her by with a critical glance, a tut and a mumbling of something incoherent but unmistakably discourteous under their breaths as they eyed the odd girl from the south with tangible irritation. In normal circumstances, Margaret would have realised her blunder, most likely blushed, and then appropriately glided out of the way with her usual elegance, but not today. The truth was that Margaret felt quite hampered by indecision, unsure of what to do. She was no longer entirely sure she could go through with it. Go to him, that is. For a start, how would he receive her? Coldly? Graciously? Awkwardly? Forgivingly? Angrily?

Margaret could scarcely fathom that her excuse for visiting the Thorntons would withstand scrutiny, especially before a man of his discerning intelligence.

She envisioned the penetrating gaze he frequently cast upon her, attempting to decipher the complex intricacies of her way of thinking. There would be a painful sort of tortured turmoil blistering there, there always was these days, ever since he had caught her in the arms of another man. She knew he did not understand her, and it was that which troubled him. He had thought that he had known her, known her in a way that a man intrinsically knows the woman he loves, but as it turned out, he had been wrong, and now he worried that she was not what he had wanted her to be, but a fraud, a deceitful phantom conjured by his lonely heart.

But that is not the only thing she saw in his eyes, no.

There was hope.

Every time she had caught him stealthily glancing her way over the past months, in those evanescent seconds of connection, she had seen it there, weak and tired as it was, but still very much alive. It was a zealous prayer that she would come to him and tell him all, alleviating his suspicions and once again reassuring him that she was, if not his own, then at least worthy of his love. It was this hope that she had to cling to, so protect it, preserve it, she most faithfully would. Therefore, with a fortifying upward tilt of her chin, Margaret picked herself up, dusted herself off, and continued on her way—Oh, wait! Was that Miss Latimer she saw in the distance? Margaret strained to see, since the figure was rather far off and walking in the opposite direction. Yes? No? Possibly? Probably not. She was supposed to be with *him*, after all.

It was an unusually quiet Sunday, and so the streets lay hushed, with many of the town's merchants indulging in their well-deserved day of rest. This tranquillity provided an effortless path for her to steer her course through the miles, her pace accelerating with each ripple of uncertainty that swept over her.

When she eventually found herself on Marlborough Street, with its grand buildings and fashionable people, Margaret passed a draper's and glanced in the window at the new designs, though they were too fussy for her taste, putting her in mind of Miss Thornton. But as she did so, she quivered to feel his tender regard once again warm the back of her neck and she nearly whimpered aloud. He was not really there, she told herself, but her proximity to him was surely playing tricks on her. With a burning flush prickling her skin and tingling the yarn of her nerves with a feathery tickle, Margaret could feel his eyes on her right there and then, sharp and soft all at once as they watched her with unfaltering intrigue. He thought she did not know he observed her thus, but she did. She had felt it even that very morning in church, his gaze swooping from floor to ceiling in restless agitation, until, at last, his eyes found their rest with her, and there they remained throughout the sermon, caressing her as they stayed fixed upon that spot where her neck dipped and her spine met her head.

Margaret knew that she ought to have been offended, she should have felt pestered by his unyielding attention, but strangely enough, she found that it brought her comfort, the tense pressure in her shoulders shrinking under the intensity of his awareness. Furthermore, Margaret knew that while some men would stare out of an acquisitive avariciousness, he did it because he could not help himself, for you see, even she could tell that if he were not looking at her, he could not settle, she being the only cure that could calm the storm that sparred within him. She could not claim to know the source of her power, nor how she wielded it with so little effort, since she had never tried to capture the mill master's curiosity or ensnare his care, her maidenly ways untrained in the brutal art of warfare that was love. All Margaret knew was that when she was near, Mr Thornton was both awakened and allayed, composed and agitated, whole and yet halved, the missing pieces that filled the jagged cracks of his being spun into the yarn of her very person, their two souls twins that were incomplete and inconsolable without the other. Yet, for all she had not courted his attention or affection, Margaret could not bring herself to relinquish it now, no, she could not wish it away, so here they were, disjointed yet allied, their bond severed by the lies that had driven them apart, a frayed link tethering them together still, ready to break at any moment if they were not careful, and careful, they had not been.

However, while Margaret may have wished to think about nothing but his gaze, she shuddered to recall that his eyes had not been the only ones to find such fascination with her today. Indeed, Margaret had been embarrassed to sense three pairs of eyes ogling her, each one narrowed as they scorched with the raging flames of envy. They belonged to three women whom Margaret hardly knew and did not care to know, for not only did she find them barely tolerable, but despite her pretence at indifference, she feared that at least one of them would come between her and her heart's most cherished desire. Margaret did not know why she both intrigued and infuriated them so, and she had no wish to be enlightened on the matter. As soon as the service had concluded, Margaret had stood up rather abruptly and made to leave so that she might hurry home and flee their scrutiny without so much as a backward glance. Only, if she had, Margaret would have seen him staring after her, his expression a stern guise, but if one looked closely, that mask of severity that polluted his handsome features bore fractures in its shield of pride, and within the fissures, one could see his pain screaming like a rampant beast. Yes, if she had looked, she would have seen him mourn her departure, her retreating figure robbing him of her company for even a few seconds longer, reminding him that they were always to live separate lives, never going here and there with each other at their side, revelling in the joy of returning home together to live out their lives as man and wife.

Oh! If only I—I mean, *she*, had looked back at him.

Well, it mattered not, but she had to see for herself, that was why she was going. Perhaps if she could see him, she could either convince him of her love, or else, convince herself that it was over, and in so, that chapter of her life, their story, it would be closed forever.

Immersed in the tumult of her doubts, Margaret scarcely noted the dynamic hum of the pulsating metropolitan life that surrounded her. The heart of Milton, unsympathetic to her tribulations, stoically bore the weight of its own concerns—with disease and poverty crying in its arms, a manufacturing city's two dependent children in need of constant attention so that they might grow and grow into insuppressible, ravenous beings.

Its momentum was dedicated to the perpetual task of reshaping itself, tirelessly adapting to the ever-evolving landscape of the world to which it forged in the furnace of industry, a world that appeared markedly distinct and unrecognisable from that of even a decade past. How pale people looked. How sickly. How ashen they appeared in this smog-ridden land that fed off their energies to fuel its own insatiable drive. Winter maintained its sovereignty in this realm, manifest in the icy air's tenacious grip on every surface and the glittering frost, like a million shards of tiny grated diamonds, adorning windowsills and rooftops alike.

Its footprints rambled and roamed the streets, permeating the core of the city with its chilling embrace, ensuring no nook remained immune to its chilling clasp.

It was towards the end of February, in that year, and a bitter black frost had lasted for many weeks. The keen east wind had long since swept the streets clean, though in a gusty day the dust would rise like pounded ice, and make people's faces quite smart with the cold force with which it blew against them. Houses, sky, people, and everything looked as if a gigantic brush had washed them all over with a dark shade of Indian ink.

However, Margaret was not to be left to her thoughts for long, for her interest was at last snatched by the sound of her name drifting towards her in the northern breeze. As the three syllables that constituted her forename coasted into her ear, her attention was drawn upward by the melodic hum of conversation approaching.

Lifting her gaze, a smile involuntarily graced her lips at the endearing scene unfolding before her. Arrayed along the street was a merry gathering of women, many of whom were familiar faces from the factory. They sallied forth, shepherded by their loved ones; mothers, sisters, and children. Margaret found herself charmed by their transformed appearance; accustomed to seeing them in the monotonous hues of grey, brown, and black factory uniforms, she now beheld them adorned in a delightful spectrum of dresses and bonnets, boasting their Sunday best. The vivid colours that emanated from the lively assembly warmed her heart, leaving her gratified and uplifted.

'Miss Hale!' cried a little boy in a frayed cap and boots too large for him when he spotted her from amidst this animated flock.

'Miss Margaret!' called his sister, scampering towards her, the brown hat atop her black curls flapping without a pin or ribbons to secure it, the girl likely unable to afford such items.

'Good day to you all,' Margaret called back eagerly, thankful for the welcome distraction their company afforded.

She attempted to paint on a cheerful smile, and it made her consider how easily those we see every day can confide or hide their true feelings, since *you cannot, read the lot of those who daily pass you by in the street. How do you know the wild romances of their lives; the trials, the temptations they are even now enduring, resisting, sinking under? Perhaps it is because when we are heavy-laden in our hearts, it falls in better with our humour to reveal our case in our own way and our own time.*

The first person to reach her was Dawn, a name perfectly aligned with her character. Much like the faithful sunrise, Dawn embodied a glow that was soft and pure. True to her nature, she took with her an optimism that cast light where there had previously been darkness. Dawn stood apart from the other factory hands Margaret had encountered in Milton. In contrast to many of her fellow workers, Dawn possessed the ability to read and write. For years, she had diligently maintained the books and handled correspondence for Slickson. Yet, her employment bore the bitter fruit of gender disparity, as she received measly wages solely because of her womanhood. The turning tide of destiny had bolstered Dawn when, in the shadows of the strike, she beheld Slickson's corruption. Boldly severing ties with her past post, she now used her skills to benefit a union charity in the nearby city of Manchester.

With exuberance, she approached Margaret, seizing her hands with gloves that must have been darned a dozen times over.

'What a welcome sight you are!' Dawn said with a broad smile, her blue eyes as bright and clear as the sky on a cloudless day.

Turning her head, Dawn waved to the others, beckoning them to join her in greeting their friend. Leading the procession was Ethel—a woman of noble qualities. Her complexion, a testament to her rich heritage encompassing Italian, Portuguese, Irish, and English stock, portrayed a striking beauty. Ethel's familial lineage could be traced back to distant lands, as her parents and grandparents had travelled across oceans to settle in England. Hints of her once vivid red hair lingered in a graceful transformation, now adorned in an attractive honey-blonde hue with subtle streaks of grey, mirroring the passage of time as she approached her seventh decade. After being deemed too old to work at Hamper's mill, Ethel had devoted countless years to the well-being of infant and ailing children, caring for the weans that were still too young to be put to work. Whenever she could, Ethel would prepare simple but hearty meals for the ageing and infirm, and of late, Margaret had been helping her visit the elderly residents of precincts such as Princeton, assisting her in carrying the pots of soup and baskets of bread. And now, as Ethel trudged the journey towards her later years, her heartfelt prayers resonated, matching a hopeful appeal for the presence of an earthly angel when her time came to need the care of others.

On arriving at Margaret's side, Ethel placed a gentle hand on her arm and patted her with the fondness of a grandmother.

'What a rare sight to see such a bonny face,' she complimented, the wise wrinkles beneath her eyes creasing. 'A country flower amongst us city weeds,' she said in light jest.

Margaret flushed. 'Not a bit of it,' she assured her.

'What brings you here today?' asked Deirdre as she joined them.

Deirdre was Ethel's daughter-in-law—a woman of Irish origin. With her petite stature and slender frame, she wore short black hair, a result of a recent illness that she had fought and survived valiantly. Margaret had quickly formed an affinity with Deirdre on her arrival in the city. Similar to Margaret, Deirdre exhibited a tendency towards shyness in larger social settings, finding solace in her own company, which sometimes led to occasions of quiet solitude. However, in the company of familiar faces, Deirdre thrived, shedding her reserved disposition and revealing a progressive outlook on life that unfailingly sought out the positive in every situation. This attitude had fortified Margaret's wavering resolution at times, and for that, she was grateful to Deirdre.

Nevertheless, Margaret did not have the chance to reply to the query regarding her occupation that afternoon, for Shawn, Deirdre's sister, answered for her with a blithe chuckle.

'Why, what always brings her here, I should think,' Shawn guessed, 'she has come to see us at the factory,' she   assumed.

Shawn embodied a vibrant personality, a departure from the individuals Margaret was accustomed to. Unlike those she had encountered before, Shawn exuded liveliness, embracing a spirited nature, unreserved and unafraid to express herself fully. She, like her sister, hailed from Ireland but had spent many years living in New York, rendering her quite novel by

Milton standards. Shawn had been drawn to the Americas as a teacher but had returned during her sister's illness, and had since become a fundamental stimulus in establishing a school for the children of the factory workers. Her wealth of experience, cultivated amidst the hustle and bustle of urban life, offered invaluable insights into the state of education in a city undergoing rapid transformation and expansion, lacking the necessary foundations to sustain such growth, often at the expense of the most disadvantaged. It had not been long before she had invited Margaret to join her, sensing that she would be a natural, both with her love of children and her charitable inclinations. In Margaret, she had found a patient, creative and encouraging teaching assistant. Still, Shawn's commitment to the cause went beyond mere aid; she became a leading presence, a pillar of stability, helping embolden both Margaret and the local children with newfound educational opportunities.

'But it is Sunday, Miss Margaret, the mill is closed,' Natalie gently reminded her, curiosity sketched on her face. She pondered the reason behind the young lady's presence in the industrial quarter on the Sabbath, the grumbles of machinery silenced, and the usual hubbub reduced to a distant drone. It was as if the looms themselves held their collective breaths, prompting Margaret to seek answers amid the unusual stillness of that particular day.

In her fifties, Natalie, a widow, gracefully defied the sands of time with her flowing, chestnut hair and expressive wide brown eyes. Her visage, reminiscent of the majestic horses that once distinguished the pastures of Helstone during Margaret's childhood, carried an enduring beauty. Originally from North Lincolnshire, Natalie had ventured to Milton in search of employment following the passing of her dearly departed husband in a tragic accident when the railway had been brought to their corner of England. He had been an engineer, and when his men had been blasting a hole through a hill in the Cheshire hamlet of Cranford, to allow the train to travel further and reach the sheltered, sleepy villages of rural England, calculations had been erroneous, resulting in the loss of more than one life. Still, despite her bereavement, behind Natalie's shy demeanour there lay a confident, comforting assurance that was quite moving.

Margaret glanced at Natalie, her typically quick tongue clipped by her secrecy.

Natalie returned her hesitant gaze, her head, which inclined to the side, offered a muted repetition of her question.

'I know why she is here,' said Inese, her eyes, which perpetually shimmered with kindness, now sparkled with the gems of mischief. 'Is it not obvious?' Inese, an effervescent lady hailing from Latvia, infused Margaret's life with delightful charm. Submerged in the fascinating history of Inese's homeland, Margaret could not help but experience a twinge of sadness upon learning the circumstances that had driven Inese to seek refuge abroad. Though Margaret had not personally encountered such dramatic upheaval, she could empathise with the idea of leaving one's home and embarking on a fresh start somewhere new and unfamiliar, determined to make the best of it.

As their friendship blossomed, Margaret evolved into more than a mere listener to Inese's tales. She became a companion, intimately sharing the substance of her friend's journey, intricately woven with strands of hope.

Fate, however, like a protective guardian, had intervened when Inese crossed paths with Natalie in Milton. Both rising valiantly to defy the challenges of life as single, unprotected women without substantial means or familial sponsorship, Inese and Natalie established a profound bond that exceeded mere companionship. Together, they founded a home, extending their haven to homeless women facing dire circumstances. This compassionate union became a refuge for those with nowhere else to turn, offering temporary shelter until they could secure employment and lodgings. Through the mist of life's uncertainties, Inese and Natalie stood as a resilient alliance, a testament to their enduring friendship and shared strength in confronting adversity.

'And why is she here, then?' asked Lucy, her red hair catching the sunlight and glinting like flames caught and bound into threads, so thin and so fine, spiders with all their skill could not hope to weave them.

'Well, why else would she be here?' Inese mused, a wink complimenting her words. 'She will be making one of her calls, as fine ladies do,' she deduced, her head jutting towards the green garrisoned gates that stood like soldiers on guard at the end of the street, overseeing the entry to Marlborough Mills.

She had not breathed a word to a living soul, but Inese knew for a fact that Miss Hale had called on that house more than once, recalling how, keeping a safe distance from the unrest, she had peered through those same gates on the day of the riot, and she had witnessed, above the crowd of scrambling people, the young woman, unmoving in her faint, being carried up the steps and into the house by a strong, dark, handsome figure. It was a figure Inese knew well, for she saw him nearly every day, standing high above them and watching them with hawk-eye vigilance, or walking amongst them, with a stern, supervising glower, a black-maned wolf stalking between white-cotton sheep. With a collection of curious eyes fixed upon her, Margaret teetered on the verge of a feeble rebuttal. However, before she could muster a response, she found herself spared as Lynda, who had just caught up with them, benevolently interposed on her behalf.

'Come,' she said, 'It is not for the likes of us to wonder who Miss Margaret pays calls to. She can visit what folks she likes,' she insisted. Her assertion carried a certain confidence, yet a close observer might notice a playful curl to her lips, revealing Lynda's long-held suspicion that Miss Hale had an admirer and was herself inclined to do a spot of admiring. Indeed, it would not surprise her in the least to learn that Miss Hale not only liked paying calls on the master but that she liked him very much as well. Lynda had noticed, on more than one occasion, the two of them engrossed, deep in conversation, only for responsibilities to force them apart, their disappointed gazes tentatively looking back at the retreating form of the other, wishing they could have stayed, wondering when their paths would cross again.

Margaret had first encountered Lynda at the recently

inaugurated public library in Milton, a haven she often visited with her young daughter to nurture their mutual love for literature. In the erudite ambience of the library, Margaret discovered a correlation of spirits with Lynda, who, along with her friend, Lucy, played a vital role at a museum devoted to celebrating the legacy of a celebrated female writer from Milton. Margaret could hardly have believed before coming here that a whole museum could be dedicated to the life and legacy of a woman, and a female writer at that, but this was a bold, brave new world, she saw that now, and she was proud to be part of it. The serendipity of their meeting not only unfurled among the shelves of books but also within the broader context of honouring the rich literary history of their vibrant town, one which was thrusting them all into an ever-changing England.

'Well,' said Anna, who was cradling her baby in her arms. 'Miss Hale may do as she likes, so long as she does not forget to visit us from time to time,' she said kindly, thinking that if she were to marry a certain master, then she would be hereabouts much more often.

However, Margaret, unconscious of Anna's insight, merely smiled at her consideration. Anna, as Margaret observed, had an understated elegance in her attire that drew admiration. Her stubbornly-straight mousy-brown hair would catch fair highlights in the sunlight. Anna's independent spirit and exceptional artistry added a loveliness that made Margaret wish for improved skills in her own artistic pursuits. Still, despite her quiet and well-spoken nature, Anna exemplified an enthusiastic personality that radiated a captivating energy, rendering her undeniably agreeable.

'Here, here!' agreed Shawn. 'We are only teasing you, Miss.'

'Only,' Deirdre spoke in a hushed tone, 'I hope... if I may, that Miss Hale is aware that we all sincerely wish her well.' Her words were accompanied by a subtle tilt of her head and a discerning gaze that conveyed an earnest understanding.

'Yes,' agreed Dawn without hesitation. 'We wish her all the health and happiness in the world because nobody deserves it as she does,' she said, quietly appreciating all that Margaret had done for them since she had arrived in their grey little patch of God's kingdom on earth.

In a society where the poor are ignored and marginalised, especially poor women, they could never have imagined that a lady as fine as she would have cared to know them and cared to care for them. To them, Miss Hale was all goodness, and there was nothing they wanted more than to see her happy, and preferably, to be settled amongst them, as one of them, for the rest of her days.

'And maybe,' said Lucy, her body circling deliberately towards the mill, 'her happiness may well be closer than she   thinks.'

Surveying the sea of smiling faces that encircled her, Margaret felt a surge of inner strength. In the company of these friends, she discovered a camaraderie that transcended social classes, rooted in the warmth of their hearts. Upon her arrival in Milton, she could never have envisioned unearthing such genuine fellowship, yet now she realised she felt more at home than ever before. In her perspective, this was the essence of sisterhood. It should not be steeped in competition or self-advancement at the expense of others. Instead, it should involve disregarding disparities in backgrounds and simply embracing each other as they were, uplifting one another in the shared spirit of womanhood. In the ancient tribes of the Amazons and across the vast expanse of Africa, women thrived in communal harmony, their bonds constructed with generational and gender-based support. Yet, amidst the shifting tides of this fallen world, where such foundations have collapsed, leaving hearts adrift in isolation, we carry the flame of unity, fuelled by the healing essence of camaraderie, striving to rekindle those sacred ties. In the course of the laughter that resonated through their conversations and the unwavering support exchanged in moments of misfortune, Margaret discovered a sanctuary of authentic relationships that surpassed the conventional expectations she had once known. It was a revelation, an unexpected gift within this new chapter, prompting gratitude for the bonds that transformed Milton from a mere spot on the map into the cherished core, the beating heart, of her unfurling story.

'There is nothing I would not do for those who are really my friends. I have no notion of loving people by halves, it is not my nature,' Margaret professed.

Feeling overcome with gratitude, Margaret thanked the women for their thoughtful words and promised to see them again soon, and hopefully, with some glad tidings, though she did not disclose what this might be. It was then, just as she was making ready to leave, that a little girl, who had remained silent thus far, tugged at her skirts, and as Margaret bent down, the child whispered a secret in her ear, one that was so delicate with the buds of faith, that it trembled on the wind.

'Are you going to marry the man?' she asked.

Margaret smiled, and leaning in closer so that only her confidante could hear, she replied with the humble truth: 'I hope so.'

The women soon dispersed, heading this way and that to attend to their own lives, and so they left Margaret to herself once more. Little by little, step by shuffling step, she walked the straight route to the mill gates. She moved slowly, soberly, the large gates seeming to intimidate her with their forbidding height. When, at last, she had reached them, and she had no more steps left, for a single more would carry her over the threshold into his world, she paused on the brink, lingering on neutral ground so that she might gather her strength once more.

It was then that she sensed a quiet, unassuming presence next to her, and turning her head sharply, Margaret found an elderly woman, with a wise, kindly face watching her intently.

'Are you quite well, my dear?' the stranger asked, concerned that the young woman appeared as queer as Dick's hatband.

Margaret thought, unsure herself.

'Oh, yes,' she replied. 'I am only…'

'Resting a moment?' the woman suggested with an understanding upward creasing of her crinkly cheeks.

Margaret's own rosy cheeks dimpled in appreciation for the woman's tact. 'Yes.'

'That is quite alright. We all need to rest sometimes.'

The stranger's eyes flitted to the gates and the house within. 'Are you not going in?'

Margaret was not sure why, but a swell of honesty sustained her. Perhaps she had spent too much of the day hiding from her feelings, concealing them from others, and both defining and defending them.

'I am not sure I feel brave enough,' she said openly.

On some such night as this she remembered promising to herself to live as brave and noble a life as any heroine she ever read or heard of in romance, a life sans peur et sans reproche; it had seemed to her then that she had only to will, and such a life would be accomplished. And now she had learnt that not only to will, but also to pray, was a necessary condition in the truly heroic. Trusting to herself, she had fallen.

The woman let out a small, light-hearted chuckle.

'If you live in Milton, you must learn to have a brave heart, Miss Hale.'

Margaret blinked. 'How do you know my name?'

The woman shook her head blithely, her grey hair peeking out from beneath her cap.

'That does not matter.'

Margaret briefly hesitated, momentarily puzzled, but soon dismissed the perishable confusion. It occurred to her that someone might have pointed her out to the woman in passing. After all, she was frequently the subject of discussion, the curious newcomer to Milton who never quite found her place. Alternatively, perhaps they had met, once upon a time. *'I would do my best,' said Margaret rather pale. 'I do not know whether I am brave or not till I am tried; but I am afraid I should be a coward.'*

'And so what if you are afraid?' the woman contested. 'Fear is good. Fear is natural. It reminds us that we are alive and have something worth living for.'

'I am sure you are right,' Margaret supposed. 'I am just not accustomed to being so unsure of my conscience and cares. I am normally quite content in myself, but lately, I have felt completely lost. This disorienting feeling is unbearable, and I long to find myself again, to rediscover my confidence and meet with the self-assured person I once was.'

The woman tutted well-meaningly. *'I hate to hear you talk about all women as if they were fine ladies instead of rational creatures. None of us want to be in calm waters all our lives.* After all, it is in times of crisis that we learn what we are made of. It is then and only then that we learn who and what we are.'

Margaret nodded. 'I have never thought of it like that before,' she conceded. 'I only wish I had someone to guide me.'

'Oh, my dear, you have a guide, right here,' the woman said, placing her wrinkled hand over Margaret's heart. *'We have all a better guide in ourselves, if we would attend to it, than any other person can be.* We like to think that someone is steering us in the right direction, even if the very notion of a straight and narrow path is nothing more than an illusion. Life is made of bumps in the road, false steps, wrong turns, and being lost in the woods. How else are we meant to find ourselves? My dear girl, there is no author of our fate, a hand that writes our story and ensures our happy ending, but that is not the case,' she assured her. 'Our lives are not like that of novels. Our destinies are not mapped out. Our choices are not manipulated. Our happiness is not predestined. You, and only you, are the author of this story.'

Margaret stood in deferential silence, immersing herself in the wisdom of those sage words.

At that moment, the woman leaned in closer, her smile shrewd, as she added: *'But then again, a girl in love will do a good deal.'*

Margaret did not reply, rendered speechless by the woman's sagacity.

'Go to him,' the old woman bid, nodding to the mill yard.

Readying to leave, the woman patted Margaret's hand, 'Screw your courage to the sticking place, my dear, and you will not fail.'

She then made to depart, walking towards two other ladies of comparable age who had observed the exchange from a nearby vantage point. Both nodded their heads in reassurance and solidarity towards Margaret.

Still dumbfounded by the peculiar events of the past few minutes, Margaret called out: 'I am sorry, I never caught your name.'

The woman turned her head, and smiling, she simply replied: '*Gaskell*…Elizabeth Gaskell.'

Chapter Seventeen

Could It Be?

It was a short time later that Margaret found herself in the Mill House. When she had arrived, she had discovered the butler employed in polishing the silverware from the dinner party, an arduous task that he seemed inclined to do single-handedly, and one which had probably been shunted with the distraction of the riot and the disturbance it had caused. Hence, when Margaret had reassured him that she knew the way to the drawing room and did not require him to escort or announce her, he had only mildly deliberated before settling himself back down on his stool, cloth in one hand, candlestick in the other. Consequently, left unaccompanied and unchaperoned, Margaret made her way through the house, the eyes of the paintings she passed, Thorntons long gone, were the only witnesses to her adventure of misadventure. As she walked leisurely towards the drawing room, she gazed in fascination at the ornaments and keepsakes she saw, imagining how they could have been part of her life story.

To think, she could have been mistress of all this.

However, it was as she was lost in these thoughts, that her subconscious embraced the ebb and flow of whispered echoes and heightened murmurs, causing her footsteps to falter and her attention to be filched, for through the haze resonated a singular voice that pierced the auditory symphony. A tender shiver cascaded down her spine, a knowing acknowledgement of its source. The voice, an obsidian serenade, shrouded her senses like the sinuous descent of warm, molten chocolate, its rich cadence meandering through the vines of her awareness. A heady intoxication seized her, casting a dizzying spell as she surrendered to its magnetic allure. Then, abruptly, she stopped, arrested by the voice's sudden, biting revelation.

'Miss Hale is...'

Margaret hardly knew what to think, her name an unexpected note that hung in the air with ambiguous implications, but before she knew what she was doing, she stepped boldly into the fray, and demanded to know with calm but firm intent: 'That I am what?'

As though propelled by an invisible force, Mr Thornton lurched forward violently, his entire being gripped by a jolt of astonishment at the unforeseen resonance vibrating throughout the shared space. It initially coasted around him, then coursed through him like a spectral draught, defying all logic. The voice that had interrupted him was calm but held a quiet authority. It could not be misconstrued as meek; rather, it emanated a native assertiveness.

Simultaneously, a collective gasp swept through the room, freezing everyone into statuesque stillness as they pivoted their focus toward the door—everyone but Mr Thornton. He lingered, his back turned to the evolving scene, yet he was not oblivious; for his every sense was acutely attuned, except his eyes, not that he needed to look at her to truly see her. In tender wonder, he closed them, granting himself a bold dose of hope, as if the very universe conspired in his favour, whispering encouraging twitters of possibility into his soul. With a hand pressed against his chest, he sensed the galloping rhythm of his heart, a phenomenon stirred solely by one person's influence.

Could it be? Could it be that she...?

Mr Thornton turned to face the source of the hallowed cadence with the measured pace of a snail. As he completed the languid rotation, a sudden cessation gripped him, his body assuming a rigid paralysis, as though struck off balance by an imperceptible and incalculable force.

There, at the other side of the room, she stood. Small, stately, surreal, dressed in a brown coat, that funny brown hat of hers in hand. The woman simply stared back at him with a stunned expression, but if Mr Thornton looked carefully, he could not help but smile, because even in her shock, she was still so majestic, fully in control of herself, unlike him.

They were within twenty yards of each other, and so abrupt was his appearance, that it was impossible to avoid his sight. Their eyes instantly met, and the cheeks of each were overspread with the deepest blush. He absolutely started, and for a moment seemed immoveable from surprise; but shortly recovering himself, advanced towards her, and spoke.

'*Margaret,*' he breathed, that unmarried word (for unmarried it was), floating into the air and causing her to tremor, the vulnerability in his husky tone of Darkshire granularity enough to make her weak at the knees.

Stepping closer, she fixed him with a firm stare, one which was uncompromising in its confidence.

She did not answer. She could not tell what words to use. She was afraid of saying anything, lest the passion of anger, dislike, indignation—whatever it was that was boiling up in her breast—should find vent in cries and screams, or worse, in raging words that could never be forgotten. It was as if the piece of solid ground on which she stood had broken from the shore, and she was drifting out to the infinite sea alone.

At last, she found her voice, and she was not afraid to use it.

'I'll ask again, Mr Thornton, what am I?' Margaret challenged. 'If you are going to talk about me, to others,' she stressed, trying not to give the gawking audience the satisfaction of her attentiveness, 'then I think I have the right to know.'

Mr Thornton gulped.

Margaret already knew what he thought of her, Mr Thornton had made it abundantly clear when they had last exchanged words—heated and heavy words. He reviled her. He thought her a wanton woman who could not be trusted. Well, be that as it may, if he had something scathing to say about her, then he ought to say it to her and her alone, since it was nobody else's concern but theirs.

The ladies all swiftly swivelled their heads from side to side as they watched, agog with exhilaration, absorbed by this unexpected addition to the afternoon, almost like they were experiencing the unveiling of an unanticipated page missing from a play, a thrilling spectacle being acted out right before their very eyes. One might think the two remaining devotees to the cause of husband-hunting would be perturbed by Margaret, Miss Hale's presence, but that was not the case, since they could see as clear as crystal that she was angry with Mr Thornton, *very* angry, so while perhaps they would be unable to crush his ardour for her, it could be that he, through the idiocy of his loose tongue, could quash any affection she may have secretly entertained on his behalf, spoiling their chances of marriage for good.

As for Mr Thornton, for once in his life, he did not need to think what to say. All at once, he marched across the room, coming to stand by her, his towering body overlooking her petite one as he stopped mere inches from Margaret. It was incredible, because while he was easily a head, shoulders and chest taller than she, Margaret had the ability at half his height to intimidate him, bringing Mr Thornton down to size. With eyes as sharp as flint, he drank her in, his orbs smouldering with a blaze born of a feral passion, the intensity of which made him appear like a man possessed. He was overwhelmed by her unforeseen manifestation in his parlour. Taking in the sight of her now, he could hardly draw breath. She was so beautiful, more so than ever, and if he tore his eyes away from her, even for a second, he feared he would go blind.

Was he bewitched by those beautiful eyes, that soft, half-open, sighing mouth which lay so close upon his shoulder all those months ago? *He could not even shake off the recollection that she had been there; that her arms had been round him, once—if never again.*

Margaret could not help her looks; but the short curled upper lip, the round, massive up-turned chin, the manner of carrying her head, her movements, full of a soft feminine defiance, always gave strangers the impression of haughtiness.

She stood *facing him and facing the light; her full beauty met his eye; her round white flexile throat rising out of the full, yet lithe figure; her lips, moving so slightly as she spoke, not breaking the cold serene look of her face with any variation from the one lovely haughty curve; her eyes, with their soft gloom, meeting his with quiet maiden freedom.* When they had first met, he had *almost said to himself that he did not like her,* that she was barely tolerable. *Before their conversation ended; he tried so to compensate himself for the mortified feeling, that while he looked upon her with an admiration he could not repress, she looked at him with proud indifference, taking him, he thought, for what, in his irritation, he told himself he was—a great rough fellow, with not a grace or a refinement about him. Her quiet coldness of demeanour he interpreted into contemptuousness, and resented it in his heart to the pitch of almost inclining him to get up and go away, and have nothing more to do with these Hales, and their superciliousness.* Perhaps if he had taken his own advice, he could have spared himself a hell-storm of grief, but he would not wish her away, not then, not now, not ever.

With his breath ragged, all he could utter was, 'I did not know you were coming here today.'

There was no accusation in his statement, no suggestion that she was not welcome in his home, it was more of an earnest need to know.

Margaret gazed back up at him, her eyes wide in awe, her neck craned, her pretty lips wetted as she struggled to find the words, too preoccupied with being hypnotised by the way he stared down at her, a curious blend of tenderness and intensity making her feel giddy, a fervent regard he had never offered her before.

Swallowing, Margaret lifted her arms and pressed a pile of books up against his chest.

'You forgot these,' she told him, 'when you read with my father last week,' she explained, her voice unsteady as they continued to lock eyes. Mr Thornton glanced down for the briefest of moments, distracted by the feeling of her hand resting against him, and what was most curious of all, was that she did not pull away, but there she stayed, lingering in their touch.

And when his eyes fell to inspect the dull stack of tomes, volumes he certainly had not needed to be returned to him so swiftly, since he could have collected them upon his next visit, something she must have comprehended, he cocked his head in bewilderment, because there, on the top, her hand shook, creeping ever so slightly, ever so steadily, towards his, and he sighed in hopeful understanding.

Seizing the books from her, he practically tossed them away carelessly on a nearby table. Returning his attention to her, he leaned in closer still.

'I need to talk to you,' he asserted throatily.

Margaret blinked. '*Now*?'

'*Now*!' he insisted.

'*Here*?' she asked, a little fretfully.

Mr Thornton shook his head sharply in disapproval.

'*No*!' he assessed promptly, 'absolutely not,' he added with just as much certainty, turning to consider their awkward surroundings.

Peering down, they both saw that their hands were loitering together, their fingers knocking as they mingled coyly, and before he knew what he was doing, Mr Thornton had turned his over, palm-up, and proffered it to Margaret. She had only looked, wondered and deliberated for a trice, because a moment later, she had placed her hand in his, and as his closed around hers, snug and safe, Mr Thornton gently pulled Margaret out of the room and led her away down the corridor.

All four women left behind (for we cannot forget them in all of this, the title of this book dedicated to two of them), remained stock-still, their jaws scuffing the floor as they gawked in disbelief. Even when they heard the master's study door close, halfway down the hallway, still they did not speak, not a single squawk or squeak.

The only person to move was Mrs Thornton, who, taking up her sewing, went to stand by the large window which gave her a hawk-like view of the yard. She often stood there. It was her spot, and it allowed her to observe the comings and goings of Marlborough Mills, ensuring that all was well, because mothers never cease to mother, no matter how old their children may grow to be. Nonetheless, little did the ladies know that not only was this a convenient position to stand if one wanted to see, but it was also ideal if one wanted to hear, and luckily for Mrs Thornton, her hearing was first-rate. With her ears pricking, she listened, and yes, just as she thought, she could catch the odd sound drifting through the walls from the study. Straining, Mrs Thornton tried to pick up whatever stray strands she could, each word or phrase a broken fragment from a sequestered conversation. Concentrating, she smiled at what she heard, and in trusting all was well, she moved away and left them to it, affording them their right to privacy, pleased that this onerous day was at last bearing fruit:

'It is about us.'

'Whether our story turns out to be synonymous with that of the hero and the heroine, we will have to wait and see.'

'Hope?'

'And what about them?'
'Witches?'
'Who was he, then?'
'A relative?'
'I am sorry.'
'All is forgiven and forgotten.'
'My dearest, loveliest Margaret.'
'Oh, John!'

Mrs Thornton breathed a sigh of relief as her son swiftly exited the room, though his departure carried the weight of abruptness and the promise of scandalous whispers. Yet, amidst the tumult, she found solace in his removal from the nest of vipers that surrounded them. It was a rare admission for her to acknowledge her own culpability, but she now identified her previous misjudgement with regret.

The unyielding bond of motherhood compelled Mrs Thornton to shield her son from further pain, especially the needless kind he had endured throughout his still rather short life. When Miss Hale had entered the picture almost a year ago and turned his life upside down and hurt him anew, the mother's bitterness toward her knew no bounds. Therefore, desperate to mend the wrongs that had been inflicted, she had wilfully chosen to believe that a lady like Miss Bingley, Miss Ingram, or Miss Latimer would suit him perfectly, envisioning them as dutiful companions who would rightly extol his virtues. Yet, upon closer examination, she saw the shallowness and lack of substance in these prospects.

John deserved more than shallow accolades and hollow companionship. He deserved depth, integrity, and a partner who would enrich his life rather than constrain it with triviality, selfishness, or deceit. Reflecting on Miss Hale's actions and character, Mrs Thornton began to see her in a new light, considering her perhaps the right woman for John, after all.

With hope kindling in her heart, she prayed that both John and Miss Hale could set aside their differences and recognise the potential for happiness they shared before it slipped away irretrievably.

It was twenty minutes later, as the remaining women peered at the clock for the hundredth time, each one of them tired and bored, but all equally refusing to budge until they received some enlightenment on the strange moment they had just witnessed, that they were startled to discern the study door once again opening, the creaking hinges a tell-tale sign that the private interview was at last over. Rearranging themselves on their chairs, they waited impatiently, and much to their relief, they detected the faint pitter-patter of feminine feet trailing away into the distance, shortly followed by the front door letting somebody out.

Ah, so she was gone. Excellent! That must mean that he had not invited her to stay, or else, she had not accepted. However, the details were of no matter, since either way, Miss Hale's departure was a good omen for these witches, meaning there was a chance for them still.

Then, all of a sudden, there was a noise, and blinking, they all sat up straight as Mr Thornton re-entered the room. There was something different about him, his steps were brisk, his manner lively, his countenance less harsh. Grabbing hold of a chair from the table, he hauled it over, and sitting beside Miss Bingley and Miss Ingram with informal ease, he slapped his thighs jovially, grinning from cheek-to-cheek as he looked at them in turn.

'Well then, ladies, where were we?' Mr Thornton asked, his eyes gleaming with impish delight. 'Tell me again, what were you saying about my fiancée?'

Chapter Eighteen

North and South

Finally, alone, they faced each other.

But not as foes this time. Simply as a man and a woman.

The air was charged with anticipation. Each heartbeat resonated in the hush, and the unspoken words trembled between them, their tension a fragile flurry of glass butterflies in the stillness. Emotions crackled in the stratosphere of their story, as if the aether itself conspired to intensify the coveted yoke of their melding. The outside world faded, leaving only the two of them in a suspended moment, on the verge of something decisive, the crescendo of their epic score, that is, if they dared to take the next step, if they dared play the final note.

As Margaret glided around the table, her movements reminiscent of an ethereal presence, her fingers nimbly caressed a chair, and a haunting familiarity settled upon her. Of course. It harked back to a significant day when he, plagued by hesitation, had approached her. In his nervousness, he had circled the table in her parlour, engaging in talk of fruit to mask his true intentions until courage found its way to his tongue.

Amidst this reminiscence, her discerning gaze caught sight of a meticulously arranged assortment of books on the table. Intrigued, she lifted them, and a sense of astonishment struck her.

'Jane Austen?' she asked, her surprise evident. 'Charlotte Brontë? You have read these?'

Suddenly, the wintry frost-bound look of care had left Mr Thornton's face, as if some soft summer gale had blown all anxiety away from his mind; and, though his mouth was as much compressed as before, his eyes smiled out benignly on his questioner.

'Aye,' said he. 'I…they have been useful.'

She looked at him searchingly.

'A man such as I can be found wanting. We lack training when it comes to affairs of the heart. We are poorly qualified. So I looked to experts for guidance. Do you, do you approve?' he solicited, strangely worried she would not.

'Oh, yes!' she affirmed. '*It is only in a novel, or, in short, only some work in which the greatest powers of the mind are displayed, in which the most thorough knowledge of human nature, the happiest delineation of its varieties, the liveliest effusions of wit and humour, are conveyed to the world in the best-chosen language.*'

His smile broke through his sober expression, tender and genuine, as he beheld her unmatched sweetness and cleverness. Admiration swelled in his breast, an adoration that was impossible to contain.

'I had a feeling you would approve,' he murmured, his relief tinged with a shy delight.

It was then that Margaret picked up another book, its spine gilded with the traces of time and tales. As she ran her fingers along its weathered edges, Margaret found herself drawn into the world of yet another literary companion. She could tell it was well-used, well-respected, well-loved. The title, a mystery awaiting unravelling, beckoned her to explore its pages, adding an extra layer of intrigue, and yet, the author's name was strangely familiar.

'I do not know this one.'

'It is called *North and South*,' he informed her.

'Do you like it?' she ventured to ask, her curiosity getting the better of her.

'Oh! I am delighted with the book! I should like to spend my whole life in reading it.'

'What is it about?' she queried, her inquisitiveness again piqued.

'Everything,' he went on enthusiastically, inspired by her interest. 'Change. Loss. Faith. Pain. Disparity. Friendship. Poverty. Family. Home. And sometimes,' he smiled, 'it is about us.'

Margaret looked at him questioningly, her eyes a canvas painted with curiosity.

'We are in it,' he explained, 'our names, that is. An amusing coincidence. But whether our story turns out to be synonymous with that of the hero and the heroine, we will have to wait and see.'

There was a further recess of reticence as she laid the book down, each passing second amplifying the suffocating tension in the room. Margaret faltered, caught in the abstract web of indecision, uncertainty etched across her features. Sensing her hesitation, he, at last, chose to take the lead, ending the deadlock of silence.

'Why are you here?' he whispered, his question barely audible as he looked at her in lingering amazement, unable to believe that she, of all people, was standing in his study.

Margaret searched her surroundings restively, as though seeking answers that she did not quite know herself.

'I—I told you,' she replied, lifting her chin so that she might assert an impression of dignity, determined that she should not appear ridiculous before him. 'I came to return your books,' she reminded him. Despite her assured tone, her words were nonetheless shaded with a subtle unease.

Upon this, Mr Thornton arched his eyebrow, observing her with a discerning gaze. He knew her better than that.

'And now, the real reason,' he remarked knowingly. The lies that had existed between them, though white with their good intentions, must now be at an end if they ever hoped to progress forward into the next unknown chapter of their entwined fates.

Initially taken aback, she appeared vaguely startled and affronted by his frankness, her sense of directness poised for a sharp retort that never came. Instead, her lips parted faintly as she responded with an aspiring uncertainty, the likes of which he had never seen in her before.

'I wanted to know whether,' she began shyly, her eyes cast to the floor with demure avoidance. Then looking up hastily, she finished with a decided effort at courage, though her voice remained tinged with faint disquiet, 'whether there was still hope for me.'

'*Hope*?' he nearly scoffed, his chords cracking with a surprise he did not even try to conceal. 'That is a word I know well,' he admitted.

He grappled with the elusive meaning behind her short but unmistakably prophetic speech, struggling to discern any clarity. Yet, in the tentative expanse of ambiguity, did any space exist for misunderstanding? What was the source of her hope? Was it tethered to her, to him, or dare he hope…*them*?

Encouraged by her admission, Mr Thornton advanced, closing the physical distance between them with just a few purposeful strides. Hitherto, he remained silent, his gaze devoted to her. In response, she locked eyes with him, her anticipation palpable as she patiently awaited the words she sensed hovering, ready to unfurl from his typically stern lips. This day, an unexpected allure emanated from his visage, enticing her like a moth drawn by a flame.

Despite her magnetic pull, Mr Thornton grappled with preoccupations, consumed by concerns about the best course of action. He felt backwards in coming forwards. Dash it all! He had wished for this moment for as long as he could remember, and now that she was here, he knew what he wanted to say, but darn it, he had no idea of how to say it.

'Miss Hale, *Margaret*,' he opened, electing to be brave, the repeated use of her name having its desired effect and causing her to look at him with flickering astonishment. Still, much to his absolution, she did not protest.

'Whatever the reason you have come to see me today, I would be a fool to waste it. So may I make a confession? Something I should have said long, long ago?'

There was an overwrought pause while he awaited her answer, and it came in the form of eyes brimming with permission.

Mr Thornton drew in a quivering breath, fighting to steady himself before embarking on what might be the most significant oration of his life thus far, and quite conceivably, of all his days.

'I now see that I have been guilty of speaking too much and too little. When we first met, I failed to be honest with you about how I felt. Then, when I ultimately found the resolve to express my desires, to confide my heart's truest wish, I spoke too hastily, without consideration. Finally, after you rejected me, I retreated into a self-imposed silence,' he acknowledged, his words remaining in the air like tenuous tendrils knotted with the intricacies of undisclosed feelings. The room seemed to absorb the weight of his revelation, the mist of which engulfed them both.

'Heaven help me! *If I* felt for *you less, I might be able to talk about it more,'* he said, mocking himself as he raked his fingers through his hair. *'But you know what I am.* And now, I must be sincere, I must be clear,' he asserted, his eyes never once leaving hers, lest the gravity of his sentiments be missed, lest his meaning be misjudged, lest their newfound connection be lost and never recovered.

It was then that he came to stand directly in front of her, and fixed her with a discernment that he had employed as both a master and magistrate, one that meant his word was his bond and could be trusted implicitly, only, now, it was attended by a soft smile that melted her resolve. Thus, he laid out his feelings as simply as he could surmise.

'Margaret: *In vain have I struggled. It will not do. My feelings will not be repressed. You must allow me to tell you how ardently I admire and love you.'*

Silent, she uttered no words, her eyes widening into lakes of wonder, a whirlpool of blue that pulled him in. Upon observing her lack of objection to this initial disclosure, his head bobbed up and down in a swift motion, emitting a gruff grunt that uncannily resembled a horse's snort. At least, he mused, he had advanced beyond previous attempts, a promising start, or so he eagerly believed.

'Very well,' said he, 'In that case, before I go any further and deepen my trench of hurt and humiliation, and before I assume to know you as I did once before and find myself mistaken, I must say this: *You are too generous to trifle with me. If your feelings are still what they were last April, tell me so at once. My affections and wishes are unchanged, but one word from you will silence me on this subject forever.*'

Margaret, *feeling all the more than common awkwardness and anxiety of his situation, now forced herself to speak; and immediately, though not very fluently, gave him to understand that her sentiments had undergone so material a change since the period to which he alluded, as to make her receive with gratitude and pleasure his present assurances.*

'Oh, my feelings!' she murmured. *'My feelings are so different...in fact, they are quite the opposite,'* she whispered intrepidly, all the previous inherent inhibition that had accompanied their relationship quite vanished.

Chapter Nineteen

The Thorn And The Rose

There was an intermission of inaction while Mr Thornton found himself stunned, his tongue rendered still, dubious of whether to continue in the spirit of caution or candour, but after inhaling a deep and fortifying breath, he chose to free the words like a liberated river of truth, flowing untrammelled from his heart.

'Margaret, I have loved you from the first moment I saw you,' he proclaimed, his hand stretched out to her and moving up and down as if to show that he loved every part of her with equal dedication. 'I may not have known it was love at first, but I knew I felt something for you that I had never felt before and never will again. I am sure of it. As I said to you that day,' he went on, defying to mention their last interview on the subject, 'I told you that I loved you as no man had ever loved a woman, and I meant it just as assuredly then as I do now. Margaret, I admire you. I respect you. I appreciate you. Darn it, I worship you! You divine creature who cannot be from this finite world, for you are too good, too pure for the likes of us scoundrels of blood and bone with our corporeal faults and corrupt failings. While we are feeble, you are fierce, and yet, you are so gentle...tell me, how can that even be?' he uttered in awestruck incredulity, more to himself than to her, his tenor elevated as if it strained into the skies for answers.

Margaret gripped the edges of her dress and nearly tore the material, for fear that she might cry out in both love and longing for this most cherished man, his emotions laid bare in their nakedness, her own dearly treasured Mr Thornton, ablaze in the light of honesty as he stood before her in all his honourable glory. However, she did not make a sound, no, she would not interrupt him, not now that he was finally saying what her heart yearned to hear.

'You are *always* on my mind, Margaret,' he went on, his attitude practically accusatory as he rubbed at his temple, almost as if to demonstrate how often his head had ached from thinking of her with such unyielding fascination. His mind had been like a maddening merry-go-round, replaying their interactions a thousand times over, much like a gardener turning over muddied dirt again and again to unearth the fertile soil he needed beneath. With distracted distress, his subconscious had sought to understand how this woman had managed to bluster into his life like a whirlwind and turn it upside down, yet somehow, at the same time, be like a breath of fresh air, effortlessly inciting and calming him.

'You are my first thought when I wake and my last thought before I sleep. Your face is all I see,' he essentially moaned, his eyes scaling the length of her, dragging with deliberate unhurriedness, all so that he might look upon her fully and unblinkingly. In doing so, he stared at her with such stark ardour and intensity of concentration that Margaret felt sure his penetrating gaze could char a cavity right through her clothes, her skin, her bones, allowing him to see into her very core. But she did not mind. She was his, body and soul, and she had nothing to hide from him. She wanted him to know her, to see her, to love her completely.

'Go on,' she urged.

He studied her, seeking any minuscule sign that the feelings he cherished for her were returned, and within the complexities of her expression, he fancied he discerned that communal connection, a bridging of their combined aspirations.

'I think I am blind to everything and everyone else now that I have been enchanted by the sunlight that is your character. Your conscience governs me, your spirit sustains me, your sweetness disarms me and leaves me a pitiful lovesick fool praying for even a second in your presence, craving just one measly ounce of your approval and affection, like some drug-dependent wretch, because I have discovered that I cannot be without you. You have ruined me, Margaret, you have stripped me of my rationality and restraint, and now I find that I need you if I hope to survive this malady that plagues me, this dissatisfaction that turns out to be my heart sickening for its aching want of you.'

His mirth echoed around them. 'God! If I did not know better, I would say you had cast a spell on me,' he laughed, amused by the prevailing theme of the day.

With the tendons of his solid jaw contracting, first tightening and then loosening, the man strangled by his infernal cravat which constricted the tide of his address of adoration, he deliberated about how to say what he must.

'You compel me to aspire to a higher self, for you embody both my angel and my accuser, seamlessly blending integrity as my anchor and intelligence as my guiding star through life's turbulent seas. You've spirited away my sanity, and I have no desire to reclaim it. I am resolute in my refusal to revert to my old ways. I do not just want you; I *need* you! In this realm of meagre mortals, Margaret, you reign as my master,' he emphasised fervently.

Mr Thornton abruptly halted in his tracks as he perceived the way her eyebrows soared in amazement at this unexpected statement, her mouth falling open in a perfect oval of an: 'O!'

It was at this point that he threw propriety to the wind and tore off his cravat, revealing his sturdy neck, his mind too harried to notice the way she gulped and stared at this exposed column of raw masculinity with evident fascination.

'You are surprised to hear me say such a shocking thing?' he surmised, momentarily imagining what the other masters would think to hear him own such a striking remark. Mr Thornton knew that he was talking radically, that he was brazenly going so far as to elevate a woman above a man, something which defied the discriminatory norms of a history in which the scales of justice were tipped most unfairly in favour of his sex, a male-dominated record of philosophy, law, and politics, which disadvantaged and degraded those who lacked the birthright of bigotry. Be that as it may, he soon dispelled those boorish pigs from his thoughts, since their obnoxious opinions were irrelevant to him, because he would never be bent or intimidated by chauvinistic minds into denouncing his deference for this beloved woman who was cleverer and more capable than the lot of those inane and incompetent brutes tossed together.

'Well, it is true, and I am not sorry for it!' he averred vehemently, the rumble of his thick northern twang vibrating in that same throat that held her interest captive.

'Most men would be, I know that. They would feel emasculated to think that they were at the mercy of a woman, that she had such absolute authority over him, but not I, *no*!' he enforced, his head shaking furiously at the conviction of his comment, his muscles tensing.

'I do not feel weakened by your sway over me. In contrast, I feel empowered by it. I feel as if knowing you and being with you allows me to be my true and full self. It was as if I were dead, but now, I am alive. Everything was and remains insipid and pointless without you, but when you draw near, you breathe meaning and warmth into me like you are my life's breath.'

Stalking towards her, Mr Thornton regarded Margaret with unfaltering affection, the intensity of which nearly caused her legs to buckle beneath her, leaving her thankful for her excessive layers of petticoats that served to hide her precarious wobbling like a plate of jelly. As he got near, Margaret's body instinctively arched towards him in greeting, her back curving in the direction of his desk, which she leaned against for support. When she did this, as she felt this spontaneous reflex that was new and strange to her—no, not strange, entirely natural, Margaret's fingers scored the surface of the table, leaving behind a vicious labyrinth of scratches on the polished top. She did not whimper as the fractured wood continued to dig into her nail bed, no, she did not cry out in pain, she cried out in pleasure. Nonetheless, her hands were soon rescued, as stepping indecently near, he boldly pried them from behind her back, and holding them in his own. Margaret could feel her skin tingling at the heat which enveloped her. Reaching out a shaky hand, he held her tenderly, first on her ring finger of all places, the introductory encounter of his rough dermis against her silky skin enough to set his soul on fire, so breathtaking as it was. As he did this, Mr Thornton tried to control himself, lest he give way to his tactless hankerings and scoop Margaret up in his arms there and then, such an act not only being inappropriate, but enough to scare his unworldly sweetheart away for good.

Mr Thornton's voice turned guttural, gruff and glorious. 'But I fear that if I do not find peace soon, I shall burn up from this all-consuming inferno which rages deep within me. It is a wildfire that nothing and no one can pacify, but you. It is unbearable, and yet, I welcome the pain, I exalt it, for within the agony of my ardour, I have the privilege of knowing you, even if you will never consent to be mine,' he described earnestly.

'But that is not all. Today, I had an epiphany that eclipsed all others,' he shared with her.

She leaned her head to the side, inviting him to continue.

'That no matter what has transpired between us, all the heartache, I have no intention of losing you completely,' he stated.

'Losing me?' she recited. 'Why should you lose me?'

'*I have a strange feeling with regard to you,*' he said with a reverent murmur, his hand, still holding hers, resting upon his heart. '*As if I had a string somewhere under my left ribs, tightly knotted to a similar string in you,*' he enlightened, his hand gently moving to rest on her breast, causing Margaret to quiver from tip to toe. '*And if you were to leave I'm afraid that cord of communion would snap. And I have a notion that I'd take to bleeding inwardly. As for you, you'd forget me.*'

Margaret trembled, her light frame shuddering against his and affecting the hairs on his body to prickle, as if his skin itched in want of her, the faintest trace of her too hot, too holy for a mere man to withstand.

'Oh, John!' she exclaimed, this being all she would say, since she was frantic with a longing to hear more, his homily more agreeable to her than anything penned by all the poets or philosophers that had ever lived. Gently squeezing his hand, Margaret mutely encouraged him to go on and on and on, for as long as he wished, because she never wanted him to stop. She longed for him to love her and make love to her with his mouth for all the days of the rest of their lives.

'I could never leave you. And you will never lose me,' she promised. 'Not when fate has conspired to bring us, a woman from the south and a man from the north, together as one. That is too great, too strong a destiny for anyone or anything to ever dissolve.' Now, let us cast aside formality and address him as John, for we are interwoven in this love story just as much as they are. The era of Mr and Miss has passed for us, bound in a narrative of which we are privy. In the pages of their intertwined chronicle, we find ourselves no longer ordinary observers, but active participants, enmeshed in the delicate strands of their emotions and experiences. As we navigate the twists and turns of their odyssey, let us revel in the conversations that overcome the barriers between storyteller and reader, where the lines blur, and we become integral characters in the unfolding tale of love.

Therefore, we will say that John took Margaret by the shoulders as his eyes, acute and alert, seeped into the caverns of her very core. She was lost to them, swimming in an ocean of cobalt blue, awash in the tenderness of his thirst for her. She struggled to catch her breath as she felt his spirit speak to her spirit, and all the emotions of his soul poured from one vessel to the other, gushing through her every nerve and vein.

'My dearest, loveliest Margaret,' John said in a rasping whisper, for he was unsure as yet whether she was truly his, his nervousness affecting his inflexion in a way which he thought most harsh and unfavourable, but little did he know that far from disliking it, the rough strum of his tenor made Margaret weak at the knees. With his fingers stroking hers, John looked down at their joined hands in dubious awe, unable to believe that Margaret was truly letting him stand so close and touch her so familiarly.

'I see now that the real question is: Is there hope not for you, or me, but *us*?'

Margaret's body almost convulsed as she felt herself overwhelmed by disbelief at her joy and she bowed her head to kiss his hand again and again, her lips anointing him with her undying devotion. How could he be unaware that she was steadfast, unyielding in her commitment, a dependable presence by his side? Not even the most untamed of horses could wrest her away from him.

'Yes,' she sniffed, her voice carrying the weight of a thousand newborn sentiments, each syllable an affirmation that resonated in the quiet space that danced between them.

Settling one calloused hand upon her cheek, his thumbs tenderly caressing the soft skin he found there, John sucked in a guttural breath as he watched Margaret's eyes flicker closed, her lashes shivering like the wings of a hummingbird.

John felt tears pricking in the corner of his eyes, and he had to suppress a laugh of rapture at this heavenly event, this miracle.

'For the first time in my miserable life, I find that I am not just existing, but I am longing to truly live, and it is all thanks to you,' he acclaimed, his eyes closing as if in meditation, his lips rotating slightly to the side as they brushed her hand in a featherlight kiss, the sensation of which extracted a strident pant from his beloved.

It was then that Margaret heard the muffled sound of chattering coming from down the corridor, and she was starkly reminded of the illusion of their seclusion.

'And what about *them*?' she inquired, her gaze flitting towards the drawing room. 'What about those other women?' Her interrogation did not arise from distrust, especially in light of all he had just confided. Instead, Margaret sought clarification. Although assured of his loyalty, she longed to dispel any lingering doubts that could potentially cast shadows on his commitment to her in the eyes of others.

He blinked his confusion. 'Margaret, those women are nothing to me,' he assured her.

'Yet somehow they are the ones who have spent the day with you,' she quietly noted. 'Since our quarrel, I always seem to find you in the company of one or other of them,' she said.

John could not deny the truth in this. 'Yes,' he admitted, 'but that is not of my choosing. If I cannot be with you, I would rather be alone,' he swore.

Still, there was a look of doubt on her face as she once again listened to the din that came from the drawing room. John huffed. Very well, thought he, she had the right to ask such a question. Ever since he had been made the Master of Marlborough Mills, he had been pursued by women, even if he had never courted their covetousness, but he would not allow the woman he loved, the only woman he had or would ever love, to feel in any way insecure because of it. Pulling her close, he held her firmly in his arms, a safe haven that murmured assurances. In that closeness, the sensory language of touch conveyed more than words ever could.

'*You hear nothing but truth from me.* I am not that sort of man. I have never known a woman, if you understand my meaning,' he admitted with awkwardness, his skin flushing beneath his clothes.

'There has never been anyone but you. I cannot imagine myself with anyone but you, and do you know why?'

Margaret shook her head.

Smiling, John gently skimmed his nose along the rim of her ear. 'Because nobody could ever hope to tolerate me like you do,' he confessed. 'Margaret, *I have blamed you, and lectured you, and you have borne it as no other woman in England would have borne it. Dare not say that man forgets sooner than woman, that his love has an earlier death. I have loved none but you. Unjust I may have been, weak and resentful I have been, but never inconstant.*'

But still, she wavered. '*Oh, Mr Thornton, John, I am not good enough!' she wailed.* Her voice was glazed with vulnerable honesty, revealing the self-doubt that writhed in the shadows of her heart.

'*Not good enough!' he laughed. 'Don't mock my own deep feeling of unworthiness.* You are the very essence of goodness, Margaret. Your very existence in my life has elevated me to a realm where love transcends all notions of adequacy, and with you, I find my truest and highest worth.'

'But John, I must tell you, I am lacking. I am not like other women, I am not fashioned from their mould,' she professed, referring to the women who sat near at hand. 'I am nothing like them,' she said, somewhat sadly, acutely aware that emulating their ways lay beyond her grasp. The nuances of dressing with elegance, playing with exquisite skill, and articulating flawless sentiments bewildered her, and she had no desire to master them. Despite intensely rejecting the idea that a woman's purpose should be confined to superficial expectations, an implicit yearning persisted within her—for him to be fiercely proud of her. In her authenticity, Margaret yearned to carve a place in his heart that appreciated her for who she truly was, imperfections and all. She aimed to cultivate a pride that emanated from the unique journey they traversed together, valuing the harmony they shared, one that was on a higher plane than the role society had intended for her.

'And thank God for that!' he hailed. 'I should not like you half as much if you were like other women. Besides, how could you think I could care for *them*?' he sneered. *'Those witches!'*

Margaret wrinkled her nose, her bafflement patent in riposte to his peculiar choice of words.

'*Witches*?' she repeated, seeking intelligibility in the midst of the unexpected term.

'Yes, for that is what they are,' he said without apology. 'That is *all* they are. Casting their spells of senselessness and spite.'

Margaret looked up at him fondly. 'And what about me? Am I a witch?' she asked, introducing a playful note into the conversation.

John let out a hearty laugh as he observed Margaret's undisguised surprise. She found his humour an endearing contrast to his usual graveness. Still, her comely lips parted in perplexity as she remained blissfully naive to the immeasurable influence she held over him.

Nevertheless, instead of reciprocating her light-hearted tease, his expression shifted to a more brooding manner.

'I sometimes wonder whether you are the greatest enchantress of them all,' he admitted earnestly.

A subtle reticence hung in the air, imbued with the tacit acknowledgement that her magic was not one of spells but of a captivating simplicity that had effortlessly charmed his heart. The warmth of their interlocked gaze held a sacred understanding, surpassing dispassionate categorisations to assume the essence of their predestined oath.

'How can you not know of the bewitching effect you have upon me?' he murmured, the strength of his feelings apparent in his racing pulse, which she could feel in his wrist that rested against her neck.

'You have bewitched me, body and soul. I love...I love...I love you,' he whispered, hardly able to breathe, the sanctity of those words overwhelming him, words which, until this day, until this very hour, he had never dared believe he could utter to her again.

In reply, she tutted, her brown curls framing her face most attractively with each movement she made.

'I am not a witch. There is no such thing,' she assured him, dispelling the myth that had clouded his mind that day. 'I am just a woman.'

John hissed, as if her words had stung him. 'Do not say that!' he begged with insistence.

'Say what?' she checked, her eyes flickering in bewilderment.

'Just a woman! I have heard nothing all day but the depreciation of women by women. Yes, you are a woman, but what a woman you are! *You are my sympathy—my better self—my good angel; I am bound to you by a strong attachment. I think you good, gifted, lovely; a fervent, a solemn passion is conceived in my heart; it leans to you, draws you to my centre and spring of life, wraps my existence about you—and, kindling in pure, powerful flame, fuses you and me in one.* So please,' he entreated, 'do not think less of yourself, not when I think the world of you.'

Margaret reached onto her tiptoes and rubbed her nose self-consciously against his, marvelling at the long shaft that was his muzzle and how she would find satisfaction in leisurely skating her smaller nose along it as often as she could.

'And there is nothing wrong with being just a woman,' she apprised confidently. 'What I mean is, there is no hidden witchcraft at work here,' she verified, her hand gracing the infinitesimal slit of space between them to reveal any invisible force that may have sought to bind them to one another through devious tricks.

'There is no sorcery. I have not cast a hex to curse you or a charm to entice you, John Thornton,' she avowed, an impish twinkle animating her eyes. 'The truth is that I am nothing exceptional. *Do not consider me now as an elegant female intending to plague you, but as a rational creature speaking the truth from her heart.* I am just Margaret. I am just a woman, standing before a man, asking him to love me as I love him. We are all

301

human, fallible to mistakes, and fallible to be mistaken, and fallible, it seems, to fall quite madly in love.'

His face was overhauled by the warmest of smiles.

'You mean to say you love me?' he recounted in awe, his features a canvas illuminated by the sympathetic touch of sunlight on a previously shadowed landscape.

'I do,' she admitted freely. *'You pierce my soul. I am half agony, half hope...I have loved none bu*t *you.'*

It was at this critical juncture, as Margaret made this declaration, this deposition, of loving him and him alone, that she realised something, and she chided herself for forgetting it until now.

'Oh!' she gasped, a hand rising to cover her mouth and stifle the shame that blundered there.

'The man!' she exclaimed, her voice filled with urgency. 'The man at the station.'

John's lips tightened into an unyielding line. He too had forgotten all about the man, surprising, given that he had been obsessing over him for months.

'Yes,' he conceded with irrepressible terseness. 'I suppose we must discuss him,' he accepted reluctantly.

Margaret was grieved on his behalf, a desire scorching within her to be close to him so that he could feel the depth of her affection for him. She could not bear for him to look at her as he had that night at Outwood, his handsome face grazed with shock and suspicion.

'And we shall,' she vowed. 'But my dearest John, I cannot wait another second to tell you, to assure you, that it was not what you imagined or implied.'

'I know what I saw,' he asserted grimly.

'But that is just it. You do not!' she insisted, her small hands balling a knot of his shirt into her fist. 'You did not see what you thought you did.'

John was further thrown by her cryptic account, which offered no real transparency.

'Who was he, then?' the magistrate in him cross-examined, fearing her pretext, her plea of defence for her extraordinary actions. He could not begin to imagine how she could justify lying to the law, and worse, to him, but he would listen, he could at least give her that courtesy.

Margaret took a deep breath, uncertain of how to explain. 'He was, is... a relative.'

John stepped back in surprise. *'A relative?'*

Margaret nodded. 'Yes, and I promise you, most faithfully, that you do not need to fear him. But John, I cannot tell you of him alone. My father must be present. He has the right to hear of it and to be apprised of your admission into the inner sanctum of our family secrets.'

John was taken aback. Ah, so her father knew? Well, he reckoned this advocated some degree of relief, because he could not credit that Mr Hale would place his daughter in danger or allow her to step out with a reprobate. And secrets? What secrets? His mind swirled with fresh curiosity. Perhaps there lurked depths to this situation that he had not initially perceived, hinting at a complexity beyond his previous assumptions.

'You will know all soon, I promise. Only, for now, will you trust me?' she implored with disarming earnestness, her tone one of desperation. John gazed down at her with adoration, his conscience stirred by the fervour in her plea. How could he resist her impassioned entreaty, when every word she spoke seemed to tug at his heart?

Bowing his head, he nimbly brushed his lips against her temple, murmuring, 'Always,' and thus, he transformed his commitment into a tender, heartfelt assurance.

Nonetheless, as his lips traced a descending path toward hers, Margaret gracefully retreated, and she interrupted him by holding up a silencing hand.

'Before you, before we, do anything like that,' she said with an air of formality, 'I must remind you that you have spoken, and I listened, so now I ask that you listen to me,' she requested. He nodded respectfully, only mildly miffed that he had been thwarted in his attempt to kiss her, but his time would come soon, he was sure of it.

'I am sorry,' was all she said, and he regarded her with bewilderment.

'You are sorry?' he reiterated. He had certainly not been expecting her to say that.

'Yes,' she maintained. 'When I first came to Milton, I was culpable of pride, and of prejudice, and I was not fair to you. You are a good man, John, the very best of men, and I am only sorry that I never saw it sooner,' she lamented.

'And now?' he asked thickly.

Margaret's laughter bubbled forth with carefree ease, like a gentle melody of amusement mingled with reprieve. She was at last able to be entirely honest with him after months of concealment. Oh, the marvel of contemplating the magnitude of change that had taken place between them!

*'Every atom of your flesh is as dear to me as my own:
in pain and sickness it would still be dear. All my heart
is yours, sir: it belongs to you; and with you it would
remain, were fate to exile the rest of me from your
presence forever.'*

'Can you forgive me?' she beseeched. 'For being so
blind? For not seeing that my whole world was standing
right before me all this time?'

Upon this realisation, John could no longer hold back,
and a solitary tear charted a path down his cheek. He
had hardly cried since his father's passing, constantly
restraining his emotions. To feel had seemed weak. To
feel had seemed a waste of time. To feel had been to
admit defeat. Yet, within the verses of the Bible, he
found solace in the wisdom that there is indeed a time
to weep, and that time had arrived. No longer did he feel
the need to hold back. He embraced a readiness to feel,
his God-given right to feel.

'If you can forgive me in kind, for my lack of trust,
and my jealousy?' he bartered, his words catching in his
throat that was choked with passion.

A sunny smile of relief brightened her face, revealing
her gleaming teeth, and in that moment, he found
himself loving her more ardently than ever before. Her
unabashed display of happiness touched his heart,
forging an even stronger bond between them.

'All is forgiven and forgotten, for love keeps no
records of wrongs,' she reminded him. 'We know better
now. We know each other better now. And we can go
hand-in-hand into the future together, leaving our
inexperience, mistakes and insecurities where they
belong: in the past.'

John nodded solemnly and kissed her on the cheek. To be sure, she spoke the truth—their mistakes were meant to stay in the past: laid to rest and never again to resurface like ghosts. Still, the realisation struck him profoundly that they had finally reached an agreement to set aside their differences and conflicts, focusing solely on nurturing their love for each other.

'But there is a further matter which I must speak of, for there must be no doubt on this score,' Margaret stated. *'I am not an angel,' she asserted; 'and I will not be one till I die: I will be myself,'* she told him, because, while she loved him with all her heart, Margaret refused to change who she was for any man. 'John, I hear you speak of me as if I were some divine being, and it gladdens me to think you hold me in such high esteem, but *you must neither expect nor exact anything celestial of me—for you will not get it, any more than I shall get it of you: which I do not at all anticipate. I am not perfect, and nor are you. We must contend ourselves with that.'*

Though John did take her speech seriously, he was forced to smirk. Bless her heart! Despite her romantic eloquence, his beloved was still gently chiding him for not embodying perfection. John reflected that while this may have stung in the past, it held no power over him now, and he hoped she would never cease urging him to strive for his utmost. However, in reply to her claim of modesty, John tugged her closer, and with a husky growl, he emphasised, 'You are perfect to me.'

He never wanted her to doubt the depth of his adulation, not his Margaret, not his muse, not his own Venus de Milo.

Margaret bestowed upon him a shy smile. *'Perhaps it is our imperfections that make us so perfect for each other,'* she mused.

John reciprocated with a puckish grin of his own, soothing her with scouring nuzzles of his jaw, the bristles softly grazing her crown.

'I am sure you are entirely right. I think you were made for me and I for you,' he affirmed. 'Very well, I agree,' he granted. 'I think you could ask anything of me and I would do it without question,' he foretold. It was little enough to ask, after all, that he accept her for who and what she was, but he had one request to make of her in return.

'Only if you will promise me one thing,' he haggled. 'That you will never change.'

Margaret's face, which had been set in seriousness moments before, broke out into the loveliest smile.

'Aye,' said she, intentionally adopting his native tongue, 'that I shall.'

Feeling coy as she basked in his unapologetic approbation, she blushed. *'Now be sincere; did you admire me for my impertinence?'* she joshed, grateful that she had found a man who would accept her just the way she was.

He chortled. *'For the liveliness of your mind, I did,'* he replied, thankful beyond words that he had found a woman who could stimulate him as she did.

With his fingers massaging hers, John concluded his testimony, his pace and pitch steadily increasing.

'I know that I have made mistakes. I know that I have been a poor and pathetic excuse for a man and an even more contemptible excuse for a prospective husband.

Still, I pledge that if you will consent to let me love you and decide to join me in this life as my equivalent, my identical yet opposite counterpart, without whom I could not be whole, then I will spend the rest of my days labouring in devotion. I wish you to be my friend, my equal, and if you agree to be my wife, you will never doubt my love for you, for it will only grow as we do,' he swore, his voice now clotted with a desperate need for her to understand.

'God alone knows how we got here. How a man like me could ever have succeeded in winning a woman like you. No!' he stopped suddenly. 'Not win. You are not a prize or possession. *Win over*,' he corrected. 'How is it that we were ever allowed to meet? How a country rose could have bloomed in the embrace of a city thorn. I do not know about these things, the science that makes it possible or the conviction that rationalises it, and I do not care. All I know is that *I ask you to pass through life at my side—to be my second self and best earthly companion.* If you say yes, we shall never again have to think of what it is to be a man or a woman, for we shall be united as one being, you and I,' he promised.

Then, bending down, he took a knee. 'There, Margaret Hale, you have brought me to my knees,' he smirked like a schoolboy, revelling in her amusement to see him do so. 'So tell me, once and for all, will you do me the honour of becoming my wife?'

Her countenance, radiant with a semblance of warmth, conveyed a message that words need not hurry; the manifest bond between them spoke volumes. In that deferred moment, their rapport blossomed, as if the cosmos itself paused to witness the beauty of two souls converging in the poetry of love.

'Of course I will,' she replied at once, for it was the easiest question she had ever been asked.

The happiness which this reply produced was such as he had probably never felt before, and he expressed himself on the occasion as sensibly and as warmly as a man violently in love can be supposed to do. Had Margaret *been able to encounter his eyes, she might have seen how well the expression of heartfelt delight diffused over his face became him; but, though she could not look, she could listen, and he told her of feelings which, in proving of what importance she was to him, made his affection every moment more valuable.*

Quite overcome by the events of the day, Margaret burrowed her head against his chest and nestled there, in the comfort of her new home, listening to the hastening rhythm of his heart. It had been a long day, and now she wanted to rest in the assurance of his love. As carefully as he could, John positioned Margaret to make her more comfortable and wrapped his arms tightly around her, as if to shelter her in a historic circle of worship, this safehold that was built just for her. Even so, much to his disbelief, Margaret, this sovereign creature, did not fight him, instead, she just allowed him to care for her. *It was too delicious to feel her soft cheek against his, for him to wish to see either deep blushes or loving eyes.*

But as John stood there, swaying on the spot, Margaret cocooned against his chest, he smiled at a memory that came flooding back to him. Shifting her hands from the orb they had formed on his front, John lifted them and set them around his neck. There he closed his eyes and relished the feeling, his mind returning to that chaotic interim when Margaret had flung her arms around him in defence before the rioters, and how he, consumed by anxiety for her safety, had not allowed himself the chance to savour the sensation, even though despite the disorientating drama of those few seconds, John had still acutely felt her touch. Oh, how John had wished with all his might at that moment that Margaret had hurled her arms around him through choice and not out of necessity. Yet now, such longing faded away into insignificance, because here she was again, with no threat of terror to overrule her actions, her arms around his neck of their own free accord, and there he hoped they would remain for the rest of their days.

Overwhelmed with emotion, John stepped away from her for a moment, briefly mourning the temporary loss of her immediate presence. The thought of being so close to her was too much. He feared he might hold her too forcefully and break her with the strength of not only his body but his irrepressible passion. Nevertheless, he swiftly returned from his desk drawer, cradling a book—the tome a lone relic from his youth, a coming-of-age gift from his father shortly before he died. This particular book safeguarded a treasure pressed between its pages, a single yellow rose from Helstone entangled with a thorn, just as he had said, the two inseparable, and he now offered it to her. A soft laugh escaped her lips, her eyes aglow with ironic delight as she gently accepted the flower. In shy response, Margaret revealed from her pocket his handkerchief, which he dotingly accepted. She then presented him with a white material rose, confessing that she had fashioned it from cotton found in his factory after her first visit there. She had not known at the time why, but as she walked through the hectic, humming walkways of Marlborough Mills, she had been fascinated, somehow knowing that this place would be inherent to her future. The exchange of these symbolic buds transformed into a tangible representation of their interlaced histories and the convergence of their worlds, the unfolding beauty of their relationship was akin to the delicate petals of a flowering bud that was soft, fragrant and open to the world, all the while joined with its resilient friend that may have appeared as a barb to the naked eye, but in truth, it was a pillar of strength, the spine of their interleaved growth. It was the marriage of the south and the north.

It was then that John noticed the tears rolling down her face, and he felt a pang of panic grip him.

'Why are you crying, dear heart?' he agonised, his thumb gently kneading her cheek and sweeping to wipe them away, the droplets of water at once soaking his jacket and seeping below onto his shirt, his clothes as proud as punch at being permitted to be the ones to dry her sorrows.

'Oh, do not worry. They are tears of joy, not sadness, and one cannot wish away tears of joy,' she reassured him. 'It is just that I suppose now *I must learn to be content with being happier than I deserve.*'

'You and I both,' he replied, the remnants of their jubilant weeping baptising them as if they were born anew as one. 'Then again, after all we have separately endured so far in the prologue of our lives; after all that we have faced, conquered and survived, I think we have earned just a little happiness all of our own.'

'That is a lovely thought, however,' pondered Margaret with her charitable mind, 'is happiness something anyone truly earns? Is it not something every person on this earth should be entitled to?'

'Aye, love, as always, you are right,' he conceded, loving her more than ever for her unyielding compassion that always thought of others before herself.

In that contemplative interval, they each realised that sometimes happiness exceeds what one believes one deserves and defies any baseless sense of worthiness.

'What happens now?' she asked, the realisation dawning that, at some point, they would have to depart from the shelter of their newfound haven, their nest in each other's arms.

John raised Margaret's head, and gazing at her intently, he sought permission to do what he had wanted to since the first day they met. With his eyes swooping to her lips, she understood his plea, but with a gentle nod, she was the one to reach up, and with the intrepid courage that was innate to her independent spirit, she placed her lips upon his.

John sucked in a sharp intake of breath. It was as if the world had stopped still, and with slow, deliberate tenderness, he kissed her for the first time, their innocent mouths melding as one, their virgin lips consecrating their love. It felt like it lasted forever, but it must have been no more than minutes, the pair lost in their love for one another, only, they were not lost, they had found their passion, their purpose, their partner.

'Go back to your father's house, just for now,' he said in answer to her question. 'I shall come to you directly,' he promised, thinking how they soon would never be parted and be always together. 'The play that has taken place here today has almost reached its end, there is just one final scene to perform before the curtain falls, and I must be the one to see our audience out.'

Chapter Twenty

Adieu

The brisk northern wind whispered through the narrow streets of Milton as Margaret emerged from the towering gates of Marlborough Mills. The cobblestone yard bore witness to her silent reverie as she left the place that would soon be her home, her gaze glancing back to take in the wonder of her happiness, her cheeks rosy with the sincere glow of contentment. The setting sun warmed her, and it made her smile to think how curious fate could be, what an unpredictable, ungovernable force it was, for when she had awoken this morning to that same sun, never could she have believed, never could she have dreamed, that she would be blessed with the love of a good man, and not only that, but the very best man who had ever lived.

She then thought the land enchanted into everlasting brightness and happiness; she fancied, then, that into a

*region so lovely no bale or woe could enter, but would
be charmed away and disappear before the sight of the
glorious guardian,* the Darkshire mountains that stood
majestically in the distance, soaring above the factory
chimneys in their proud permanence, a melding of old
and new, nature and industry. *Now she knew the truth,
that earth has no barrier which avails against agony.*

The sky above, adorned with hues of twilight, seemed
to reflect the kaleidoscope of sentiments absorbed by
her heart, one that was now at peace, though it danced
in tandem with the lightness of her steps, for within its
chambers echoed the blissful revelation that John, the
master of this little world, harboured a true affection for
her. She had once thought him selfish and severe,
incapable of thinking in terms other than buying or
selling, but oh, how wrong she had been. He was a man
of great honour, intelligence and sensitivity, and she
vowed to spend the rest of her life – *no*, the rest of *their*
lives together, making him feel as safe and treasured as
he made her feel. Their love a solid, sacred ground.

Margaret's testimony washed over her like a gentle
wave of empowerment. While she might not fit the
traditional mould of a heroine, today, she embraced her
own narrative with pride. At this moment, she
embodied the essence of strength and resilience.

Reflecting on the stories that shaped her journey,
Margaret saw them as intricate maps guiding her
through life's labyrinth. Each tale, penned by the
courageous voices of women before her, served as a
beacon of inspiration. They whispered secrets of self-
discovery, urging her to embrace authenticity and
vulnerability.

In the embryonic whispers and loud roars of those stories, Margaret found her own voice. They were more than just words on a page; they were love letters penned by history's female writers, urging her to claim her place in the world. With every turn of the page, they imparted lessons of growth and promise, affirming that with an unshakable belief in oneself, anyone can become the protagonist of their own narrative.

It was as Margaret turned a corner, exiting this chapter of her story and ready to step boldly onto the parchment of an unwritten future, that I, your narrator, must say farewell.

But, before we bid adieu to our lovers, poised at the threshold of their shared journey, let me express my deepest gratitude for your companionship within these pages. In this humble tale of maturity, self-discovery, and womanhood, may you find solace, inspiration, and the balm of kindred spirits. The tale of Margaret Hale and John Thornton, united with fibres of hope and faith, revealed itself to be a testament to the transformative nature of a love that defies all and surmounts the impediments of class and context, removing the barriers of time and text. And, it is here that I confide, I confess, my identity, and perhaps reveal how I came to know so much about our friends' story and justify why I should care about them so dearly. Therefore, with my concluding meeting of paper and ink, I declare to you, with a heart overflowing with joy:

Reader, I married him.

The End

A Gaskell, Austen and Brontë Crossover

The Three Witches

Damn Her And Her Fine Eyes!

Caroline Bingley's Story

As Caroline Bingley sat at the breakfast table of her Chelsea house, nibbling crossly at the corner of a crumpet that had, much to her irritation, not been toasted to her exact specifications, she cast a disdainful glance at the window where the rain lashed, wiggling down the panes like a cluster of translucent worms in a race. A loathing for rain gripped her; it had a knack for spoiling the exquisite hems of her silken gowns. To compound matters, the inclement weather dampened the likelihood of a certain gentleman making social calls when in town, meaning that he was less likely to find the opportunity or impulse to request her hand in marriage.

Nevertheless, at least she could find some slight solace in the fact that she was in London, once again supplanted in civilisation. The busy thoroughfare outside, with its harried hum, provided a congenial symphony of urban sophistication that matched the melody of her character. She admired the symmetry and uniformity of cities, the way they edited disorder, eradicated it, rather, and corrected it with exactness in the form of straight streets and shiny marble buildings. Indeed, Caroline found relief in the cacophony, grateful for the absence of the insufferable chirping that inundated the trees around Netherfield Park. Those horrid little birds, with their audacious insolence, seemed to have claimed the wildlife-infested land as their own, as if they held some preposterous entitlement to the grounds that predated and predestined hers.

'Ugh! Nature!' she exclaimed with an air of exasperation, her sensibilities offended by the very idea of such insubordination. Was there ever anything more unnatural? Caroline's contemplation was accompanied by a contemptuous grimace that etched itself upon her refined features and attempted to sink into her skin as wrinkles set in stone. In her discerning estimation, nature appeared as an unwelcome intrusion into the cultivated realm of elegance she sought to establish. The very notion of untamed creatures asserting their presence in domains of genteel living struck her as a direct affront to the principles of propriety she held dear. Moreover, the expansive grounds provided ample space for walking, a most irksome exercise. Legs had been made by God to wear fine silken stockings, *not*, to be used for traipsing about. Besides, it afforded obstinate and headstrong women, who refused to adhere to conventional decorum, the freedom to wander and captivate the notice of eligible bachelors.

Yes, nature should be kept in its place.

With a dismissive shake of her head, Caroline deftly dabbed at her mouth to rid it of the lingering smears of jam and put her mind to contemplating much pleasanter concerns. Pondering the allocation of her precious time, she resolved to dedicate it exclusively to the most superior pursuits. Perhaps a leisurely shopping expedition, a scenic drive through St James's Park, or the attendance of an elegant luncheon with the potential for disseminating some tastefully malicious gossip. After all, *for what do we live, but to make sport for our neighbours, and laugh at them in our turn?* Though, Caroline would personally omit any suggestion that she could ever make sport for others, for one so exemplary as she could only be talked of with the utmost admiration, and, of course, envy.

Yet, the most alluring prospect of all, was the idea of reclining on her sumptuous settee, allowing her thoughts to luxuriate in contemplation of the handsome Fitzwilliam Darcy and the abundance of his marvellous wealth. In this quest for elevated indulgence, Caroline envisioned her day unfolding with an exquisite fantasy.

Cue breathy sigh.

In Caroline's case, the saying was truer than true: *A lady's imagination is very rapid; it jumps from admiration to love, from love to matrimony in a moment.*

As she thought this most deliciously delightful thought, her quixotic musings were interrupted as the door opened abruptly, and her brother marched right on in, as if he owned the place, even if he did, in fact, own the place. Caroline's giddy grin flopped into a frown.

'Charles,' she nipped, declining him the courtesy of a "good morning," and doing her best to perfect her pitch so that it sounded as peeved as possible, a proficient art that any finishing school worth its salt would teach a respectable young lady, and needless to say, Caroline Bingley was the very best there ever was at spouting a cynical and sneering jibe.

However, much to her dissatisfaction, her brother was not the least bit perturbed by her artful attempt at rudeness, and as she looked up, a disgruntled Caroline discerned the sparkle in his irritatingly lively eyes, his cheeks pink and plump, just like a baby's bottom. With her flawless skin turning scarlet in provocation, Caroline scowled, and if one listened carefully, then one would swear that she snarled too.

'What is the matter with you?' she bit out with a wasp-like sting, sipping her coffee and swirling the tart brew around her mouth. Caroline was never happy with her brother at the best of times, but she had made a vow to permanently dislike him -no, wait, detest him, - ever since he had become engaged to that Bennet creature and thus degraded the Bingley name by association. What would people think of them? He was entering into a marriage with a family lacking any distinguished pedigree, accompanied by a mother of unapologetic vulgarity and sisters spanning the spectrum from mind-numbingly mundane to outrageously shocking. His ill-advised match (to put it mildly), blatantly invited the scrutiny of public opinion.

As Charles roamed back and forth with eager agitation, his curly hair caught the rays of the sun which shone through the window, affecting the red strands upon his head to gleam like fine wires of copper -how common! With her narrowed eyes tracking him as he paced about the lavishly decorated morning room like a buffoon, practically prancing as he went, Caroline grumbled, a slight growl seeping out from between her gritted (yet perfectly straight and white), teeth.

Charles, exuding an unrestrained exuberance akin to a poorly trained puppy, could hardly contain the bubbling excitement coursing through him from tip to toe. As he clapped his hands and licked his lips, the man energetically rolled on the balls of his feet, preparing to unleash his most remarkable announcement with an infectious zeal that promised to captivate the attention of his sibling.

'I have something to tell you,' he started, his face awash with animation. 'It is about our dear friend, Darcy.'

Caroline, who had been drinking her coffee, suddenly stopped and stilled, a generous mouthful of hot, brown, sugary liquid now stuck in her gossiping mouth while she waited with bated breath.

Oh! What was this? The tantalising mystery hung in the air, supplemented by a cascade of questions. Was it something truly ominous? Was Mr Darcy unwell, or worse, involved in an accident that had permanently disfigured his handsome face? The belief seemed implausible and it did not tally with her brother's jovial demeanour. It had to be something delightful, Caroline reassured herself. Could it be that his horrid aunt had passed away, leaving him a substantial fortune and the grand estate of Rosings Park? Or, perhaps he had finally persuaded Charles to relinquish his intentions of marrying Jane Bennet and instead consider uniting with Mr Darcy's sister, Georgiana? The prospect of such a twist in fate enthralled Caroline, and she found herself favouring the notion.

'You will never guess!' he taunted good-naturedly.

Good heavens! What could it possibly be, thought she?!

Charles was grinning from ear to ear like a Cheshire Cat who had well and truly got his cream, and after letting out a strident chuckle of joy, one which can only derive from a person with the most gentle and generous of hearts, he cheerfully revealed, 'Why, he is engaged to be married!'

In a mere twinkling of an eye, Caroline spat out her coffee, the contents spilling out, rather like...well, I am sorry to have to say it and be so uncouth (especially over the breakfast table), but rather like an animal spraying its...well, you know what.

Coughing and spluttering, Caroline nearly choked, her countenance flushing a vivid hue resembling rhubarb.

'*Engaged*!' she blustered, the word struggling to escape, its two syllables momentarily lodged in the recesses of her throat, threatening to do her in.

Charles' head bobbed with such fervour that it seemed a marvel it did not dislodge from its figurative perch altogether. The vigour of his nodding left Caroline feeling distinctly woozy.

'Yes!' he confirmed merrily. 'Is it not wonderful? And to think, he and I will be like brothers since we shall marry two sisters, the dearest ladies in all the world, Jane and Elizabeth Bennet!' he cried, overjoyed by this most agreeable turn of events.

'Oh! I must go and tell Louisa!' he said, opening the door and skidding off down the hallway to speak with his other sister.

Left alone once more, Caroline sat there in stunned silence, her mind seething, pounding in the stillness of her solitude. Clutching onto the coffee cup which still reposed in her well-polished hand, she tightened her grip, and before she knew it, the fine china had shattered, sending fragments of Royal Doulton across the table in a furious frenzy. As these pent-up passions erupted within, Caroline found herself utterly devastated. Her nostrils flared, her eyes bulged, and her chest heaved with the intensity of the agitation she felt, not to forget the mephitic anger. The world around her seemed to blur as her mind reeled from the overwhelming spate of feelings. In a moment of unbridled release, all she could do was unleash the loudest and most unladylike scream that had ever escaped her pretty yet petty lips.

The reverberations of her shriek boomed through the room, setting the delicate glass of the windows aquiver, causing the chandelier to sway precariously, and even affecting the water goblets on the table to shudder in fright. The physical manifestations of her emotional outburst mirrored the chaos she suppressed inside, leaving an aftermath of trembling fragility in the once-stately room.

She was experiencing not only humiliation but, on a deeper level, a twinge of heartbreak. Had she ever genuinely loved Mr Darcy? Perhaps not, but she desired him fervently, making the prospect of him marrying another, especially someone as unsuitable and wholly unexpected as Elizabeth Bennet, particularly painful. The impulse to cry overtook her, a tumultuous wave labouring to breach the walls of her composure. With unyielding determination, she resisted, refusing to yield to the dander that loomed. How could she see him again after this? And, perhaps more daunting still, how could she face herself? The relics of her broken aspirations recoiled and cowered in her wake, casting shadows over the demoralising prospect of a fractured self-image that was beyond repair. She would never be a Darcy. She would never live at Pemberley. And worst of all, she would never have ten thousand a year.

Caroline remained unmarried, never encountering a man who could command her admiration as Mr Darcy had. On the rare occasions when she approached the brink of such a connection, her spiteful tongue promptly repelled any potential suitors. They considered her an embittered spinster, which was exactly what she was. Gradually, even her sister wearied of her escalating animosity. She found herself unable to visit her brother, whose happiness had flourished in stark contrast to her own diminishing prospects. His joy had become entangled with the Bennet family, a name she abhorred. *There is, in every disposition a tendency to some particular evil, a natural defect, which not even the best education can overcome. And her defect was a propensity to hate everybody.*

Over the passing years, Caroline withdrew into a reclusive existence, her mind even going so far as to fondly recall her days at Netherfield, wondering how different everything could have been if she had simply made peace with those around her. Still, the resentment continued to poison her gradually. Each encounter with a woman of striking beauty, who thought and spoke her mind, evoked an involuntary hiss, a testament to the venom that had bled into her solitary existence, and she would be known to boo: 'Damn her and her fine eyes!'

I Am Not An Angel

Blanche Ingram's Story

Agitated, Blanche Ingram paced the expanse of the grand drawing room of her family's Yorkshire estate, her manner ominously similar to a tiger locked in a cage, ready to strike out at any moment. The ornate clock on the mantelpiece marked the passage of time with each restless second, its resonance seemingly antagonising her mounting impatience, mocking her with the tick-tock click of its mechanical tongue. She had never been a patient person, her lack of tolerance abetted by the fact that her every whim and fancy had been indulged immediately since she was old enough to point and give orders. However, today, her fortitude was being sorely tested. Exhaling sharply, Blanche chastised herself for indulging in such frivolous thoughts, staunchly rejecting the disquieting possibility that had unexpectedly invaded her consciousness, unsettling her profoundly, just moments after her morning ride and upsetting the balance of her entire day. It simply could not be true, and she would not let it be so!

At last, the door creaked open, and Blanche's younger sister, Henriette, appeared with a hesitant smile that was pitiful in its masquerade. Blanche's expression turned icy, and her eyes fixated on every twitch of Henriette's manner, struggling to draw any intelligence out of her. It was like drawing blood from a stone, something she would be hurling if she did not get answers soon.

'Well? What news do you bring?' Blanche interrogated, her tone akin to the regalness of a queen addressing a lowly courtier. Nevertheless, there was an unmissable edge to her voice, a nervous convulsion that she could not suppress.

Her sister faltered for a trice before composing herself. After the silence between them lingered awkwardly, agonisingly suffocating, as a corset is around bruised ribs, Blanche could not stand it any longer.

'Speak!' she demanded, her voice like a whip that sliced through the air. 'Out with it!'

'Blanche,' Henriette started with discernible wariness, this alone being enough to arouse suspicion. 'I heard it from the maids in the kitchen: Mr Rochester *is* to marry Jane Eyre.' Blanche was struck with a swell of shock, her mind suddenly shrouded in a thick, disorientating fog of incomprehension. She stood as still as a statue rendered of the harshest stone, unable to process the erratic emotions coursing through her. Seeking some semblance of control, she scrunched her hands tightly behind her back, feeling her nails dig into her palms as if trying to ground herself against the tangle of thoughts howling in her breast. She bit her lip as she felt a thin river of red trickling down her fingers. With a steadying breath, she tried to dispel her distress, but it was no use. As soon as Henriette had mentioned that woman-*that thing!-,* everything seemed to dissolve around her, all her hopes, all her expectations, all she had ever known.

Jane Eyre?

'The governess?' Blanche hissed, her tongue quivering like that of a snake, her voice laced with disdain as if the word were tainted with a bitter tang.

So, she had been right. The clandestine glances the pair had shared had not escaped her notice. At first, Blanche had assumed that Mr Rochester was perhaps using the governess's services in a way that the master of the house was entitled to, and, as such, there was a mild, pitiful fondness between them. But then, she had seen them, or thought she saw them, from afar as she rode past the hall one day, the two of them walking arm-in-arm, their heads bent together in intimate conversation. It had been so surprising, so shocking, that Blanche had almost been thrown from her horse, but she had quickly cantered away and told herself that she was imagining things, the heat of the English summer befuddling her senses.

But, as it turned out, she had been right.

Could it be true? That plain, insipid mouse, was going to be the mistress of Thornfield Hall? Blanche's eyes widened with the disbelief flooding through her veins, replacing her blood as her vital life force. The colour drained from her typically fair complexion, leaving her looking ghostly pale, except for the angry splotches of scarlet on her cheeks. She could feel her features contorting into an expression of indignation, giving her a blotched, bloated appearance that was a far cry from her usual beauty. Blanche shook her head adamantly, her blonde curls bouncing in their tight ringlets.

'No, it cannot be so. How on earth did she manage to ensnare him? It's preposterous! I will not believe it! It must be no more than gossip! Rumours spread by those with nothing better to speak of!'

Her sister nibbled nervously on the corner of her lip, knowing her elder sibling's vanity all too well.

'It seems he has quite fallen in love with her, Blanche. They are to be married in a fortnight,' she foretold.

Blanche could feel the heat rising within her, a potent, poisonous combination of wrath and mortification. How could Mr Rochester, a man of wealth and stature, choose such a drab creature as that over the refined and accomplished Blanche Ingram, the most desirable young lady in the county? The injustice of it all charred like inflamed bile in her chest, her heart, if she even possessed such a human, humane entity, clenching painfully in its bony confine.

If only Mr Rochester had been wiser, he may have realised it was foolish, dangerous, even, to toy with a woman such as Blanche Ingram. *It does good to no woman to be flattered [by a man] who does not intend to marry her; and it is madness in all women to let a secret love kindle within them, which, if unreturned and unknown, must devour the life that feeds it; and, if discovered and responded to, must lead, ignis-fatuus-like, into miry wilds whence there is no extrication.*

'All I can think is that he must be quite mad,' Blanche insisted, rubbing her temple, for her head now ached something dreadful. 'To think that he would choose a servant over me!' she scoffed. 'It is inconceivable!'

Unknown to Blanche, her words, though untrue, would prove to be prophetic, for at this point, she, nor others of Mr Rochester's acquaintance knew of his dark secret, that he kept a wife, a mad woman, in his attic. Once this revelation had become public knowledge, Blanche had been naturally horrified. Nevertheless, she had swiftly used it as a further reason to insist that he must be disturbed, as if mental illness were catching. Henriette shifted uncomfortably, caught in the inner struggle between her allegiance to her sister and the unyielding pull of the truth. The weight of this internal conflict lingered in her gaze, revealing the complex web of emotions weaving through her as she grappled with the diplomatic balance between loyalty and honesty.

'Perhaps there is something about Miss Eyre that captivated him,' she suggested, remembering the way he had looked at the governess during a recent dinner party they had all attended, his eyes gleaming with awe and admiration as they flitted in constant fascination towards the unassuming yet profound young woman who had watched them from the wings. Her presence had been ethereal, reserved yet modestly mesmeric. She now recalled that he had especially requested that the quiet governess join them after dinner, a curious fancy, she had thought at the time, and now she understood why. He could not bear to be parted from her.

'Love is a mysterious thing, after all,' she said with a soft smile, silently praying she would one day find a man who loved her so.

Blanche sneered at the notion. '*Love*?! What does love have to do with it? Marriage should not be built on something as changeable as love!' she decreed. 'Love is fictional. Society. Status. These are what bring us stability. These are what remain when our looks fade and men look elsewhere and cast us aside.'

Blanche refused to have a marriage like that of her parents, one where the woman was meek and the man had turned to someone more impressive for companionship.

Her sister let out a resigned sigh, fully aware that endeavouring to reason with her in such moments was as futile as trying to fly. Blanche, driven by her pride, would remain oblivious to the concept that someone might be prized for their character rather than their riches or lineage. Despite numerous attempts to broaden her perspective, Blanche's stubborn convictions persisted, casting a gloom over the possibility of valuing true worth beyond superficial credentials. Though it was difficult to admit, her sister accepted that there was a barrenness to Blanche, a hollowed-out shell where her soul ought to have been. Her sister often wondered, worried, whether it would ever be filled, or whether, as she feared, it would continue to grow into a chasm that consumed her, rotting her gradually, like a cavity willowing away a tooth.

As the days passed, Blanche's hostility only intensified. She watched with seething jealousy as the household prepared for the approaching nuptials of Mr Rochester and Jane Eyre, the world around her a flurry of contentment. The murmurs of the town's tittle-tattle reached her ears of how happy the couple were, of how perfect they seemed for one another regardless of their differences in circumstance, each stray word adding fuel to the fiery tempest of her ire.

Her despair only gained a brief respite of relief, when, much to the shock of all who were privy to the scandal, it proved that the master was already married, and in the aftermath of his devious plan to commit bigamy, the governess had fled, presumed never to return. Nevertheless, fate, that old romantic, intervened, and after a fire that devastated Thornfield Hall, his unfortunate wife died, and, left as a blind and broken invalid, Blanche judged that he had been righteously punished for snubbing her. However, loneliness was not to be his calling, for it was not long before his faithful love returned, promising to love him unconditionally and eternally.

On the eve of the long-awaited wedding, one that finally took place despite the impediments that life had thrown in the path of the bride and groom, Blanche stood by the window, surveying the sun as it dipped below the horizon. As the orange star set, her sister entered the room with a tentative expression. Blanche's resentful gaze met her sister's anxious eyes, and in that charged moment, the air in the room seemed to fizzle with an implicit, smothering tension. The impending union had become not just a thorn in Blanche's side, but a relentless typhoon that threatened to engulf her and drag her down into the depths of obsessive jealousy.

'Blanche, I understand your disappointment, but dwelling on this will only bring you further anguish,' her sister urged. 'Forget him. Forget her. Find your own happiness, I beg of you.'

'No, sister! *I am not an angel*, she asserted; '*and I will not be one till I die: I will be myself*. I am a woman in all her glory, and a woman scorned is what I am! I will not be defeated by some insignificant nymph,' Blanche bit back with the ferocity of an injured wolf. 'Mr Rochester may have made a foolish choice, but I will not let that define my future. From this day on, I vow never to let another woman, especially a nobody, get in my way of making a fine match. I will marry a man of prominence, I will be beloved, and I will do whatever it takes to secure my place in society.'

At this, Henriette retreated, accepting with sadness that the battle was lost. She understood, all too easily, the wilful resolve engraved in her sister's eyes, those specks of spite that danced upon her iris like flecks of dust from crumbled dreams. She knew that Blanche was not one to be easily swayed once her mind was set, so she left her alone, the aura of her sister's fury creating a permanent barrier between them from that day on.

From that moment, Blanche clung to her promise to herself, determined to rise above the humiliation and secure a future that would obliterate the triumph of another from her mind forever. In the months that followed, Blanche immersed herself in the social season, attending every event in the hope of attracting a suitor of significant standing. She adorned herself in the most fashionable gowns, her demeanour exuding an air of unapproachable superiority. In this façade, Blanche became the epitome of grace and charm, masking the turmoil that devoured her. She entertained countless followers, but her heart was no longer in the pursuit of genuine affection. It was a game of one-upmanship, a mêlée to prove to herself and society that she was worthy of a match that would erase the memory of her degradation.

However, despite her efforts, Blanche found herself haunted by the ghost of her disgrace. The vaguest mention of the subject was enough to send a chill down her spine. She became increasingly consumed with unravelling the mystery of Jane's allure, determined to understand what had influenced a man of Mr Rochester's mysterious appeal. This preoccupation reigned supreme over her pleasure in life, and perhaps, even her sanity.

As the years passed, Blanche's relentless search for validation took its toll. Despite marrying into affluence, she found herself living in a gilded cage, surrounded by opulence but devoid of true serenity and substance.

In the end, Blanche Ingram became a cautionary tale among the elite, a woman who had sacrificed love for the sake of approval. The drawing room of her family estate, once filled with the promises of a glittering future, now resonated with the meaningless hark of a victory that had ultimately left her empty and unfulfilled. The echoes of her oath rumbled through her lonely castle on the moors, a constant reminder of the lengths she had gone to escape the shadow of Jane Eyre.

The Ice Queen

Ann Latimer's Story

The Swiss finishing school nestled in the Alps, decorated in pure, pristine white snow, as pure as the virginal ladies who dwelt within, was where the ice queen was formed. The secluded chateau was a beacon of refinement that called to the families of the newly rich, inviting them to send their daughters to be finished and ready to send out into society as docile, dutiful dolls to dangle off the arms of their future husbands.

It was a place where girls like Ann Latimer sought to not only polish their manners but also discover that indefinable charm that would make them the epitome of grace, the woman out of all of the women he could choose from, that a man would wish to be his wife. Ann, with her blonde hair and serene grey eyes, stood out amongst her fellow schoolgirls, her delicate features hinting at a vulnerability that belied her seemingly composed exterior. She was a jovial soul, gentle, and full of hope. And, oh, how she loved to talk.

It was against this backdrop that Ann met John Willoughby, the son of one of the patrons. He was a striking young man, so impressive, in fact, that one would think he had stepped right out of a novel. He was adept at giving charming compliments, his disarming gaze was like a ray of sunshine, and if he should look at you, your heart would be sure to flutter in your breast with a swoon. Tall and confident, with a gleam in his hazel eyes, John possessed the kind of charisma that drew people in effortlessly.

They had first encountered one another at a ball, and under a canopy of twinkling stars, they had embraced, spinning and swaying as one, their awe-struck shyness speaking for itself and speaking volumes as they danced the night away.

Ann, in her endearing unworldliness, found herself utterly captivated by his innate magnetism. Their acquaintance blossomed into companionship during afternoon strolls through the snow-covered grounds. John's words dripped from his lips with the pleasantness of golden honey, and he spoke of a tenderness so profound that it seemed to reach higher than the very mountains that surrounded them, touching the heavens with its celestial poetry. Ann, with her romantic sensitivities, was enchanted, and she found herself quite hopelessly in love.

As winter turned to spring, the two became inseparable. Ann's laughter was like sweet music as she shared her heart's most sacred confidences with John amidst the blooming flowers of the Swiss countryside, the vivid petals peeking open to smile at them coyly. The school hummed with excited whispers of their romance. Much to her delight, Ann became the affectionate envy of all the other girls, for it seemed that she had truly found the love story she had always wished-for, ever since she was a child, and her mother had told her she was not pretty enough to ever find true happiness.

However, unbeknownst to Ann, the charming John harboured a dark secret. His affections were not stirred by love but were goaded by a more sinister motive. In the dimly lit nooks of the school grounds, he would converse with a mysterious stranger, a crook, a man with a shadowed face, discussing a plan that would ultimately shatter Ann's world. It was one evening when she was hidden behind shelves of leather-bound books, that Ann heard voices drifting up from beneath an open window, and leaning closer, she listened as John spoke of an impending fortune that would come his way.

'She believes every word, the stupid child. Once we marry, her father will bestow a generous dowry on her that I will seize at once, and when he dies, I will have the lot,' John sneered, his brashness a repugnant edge that raked against their uplifting surroundings.

'And will it be enough to pay off your debts?' the reprobate interrogated with a hoarse voice that was lined with whisky.

'Yes, and more!' John replied with scorn. 'I will be as rich as Croesus!'

'And what of the girl?' questioned his friend, a loathsome jeer strumming his husky throat.

'I do not care!' scoffed John without remorse. 'She will be of no further use to me. I will leave her in her drab little Milton, that dreary smog-ridden backwater and I will go to the continent, to civilisation, and amuse myself with drink, cards and women, then I will never have to see her plain face again.'

The two men shared a mocking, sickly laugh that ricochetted in the courtyard, amplifying their malice.

Ann's breath mingled with the cold wind of the night and caught sharply between her ribs as it sought to choke her. No! It could not be! The man she had given her heart to, the one who had promised her devotion as timeless as the snow-capped peaks, was nothing more than a charlatan. His intentions were as cold as the Swiss air, and the reality of his deceit seeped into her very soul, a once fiery passion that had crumbled into ice.

The days that followed were a blur for Ann. The vibrant colours of the landscape faded into muted sepia, mirroring the despair within. She struggled to maintain appearances, attending her lessons with a desolate spirit, her sparkling eyes of days gone by now dulled by the dusk of betrayal.

Word of Ann's heartbreak spread through the school like wildfire. The sympathetic glances and hushed chattering that followed her every move became a constant reminder of the tenderness she had lost and the bitter sting of humiliation that would forever plague her. She bore the scratches of her experiences, marked by the trials that had shaped her. Her youth was tainted, her innocence scarred. She was *so tired - so tired of being whirled on through all these phases of her life, in which nothing abides by her, no creature, no place; it is like the circle in which the victims of earthly passion eddy continually.*

In the loneliness of her room, Ann wrote letters to her father, her pen becoming the vessel of pain as she attempted to make sense of her crushed faith in the legitimacy of love that lay in John's wake. However, she could not adequately express her sorrow, nor could she bear to confide her indefensible foolishness, and so, Ann, a formerly forthcoming, effervescent essence, dwindled into silence, a subdued figurine who hardly ever spoke, and she retreated further and further into herself.

The final day at finishing school arrived, denoted by tearful farewells and promises of everlasting friendship. Ann, however, stood apart, a solitary figure on the balcony, gazing at the mountains that had witnessed the unravelling of her dreams. As the school gates closed behind her, Ann carried the burden of her wearied heart back to England, believing with inconsolable finality that her hopes for happiness were blighted, her future disfigured, and her heart, eternally broken.

'But the future must be met, however stern and iron it be,' she whispered to herself as her past faded into view.

The steam engine screeched as it chugged across the country, carrying Ann back to Milton, the town of her birth. Standing on the platform of the busy railway station of Outwood, the smoke billowing from the factories in the background, her gloved hands clutched the edges of her travelling cloak as she prayed that this next chapter of her life would be kinder than the last.

'Come! Poor little heart! Be cheery and brave,' she told herself. *'We'll be a great deal to one another, if we are thrown off and left desolate.'*

Her resolve was firm, remembering the promise she had made her mother, that one day she would return in triumph, a daughter she could finally be proud of, a member of the esteemed cotton merchant class, taking up her rightful place as a leading lady of Darkshire.

As a child, Ann's father had not been the banker of prominence he was now, so she had grown up watching the grandeur of the city's emerging elite from a distance. Their elegant houses and opulent lifestyles fuelled her aspirations. She vowed to elevate herself, to be crowned the diamond of Milton society. And, in her mind, there was no one more fitting to share that life with than John Thornton, the prominent mill master, and, more importantly, a man who could not have been further removed in nature from John Willoughby. Unlike his peers, he was young, energetic, serious, and intelligent. What was more, Ann admired him greatly, and there was something in the assurance of his dependable nature that made her believe he would be a faithful husband, and perhaps, one day, her wounds would heal. Thus, with scarcely a moment's pause, Ann promptly turned her attentiveness towards capturing the attention, and, in time, affections, of John Thornton.

Nevertheless, life has a way of taking us by the hand and leading us down unexpected and unfamiliar paths. So it was in this vein that Ann's vision of her providence took a surprising turn. While she had firmly believed that she was qualified in every way to be the perfect bride for him, what with being native to Milton, accomplished, nice-looking and reserved, she quickly found that his love was not only elusive but lay in an entirely different direction, for he fell in love with another.

In the aftermath of this second rejection, Ann could admit that she was consumed by feelings of resentment, and it would have been all too easy for her to be sucked into a bog of odium that drowned her. Nonetheless, she chose to confront this emotional turmoil head-on. With a remarkable effort at resilience, she made a conscious decision to release the shackles of discontent, and, instead, embraced the empowering choice to forge ahead on a course of self-discovery and renewal.

A year passed, and Ann found herself preparing for her wedding day. The man awaiting her at the altar was not a cotton master, and he was hardly what one would call prosperous or influential, but he embodied a genuine fondness that had grown between them. His name was Charles, a modest solicitor with a considerate heart that made her indifferent to his lack of status and wealth. Indeed, the initial disappointment of straying from her childhood ambitions had given way to a deeper understanding of true companionship.

As Ann walked down the aisle, the silk of her wedding gown rustling softly, she saw familiar faces in the pews, the whole of the town having come to rejoice in her day. Among them were John Thornton and his wife, Margaret. Her heart skipped a beat when she noticed them amongst the gathering, the sea of fine dresses and starched suits, but she steadied herself, unwilling to let old feelings resurface. Ann could not deny the fleeting pang of nostalgia that gripped her. She remembered the days when she imagined herself in Margaret's place, the lady of the mill owner's heart and home.

Yet, as Ann continued her graceful descent towards Charles, she felt a warm glow of peace, trusting that this was all part of her story. The ceremony proceeded, and as the vows were exchanged, Ann and Charles looked into each other's eyes with devout adoration. Finally, the congregation erupted into applause when they were pronounced husband and wife, and the newlyweds shared a tender kiss, sealing the promise of a life together.

In the months that followed, Ann settled seamlessly into married life with her husband. Their home, though not as grand as those of the cotton masters, was enriched by laughter, as well as the sincere thrum of mutual respect and friendship. Charles proved to be a loving and devoted partner, a man who cherished her for the person she was, rather than the ideal image he could mould her into.

Occasionally, Ann would catch glimpses of John and Margaret during social events from afar, their lives continuing on parallel tracks as they lived the pages of their distinct narratives. *As she realised what might have been, she grew to be thankful for what was.* She could have married one of two Johns, neither of whom loved her; one, because he was a heartless scoundrel, and the other, a man with a heart of gold, but he simply could not offer such a gift to her, for it belonged to another.

And so, it was on one afternoon, many moons later, as Ann strolled through Milton's bustling market square with Charles, that she noticed John approaching with Margaret at his side. The couples exchanged genial greetings and glad tidings, and Ann could not help but reflect on the twists of fate that had brought them all to this point. As the conversation flowed, Ann felt a sense of closure. The dreams of her youth had transformed into a reality far richer than she could have imagined. She looked at John and Margaret, her heart full of gratitude for the role they unknowingly played in her journey, and, in all honesty, she could say she wished them well.

Quotes

This book features a curated selection of quotes from the original texts upon which it draws inspiration. The aim is not to replicate the authors' works but rather to pay homage to their literary prowess by seamlessly intermingling their narratives and dialogues with my own humble contributions.

By including these quotes, the intention is to illuminate the enduring brilliance of these authors and showcase how the essence of their writing transcends the boundaries of time and text. This serves to deepen our appreciation for their craft and the profound impact of their words on literary culture.

Furthermore, recognising that some readers may not have encountered the original works, I hope that this inclusion may serve as an invitation for them to explore these remarkable literary treasures. The novels of Gaskell, Austen and Brontë hold a unique charm and depth that deserve to be experienced by all.

Throughout *The Three Witches of Milton*, diligent efforts have been made to distinguish the incorporated quotes by presenting them in italics, thus signalling their origins from the works of Gaskell, Austen and Brontë. However, it is acknowledged that occasional limitations in font embedding may affect the presentation of the final product. Therefore, for readers' convenience, a comprehensive list of the included quotes is provided below for reference.

CHAPTER 1: THERE IS A TRUTH UNIVERSALLY ACKNOWLEDGED

'It is a truth universally acknowledged, that a single man in possession of a good fortune, must be in want of a wife.'
(Jane Austen, Pride and Prejudice)

CHAPTER 2: NINE MINUTES EARLIER

'Ah! There is nothing like staying at home, for real comfort.'
(Jane Austen, Emma)

'So foul and fair a day I have not seen.''
(William Shakespeare, Macbeth)

CHAPTER 3: THESE THREE WITCHES

'Happiness in marriage is entirely a matter of chance.
If the dispositions of the parties are ever so well known
to each other, or ever so similar beforehand, it does not
advance their felicity in the least.'
(Jane Austen, Pride and Prejudice)

'A lady's imagination is very rapid; it jumps from
admiration to love, from love to matrimony in a
moment.'
(Jane Austen, Pride and Prejudice)

'There will be little rubs and disappointments
everywhere, and we are all apt to expect too much; but
then, if one scheme of happiness fails, human nature
turns to another; if the first calculation is wrong, we
make a second better: we (as women), *find comfort*
somewhere.'
(Jane Austen, Mansfield Park)

'It seemed as if it fascinated him to see her push it up
impatiently, until it tightened her soft flesh; and then to
mark the loosening — the fall. He could almost have
exclaimed — 'There it goes, again!'
(Elizabeth Gaskell, North and South)

'*For you see, young ladies have a remarkable way of letting you know that they think you a "quiz" without actually saying the words. A certain superciliousness of look, coolness of manner, nonchalance of tone, express fully their sentiments on the point, without committing them by any positive rudeness in word or deed. But they would not succeed where he was concerned. To* women who only sought to please him *by their faces,* he *was the very devil when* he *found out that they* had *neither souls nor hearts — when they open to* him *a perspective of flatness, triviality, and perhaps imbecility, coarseness, and ill-temper: but* in contrast, *to the clear eye and eloquent tongue, to the soul made of fire, and the character that bends but does not break — at once supple and stable, tractable and consistent —* Mr Thornton would be *ever tender and true.*'

(Charlotte Brontë, Jane Eyre)

'*She never called her son by any name but John; 'love' and 'dear', and such like terms, were reserved for Fanny.*'

(Elizabeth Gaskell, North and South)

'*I am the mother that bore you, and your sorrow is my agony; and if you don't hate her, I do.*'

(Elizabeth Gaskell, North and South)

'*Then, Mother, you make me love her more...She is unjustly treated by you, and I must make the balance even* by loving her twice as much to make up for it.'

(Elizabeth Gaskell, North and South)

'A mother's love is given by God, John. It holds fast forever and ever. A girl's love is like a puff of smoke,' she said, blowing her words like hot air, *'it changes with every wind. And she would not have you, my own lad, would not she?'*

(Elizabeth Gaskell, North and South)

CHAPTER 4: THIS WAR OF WOMEN

'...unsocial, taciturn disposition, unwilling to speak, unless I am expected to say something that will amaze the whole room, and be handed down to posterity with all the eclat of a prover.'

(Jane Austen, Pride and Prejudice)

'Let me persuade you to follow my example, and take a turn about the room. I assure you it is very refreshing after sitting so long in one attitude.'

(Jane Austen, Pride and Prejudice)

'but depend upon it, he means to be severe on us, and our surest way of disappointing him will be to ask nothing about it.'

(Jane Austen, Pride and Prejudice)

'I have not the smallest objection to explaining them,' said he, as soon as she allowed him to speak. *'You either choose this method of passing the* afternoon *because you are in each other's confidence, and have secret affairs to discuss, or because you are conscious that your figures appear to the greatest advantage in*

walking; if the first, I would be completely in your way, and if the second, I can admire you much better as I sit by the fire.'
(Jane Austen, Pride and Prejudice)

'Oh! shocking!' cried Miss Bingley. 'I never heard anything so abominable. How shall we punish him for such a speech?'
(Jane Austen, Pride and Prejudice)

'He knew that it does good to no woman to be flattered by a man who does not intend to marry her; and it is madness in all women to let a secret love kindle within them, which, if unreturned and unknown, must devour the life that feeds it; and, if discovered and responded to, must lead, ignis-fatuus-like, into miry wilds whence there is no extrication.'
(Charlotte Brontë, Jane Eyre)

'How very ill Miss Hale (Miss Bennet) looked...I have never, in my life, seen a woman so altered as she is since the winter!'
(Jane Austen, Pride and Prejudice)

CHAPTER 5: WHO ELSE?

'No one who had ever seen Catherine Morland in her infancy, would have supposed her born to be a heroine... But from fifteen to seventeen she was in training for a heroine...'
(Jane Austen, Northanger Abbey)

'To begin with the old rigmarole of childhood. In a
country there was a shire, and in that shire there was a
town, and in that town there was a house, and in that
house there was a room, and in that room there was a
bed, and in that bed there lay a little girl.' (Adapted)
(Elizabeth   Gaskell,   Wives   and   Daughters)

CHAPTER 6: THE VANQUISHED HERCULES

'He shrank from hearing Margaret's very name
mentioned; he, while he blamed her – while he was
jealous of her – while he renounced her – he loved her
sorely, in spite of himself.'
(Elizabeth Gaskell, North and South)

'...for a charm of powerful trouble, like a hell-broth
boil and bubble.'
(Shakespeare, Macbeth)

'She is always so grave and disapproving, It is not as
if she will ever get a husband!'
(Sandy Welch, BBC North and South, 2004)

'…your sister and I *were agreeing that we would*
hardly know her again.'
(Jane Austen, Pride and Prejudice)

'I noticed no great difference.' (Altered from prose).
(Jane Austen, Pride and Prejudice)

CHAPTER 7: A VERY DIFFERENT CLOTH

'What could it be? Why did she care for what he thought, in spite of all her pride in spite of herself? She believed that she could have borne the sense of almighty displeasure, because He knew all, and could read her penitence, and hear her cries for help in time to come. But Mr Thornton - why did she tremble, and hide her face in the pillow? What strong feeling had overtaken her at last?'
(Elizabeth Gaskell, North and South)

'...she lay down and never stirred. To move hand or foot, or even so much as one finger, would have been an exertion beyond the powers of either volition or motion. She was so tired, so stunned, her feverish thoughts passed and repassed the boundary between lucidity and irrationality, and kept their own miserable identity.'
(Elizabeth Gaskell, North and South)

'Looking back upon the year's accumulated heap of troubles, Margaret wondered how they had been borne. If she could have anticipated them, how she would have shrunk away and hid herself from the coming time!'
(Elizabeth Gaskell, North and South)

'Do you think if I could help it, I would sit still with folded hands, content to mourn? Do you not believe that as long as hope remained I would be up and doing? I mourn because what has occurred cannot be helped.

The reason you give me for not grieving, is the very sole reason of my grief. Give me nobler and higher reasons for enduring meekly what my Father sees fit to send.'
(Elizabeth Gaskell, Mary Barton)

'A ruffled mind makes a restless pillow.'
(Charlotte Brontë, The Professor)

'I am so tired, so tired of being whirled on through all these phases of my life, in which nothing abides by me, no creature, no place; it is like the circle in which the victims of earthly passion eddy continually.'
(Elizabeth Gaskell, North and South)

'...day by day had, of itself, and by itself, been very endurable--small, keen, bright little spots of positive enjoyment having come sparkling into the very middle of sorrows.'
(Elizabeth Gaskell, North and South)

'She liked the exultation in the sense of power which these Milton men had. It might be rather rampant in its display, and savour of boasting; but still they seemed to defy the old limits of possibility, in a kind of fine intoxication, caused by the recollection of what had been achieved, and what yet should be.'
(Elizabeth Gaskell, North and South)

CHAPTER 8: A PAIR OF FINE EYES

'Of all the trite, worn-out, hollow mockeries of comfort that were ever uttered by people who will not take the trouble of sympathising with others...'
(Elizabeth Gaskell, Mary Barton)

'...he would rather have heard that she was suffering the natural sorrow. In the first place, there was selfishness enough in him to have taken pleasure in the idea that his great love might come in to comfort and console her; much the same kind of strange passionate pleasure which comes stinging through a mother's heart, when her drooping infant nestles close to her, and is dependent upon her for everything.'
(Elizabeth Gaskell, North and South)

'Margaret, with her superb ways of moving and looking, he began to feel ashamed of having imagined that it would do very well for the Hales, in spite of a certain vulgarity in it which had struck him at the time of his looking it over.'
(Elizabeth Gaskell, North and South)

'...she might droop, and flush, and flutter to his arms, as to her natural home and resting-place.'
(Elizabeth Gaskell, North and South)

'One moment, he glowed with impatience at the thought that she might do this, that she might confess that she cared for him too, then *the next, he feared a passionate rejection, the very idea of which withered up*

his future with so deadly a blight that he refused to think of it.'

(Elizabeth Gaskell, North and South)

'...she has nothing else, in short, to recommend her, but being an excellent walker. Why, I shall never forget her appearance this morning. She really looked almost wild.'

(Jane Austen, Pride and Prejudice)

'Yes, and her petticoat; I hope you saw her petticoat, six inches deep in mud, I am absolutely certain!'

(Jane Austen, Pride and Prejudice)

'Your picture may be very exact, but this was all lost upon me. I thought Miss Hale looked remarkably well when she came into church this morning. Her dirty petticoat quite escaped my notice.'

(Jane Austen, Pride and Prejudice)

'To walk three miles, or four miles, or five miles, or whatever it is, above her ankles in dirt, and alone, quite alone! What could she mean by it? It seems to me to show an abominable sort of conceited independence, a most country-town indifference to decorum!'

(Jane Austen, Pride and Prejudice)

'I am afraid...that her adventures may rather have affected your admiration for her eyes.'

(Jane Austen, Pride and Prejudice)

'*...they were brightened by the exercise.*'
(Jane Austen, Pride and Prejudice)

'*For my part, I must confess, I never saw any beauty
in her face. Her features are not at all handsome. Her
complexion has no brilliancy. Her nose wants character
– there is nothing marked in its lines.*'
(Jane Austen, Pride and Prejudice)

'*Oh, her teeth are tolerable, I suppose, but nothing out
of the common way.*'
(Jane Austen, Pride and Prejudice)

CHAPTER 9: MASQUERADE

'She *valued* her *own independence so highly that* she
could *fancy no degradation greater than that of having
another man perpetually directing and advising and
lecturing* her, *or even planning too closely in any way
about* her *actions. He might be the wisest of men, or the
most powerful*—but she *should equally rebel and resent
his interference.*'
(Elizabeth Gaskell, North and South)

'*I can live alone, if self-respect, and circumstances
require me so to do,*' she would whisper to herself. *I
need not sell my soul to buy bliss. I have an inward
treasure born with me, which can keep me alive if all
extraneous delights should be withheld, or offered only
at a price I cannot afford to give.*'
(Charlotte Brontë, Jane Eyre)

'The more she saw of the world, the more she was *dissatisfied with it; and every day confirmed* her *belief of the inconsistency of all human characters, and of the little dependence that can be placed on the appearance of merit or sense.'*
(Jane Austen, Pride and Prejudice)

'The French girls would tell you, to believe that you were pretty would make you so.'
(Elizabeth Gaskell, Wives and Daughters)

'She *was at an age when any apprehension, not absolutely based on a knowledge of facts, is easily banished for a time by a bright sunny day, or some happy outward circumstance.'*
(Elizabeth Gaskell, North and South)

CHAPTER 10: GENTLEMAN AND HIGHWAYMAN

'… *she gives herself airs, and they're not rich – never have been*!'
(Sandy Welch, BBC North and South, 2004)

'And *she cannot even play the piano!'*
(Sandy Welch, BBC North and South, 2004)

'Go on, Fanny. What else does she lack to bring'er up to your standard?'
(Sandy Welch, BBC North and South, 2004)

'I heard Miss Hale say she cannot play herself, John.'
(Sandy Welch, BBC North and South, 2004)

'No one can be really esteemed accomplished and fit
for society *who does not greatly surpass what is usually
met with. A woman must have a thorough knowledge of
music, singing, drawing, dancing, and the modern
languages, to deserve the word; and besides all this, she
must possess a certain something in her air and manner
of walking, the tone of her voice, her address and
expressions, or the word will be but half deserved.'*
(Jane Austen, Pride and Prejudice)

*'People who are only in each other's company for
amusement never really like each other so well, or
esteem each other so highly, as those who work
together, and perhaps suffer together.'*
(Charlotte Brontë, The Professor)

*'I am no longer surprised at your knowing only six
accomplished women, I rather wonder now at your
knowing any.'*
(Jane Austen, Pride and Prejudice)

*'People may talk as they will about the little respect
that is paid to virtue, unaccompanied by the outward
accidents of wealth or station; but I rather think it will
be found that, in the long run, true and simple virtue
always has its proportionate reward in the respect and
reverence of everyone whose esteem is worth having.
To be sure, it is not rewarded after the way of the world
as mere worldly possessions are, with low obeisance*

and lip-service; but all the better and more noble qualities in the hearts of others make ready and go forth to meet it on its approach, provided only it be pure, simple, and unconscious of its own existence.'
(Elizabeth Gaskell, Ruth)

'...she must yet add something more substantial, in the improvement of her mind by extensive reading.'
(Jane Austen, Pride and Prejudice)

'I declare after all there is no enjoyment like reading! For the person, be it gentleman or lady, who has not pleasure in a good novel, must be intolerably stupid.'
(Jane Austen, Northanger Abbey)

'How much sooner one tires of anything than of a book! When I have a house of my own, I shall be miserable if I have not an excellent library.'
(Jane Austen, Pride and Prejudice)

'It is happy for you that you possess the talent of flattering with delicacy. May I ask whether these pleasing attentions proceed from the impulse of the moment, or are the result of previous study?'
(Jane Austen, Pride and Prejudice)

'My temper I dare not vouch for. It is, I believe, too little yielding— certainly too little for the convenience of the world. I cannot forget the follies and vices of others so soon as I ought, nor their offences against myself. My feelings are not puffed about with every attempt to move them. My temper would perhaps be

called resentful. My good opinion once lost, is lost forever.'
  (Jane Austen, Pride and Prejudice)

'A man should pay no heed to his good looks, he should only possess strength and valour. Gentleman or highwaymen, his beauty lies in his power.'
  (Charlotte Brontë, Jane Eyre)

'Miss Ingram was a mark beneath jealousy: she was too inferior to excite feeling. Pardon the seeming paradox; I mean what I say. She was very showy, but she was not genuine; she had a fine person, many brilliant attainments, but her mind was poor, her heart barren by nature; nothing bloomed spontaneously on that soil; no unforced natural fruit delighted by its freshness. She was not good; she was not original; she used to repeat sounding phrases from books; she never offered, nor had, an opinion of her own. She advocated a high tone of sentiment, but she did not know the sensations of sympathy and pity; tenderness and truth were not in her.'
  (Charlotte Brontë, Jane Eyre)

'I do not look on self-indulgent, sensual people as worthy of my hatred; I simply look upon them with contempt for their poorness of character.'
  (Elizabeth Gaskell, North and South)

'There is nothing like wounded affection for giving poignancy to anger.'
  (Elizabeth Gaskell, Wives and Daughters)

'*It is in vain to say human beings ought to be satisfied with tranquillity: they must have action; and they will make it if they cannot find it. Millions are condemned to a stiller doom than mine, and millions are in silent revolt against their lot. Nobody knows how many rebellions besides political rebellions ferment in the masses of life which people earth. Women are supposed to be very calm generally: but women feel just as men feel; they need exercise for their faculties, and a field for their efforts, as much as their brothers do; they suffer from too rigid a restraint, too absolute a stagnation, precisely as men would suffer; and it is narrow-minded in their more privileged fellow-creatures to say that they ought to confine themselves to making puddings and knitting stockings, to playing on the piano and embroidering bags. It is thoughtless to condemn them, or laugh at them, if they seek to do more or learn more than custom has pronounced necessary for their sex.*'
(Charlotte Brontë, Jane Eyre)

'She is *no bird; and no net ensnares* her…she is *a free human being with an independent will.*' *(Adapted)*
(Charlotte Brontë, Jane Eyre)

'*But afterwards she seemed to improve on you, and I believe you thought her rather pretty at one time.*'
(Jane Austen, Pride and Prejudice)

'Yes, I did...But that was only when I first knew her...But *it is many months since I have considered her as one of the most handsome women of my acquaintance.' (Adapted)*

(Jane Austen, Pride and Prejudice)

CHAPTER 11: BARELY BEAR

'*Mr Thornton was perhaps the oldest of Mr Hale's pupils. He was certainly the favourite. Mr Hale got into the habit of quoting his opinions so frequently, and with such regard, that it became a little domestic joke to wonder what time, during the hour appointed for instruction, could be given to absolute learning, so much of it appeared to have been spent in conversation.'*

(Elizabeth Gaskell, North and South)

'*...straight brows* which *fell over the clear deep-set earnest eyes, which, without being unpleasantly sharp, seemed intent enough to penetrate into the very heart and core of what he was looking at. The lines in the face were few but firm, as if they were carved in marble, and lay principally about the lips, which were slightly compressed over a set of teeth so faultless and beautiful as to give the effect of sudden sunlight when the rare bright smile, coming in an instant and shining out of the eyes, changed the whole look from the severe and resolved expression of a man ready to do and dare everything, to the keen honest enjoyment of the moment,*

which is seldom shown so fearlessly and instantaneously except by children.'
  (Elizabeth Gaskell, North and South)

'Margaret liked this smile; it was the first thing she had admired in this new friend of her father's; and the opposition of character, shown in all these details of appearance she had just been noticing, seemed to explain the attraction they evidently felt towards each other—'
  (Elizabeth Gaskell, North and South)

'What could he mean by speaking so, as if I were always thinking that he cared for me, when I know he does not; he cannot. ... But I won't care for him. I surely am mistress enough of myself to control this wild, strange, miserable feeling.'
  (Elizabeth Gaskell, North and South)

'The vehemence of emotion, stirred by grief and love within her, it *was claiming mastery, and struggling for full sway; and asserting a right to predominate: to overcome, to live, rise, and reign at last; yes,--and to speak.'*
  (Charlotte Brontë, Jane Eyre)

'I don't want to possess you!'
  'I came... because... I think it... very likely... I know I've never found myself in this position before. It is... difficult to find the words...'
  'My feelings for you... are very strong...'
  'I wish to marry you because I love you!'

'I spoke to you about my feelings because I love you. I had no thought for your reputation.'

'You must have to disappoint so many men who offer you their heart.'

(Sandy Welch, BBC North and South, 2004)

'One word more. You look as if you thought it tainted you to be loved by me.'

'I am a man. I claim the right of expressing my feelings.'

'You cannot avoid it.'

'Nay, I, if I would, cannot cleanse you from it.'

'...do not be afraid of too much expression on my part.'

(Elizabeth Gaskell, North and South)

'She disliked him more for having mastered her inner will. How dared he say that he would love her still, even though she shook him off with contempt? She wished she had spoken more - stronger. Sharp, decisive speeches came thronging to her mind, now that it was too late to utter them. The deep impression made by the interview was like that of a horror in a dream; that will not leave the room although we waken up, and rub our eyes, and force a stiff rigid smile upon our lips. It is there - there, cowering and gibbering, with fixed ghastly eyes, in some corner of the chamber, listening to hear whether we dare to breathe of its presence to anyone. And we dare not; poor cowards that we are!'

(Elizabeth Gaskell, North and South)

'..even before he left the room, - and certainly, not five minutes after, the clear conviction dawned upon her, shined bright upon her, that he did love her; that he had loved her; that he would love her. And she shrank and shuddered as under the fascination of some great power, repugnant to her whole previous life. She crept away, and hid from his idea. But it was of no use.'
(Elizabeth Gaskell, North and South)

CHAPTER 12: PERHAPS, PERHAPS...PERHAPS NONE

CHAPTER 13: THE BLUE DEVIL

'Miserably disturbed! that is not strong enough. He was haunted by the remembrance of the handsome young man, with whom she stood in an attitude of such familiar confidence; and the remembrance shot through him like an agony, till it made him clench his hands tight in order to subdue the pain.'
(Elizabeth Gaskell, North and South)

'The very falsehood that stained her, was a proof how blindly she loved another--this dark, slight, elegant, handsome man--while he himself was rough, and stern, and strongly made. He lashed himself into an agony of fierce jealousy. He thought of that look, that attitude!-- how he would have laid his life at her feet for such tender glances, such fond detention! He mocked at himself, for having valued the mechanical way in which

*she had protected him from the fury of the mob; now he
had seen how soft and bewitching she looked when with
a man she really loved. He remembered, point by point,
the sharpness of her words--'There was not a man in all
that crowd for whom she would not have done as much,
far more readily than for him.' He shared with the mob,
in her desire of averting bloodshed from them; but this
man, this hidden lover, shared with nobody; he had
looks, words, hand-cleavings, lies, concealment, all to
himself.'*

  (Elizabeth Gaskell, North and South)

  'Please! Stop. Pray, please don't go any further.'

  *'Please don't continue in that way. It is not the way of
a gentleman.'*

  *'It offends me that you should speak to me as if it were
your duty to rescue my reputation!'*

  *'You think that because you are rich, and my father is
in reduced circumstances, that you can have me for
your possession! I suppose I should expect no less from
someone in trade!'*

  'I do not like you, and never have.'

  (Sandy Welch, BBC North and South, 2004)

  'Your way of speaking shocks me. It is blasphemous.'

  (Elizabeth Gaskell, North and South)

CHAPTER 14: LOVE HER WELL

*'Reserved people often really need the frank
discussion of their sentiments and griefs more than the*

expansive. *The sternest-seeming stoic is human after all, and to burst with boldness into the silent sea of their souls is often to confer on them the first of obligations.'*
(Charlotte Brontë, Jane Eyre)

'Angry people are not always wise.'
(Jane Austen, Pride and Prejudice)

'Life appears to me too short to be spent in nursing animosity or registering wrongs. We are, and must be, one and all, burdened with faults in this world: but the time will soon come when, I trust, we shall put them off in putting off our corruptible bodies; when debasement and sin will fall from us with this cumbrous frame of flesh, and only the spark of the spirit will remain,--the impalpable principle of light and thought, pure as when it left the Creator to inspire the creature: whence it came it will return; perhaps again to be communicated to some being higher than man--perhaps to pass through gradations of glory, from the pale human soul to brighten to the seraph! Surely it will never, on the contrary, be suffered to degenerate from man to fiend? No; I cannot believe that: I hold another creed: which no one ever taught me, and which I seldom mention; but in which I delight, and to which I cling: for it extends hope to all: it makes Eternity a rest--a mighty home, not a terror and an abyss. Besides, with this creed, I can so clearly distinguish between the criminal and his crime; I can so sincerely forgive the first while I abhor the last: with this creed revenge never worries my heart.'
(Charlotte Brontë, Jane Eyre)

'He is the personification of sensible silence.'
(Elizabeth Gaskell, Wives and Daughters)

CHAPTER 15: SISTERHOOD

'Which of all my important nothings shall I tell you first?'
(Jane Austen in a letter to her sister, Cassandra)

'It is the town life,' said she. 'Their nerves are quickened by the haste and bustle and speed of everything around them, to say nothing of the confinement in these pent-up houses, which of itself is enough to induce depression and worry of spirits.'
(Elizabeth Gaskell, North and South)

'I cannot fix on the hour, or the spot, or the look, or the words, which laid the foundation. It is too long ago. I was in the middle before I knew that I had begun.'
(Jane Austen, Pride and Prejudice)

'She *had not intended to love him; the reader knows* she *had wrought hard to extirpate from* her *soul the germs of love there detected; and now, at the first renewed view of him, they spontaneously revived, great and strong!'*
(Charlotte Brontë, Jane Eyre)

'She began now to comprehend that he was exactly the man who, in disposition and talents, would most suit her. His understanding and temper, though unlike her

own, would have answered all her wishes. It was a union that must have been to the advantage of both: by her ease and liveliness, his mind might have been softened, his manners improved; and from his judgement, information, and knowledge of the world, she must have received benefit of greater importance.'
(Jane Austen, Pride and Prejudice)

'Margaret was not a ready lover, but where she loved she loved passionately, and with no small degree of jealousy.'
(Elizabeth Gaskell, North and South)

'It is right to hope for the best about everybody, and not to expect the worst. This sounds like a truism, but it has comforted me before now, and some day you'll find it useful. One has always to try to think more of others than of oneself, and it is best not to prejudge people on the bad side.'
(Elizabeth Gaskell, Wives and Daughters)

'I saw he was going to marry her, for family, perhaps political reasons, because her rank and connections suited him; Margaret felt he had not given her his love, and that her qualifications were ill-adapted to win from him that treasure. This was the point--this was where the nerve was touched and teased--this was where the fever was sustained and fed: she could not charm him.'
(Charlotte Brontë, Jane Eyre)

'If she had managed the victory at once, and he had yielded and sincerely laid his heart at her feet, I should

have covered my face, turned to the wall, and (figuratively) have died to them. If Miss Ingram had been a good and noble woman, endowed with force, fervour, kindness, sense, I should have had one vital struggle with two tigers--jealousy and despair: then, my heart torn out and devoured, I should have admired her--acknowledged her excellence, and been quiet for the rest of my days: and the more absolute her superiority, the deeper would have been my admiration--the more truly tranquil my quiescence. But as matters really stood, to watch Miss Ingram's efforts at fascinating Mr Rochester, to witness their repeated failure--herself unconscious that they did fail; vainly fancying that each shaft launched hit the mark, and infatuatedly pluming herself on success, when her pride and self-complacency repelled further and further what she wished to allure--to witness THIS, was to be at once under ceaseless excitation and ruthless restraint.'

(Charlotte Brontë, Jane Eyre)

'Because, when she failed, I saw how she might have succeeded. Arrows that continually glanced off from Mr Rochester's breast and fell harmless at his feet, might, I knew, if shot by a surer hand, have quivered keen in his proud heart--have called love into his stern eye, and softness into his sardonic face; or, better still, without weapons a silent conquest might have been won.'

(Charlotte Brontë, Jane Eyre)

'I know I must conceal my sentiments: I must smother hope; I must remember that he cannot care much for me. For when I say that I am of his kind, I do not mean

that I have his force to influence, and his spell to
attract: I mean only that I have certain tastes and
feelings in common with him. I must, then, repeat
continually that we are forever sundered: − and yet,
while I breathe and think, I must love him.'
(Charlotte Brontë, Jane Eyre)

'He is not to them what he is to me,' I thought: 'he is
not of their kind. I believe he is of mine; − I am sure he
is, − I feel akin to him, − I understand the language of
his countenance and movements: though rank and
wealth sever us widely, I have something in my brain
and heart, in my blood and nerves, that assimilates me
mentally to him.'
(Charlotte Brontë, Jane Eyre)

'I dare say there's many a woman makes as sad a
mistake as I have done, and only finds it out too late.'
(Elizabeth Gaskell, North and South)

'I could not unlove him now, merely because I found
that he had ceased to notice me.'
(Charlotte Brontë, Jane Eyre)

'One word more. You look as if you thought it tainted
you to be loved by me. You cannot avoid it. Nay, I, if I
would, cannot cleanse you from it. But I would not, if I
could. I have never loved any woman before: my life has
been too busy, my thoughts too much absorbed with
other things. Now I love, and will love. But do not be
afraid of too much expression on my part.'
(Elizabeth Gaskell, North and South)

'There is a stubbornness about me that never can bear to be frightened at the will of others. My courage always rises at every attempt to intimidate me.'
(Jane Austen, Pride and Prejudice)

'It darted through her with the speed of an arrow that Mr Knightley must marry no one but herself!' (Adapted)
(Jane Austen, Emma)

CHAPTER 16: THE AUTHOR OF THIS STORY

'It was towards the end of February, in that year, and a bitter black frost had lasted for many weeks. The keen east wind had long since swept the streets clean, though in a gusty day the dust would rise like pounded ice, and make people's faces quite smart with the cold force with which it blew against them. Houses, sky, people, and everything looked as if a gigantic brush had washed them all over with a dark shade of Indian ink.'
(Elizabeth Gaskell, Mary Barton)

'...you cannot, read the lot of those who daily pass you by in the street. How do you know the wild romances of their lives; the trials, the temptations they are even now enduring, resisting, sinking under?'
(Elizabeth Gaskell, Mary Barton)

'When we are heavy-laden in our hearts, it falls in better with our humor to reveal our case in our own way and our own time.'
(Elizabeth Gaskell, Mary Barton)

'There is nothing I would not do for those who are really my friends. I have no notion of loving people by halves, it is not my nature.'
(Jane Austen, Northanger Abbey)

'On some such night as this she remembered promising to herself to live as brave and noble a life as any heroine she ever read or heard of in romance, a life sans peur et sans reproche; it had seemed to her then that she had only to will, and such a life would be accomplished. And now she had learnt that not only to will, but also to pray, was a necessary condition in the truly heroic. Trusting to herself, she had fallen.'
(Elizabeth Gaskell, North and South)

'If you live in Milton, you must learn to have a brave heart, Miss Hale.'
(Elizabeth Gaskell, North and South)

'I would do my best,' said Margaret rather pale. 'I do not know whether I am brave or not till I am tried; but I am afraid I should be a coward.'
(Elizabeth Gaskell, North and South)

'I hate to hear you talk about all women as if they were fine ladies instead of rational creatures. None of us want to be in calm waters all our lives.'
(Jane Austen, Persuasion)

'We have all a better guide in ourselves, if we would attend to it, than any other person can be.'
(Jane Austen, Mansfield Park)

'But then again, a girl in love will do a good deal.'
(Elizabeth Gaskell, North and South)

'Screw your courage to the sticking place.' (Adapted)
(William Shakespeare, Macbeth)

CHAPTER 17: COULD IT BE?

'They were within twenty yards of each other, and so abrupt was his appearance, that it was impossible to avoid his sight. Their eyes instantly met, and the cheeks of each were overspread with the deepest blush. He absolutely started, and for a moment seemed immoveable from surprise; but shortly recovering himself, advanced towards her, and spoke.'
(Jane Austen, Pride and Prejudice)

'She did not answer. She could not tell what words to use. She was afraid of saying anything, lest the passion of anger, dislike, indignation - whatever it was that was boiling up in her breast - should find vent in cries and screams, or worse, in raging words that could never be

forgotten. It was as if the piece of solid ground on which she stood had broken from the shore, and she was drifting out to the infinite sea alone.'
(Elizabeth Gaskell, Wives and Daughters)

'Was he bewitched by those beautiful eyes, that soft, half-open, sighing mouth which lay so close upon his shoulder only yesterday? He could not even shake off the recollection that she had been there; that her arms had been round him, once—if never again.'
(Elizabeth Gaskell, North and South)

'Margaret could not help her looks; but the short curled upper lip, the round, massive up-turned chin, the manner of carrying her head, her movements, full of a soft feminine defiance, always gave strangers the impression of haughtiness.
She stood *facing him and facing the light; her full beauty met his eye; her round white flexile throat rising out of the full, yet lithe figure; her lips, moving so slightly as she spoke, not breaking the cold serene look of her face with any variation from the one lovely haughty curve; her eyes, with their soft gloom, meeting his with quiet maiden freedom.* When they had first met, he had *almost said to himself that he did not like her before their conversation ended; he tried so to compensate himself for the mortified feeling, that while he looked upon her with an admiration he could not repress, she looked at him with proud indifference, taking him, he thought, for what, in his irritation, he told himself he was - a great rough fellow, with not a*

grace or a refinement about him. Her quiet coldness of demeanour he interpreted into contemptuousness, and resented it in his heart to the pitch of almost inclining him to get up and go away, and have nothing more to do with these Hales, and their superciliousness.'

(Elizabeth Gaskell, North and South)

CHAPTER 18: NORTH AND SOUTH

'It is only a novel... or, in short, only some work in which the greatest powers of the mind are displayed, in which the most thorough knowledge of human nature, the happiest delineation of its varieties, the liveliest effusions of wit and humour, are conveyed to the world in the best-chosen language.'
(Jane Austen, Northanger Abbey)

'Oh! I am delighted with the book! I should like to spend my whole life in reading it.'
(Jane Austen, Northanger Abbey)

'Suddenly, the wintry frost-bound look of care had left Mr Thornton's face, as if some soft summer gale had blown all anxiety away from his mind; and, though his mouth was as much compressed as before, his eyes smiled out benignly on his questioner.'
(Elizabeth Gaskell, North and South)

'If I felt for you less, I might be able to talk about it more.'
(Jane Austen, Emma)

'In vain have I struggled. It will not do. My feelings will not be repressed. You must allow me to tell you how ardently I admire and love you.'
(Jane Austen, Pride and Prejudice)

'You are too generous to trifle with me. If your feelings are still what they were last April, tell me so at once. My affections and wishes are unchanged, but one word from you will silence me on this subject forever.'
(Jane Austen, Pride and Prejudice)

'...feeling all the more than common awkwardness and anxiety of his situation, now forced herself to speak; and immediately, though not very fluently, gave him to understand that her sentiments had undergone so material a change since the period to which he alluded, as to make her receive with gratitude and pleasure his present assurances.'
(Jane Austen, Pride and Prejudice)

'My feelings are so different...in fact, they are quite the opposite.'
(Andrews Davies, BBC Pride and Prejudice, 1995)

CHAPTER 19: THE THORN AND THE ROSE

'I have a strange feeling with regard to you, as if I had a string somewhere under my left ribs, tightly knotted to a similar string in you,' he enlightened, his hand gently moving to rest on her breast, causing Margaret

to quiver from tip to toe. 'And if you were to leave I'm afraid that cord of communion would snap. And I have a notion that I'd take to bleeding inwardly. As for you, you'd forget me.'
  (Charlotte Brontë, Jane Eyre)

  'I have blamed you, and lectured you, and you have borne it as no other woman in England would have borne it.'
  (Jane Austen, Emma)

  'Dare not say that man forgets sooner than woman, that his love has an earlier death. I have loved none but you. Unjust I may have been, weak and resentful I have been, but never inconstant.'
  (Jane Austen, Persuasion)

  'Oh, Mr Thornton, I am not good enough!'
  'Not good enough! Don't mock my own deep feeling of unworthiness.'
  (Elizabeth Gaskell, North and South)

  'You have bewitched me, body and soul. I love...I love...I love you.'
  (Deborah Moggach,, Pride and Prejudice, 2005)

'You are my sympathy - my better self - my good angel; I am bound to you by a strong attachment. I think you good, gifted, lovely; a fervent, a solemn passion is conceived in my heart; it leans to you, draws you to my centre and spring of life, wraps my existence about you - and, kindling in pure, powerful flame, fuses you and me in one.'
(Charlotte Brontë, Jane Eyre)

'Do not consider me now as an elegant female intending to plague you, but as a rational creature speaking the truth from her heart.'
(Charlotte Brontë, Jane Eyre)

'You pierce my soul. I am half agony, half hope...I have loved none but you.'
(Jane Austen, Persuasion)

'I am not an angel,' she asserted; 'and I will not be one till I die: I will be myself.'
(Charlotte Brontë, Jane Eyre)

'You must neither expect nor exact anything celestial of me—for you will not get it, any more than I shall get it of you: which I do not at all anticipate. I am not perfect, and nor are you. We must contend ourselves with that.'
(Charlotte Brontë, Jane Eyre)

'Every atom of your flesh is as dear to me as my own: in pain and sickness it would still be dear.'
(Charlotte Brontë, Jane Eyre)

'All my heart is yours, sir: it belongs to you; and with you it would remain, were fate to exile the rest of me from your presence forever.'
(Charlotte Brontë, Jane Eyre)

'Perhaps It is our imperfections that make us perfect for each other.'
(Douglas McGrath, Emma, 1996)

'Now be sincere; did you admire me for my impertinence?'
'For the liveliness of your mind, I did.'
(Jane Austen, Pride and Prejudice)

'I ask you to pass through life at my side—to be my second self and best earthly companion.'
(Charlotte Brontë, Jane Eyre)

'The happiness which this reply produced was such as he had probably never felt before, and he expressed himself on the occasion as sensibly and as warmly as a man violently in love can be supposed to do. Had Margaret been able to encounter his eyes, she might have seen how well the expression of heartfelt delight diffused over his face became him; but, though she could not look, she could listen, and he told her of feelings which, in proving of what importance she was to him, made his affection every moment more valuable.'
(Jane Austen, Pride and Prejudice)

'*It was too delicious to feel her soft cheek against his, for him to wish to see either deep blushes or loving eyes.*'
(Elizabeth Gaskell, North and South)

'*I must learn to be content with being happier than I deserve.*'
(Jane Austen, Pride and Prejudice)

CHAPTER 20: ADIEU

'*She then thought the land enchanted into everlasting brightness and happiness; she fancied, then, that into a region so lovely no bale or woe could enter, but would be charmed away and disappear before the sight of the glorious guardian mountains. Now she knew the truth, that earth has no barrier which avails against agony.*'
(Elizabeth Gaskell, Ruth)

'*Reader, I married him.*'
(Charlotte Brontë, Jane Eyre)

DAMN HER AND HER FINE EYES: CAROLINE BINGLEY'S STORY

'*For what do we live, but to make sport for our neighbours, and laugh at them in our turn?*'
(Jane Austen, Pride and Prejudice)

'A lady's imagination is very rapid; it jumps from admiration to love, from love to matrimony in a moment.'
(Jane Austen, Pride and Prejudice)

'There is, in every disposition a tendency to some particular evil, a natural defect, which not even the best education can overcome. And her defect was a propensity to hate everybody.'
(Jane Austen, Pride and Prejudice)

I AM NOT AN ANGEL: BLANCHE INGRAM'S STORY

'It does good to no woman to be flattered [by a man] who does not intend to marry her; and it is madness in all women to let a secret love kindle within them, which, if unreturned and unknown, must devour the life that feeds it; and, if discovered and responded to, must lead, ignis-fatuus-like, into miry wilds whence there is no extrication.'
(Charlotte Brontë, Jane Eyre)

'I am not an angel,' I asserted; 'and I will not be one till I die: I will be myself.'
(Charlotte Brontë, Jane Eyre)

THE ICE QUEEN: ANN LATIMER'S STORY

'Nothing had been the same; and this slight, all-pervading instability, had given her greater pain than if all had been too entirely changed for her to recognize it... ...I am so tired - so tired of being whirled on through all these phases of my life, in which nothing abides by me, no creature, no place; it is like the circle in which the victims of earthly passion eddy continually.'

(Elizabeth Gaskell, North and South)

'But the future must be met, however stern and iron it be.'

(Elizabeth Gaskell, North and South)

'Come! Poor little heart! Be cheery and brave,' she told herself. 'We'll be a great deal to one another, if we are thrown off and left desolate.'

(Elizabeth Gaskell, North and South)

'As she realised what might have been, she grew to be thankful for what was.'

(Elizabeth Gaskell, North and South)

Glossary of Terms

This story has included a series of Regency, Victorian and Mancunian terms so that it might seek to link the past and the present through the use of authentic words and dialect. Details of the phrases and their meanings can be found below.

CHAPTER 1: THERE IS A TRUTH UNIVERSALLY ACKNOWLEDGED

Reaper of the Ring: A Regency phrase that refers to someone who marries for personal gain and selfishly reaps the benefits of marriage whilst disregarding the wants or welfare of their spouse.

CHAPTER 2: NINE MINUTES EARLIER

Dreich: Shetland word meaning dreary.

Cockcrow Edition Rags: Victorian newspapers that came out at first dawn, were particularly popular with businessmen and politicians.

CHAPTER 3: THESE THREE WITCHES

Bit o' Raspberry: An attractive girl, originally a raspberry jam as this was considered the most flavoursome of preserves, so the prettiest of the girls were a bit o' raspberry.

Lather Up The Bacon: Too much extravagance.
Prince of the Penny: Regency term to describe a man who was well off.

Chuckaboo: A nickname given to a close friend.
Mithering: Bothering.

CHAPTER 4: THIS WAR OF WOMEN

Jelly-Doll: The jelly part of the phrase refers to someone unpredictable and unsteady in their actions and temperament, like a plate of jelly. The doll could either refer to the person as being attractive or them being easy to manipulate as if they had no mind or will of their own.

Wooden Spoon: A particularly stupid person.

Foozler: Someone who was likely to mess things up, such as being clumsy or making mistakes.

Porky-Pinched: When someone has a deep blush. Porky refers to the pink colour of pork and pigs and pinched refers to the way women would pinch their cheeks to entice a natural blush.

Hornswoggles: People who are adept at cheating others and getting their way as a result of devious means.

Gal-Sneaker: A man devoted to the art of seduction.

CHAPTER 5: WHO ELSE?
Skivvy: Lowly servant.

Plume-swish: A servant who typically attends to tasks such as dusting. The term derived from the growth of the expendable income in the Victorian period, allowing people to acquire more ornaments and luxury items in their homes, all of which required a greater level of cleaning.

CHAPTER 6: THE VANQUISHED HERCULES
Bluestocking: A woman with unfashionably intellectual and literary interests.

CHAPTER 7: A VERY DIFFERENT CLOTH
A watering pot: One who weeps too much and too often.

CHAPTER 8: A PAIR OF FINE EYES
'Had-yur-wheest!: Be quiet, hold your tongue.

Champagne weather: Heavy rain.

Raily-daily-Abigail: A maid.

Skiv: A Regency word that is a shortened version of "skivvy," referring to the lowest form of domestic staff.
Sally-shiggle: A dance named after Sally Epsworth, the early 18th-century music hall dancer.

Squiffy: Squiffy is a term that was first invented by Elizabeth Gaskell and appears in one of her letters. It was originally used to mean someone who appears drunk, but can also refer to a screwed-up facial expression.

Cinder: Comes from Cinderella, which means a person who works in a dirty way, domestically.

Batty-fang: To thrash someone thoroughly, either physically or verbally.

Scotched: For something to be spiked or laced with something strong.

Parish Pick-Axe: A prominent nose.

Poked-up: Embarrassed.

CHAPTER 9: MASQUERADE
None.

CHAPTER 10: GENTLEMEN AND HIGHWAYMEN
Sauce-box: A talkative person, often prone to gossiping or speaking in a way that is silly or indiscreet.

CHAPTER 11: BARELY BEAR
Collie-Shangles: An argument.

Scrikin: Crying.

CHAPTER 12: PERHAPS, PERHAPS...PERHAPS
None.

CHAPTER 13: THE BLUE DEVIL
A bird of paradise: A loose woman.

Fudge: False rumours.

Be fudged: Be quashed.

A fit of the blue devils: Depressed.

CHAPTER 14: LOVE HER WELL
Wheeze-sneeze: Silly, senseless talk that is often nonsense or malicious.

A Gabster: A talkative person.

CHAPTER 15: SISTERHOOD
Beau monde: A person of fashion.

Pink of the Ton: Being at the height of fashion.

Camouflet Intentionnel: Deriving from French, it means an intentional snub. The term was often used throughout the 19th century to refer to people being deliberately excluded from society.

Plump in the pockets: Wealthy.

Too smoky by half: Suspicious.

Coffee sisters: Women who enjoy sitting around together to gossip.

Cheek-achers: Women who enjoy saying unkind things about others to make them blush or frown, causing their cheeks to ache or turn red.

CHAPTER 16: THE AUTHOR OF THIS STORY
Lollygag: Go about lazily or sluggishness.

Queer as Dick's hatband: To look unwell, rather faint and weak.

CHAPTER 17: COULD IT BE?
None.

CHAPTER 18: NORTH AND SOUTH
Yoked: Married

CHAPTER 19: THE THORN AND THE ROSE
None.

CHAPTER 20: ADIEU
None.

DAMN HER AND HER FINE EYES: CAROLINE BINGLEY'S STORY
None.

I AM NOT AN ANGEL: BLANCHE INGRAM'S STORY
None.

THE ICE QUEEN: ANN LATIMER'S STORY
None.

Acknowledgements

I would like to thank Sandy Welch for granting permission for this book to be written since it contains references to her exceptional screenplay. I would also like to thank her for the wonderful opportunity to meet her in 2022 so that I could interview her about her time working on *North and South* whilst also supporting Elizabeth Gaskell's House. It was a privilege and a pleasure, so from one writer to another, thank you.

Nancy, I extend my heartfelt gratitude to you for your meticulous proofreading of this story. Your generous investment of time and effort in reviewing this book, providing detailed corrections, and offering thoughtful feedback is deeply appreciated. Your support and dedication have been invaluable throughout this process. Thank you sincerely for your contributions.

I also want to express my heartfelt appreciation to the remarkable people who have been devoted readers over the years, offering unwavering support, guidance, and encouragement. Your presence has been instrumental in shaping my work and uplifting me during moments of fatigue or doubt. To Rhona, Denise, Helena, Deirdre, Catherine, Anna, Michelle, Dawn, Halin, Julia, Katlyn, and to those quietly yet faithfully following my journey, I am deeply grateful. Your continued backing means the world to me, and I invite you to stay for the adventures that lie ahead.

Lastly, I extend my gratitude to the women who generously allowed me to include their names as cameo characters in the chapter, "The Author of This Story." Thank you to Dawn, Ethel, Deirdre, Shawn, Natalie, Inese, Anna, Lucy, and Lynda, for becoming a part of this narrative and adding a personal touch. I wanted to include you as representatives of the enduring fans of these authors and their works—fans from diverse generations, countries, and cultures. It is a real honour to have you be part of this.

Declaration

While *The Three Witches of Milton* has been written entirely by myself, I must give Elizabeth Gaskell, Jane Austen and Charlotte Brontë full credit and applause for writing the original novels on which it is based. Again, while the majority of the story contains my own words, there are some quotes from the primary texts penned by these three writers, all presented in italics to give recognition to the authors and highlight them for the benefit of readers.

This book has taken the liberty of referring to the fictional character of Ann Latimer, a person who does not exist in the original novel, but is a creation of Sandy Welch's for the 2004 BBC screen adaptation of *North and South*. I would like to note that while Sandy Welch and the BBC have granted permission for this book to be published, they have no further association with this work.

Again, while Elizabeth Gaskell's House, Jane Austen's House and the Brontë Parsonage have all recognised this book and have accepted the royalties gift, this book has no commercial connection with any societies or trusts relating to any persons or organisations that may have been involved in the writing and creating of the novel or the series. Any promotion or support shown by them following its publication will be by their own choice and discretion.

About the Author

Greetings, I'm Caroline Malcolm-Boulton, also known as The Scribbler CMB. Born in 1993, I proudly hail from Scotland, where I reside with my husband and our cherished daughter.

Raised in a family that revered the English classics, I was immersed in a world where we avidly read these tales and watched their adaptations. The works of Gaskell, Austen, Brontë, and other literary luminaries hold a cherished place in my heart, but among them, *North and South* stands as my perennial favourite.

For the past eighteen years, my fascination with *North and South* has deepened. I've delved into its pages repeatedly, studied its nuances at university, and even participated in a touring stage adaptation, contributing to the script and portraying Fanny Thornton in 2015. Now in my thirties, I work part-time as a freelance Arts and Film & Television journalist, dedicating considerable time to exploring the life and legacy of

Gaskell, including supporting Elizabeth Gaskell's House through various events.

But what about writing *North and South* retellings and continuations? Despite my admiration for this Victorian classic spanning nearly two decades, it wasn't until 2020 that I discovered fan fiction. Initially sceptical, the onset of Covid-19 prompted me to explore this genre, leading to one of the most enriching experiences of my life.

Inspired by the diverse interpretations of fellow fans, I embarked on my own writing journey. It has been a transformative experience, fostering personal growth as both a writer and reader, and connecting me with kindred spirits in the fandom. Encouraged by this journey, I advocate for others to embrace writing as a means of nurturing cognitive and creative well-being. Fan fiction, in particular, offers a unique avenue for creative expression and exploration.

While some may approach fan fiction with hesitation, I wholeheartedly recommend embracing its potential. Reading fan fiction feels like returning to the comfort of familiar characters and settings, akin to coming home. Among these beloved characters, none hold a more special place in my heart than John and Margaret.

In essence, I am simply a woman who finds joy in reading and writing, and that was probably all I really needed to say.

Contact:

Email: caroline.malcolmboultonmedia@gmail.com
X (Formerly Twitter): @TheScribblerCMB
Facebook Arts Page: @TheScribblerCMBArts
Facebook Writing Page: @TheScribblerCMBWriter
Instagram: @TheScribblerCMB

Printed in Great Britain
by Amazon